VACANT EYES

A THRILLER BY
SIDNEY SPIES

A DELL BOOK

Published by
Dell Publishing
a division of
Bantam Doubleday Dell Publishing Group, Inc.
666 Fifth Avenue
New York, New York 10103

ISBN: 0-440-20985-4

Printed in the United States of America

To Rita, whom I've loved for as long as I can remember.

Without the support and encouragement of my agent, Larry Gershel, this book could not have been written. Likewise, the editorial advice and criticisms of Joan Sanger and Stef McDonald were invaluable.

Nancy Boyarsky and Nadine Leveille have been immense resources throughout the writing. I also owe thanks to the other members of my writing group—Tony Finizza, Barry Haworth, and Carol O'Connell.

Technical computer advice was furnished by Robert Spies. The material on neurotransmitters was gleaned from a large number of sources in medical literature; particularly valuable was the extensive review on CRH defects in dementia by Dr. Errol De Souza in Hospital Practice, September 1988.

Finally, Rita Spies was an unfailing source of advice, support, and motivation.

PART ONE

PART ONE

1

Code Blue in emergency room!

The terse, demanding announcement broke into the background clamor of coughs, voices, beeping electronic monitors, whooshing respirators, groans.

". . . blood pressure seventy-eight over sixty, pulse one hundred thirty and thready . . . skin loose, pigmented in the folds." Seated at the long, cluttered nurses' desk at the hub of the chrome-and-glass intensive care unit, Dr. Karen Formaker dictated her consultation note. When she finished, she impatiently riffled back through the chart for the order sheets. She couldn't allow the intern to hold off treatment any longer to await the refined tests of adrenal function—the case was an adrenal crisis until proven otherwise. Here at University Hospital, the heart of medical academia, a patient could die while awaiting completion of the elaborate workups that looked so good on grand rounds.

Code Blue in emergency room!

Her pen pressed through the three copies of the order sheet: "200 mgm hydrocortisone IV stat."

The refrain on the speaker system ended. Two years ago, when she had been a third-year resident in internal medicine, Karen would have been expected to drop everything and rush to the emergency room along with the on-call pharmacist, respiratory therapy technician, and intensive care nurses. But now, near the end of her second year of fellowship in endocrinology, she wasn't needed. A few more years in Endocrine, and she might forget how to handle a real emergency—except a diabetic coma or an adrenal failure like the one she'd just seen.

The staccato beep of her pager broke through. She shut it off and glanced down at the LED readout. Extension 5200. *Shit! That's the emergency room.*

She checked the overhead wall clock. Four forty-five. Tonight she and Hank would blow a half-week's pay on dinner at L'Ermitage to celebrate the still incredible offer from Dr. Berkholt. Since he'd first broached it six days ago, she'd been walking on air. In the guise of Arnold Berkholt, God had smiled down on her and honored her with a position by his side. In another six weeks, when her endocrine fellowship ended, she'd become Dr. Berkholt's associate.

Reservations were at eight. Beneath her white lab coat she already wore her blue silk pullover blouse and wool royal-and-black skirt so she wouldn't need to change when she finished at the hospital. She impatiently punched the dial-tone buttons. What the hell would the ER need her for?

The phone was answered by Debbie, the young, blondish ER nurse who hovered worshipfully near Karen whenever she made a visit to the emergency room. She sounded close to crying. "Dr. Formaker—Dr. Ezekial wants to talk to you."

Karen briefly wondered why Debbie called her Dr. Formaker. Like most of the nurses who'd been around University for a while, Debbie called her Dr. Karen to distinguish her from her older sister. Susan had gone through residency here in Obstetrics four years earlier and stayed on as a member of the faculty. After she married Duane Dreyer, she had continued to use her maiden name professionally.

Ezekial's deep, resonant voice came through the phone. "I need you here, Karen."

She continued scribbling on the order sheets. "What've you got, Zeke?" Malcolm Ezekial had been in the internship group before hers, finished two years of emergency room residency, and was now full time in the ER department. She'd never witnessed an urgent situation he couldn't handle.

"It's Susan."

She stopped writing. Why would Susan need her in the emergency room? And why hadn't Susan herself phoned? "Okay, Zeke—tell her I'll finish up this patient and be right down."

Ezekial's voice dropped lower. "Karen, it was a car accident. Susan's hurt."

The pen dropped onto the desk as her hand lost its grip. A hollow feeling carved a wedge in her stomach.

She shoved the chart across the desk to the charge nurse. "Give him the IV hydrocortisone. If I'm not back in twenty minutes, call Dr. Percy Barnes to take over." At a run, she started down the hall.

Two ambulance paramedics lounged outside the ER entrance. She'd seen the lanky, crinkle-faced one here many times before. He nodded toward the broad ER door. The line of his lips stretched and shortened in rapid strokes as he spoke with an empty cigarette holder clenched between his teeth. "Two of 'em. Wrong direction on the freeway. Woman was thrown."

The hollow wedge in her belly became a deep, gaping vacuum. She pushed through the wide door—and entered the familiar maelstrom of University Hospital Emergency Room.

Only this time something was different. It was as if she'd thrown a switch, shutting off all sound. Figures in white coats and uniforms turned silently toward her and stopped, suspended. The room was a wax museum of figures frozen in the white glare of overhead fluorescents. Wide, fixed eyes stared. Voiceless mouths gaped.

Debbie was in front of her. Her hands reached out, hovered, withdrew. "It's Dr. Formaker—I mean, Dr. Susan." Tears made her glistening eyes melt and buckle. She gave a sideways, birdlike motion of her head. "They're working on her in room three."

The frozen wax figures faded. Karen burst through the door to three.

A white-coated crowd milled around the examining table. At the head of the table, the chief anesthesiology resident squeezed and released a ventilator bag. Its black tubing disappeared into a white sea. The senior ER nurse, Stan, stood on a footstool. With arms extended straight, right hand atop left, he rhythmically compressed the center of a breastbone. His face was covered with sweat. His head bobbed up and down with every press. "One, two, three, four, five, pause, one, two, three, four five, pause. . . ." With each bob a jagged streak broke a white line on a monitor screen.

Susan.

Zeke broke from the cluster. He was a tall man with pure white hair. It could have been the flowing white hair of an aging patrician, but his face was unlined, startlingly young. His lips were a narrow line. He reached for her hand, but like Debbie—as if he had seen something in Karen's eyes that gave pause—his hand stopped in midair and fell to his side. "It's not good," he said.

Through the unearthly quiet of the examining room she recognized the voice of Roger Harriman, cardiology fellow. "Hold off for a minute, Stan," he said.

The tall, muscular nurse straightened up with a groan and massaged his knuckles. Karen stared dumbly at the screen. A straight white line crossed a green background.

Twenty seconds.

"Okay, get back to it." Harriman sighed. Stan bent over. One, two, three, four, five, pause, one, two, three, four, five, pause. . . .

Karen didn't remember moving, but the white-frocked crowd melted before her, and she was at the side of the table. "Susan." Her voice sounded distant and strange, like an echo in a hollow chamber. The black ventilator tube protruded from the side of her sister's mouth. Blood trickled from beneath the large gauze pad draped loosely over her forehead. She reached and touched the forehead. The blood was sticky, already cool.

Karen was thirteen. In a drizzling rain, her big sister parked in the three-minute zone in front of the Studio City post office in northwest Los Angeles. "Wait here, Kare." Susan disappeared into the building. Karen remembered the letter to mail and scooted from the car. She slipped on the wet stairs, and when she tried to get up, blood was gushing from her forehead.

"Let me help you, little lady." The fat man bent down and lifted her to her feet.

Susan burst from the post office. "What have you done to my sister?" she screamed. And she was hitting the poor man with her purse, swinging wildly and hitting him again and again as he staggered back, shielding his face. . . .

Karen lifted the thick gauze pad. The gaping vacuum in her belly became a cold block of ice. The left side of Susan's skull was caved in. Pink-gray gelatin oozed from a rent in the hollow.

Mechanically, she replaced the gauze drape. Although her knees threatened to buckle, her hand was steady. It was a robot's talon, it wasn't part of her. Fingers of the talon lifted eyelids and uncovered round, black pupils, wide and depthless, unmoving in the glare of the overhead surgical lamp. The fingers let loose. The lids slid partway back.

Zeke's hand rested lightly on her shoulder. She wanted to turn and slap it off. But she stared—at Susan's blood trickling down from her forehead to stain the stiff, white examining table paper.

What have you done to my sister?

"I'm sorry, Karen," he said.

"How long?" Karen lifted her eyes to Harriman, who stood quiet and impassive across the body.

"I've been here ten minutes," he said. "Maybe eighteen total since she arrived. Paramedics estimate another twenty-two in the field."

She turned to Zeke. "No heartbeat in that time?"

Zeke pressed his lips together and shook his head.

Her eyes reached only to the level of the triangle between his collarbones. She stared at the triangle. "Oh," she said.

Zeke looked at Harriman.

"We were waiting for you before stopping," Harriman said.

Karen still had Susan's red raincoat in the trunk of her car. She'd borrowed it last week when she'd had to rush off to a meeting at St. Vincent's. She'd kept meaning to return it. Numbly, she nodded.

Harriman motioned toward Stan, a casual little gesture as if waving off a fly. Stan straightened up, stepped from the stool. The anesthesiologist let the ventilator bag drop, then disconnected it from the tracheal tube. Harriman turned and looked at the monitor.

Every set of eyes in the room fastened on the straight, white line on the screen.

After four minutes the first of the attendants began filing from the room. Harriman gave a bare nod. "I'm sorry. I wish we could have done something." He left.

Finally, only Zeke and Debbie remained behind with her.

Karen reached out and closed the eyelids over the black half-moons. She continued staring at the closed lids.

"What happened?" she asked.

"She'd been up all night with a breech delivery," Zeke said. "Duane picked her up. The cops figure she crawled into the back seat to sleep while he drove."

"How bad was he hurt?"

"There aren't many findings. He's got a bruise on his head. . . ." Zeke frowned. "Something's strange about him, Karen."

Her hands tightened as she continued looking at the still, wax face of her sister. "Drunk?"

Zeke shrugged. "No smell of alcohol. We're getting a drug panel."

She slowly lifted her face, looked first at Zeke, then at Debbie. Each word escaped through clenched teeth. "Where is he?"

"Dr. Dreyer?" Debbie's voice caught. "He's in one."

Zeke spoke softly. "Karen, maybe you should wait until morning."

"I'll go talk to the son of a bitch now," Karen said.

2

The door to room one was closed. Karen shoved it viciously. It swung wide and crashed against the wall.

Seated in a bedside chair, both of Duane Dreyer's hands jerked upward in sudden alarm. He recognized Karen and smiled weakly. Dr. Michael Werner, associate professor of neurology on the medical school faculty, stood next to him.

Cold rage gripped at Karen's throat and tightened her voice. "I'll come back when you're through."

Werner was a large, athletically built man with square shoulders, square chin, trimmed black beard, and thinning hair. "I'm finished for now." His face was grim as he deposited a reflex hammer, tuning fork, and pinwheel into a black leather bag. "I'll be at the nurses' desk."

After he closed the door behind him, she faced her brother-in-law. Duane Dreyer was a slim man of average height, but his erect carriage and smartly tailored suits had always given him the appearance of tallness. He'd been Karen's favorite attending man when she started her residency at University Hospital nearly five years earlier. She'd introduced him to Susan. He was bright, caring, articulate—and had a wide fund of knowledge that spanned the entire field of internal medicine. Her chief, Dr. Berkholt, had recognized this when he recommended Duane for full professorship status at the age of thirty-eight and appointed him chief of medicine at Collier Hospital, one of the two chronic care hospitals in the large Cinema Acres Retirement Community. It was Berkholt himself who a year earlier had engineered the affiliation of Cinema Acres with the medical school as its geriatric teaching unit.

There was nothing impressive about Duane today. A discolored swelling covered the right side of his forehead. A small crust of blood lined his upper lip. He wore a baggy white patient's gown, beneath which his knees protruded like pink doorknobs. His smile of recognition was replaced by a bewildered look. "Where's Susan, Karen?"

When she'd started her residency, Karen had wanted to emulate him. Now her tight fists trembled at her side as she struggled to keep from striking him. She spat out her words. "Susan's dead, Duane."

His eyes widened, and his face crunched up. "Dead? Susan can't be dead." He started to rise but settled back into the chair and looked up at Karen.

"Yes, dead. Killed when she was thrown from the car you were driving." She bent forward over him, her body a taut steel spring. "What happened, Duane? I want to know what happened."

His mouth fell open. His eyes stayed wide. "I—I don't know."

She grabbed his shoulders and shook him. His head lolled like a loose rag doll's. "What have you been taking, you bastard? What are you on?"

Tears glistened in his eyes. "I don't understand."

She stared at him, then shoved him back into his chair. "God damn you!" She turned away. She'd be sick in front of him if she stayed. She headed for the door.

"Karen?"

At the sound of his voice the rage rose again like the bile that was stuck in her throat. She turned back.

He hadn't risen from the chair. The lines had disappeared from his face and left him looking almost childlike. He gave a weak smile. "Karen, would you call Susan?"

Mike Werner was at the nurses' station dictating his report on Duane. He signaled to Karen and pointed at a nearby chair. She sat down heavily.

When he finished the dictation, he turned to her. He reached out a hand and rested it on her arm. "How're you doing, Karen?"

Her arm reflexively drew back. The last thing she wanted was sympathy. She was too close to sickness and to tears already. She struggled to keep her voice from catching. "What the hell is he on, Mike?"

Werner withdrew his hand. "The drug screen was totally negative. And blood alcohol level was zero."

She stared at him.

He nodded grimly. "What else could it be? Maybe a temporal lobe tumor? A bleed—a subdural hematoma?" He shook his head. "I just reviewed the CAT scan. Normal."

She shaped each word slowly and deliberately. "Mike, he's not normal."

Werner pursed his lips. "Has Duane been acting strangely—before today?"

For the first time since she'd answered the ER page, a feeling of uncertainty dug at her—and with it, a rush of fear. Of desperation. *No. I don't want to hear anything that might make me hate him less.* "I—I don't know. The service has been busy—I haven't seen him and Susan much."

"When was the last time?"

She let out a deep breath. Her voice dropped. "It's been a few weeks. Last Friday I was scheduled to discuss a case on his service. He didn't show up. That wasn't like him. Didn't call, didn't leave a message—just didn't show up."

"Did you talk to your sister about it?"

Karen answered slowly. "I had lunch with her Saturday."

The memory of that day flooded back. She'd run into Enrique's Coffee Shop in Westwood Center, just outside the university campus, prepared to apologize to Susan for being a half hour late—teaching rounds with Dr. Berkholt had stretched much longer than she'd expected. The house staff had had a hundred questions, and Dr. Berkholt had generously deferred many of them to "my colleague, Dr. Formaker." That was the day after he'd offered her the position as his associate.

Her apologies weren't necessary. Susan hadn't yet arrived. She showed up a few minutes later. "I'm sorry, Kare," she said.

Susan had never looked so tired, even during the thirty-six-hour on-call schedules of obstetrics residency. A twinge of concern struck Karen after the hostess seated them. Whatever was bothering Susan, it was more than fatigue. She felt Susan's troubled thoughts, and along with them a current of fear.

Their mother had died when Karen was five. Susan, four years older, had filled the vacuum. She was mother, sister, closest friend, confidante. Somehow this closeness had given the two sisters the kind of extrasensory perception of each other's inner thoughts that is sometimes found in identical twins. "What is it, Susan?"

Susan frowned. A crease appeared under each cheekbone, almost a half-moon. Karen had identical creases when she frowned. One glance, and there could be no doubt that the two of them were sisters. The same straight golden-brown hair. The same alive, brown eyes, slightly upswept, freckled nose, hips a little too broad for an otherwise slim figure. The main difference was that at five foot three, Susan was almost three inches taller. Karen had accused her of hogging all the tall genes in the family.

The half-moon creases beneath Susan's cheekbones were more prominent than usual. "It's Duane."

"Duane? Has he been sick?"

Susan bit her lip. "I don't know. Something's strange about him the past few weeks. I can't pinpoint it. He's been acting troubled, almost frightened. I tried to get him to talk about it, but he backed off. And then, two days ago . . ." Susan looked off into the distance. Tears glistened in her eyes.

"What happened?" Karen asked quietly.

"I'd slept in. I'd been up until four with an emergency cesarean." She swallowed and continued staring into the distance. "I got a call from the resident on his service at ten. Duane was supposed to lead the nine o'clock attending rounds. He hadn't shown up."

Susan looked back at Karen. Her lips tightened. "He's never missed an appointment, Karen. When I got home that night, he was already home. I asked him how his day went. He said okay. I asked about attending rounds. He said they went fine. Just fine."

"What are you thinking about?"

Susan swallowed. "I don't know. I thought maybe . . . he's involved with someone else."

Karen reached for her sister's hand. "There must be a hundred simpler explanations. But Susan, rather than let it torture you, don't you think you ought to confront him?"

Susan bit her lip. "I'm not sure I'm ready—I mean, to find out." She studied her folded napkin on the table. "Whatever it is, it's tearing him apart. Last night I got a call to go to the hospital around three. Duane wasn't in bed. I heard something that sounded like a sob coming from the living room and went to investigate. I found him sitting on the couch with his head in his hands, and every few seconds his shoulders would heave. I came up and touched him on the shoulder. He gave a gasp and leaped from the couch as if he were in terror. He said he was just having a bad dream."

Mike Werner gazed at Karen sadly. "Did Susan say anything at all about drugs? Pot? Any clue?"

"I asked her, Mike. She said Duane doesn't even take aspirin. She had checked his medicine cabinet and the bathroom drawers, all the same. Not a trace."

Werner's lips tightened. "So far it's one blind alley after another."

Karen looked intently at him. "Could he have been on something that wouldn't show up in a drug screen?"

Werner toyed with his pen. "Were you at grand rounds Wednesday?"

"The pulmonary fibrosis? I missed it. I remember, because I'd consulted on the case. I was trapped with a diabetic ketoacidosis in ICU."

"I was on the panel with Duane, Karen. He presented the case." Werner paused and pursed his lips. "You know his usual delivery?"

"Sure, it's one of the things I've admired about him. He can discuss a case in almost any field as if he'd written the original paper on it."

"Exactly. Standing on the podium, he hadn't changed—immaculately dressed, ramrod straight, same mellifluous voice. And the same beautiful delivery—crisp, clear-cut, logical. As long as he read from his written report."

"What do you mean?"

"With the first question in the discussion period afterward, he confused the case with a bronchogenic carcinoma. He didn't know any of the lab results he'd just read off. Then all of a sudden, he called me up to the podium. There wasn't even a neurologic aspect to the case." Werner turned from Karen and gazed down the hallway. "Duane and I were in the same medical school class. Each of us was best man at the other's wedding. He's my closest friend." He took in a deep breath and turned back to her. "Karen—he walked off. He didn't say a word to me. He just left me up there at the podium and walked off."

As Karen stared at Mike Werner, his words began to blur.

The realization struck again with fresh force. *Susan's dead!* Nothing would bring her back.

She didn't want to listen to Mike any longer. All she wanted now was to get away and tend to her own private grief. She shook her head; her voice rose. "I don't understand what you're talking about. Just a few weeks ago I made rounds with Duane and Dr. Berkholt at Collier Hospital. Duane knew every case as if the patient were his personal charge. He could run off a page of lab results without looking at the chart."

"Yes, he could. A month ago."

Nothing made sense. She had to get away. "Mike, what besides drugs could do this to a man?"

"I don't know, Karen." Werner shook his head slowly. "I don't know."

3

Susan had long made it clear that she'd opt for cremation. "We'll have a hard enough time finding room for the living on this planet without reserving more space for the dead," she'd said. The ceremony was scheduled for the second day following her death. Karen limited the ceremony to a nonsectarian memorial service.

The mortuary was a U-shaped, one-story, Spanish-style building with freshly painted white stucco walls and a red tile roof. A small courtyard occupied the space between the sides of the U. Across the street was a tiny park with green lawn, palm trees, and a central patch of rose bushes. The small complex, tucked between the highrise office buildings and condominiums of West Los Angeles, concealed a soft glimpse of Southern California's past.

The mortuary chapel overflowed with University Hospital house staff and attending faculty. Brightly polished mahogany benches flanked the central aisle. Banks of roses, gardenias, and azaleas lined each side of the platform. At the head of the chapel, velvet drapes of dark purple walled off the coffin. In front of the drapes stood a tall crystal vase of tiger lilies that Karen had carefully placed. Tiger lilies had been Susan's favorite flower.

Karen sat next to the aisle, front row left. At her side was Hank Merrill, the intense but outwardly easygoing biostatistics expert with whom she shared an apartment. Duane hadn't appeared. As of morning, he was still hospitalized. She hadn't been able to bring herself to go back to see him.

A series of friends and fellow doctors followed one another to the podium to pay tribute to Susan.

The most moving eulogy was Dr. Berkholt's.

Fifty-eight-year-old Arnold Berkholt was a giant figure in medicine—

chairman of the Department of Endocrinology, co-winner of the 1979 Nobel prize for his pioneer work on brain hormones, author of the definitive textbook in his field, editor of the *American Journal of Endocrinology*. His rich baritone filled the chapel. "I grieve for the senseless loss of a beautiful woman who graced our hallways and enriched our lives. Even more, I grieve for the loss to humanity of an idealistic, dedicated doctor who, in her youthful years, had already shown the capacity for greatness."

He paused, and Karen could hear the coughs and sniffles and muffled sobs that rustled through the hall. "I had the privilege of working with Susan Formaker when she rotated through my service during her first year of residency. I not only watched but *felt* her strength, enthusiasm, and vitality—that wonderful zest for life that's found only in a gifted few —as it spread from her to everyone with whom she worked. I've had close opportunity to observe those same qualities as they've been handed on from her to her younger sister, whom I'll soon have the honor of calling my associate."

He turned slowly until he faced the closed velvet drapes behind the pulpit. "We shall sorely miss you here at University Hospital, Susan Formaker. We shall miss your talent and your wisdom, your laughter and your spirit. You ennobled us with your presence. For the all too few years you were with us, we were richer. The world is poorer from your loss."

Karen swallowed. She stared hard at the drapes, trying to concentrate, as if from behind that wall of velvet she could once again will her sister's thoughts to her. But it was of no use. The tears welled up; she couldn't force them back.

She felt Hank's hand take hers, and she turned to him. He was slim and fairly tall, with dark hair that was usually brushed loosely to the side but never quite combed. He had wide, dark brows. A full, brown moustache curved slightly downward at the angles of his lips. His relaxed good looks and a casual trace of Texas still left in his speech put people at ease —except when he was in one of his withdrawn, remote phases. Then the fine crinkles at the corners of his lids would disappear, and his eyes would become cool and distant.

His gaze was fixed on Karen. She wiped her eyes with a finger and gripped his hand. Except for Duane, Hank Merrill was the closest to family she had left.

Although she and Hank had lived together for the past five months, Hank would frown if he could read her thoughts. *Family* wasn't part of his vocabulary. Family meant commitments. Commitments were fences. Hank Merrill had made it clear that he wanted no fences around him, asked none of her.

At first that had been fine with Karen. In fact, it had been part of the attraction.

She could remember only once when the topic of marriage had come up. It had been a little over three months ago, after Duane and Susan's fourth-anniversary dinner party. Five other couples attended. Karen handled the preparation and cooking, along with Mike Werner's wife. Shrimp, Cornish hens, and grilled mushroom caps were washed down with liberal amounts of champagne.

After dinner, Susan took Karen aside in the kitchen. "Thanks, little sister," she said. "Some day, I hope I'll get a chance to do the same for you and Hank."

Karen shook her head. "I wouldn't count on it, Suze. Hank and I don't seem to be the marrying type."

"I said that once," Susan said. "You just wait." She looked toward the dining room. "I really like him, Karen."

Karen grinned. "You do?"

Susan nodded firmly.

Karen and Hank got back to their apartment after midnight. They climbed into bed. Hank slipped an arm under her shoulders. "It was a neat party," he said.

She still felt a glow from the wine and the intimacy of the evening. She rubbed her cheek against his arm. "Susan said she'd like to someday throw an anniversary party for us."

"Why not?" he said. "We can start a movement to popularize Sylis anniversaries."

Karen lifted her head. "What the hell is a Sylis?"

He grinned a triumphant *gotcha!* grin. "The parent organization of Single Yuppies Living in Sin."

A strange feeling, something close to disappointment—or anger—gnawed at her. She tried to keep her voice light. "I meant a real anniversary. Of a wedding."

Hank pulled her closer. "You're great in bed, Formaker. We're too smart to let anything like marriage wreck a good arrangement."

"You're right, Merrill. We're too smart for that." She pulled away from him and turned over.

Hank lifted himself up in bed and rested a hand on her shoulder. "I'm sorry."

"Forget it," she said.

"I mean it, Kare. I'm truly sorry. I don't know what comes over me when I talk this way."

"I don't either. But it's pretty damned callous."

He looked down at her with sadness in his eyes. "It's just that I wouldn't ever again want to screw up two lives."

"Sure."

He slowly stroked her arm. "Please try to understand. You're very important to me. You're the most important person in my life."

"Good night." She closed her eyes tightly.

But she was far from sleep.

Hank rarely talked about his past marriage, and then only when he'd had too much to drink. Her name was Terri. A sweet, home-town girl. They'd started dating in high school in Dallas. After graduation, both had enrolled in Southern Methodist University. Hank's father was a prominent Dallas ophthalmologist. His ophthalmology clinic had expanded into the Merrill Eye Center, with fifteen physicians and a referral base that encompassed the entire Southwest. He expected Hank to marry Terri and become a doctor.

Though Hank had been in premed, his mania was computers, and he was considered a genius in math. But everyone knew Hank would go into medicine, just as everyone knew Hank and Terri would marry. His father would support the two of them while they finished SMU and Hank went through medical school. He'd have a place waiting for Hank in the Eye Center.

Just as planned, Hank and Terri had married near the beginning of their senior year. Hank promptly flunked comparative anatomy and barely passed zoology three. He developed a migraine in the middle of the Medical College Admissions Test and couldn't complete it. When the MCAT was offered again four months later, he didn't show up for it. By then, Terri had announced that she was having an affair with a twenty-eight-year-old rock singer, and Hank had dropped out of college.

When he and Terri were divorced, Hank had been twenty-two.

Sitting in the front row of the mortuary, Karen felt vulnerable. She looked at Hank. His eyes were still on her. She swallowed. *There's no one but me. What about getting married? I've no family left now. What's wrong with wanting my own?*

As if he'd read her mind, his eyes clouded. He turned away and looked toward the podium.

After the ceremony, Karen found Dr. Berkholt waiting for her next to the small fountain in the mortuary courtyard.

He'd seemed remote and unreachable until only six days ago when he'd called her to his office on the eighth floor of the medical school and offered her the job. "I believe I'm nearing a breakthrough, Karen. But the work has split along two channels, and each needs full-time attention. First, there's the basic laboratory research, which, as you know, has focused on CRH and its analogs. Second, and equally important, is the clinical practice—without the patients, the research becomes an empty exercise. I can no longer keep up with both, and I'm asking for your help. I'll want you to maintain a working knowledge of the research, but mainly I'll ask you to take over the clinical side, the everyday nuts-and-bolts of seeing the patients."

In the days since that interview, Karen had begun seeing new consults in his office. Two nights ago, when she had worked particularly late, he had dropped by, and they drove to a nearby coffee shop where, for the first time, they had talked of their personal lives. He was fifty-eight and lived alone. He'd once been married and had a child who'd died of a congenital heart malformation in infancy. The medical school had offered him chairmanship of the Department of Medicine, but he'd refused it for fear it would take too much time away from his research on the brain hormone CRH.

As the days passed, in spite of her growing feeling of closeness to him, Karen couldn't address Arnold Berkholt by his first name, as she did all of her other attending men. She probably never would. There was something imposing about him that wasn't easily put into words. If she were trying to describe his physical appearance, she'd have difficulty finding anything out of the ordinary to say about it. He was of average height and had a full head of dark hair barely beginning to gray. His face was finely pitted, skin the texture of ripened orange peel. His nose was sharp, slightly curved, fitted between wide-set gray eyes and prominent dark brows. He dressed well but not spectacularly. There was nothing distinctive about him physically.

But once he began to speak, Arnold Berkholt could have been ten feet tall. He had a clear, natural eloquence. His rich, modulated voice radiated strength and confidence. It hardly ever rose in volume, but with his first words a crowded room would become silent.

Karen walked up to him now, where he waited for her by the courtyard fountain. "That was a beautiful tribute you paid my sister," she said.

"She was a beautiful person."

She had no fear of his sympathy. There was no sentimentality in Berkholt's steady slate-gray eyes, only a comforting strength. At least for the moment, tears were behind her. "Thank you," she said quietly.

Berkholt nodded toward the small park across the street. "Do you feel like walking?"

They crossed, then strolled the gravel paths. "Have you seen Duane?" he asked.

Her voice tightened. "Not since the emergency room."

"I've been to his room," Berkholt said.

"Oh?"

"I know you blame him for Susan's death, Karen. But I was heartsick at what I found. Something terrible is happening to him. Something that so far makes no sense. He can't remember the accident. He can't even understand that Susan's dead." His voice dropped. "Duane and I have worked together since he joined the faculty. I took him under my wing. He's almost young enough to fill the role of the son I lost."

She wasn't prepared for the wrenching sadness in his voice. Her step slowed, and she rested her hand on his arm for a moment. "I'm sorry. I'd forgotten just how close you were."

"I was hoping we could blame his head injury for some of his behavior. But in two days he's grown considerably worse. And the injury doesn't seem enough to explain it."

"Has Mike Werner come up with anything?" she asked.

"He's brought in some of the best people on the faculty. But so far, nothing."

Karen slowly shook her head. "I just can't get myself to forgive him, Dr. Berkholt."

"With your loss, I can understand that." Dr. Berkholt looked straight ahead as they walked. "Actually, Duane's not the reason I've been waiting to talk to you. I have a major request to make." He paused for a moment. "I regret the heavy load that even making the decision will place on you."

She stopped walking and turned to look at him.

His face was solemn. "Duane's illness creates a terrible vacuum at a time when our work can least afford it. I want you to become my associate as of now, and take over his job as Chief of medicine at Collier Hospital."

She stared at him. Collier Hospital was the chronic care dementia hospital at the huge retirement complex of Cinema Acres.

He continued. "I realize it's an unfair load to dump on you at a time when you're already weighed down by grief. I'm asking a great deal—in addition to your work at Collier, you'll still be seeing my private patients at the medical school."

"But Collier already has a medical staff. All of them have more experience with dementia patients than I have."

"Karen, Collier Hospital may soon become more than just another storage place for crumbling minds. As you know, it will be the trial hospital for our first CRH studies on humans. When I asked you to become my associate, it wasn't a casual decision on my part. In the ten years I've been here, you've done the finest work of anyone who's served a fellowship in my department. And as far as Collier Hospital is concerned, you've studied CRH more intensively than any doctor at the medical school other than myself." He paused. "That's why I'm asking you to take on the job."

She gazed hard into his eyes. They held pain but also a reassuring firmness. "I'll need a day before I can give you an answer," she said.

"Of course," he said gently.

4

Karen walked slowly back to the parking lot. Her mind was still too numb from the funeral services to digest Dr. Berkholt's offer. She gave a breath of relief when she saw Hank waiting for her by the car.

He lifted his arms. She fell into them.

His lips brushed her hair as he spoke. "I'm going to miss her, too, Karen."

"It was a good ceremony," she said.

"Yes, it was." His hand stroked slow circles over her back.

Karen lifted her head and looked up at him. "Let's go to Palisades Park. I'd like to look at the ocean."

He wiped back a strand of her hair and kissed her on the forehead. "Sure."

They drove along San Vicente to Palisades Drive. Hank parked his Tercel and slipped a quarter into the parking meter. They crossed the grass to the fence at the edge of the bluff.

The autumn air was clear enough for Karen to see the outline of Catalina Island in the distance. As sunset approached, the long, linear clouds capping the horizon took on their first hue of orange. She held onto the guardrail. Many times she and Susan had come here with brown bag lunches to gaze at this same scene. While Susan was in her first two years at the medical school and Karen was an undergraduate at UCLA, they'd come almost daily. Then the time pressures of Susan's clinical years—and later Karen's—had broken up their noon get-togethers. But still, whenever there were decisions to be made, they had found time to meet here. It was as if the fresh salt air and the background splash of the waves were part of the decision-making process. It was here, a little over four years ago, that Susan had told her that Duane had asked her to marry him. Two days before the wedding, in this same spot, Susan had poured out her sudden flood of qualms about the upcoming marriage. Karen assured her that they'd still be together, that she and Duane had already become good friends, that marriage wouldn't divide the two sisters. And it was here, only six months ago, that Karen had told Susan she was thinking of moving in with Hank. She knew she was leaving herself open for hurt; Hank had been too wounded in his marriage to Terri to ever make a commitment. Susan had wrapped her arm around her. "Wounds heal, Kare," she'd said. "Hank loves you. I see it in the way he looks at you and the way he comes to life when you're around. You can't always stay protected—you've got to follow your feelings."

Karen turned to Hank. He was gazing out into the distance. His brown hair waved in the ocean breeze. "Dr. Berkholt wants me to take over Duane's job," she said.

Hank looked at her in surprise. "At Collier?"

She nodded.

"But what about your work as his associate?"

"That's part of it. He's going to be starting a major new research project at Collier. It involves working with the brain hormone that was the main thrust of my research year. The two jobs would fit together."

"What did you tell him?"

"I couldn't think, Hank. I told him I needed a day."

"A day isn't very long."

"The new project's due to start in two weeks."

His eyes studied hers. "How do you feel about it?"

"I'm honored." She shook her head. "But I don't know if I'm qualified."

"It sounds good, Karen. And it's not as if you're standing alone. You've got the big man's full support behind you."

Her lips tightened. "Damn it, I have to make it on my own merits. I won't stand on anyone else's coattails."

"That's not what I said. Look, Berkholt picked you over at least twenty others from your residency group, all of whom would have given their eyeteeth for the endocrine fellowship. He's already told you he wants you in charge because you know about the stuff he'll be working with there. And he obviously thinks you're good enough to be his associate—which I'd like to point out is a first. How much more reassurance can you ask?"

She took his hand and smiled. "I don't know. But that sure helps."

After they stopped for dinner, Hank dropped her off at the apartment while he went by the med center to check on a download from the central mainframe.

They shared a one-bedroom apartment on the crowded West Side, five miles south of the medical center. Computer furniture and equipment crowded their otherwise sparsely furnished living room. In the kitchen the telephone answering machine flashed, its readout indicating nine messages. As Karen listened to a series of condolences, she suddenly found herself sobbing.

One message caught her. It was from Bill Horlich. She wiped her eyes and quickly jotted down the number.

She bit her lip as she dialed. God, it would be good to talk to Bill now.

He'd come to University Medical Center for a fellowship in infectious disease during Karen's last year of residency. He'd just finished his own internal medicine residency at Massachusetts General Hospital. When she first saw him, he looked more like a tight end for the Los Angeles Rams than a doctor—six foot four, black, broad shouldered, two hundred twenty pounds of muscle.

Karen had had little contact with him until her strange illness. It was in August, over two years ago, shortly after she had started her fellowship. She and Hank were returning from a ten-day Sierra Club wilderness trip in the Sawtooth Mountains of Idaho. Wearing daypacks while mules carried their duffel bags, they'd hiked ten miles to the shores of remote Cramer Lake, where the granite spires of Mount Cramer formed a cathedral background to clear sapphire waters. People had just begun to refer to them as a couple. They had made no special arrangements—as a matter of fact, the only spoken agreement between them was Hank's first of several "no commitments" declarations. They'd brought separate backpackers' tents—but by the fourth day of the Cramer Lake trip, Karen's tent was being used only for storing supplies, and nights found the two of them bundled together in Hank's.

On the flight back from Idaho Falls, Karen had had her first chill. She shook hard, her teeth chattering like castanets. She had a pounding headache. Every muscle felt as if she'd just fought and lost a wrestling match with one of the Sawtooth grizzlies.

Hank was worried sick. He wanted to take Karen directly to be checked over by Duane, but she assured him she only had the flu, and by the time she returned to work two days later, she was well. Four days later, however, the shaking chills returned, with temperature spikes to 104 degrees. She saw the senior resident on internal medicine. The examination was unremarkable. Her white cell count was normal at 7200. Liver function tests were normal. By the time the studies were completed, her fever had cleared. Her muscles felt washed out but no longer ached. The senior resident shrugged. Just another flulike viral syndrome.

When the chills and fever again recurred four days later, Susan had insisted that Karen move in with her and Duane. This time the senior resident threw the book at her: chest film, blood and urine cultures, stool cultures, malaria smears, full chemistry panel, blood serologies for influenza, HIV, Epstein-Barr, toxoplasma, Rocky Mountain spotted fever, typhus. All normal.

Again, the fever cleared. Karen returned to work.

When the chills returned four days later and her temperature spiked to 105.6 degrees, she was hospitalized. That was when Bill Horlich was called in.

Her last chill had just ended and her fever was falling when he reviewed her history with her. Point by point he went over her exposures. She'd drunk only boiled or heavily iodinated water on the trip. Sure, there'd been a few mosquito bites, but malaria hadn't been reported indigenous to the Rockies during this century. None of the other eighteen people who'd taken the trip had developed anything more than a cold.

Bill's examination had been remarkably gentle for so massive a man. He had checked every inch of her skin, studying particularly a pink pinpoint on her left thigh. He felt carefully for nodes. His fingers probed beneath her rib cage for the tip of her spleen and liver

When he finished, Karen's findings remained remarkably normal. He went over her lab reports in intricate detail, then headed for X-ray to review her chest film and to the lab to look at her blood slides.

Forty minutes later, he had returned to her hospital room. "Are you up to dropping by the lab with me?" he asked.

She didn't question why. Bill radiated a feeling of confidence, and she felt more secure than she'd felt since the first recurrence of chills. In robe and slippers, she took the elevator with him to the huge University Hospital laboratory. In Hematology, the chief technician stood by a microscope while other technicians were taking turns looking in. When he saw Bill, the chief technician shook his head. "I don't know how I could've missed it," he said.

"Let's let Dr. Formaker have a look," Bill said in a casual tone. He motioned to the microscope.

Karen peered in. The slide was a malaria smear—which is prepared no differently from a routine blood count stain, except that the blood is smeared on the glass slide more thickly. She moved from one field to another. Normal white blood cells. None of the red blood cells contained any of the tiny violet staining parasites that she'd read about but never seen, as diagnostic of malaria.

Finally, she gave up and lifted her head from the microscope. "I don't see anything wrong, Bill."

The chief technician smiled in relief.

"Borrelia, Karen," Bill Horlich said softly.

She blinked. *Borrelia hermisii.* Tick-borne relapsing fever. She quickly put her eyes back to the microscope. There they were! Tiny, thin blue spirals scattered throughout the field. The classic spirochetes of *Borrelia.*

She looked up at Bill, wide-eyed. "I didn't see them the first time."

"None of us did," said the technician. "But now they practically jump out at me every time I recheck the slides."

"It's one of the axioms of medicine," Bill said. "We're usually blind to anything we're not looking for. If there were a single malaria parasite on that slide, there'd be no chance on earth it would have gone undetected. But we're not accustomed to looking for spirochetes."

"Borrelia," Karen said quietly. "The tick that transmits it is a night feeder. Drops off after a couple hours. Usually wouldn't be noticed."

"Exactly," Bill said. "Perhaps the pinpoint on your thigh is what's left of its signature. Or maybe it's just coincidence. But we've got the answer, Karen."

Once the diagnosis was established, treatment was simple. Doxycycline, a hundred milligrams twice a day for ten days. The fever didn't recur after the first day.

During the remainder of his two-year fellowship, until he went to Atlanta to take a job with the Centers for Disease Control, Bill Horlich was Karen and Hank's closest mutual friend.

She'd phoned him the night Susan died and left word on his answering machine. Tonight, she gave a deep breath of relief when she heard his familiar deep, resonant voice.

"Bill, I can't tell you how much it meant to me when I heard your message."

"I just got back from Stockholm this afternoon, Karen. I was stunned. I'm so very sorry."

"I shouldn't have given you the news on an answering machine," she said. "I should have waited until I could talk to you." A warmth sprang up behind her eyes, and her throat got tight. "But it was so sudden. I—couldn't think."

"You did right, I'd have been hurt if you hadn't called. Tell me what happened."

Once, while she was describing what she found in the emergency room, her voice broke, and she had to pause. When finally she finished, Bill spoke slowly. "I don't understand about Duane."

"None of us do. At first I hated him. All I could think of was that he caused Susan's death." She swallowed. "Now I don't know."

"What are your plans now?"

"Dr. Berkholt wants me to take over as chief of medicine at Collier Hospital." She told him about the project.

"It sounds like a fine opportunity."

She gazed at the dark outside the window. "That's what Hank thinks. But I don't know if I'm ready. I haven't had enough time to mourn Susan."

"From what I remember of Susan, she'd rather you got on with your life."

"I guess you're right, Bill."

"Karen, I can chuck things and come there tomorrow."

She smiled. For some reason, all at once, she felt more at peace than she'd felt since Susan died. "Thanks, Bill. But the funeral's over, and you must be swamped with work after being away in Stockholm. I'm going to be fine."

"You'll call me if you can use me?"

"I promise."

After she hung up, she sat quietly for a moment.

She lifted the notepad pencil. Her hand tightened around it.

Then she picked up the phone to call Dr. Berkholt.

5

University Medical Center was an extensive gridwork of connected buildings that housed the medical and dental schools, University Hospital with all its divisions, and the large Neuropsychiatric Institute. On that campus in West Los Angeles, Karen had spent the last nine years, starting there as a medical student four years after Susan. She had graduated second in her class, stayed on for three years of residency, then turned down an offer to become chief resident so she could take a fellowship in endocrinology. Now she was there as Dr. Berkholt's associate, with her fresh appointment as assistant professor of medicine on the medical school faculty.

Her duties at Collier Hospital were scheduled to start in two days. She made preparations to transfer her current endocrine service cases to Percy Barnes, the endocrine fellow who, like Karen before him, was spending the first year of his fellowship in laboratory research. With Karen leaving the fellowship, he would move up to his clinical year two months early.

Karen used a wheelchair to carry her books and papers from her metal desk in a basement house staff room to her new private office in Dr. Berkholt's eighth-floor suite in the medical school. After downing the hospital cafeteria's "diet special" of tuna salad, broccoli soup, and a small apple, she met Barnes in her old basement office. He was a short, bony man with long black hair and large eyes centered behind thick, plastic-rimmed glasses. He was so soft-spoken that Karen often had to strain to hear him.

"I'm really sorry about Susan, Karen," Barnes said.

"I saw you at the funeral, Percy. I appreciated it."

"She was a neat lady."

"That she was," Karen said quietly.

Barnes shifted feet. He squinted behind his heavily magnified glasses as he looked around the cramped, windowless room. "So this is the office?"

"Yep. You see it all in one glance."

"You don't get claustrophobic?"

"It's not as bad as it looks," Karen said. "Every so often the keeper of the dungeon comes around, throws you scraps, and refills your water bowl."

Barnes shrugged. "At least I'll get a chance to deal with real live patients again. How long will it take me to wipe the CRH analog formulas from my mind?"

"It's too late, Percy. The lab year in endocrine fellowship brands the CRH formulas indelibly onto your brain. Like a Circle K brand on your butt. You'll think about them, dream about them, see their letters in your bowl of cereal every morning. Like me, you're doomed to wander the rest of your life with CRH formulas cluttering your mind."

Barnes looked at her with his wide owl-eyes and slowly nodded.

"Okay," Karen said as the sadness returned in a sudden rush, "let's go over the patients you'll be following."

Karen finished early the final afternoon before starting her new job at Collier Hospital. She walked into the apartment long before the time when Hank usually returned. She changed into sweats, went to the kitchen, and peered into the freezer. The only instant dinner on the nearly bare shelves was Mrs. Garcia's Cheese Enchiladas. She pulled it out, tore off the aluminum foil cover, checked the directions, and popped it into the microwave. She set the timer for six minutes, opened a Pepsi, and sat at the small Formica-topped table.

She'd learned soon after she and Hank had moved in together not to wait for him for dinner. It wasn't unusual for him to come home after nine. That wasn't what held her back—her own schedule involved demanding hours as well. But Hank had made it quite clear that he didn't like the idea of Karen holding a meal for him. It was another part of his thing against commitments.

After his divorce from Terri, he had gone through a period of desolation. He left home, drank heavily, worked odd jobs, slept in fleabag rooms. He completely severed the ties of family financial support. Not that his father would have continued supporting him, anyway. When Hank dropped out of premed, his father became apoplectic. Hank was throwing away the opportunity for prestige and wealth waiting for him in his reserved niche in the Merrill Eye Center. Had he any idea what it was like to struggle for a living, as his father had struggled when he worked his way through college and starved through medical school on the sole support of the GI bill?

In time, Hank picked up the pieces of his life and headed for Los Angeles. He got a job in computer programming for the biotechnology division of Jet Propulsion Labs. His genius in mathematics and wizardry in computers quickly became evident. After six months, JPL sent him part time to California Institute of Technology for advanced studies. There, his lack of a bachelor's degree was ignored and he was placed on track for a graduate degree in computer science. Within a year he had his master's and became a teaching assistant at CalTech.

He was working toward his Ph.D. in biostatistics when he met Karen.

She was a resident on cardiac care ICU. In the wee morning hours when she was giving an intravenous clot dissolver to an acute coronary, the computerized monitor console for the CCU had gone haywire. Karen was fully aware that for the first few hours after the dissolver, deadly heart rhythm disturbances were common. The charge nurse ran up with a crash cart and wired the patient to its emergency portable monitor.

Karen sat by the small monitor, watching tensely as the number of threatening premature ventricular beats increased. "Can't we get someone out?" she asked.

"I'll try Bioengineering," the nurse said.

Within forty minutes, a young man of slim, gangly build appeared. His dark hair was tousled, as if he'd come straight from bed. His moustache was full and straggly. He wore a loose, wrinkled flannel shirt, faded denim jeans, and jogging shoes. Strapped to his shoulders was a frayed green nylon daypack. After the chief nurse spoke to him, he ambled up to Karen. "Got a problem, doc?" His voice revealed a slight southern twang. Fine crinkles spread from the corners of his dark blue eyes.

"Yes, I have a problem," she said stiffly. Why the hell couldn't this have happened during the daytime when they could've gotten someone experienced? This guy looked as if he'd just come in from a junior college track meet. She turned back to the monitor on the crash cart. "I've got a patient who can die with ventricular fibrillation any minute, and the only way I can monitor him is on this Mickey Mouse outfit."

He made a sucking noise between his teeth and bent forward over her shoulder. He pointed at two wide, jagged patterns crawling side by side across the screen. "That what you're worried about?"

Karen gritted her teeth. That was exactly what she was worried about. "Look, what I need is someone to fix the monitor system. What I *don't* need right now is a kibitzer."

He nodded sagely. "Let me see what I can do." He shrugged off his daypack, pulled out two screwdrivers and a long-nose pliers, and crawled beneath the wide console.

In less than six minutes the row of twelve screens lit up. He appeared from beneath the equipment. "Loose chip," he drawled. "Nothing needed replacing."

Karen checked the patient's heart and lungs while the nurse reconnected him to the central monitor system. She reduced the lidocaine drip from four to three milligrams per minute, then turned to the slim young man, who'd just finished zipping shut his daypack. "Sorry if I snapped," she said with a smile. "You did a great job. Actually, you saved me from an acute panic attack." She held out her hand. "I'm Karen."

"Hank," he said. "Hank Merrill. You hungry?"

She glanced at the wall clock. Five thirty. "Not much point in going back to bed now, is there?"

He shook his head. "Nah. I've got a seven-thirty seminar, and there's probably a slew of patients who'll be waiting for you."

There *was* something appealing about those crinkles at the corners of his eyes. "Yep, I am pretty hungry," she said.

Karen tried to read while she picked at her TV dinner. She'd brought home the last six issues of *Journal of Geriatrics* from the library. But she was halfway through the first when she realized she hadn't retained a word. She turned the TV on to a *Lucy* rerun. It was no better. Her thoughts shifted between memories of scenes with Susan and her fears of the scene she'd face tomorrow at Collier Hospital.

She jumped up from the couch when she heard Hank fumbling with his keys. She restrained herself from running to the door to open it.

He threw his daypack onto a chair and gave her a quick kiss on the lips. "How are you?"

She shrugged. "Okay. I finished turning over my endocrine cases to Barnes and had only two consults for Dr. Berkholt."

He took her hands. "It had to be rough, this soon after Susan."

"By now, everyone's run out of condolences. Actually, that makes it easier."

He smiled gently. "I can understand that."

"I'd feel a lot better if this were tomorrow night."

"You mean, after you get through your first day at Collier?"

She nodded.

"You'll have it all under control in a couple of days."

"Come on, Hank. At thirty-one, I'm four years younger than any other doctor on the staff. And I'm gonna be in charge?"

"Thirty-one, huh. That sounds kinda old to me." Hank was two months younger than Karen.

She frowned. "When I told Dr. Berkholt I'd take the job, I felt I could've done anything. The man has that effect on you. But that's worn off. Oh, I realize that Collier's only an old-age hospital, but he intends to make it a major geriatric research center. I didn't expect so much so soon. I'm scared." She jammed her hands into the pockets of her sweatjacket. "Ahhh, shit. I'm just at loose ends, waiting. I'll probably be better after I get started."

"Sure you will." Hank sat on the couch. "As long as we're at it, what stuff *will* you be working with?"

"CRH. I've told you about it. I had the damned stuff coming out of my ears my entire year in endocrine lab."

"I remember your using the letters," Hank said. "But I thought maybe you were an officer in a California Republican Home."

In spite of herself, she smiled. "Go jump off a log."

He stroked his chin. "Or maybe a Constipation Rehab Hostel?"

Karen sighed. "Okay, you want a crash course in pop neuroendocrinology, you'll get one." She dropped down next to Hank on the couch. "CRH stands for corticotropin releasing hormone. It's a hormone put out by the brain that stimulates the pituitary gland. Dr. Berkholt showed that CRH also has a role in the basic workings of the brain itself." She turned to Hank, and her voice livened as she warmed to the subject. "You see, all brain function requires the stimulation of one brain cell by another. Multiply that by billions, and you have the machinery to create a thought, or an emotion, or a set of directions to a muscle to tell it to move a finger or blink an eyelid." She pulled her legs up under her on the couch. "How does one brain cell stimulate another? It does it by releasing chemicals called neurotransmitters. About twenty of them have been discovered so far. CRH is one."

"And what does that have to do with an old-age hospital?"

"That's just what we want to find out. If we succeed, it may provide a key to Alzheimer's disease. On autopsies, brains of Alzheimer's patients show lower amounts of many neurotransmitter chemicals than normal brains. One that's particularly low is CRH—Dr. Berkholt's baby. We're going to try to find a way to replace CRH in Alzheimer's brains and see if it can reverse the disease. In a nutshell, that's what we'll be doing at Collier Hospital."

Hank nodded. "Very interesting." He reached out a hand and began to stroke the back of her neck.

"You're trying to distract me," she said.

"Uh-huh." He continued stroking.

She felt her muscles start to relax. "Don't you want to know how we're gonna get the CRH into brains?"

He began to gently massage. "Of course I want to know."

She hunched her shoulders sensuously. "Well, I haven't finished telling you."

His hand slowly moved down her back. "Go on," he said.

She twisted from side to side as he continued kneading her tight muscles. "You don't really give a damn about CRH, do you?"

He pulled her toward him. "Uh-unh."

He kissed her. His lips were warm and moist. Her body began to tingle in familiar places. With a will of its own, it pressed against him.

"There's a lot more about CRH you should know," she said.

"Uh-huh," he said.

6

Karen didn't look forward to the breakfast meeting scheduled for her first day at Collier Hospital. The hospital administrator had said it would be a fine opportunity for her to meet the four full-time staff doctors. But this morning, as she donned an austere gray wool gabardine suit and black patent pumps, she thought that she'd feel a hell of a lot better if she were meeting them one at a time. She was in no mood to face four-to-one odds her first day on the job.

On a sparkling clear autumn morning, she arrived on the Cinema Acres campus ten minutes early and walked a full circle around the Collier Hospital grounds before entering the building. The last thing she wanted was to get there early and have to make small talk before the meeting. If only she were older, or more glib, or taller.

The delay was a serious mistake. She opened the door to the conference room to find all four doctors waiting. Conversation instantly died. Eight eyes turned to her. The room was bathed in silence.

At the center of the room a rectangular table of polished oak was surrounded by five chairs, with a place setting in front of each. Two doctors sat on each side of the table like judges at a tribunal. The only empty chair was at the head of the table. It was tall, massive, straight-backed. Karen had seen the same chair in a photograph of the gas chamber in San Quentin.

As she closed the door behind her, its hinges creaked in the tomblike silence of the room. She gave a quick, longing glance at the window and had to resist the urge to run back out to the rolling, green lawns she'd just left. She swallowed and began the interminable walk to the chair at the head of the table.

* * *

Cinema Acres, the next-to-final resting place for aging movie and television performers, was located in the foothills of the Santa Monicas, three miles west of University Medical Center. Canyon oaks, sycamores, and broadly branching coral trees dotted wide expanses of rolling fields. A network of gravel paths added to the sylvan feeling of the grounds. If a newcomer could ignore the sounds coming from the freeway a half-mile to the south, he could imagine that he was strolling along remote pathways far out in the countryside.

The buildings of Cinema Acres were divided into three sections.

In the ranch-style cottages of the ambulatory section lived those who were afflicted with chronic illnesses but could still get around on their own. University Medical Center's interns and residents who rotated through the busy outpatient clinic service dubbed them the Cinema Achers.

The small acute care hospital was for patients who had been transferred temporarily from one of the other divisions because of acute illness or need for surgery.

The third and largest division of Cinema Acres comprised the two convalescent hospitals. Both housed chronically ill patients who didn't require acute measures but were too ill or disabled to manage without daily nursing care. Philips Hospital, with one hundred fifty beds, housed the disabled but mentally intact: strokes, cancers, emphysemas, fractured hips, crushed spines. One-hundred-thirty-five-bed Collier Hospital, where Karen was now taking over as chief of medicine, housed the demented. Currently, all of these were classified as Alzheimer's. Collier Hospital was the largest Alzheimer's hospital in the country to be affiliated with a medical school.

The attending staffs had been weak until Dr. Berkholt lent his name to Cinema Acres two years before and added the large complex to the medical school hierarchy. Before then, the staff doctors at the three hospitals had consisted of aging, semiretired men, who the nurses said were often hard to tell apart from the patients. With the infusion of prestige and grants Berkholt brought, a marked improvement in quality followed. Every doctor on the staff held a faculty appointment at the medical school.

The full-time medical staff at Collier Hospital consisted of three internists and one psychiatrist. These were the men whose eyes were trained like searchlights on Karen as she closed the door to the conference room behind her.

She cleared her throat and gave a weak smile. As she headed for the empty chair, the room remained quiet.

Then, suddenly, they were all up and speaking at the same time.

"No, no, call me Frank."

"Wait'll the patients see the good-looking new doctor in charge. You bet they'll brighten up."

"It ees my pleasure, *doctora. . . .*"

"Better wear a name tag to let the nurses know you're not one of the students."

"Don't worry, you'll get used to the gaff."

Hands extended toward her. On the first go-round, faces passed in a blur, but the names were familiar to her from her study of the directory of the medical school faculty the night before.

On her left sat Frank Terhune, thirty-nine-year-old internist, one of the first diplomats of the recently established American Board of Geriatrics. Terhune doubled as attending physician at both Collier Hospital and at Cinema Acres' small acute care hospital. An up-and-comer, rumors were that he had his eye on the heavily endowed Harrington Chair of Geriatrics at the medical school when the present holder finished his three-year tenure. "We were working on some changes in the intake protocol when Duane, ah, had his problems," he said. "I'd pointed out to him that an overnight stay at the medical center could replace most of the four to five days of transporting new patients to University for studies."

"Come on, Frank, give Karen a day before you bombard her." That had to be Ron Olsen, thirty-five-year-old psychiatrist. Excluding Karen, he was the youngest doctor there. By any woman's criteria, he'd be considered handsome. He was tall, about six feet, with an athletic build, startling red hair, neatly trimmed beard, unlined cheeks and forehead. He smiled at her. His teeth were incredibly white. "Frank's always in a hurry. Take plenty of time to get your sea legs."

Karen smiled back gratefully, then blinked. For a moment, she thought Olsen had winked at her. No, of course not. She cleared her throat and sat up in her chair.

A worker from the kitchen wheeled in a cart with a coffee urn, a pitcher of orange juice, and a blackboard breakfast menu. The woman poured, then took orders. Karen ordered a cheese omelette, hash browns, rye toast.

"For a hospital, the food's better than most," said the gaunt, gray-haired man at her far right. The right side of his face sagged, causing that corner of his mouth to droop so that his words seemed to come out of a slitlike opening in the left corner. A cane was propped against the table next to him. He must be Bernard Eisenberg. At sixty-four, he was on the opposite end of the academic ladder from Frank Terhune. He was the only doctor who'd been on the staff of Collier Hospital since it opened seven years ago. He'd been a professor of rheumatology at a midwestern medical school, when he'd suffered a stroke. For him, Collier was a haven where he could slow the pace.

She looked at the one person who hadn't spoken since the first introductions. Alberto Ruiz was a short man with thinning brown hair, narrow eyes, prominent cheekbones, sunken cheeks, and shoulders that seemed too wide for his height. His specialty was infectious disease. He'd come here a year or so ago from the Universidade de São Paulo in Brazil, where he'd published a number of papers on viral diseases. He caught Karen's look and gave a short mechanical nod.

"It will be a pleasure working with all of you," she said, glancing toward the kitchen worker who was leaving to get their breakfasts, "although it may take me a while to get used to this luxury."

Ruiz spoke up for the first time. "What ees the substance of your interests, Dr. Formaker?" His accent was heightened by his slow, deliberate pronunciation.

Karen was grateful for the opportunity to escape to a topic she was familiar with. "I'm working with CRH—corticotropin releasing hormone —secreted by the midbrain. Most think of it only in its role of pituitary stimulation, but we're beginning to realize an even broader role as a neurotransmitter." *Shit, I'm overexplaining.* "I spent a year working with it in Dr. Berkholt's lab."

"Well," Terhune said dryly, "I'm sure that working with Berkholt didn't delay your getting a faculty appointment at the med school."

She felt her face flush. The son of a bitch was making a dig at her youth. She rose from her chair and continued speaking as if he hadn't interrupted. "The most widely studied neurotransmitter has been acetylcholine. Most of the research looking for a correctable deficiency in Alzheimer's has involved trying to replace it. For a number of reasons that we know—and probably many that we don't yet know—that work has been fruitless. Dr. Berkholt is one of the researchers who's proved that CRH, as well as acetylcholine, is deficient in Alzheimer's. His upcoming research protocol at this hospital has two goals: first, to determine how best to replenish CRH in the Alzheimer's-afflicted brain; second, to see if doing so will reverse the dementia."

Her throat was dry. As she reached for her orange juice, she was relieved to see that her hand didn't shake. "In his original work on CRH, Dr. Berkholt created a purified form of it, which we've already tried extensively on a number of animal models. The results have universally been the same: CRH taken by mouth is destroyed in the intestine—and, given by injection, it can't pass from the bloodstream into the brain. For practical purposes, this means that CRH itself is useless to replenish brains deficient in it. Our current work in endocrine lab has been an attempt to get around that impasse by creating analogs of CRH."

Ron Olsen interrupted. "Whoa, Dr. Formaker. You must remember you have in your audience a psychiatrist who's been away from clinical medicine a few years. What's an analog?"

"I had to look the word up, too, when I started endocrine fellowship," Karen said. "It goes back to freshman pharmacology. An analog of CRH is a chemical that's almost identical to it, but with its formula slightly altered to allow it to do things CRH can't. In endocrine lab, we were searching for a CRH analog that would cross the barrier from blood to brain. So far, we've created six that will do just that.

"All of our work on CRH analogs has been on animals, principally rats. But Alzheimer's, at least until it's far advanced, is a disease that affects only the intellect. What this boils down to is that we've gone as far as we can with animal models—we have to work with patients. That's what's behind the projected protocol for Collier Hospital."

The door to the conference room opened, and the kitchen worker pushed in a cart holding five breakfast trays, each with a silver dome over a plate.

Karen sat. "I'm sorry. I didn't intend to launch into a full-fledged speech."

Alberto Ruiz, who'd been looking at her with narrow, unblinking eyes, spoke in precise English. "It ees good that you did so, Dr. Formaker. We have need of a better understanding of the changes that will be happening at our hospital."

Frank Terhune cleared his throat grandly. "Alberto's right, Karen. Particularly since we seem to be on the verge of becoming a cage for a hundred and thirty-five guinea pigs."

Karen's self-consciousness melted under a thin flame of anger. She hadn't liked this man from the first words he'd spoken. "I'm not certain that I understand you, Dr. Terhune."

Terhune shrugged. "It sounds as if Berkholt is stationing you here to use our patients in place of your white rats."

Karen's voice hardened. "I can assure you that no patient will be admitted to our protocol until his closest relative has signed a clearly worded, informed consent."

Terhune smiled knowingly. "With the hype and attention Berkholt has already gotten from the media on his project, I doubt that many relatives will refuse."

Karen barely noticed the kitchen worker set a breakfast tray in front of her. "And is that so bad? What have you to offer these patients, Dr. Terhune? Anything more than room and board? Restraints when necessary? Antibiotics for their terminal pneumonias and bedsores and urinary tract infections?" She sat forward on the edge of her chair. "This is a protocol for patients for whom there's no known treatment, and for whom there's no future. I realize that when Dr. Berkholt's project is completed, there may still be no known effective treatment. But there never can be one unless clinical trials such as the CRH trial are undertaken. In the meantime, Dr. Terhune, we'll be offering the only encouragement any of us can offer at this stage—a glimmer of hope in a disease that's robbed every vestige of it from its victims."

Terhune's face turned red. He unfolded his napkin and angrily laid it on his lap. "We shall see."

7

After breakfast, Karen would have welcomed a few minutes of solitude to relax the tight muscles of her neck. Ron Olsen, however, insisted on personally escorting her down the hall to meet the chief nurse.

"You did a good job of handling Frank," he said.

Karen's face still felt flushed. "I didn't mean to lose my cool."

"Don't let it bother you. Frank asked for it." Olsen smiled secretively. "Now, I hope you're prepared to face your second ordeal of the morning."

Karen didn't tell him that her only ordeal was already over. Dealings with nurses didn't bother her. She'd had a comfortable relationship with every nursing staff she'd ever worked with. Nurses generally responded to her open, uncondescending style.

The office of the chief nurse was in the center of the long, connecting corridor. The door was open. Olsen motioned her in.

Behind a wide, uncluttered oak-paneled desk sat a commanding-looking woman in her fifties. She had straight black hair, an aquiline nose, and thin bloodless lips. Her white uniform was crisp and wrinkle free, her triangular white hat sharply creased. She looked up from a pad she was writing on. Her eyes passed coolly over Karen and settled on Ron Olsen. Karen thought she saw a look of disapproval in them. "Good morning, Dr. Olsen."

"Ms. Wagoner," Olsen announced, "I want you to meet our new chief of medicine, Dr. Karen Formaker. Dr. Formaker, Ms. Sybil Wagoner."

Wagoner's eyes shifted back. Karen felt her own five-foot-quarter-inch height slowly shrink under the nurse's gaze.

"How do you do?" Karen said.

"I was expecting you, doctor." Wagoner rose from her chair.

Karen blinked. Wagoner's starched body wouldn't stop lengthening. It finally reached full height at five feet eleven. "Oh," Karen gulped.

Wagoner towered over her as she stepped from behind her desk. "Where would you like to start rounds?"

Karen struggled to keep her voice strong. "I don't think it's necessary for me to take your time now, Ms. Wagoner. If you'll show me to my office, I'm sure I can find my way around the hospital myself."

Ice dripped from Wagoner's voice. "I think it would be proper, doctor, for me to show you around the first time."

Ron Olsen appeared to be having trouble with his mouth. It kept threatening to smile, and he kept raising his hand to wipe it. "I'll leave you two to your business," he said, and left the room at a quick step.

Karen took a deep breath. "Very well, Ms. Wagoner. Why don't we just make a thumbnail run? I'll make more detailed rounds later on my own."

"Whatever you say, doctor."

They started rounds on Wing A.

Collier Hospital was a stretched-out single-story structure with a long main corridor and three legs. The corridor held the business office, staff cafeteria, chief nurse's office, examining rooms, and doctors' offices. Each leg housed a combined dining and recreation hall and rooms for forty-five patient beds.

"Many of the patients are in the recreation hall at this hour," Wagoner said as she led Karen into a wide room.

Karen looked around with a sense of foreboding. The whole hospital carried an atmosphere of decay. She wasn't sure why. The floors were clean, the halls and recreation room were freshly painted, the furniture was relatively new, and nicely framed paintings lined the walls. Obviously, Collier Hospital didn't suffer any financial woes.

Maybe it was the smell. From the moment Karen entered the patient wing, she picked up the slightly sweet, offensive scent that characterizes every hospital that houses incontinent patients. From deodorant wicks and aerosol sprays, a chemist's translation of "wild lilac" or "spring jasmine" had combined with the ammonia smell of old urine to create the vaguely sickening odor that no modernization of facilities can hide.

But the atmosphere of decay was more than the deodorized smell. It was the people, too. Bent figures in baggy clothes shuffled to and fro. The walls of the recreation hall were lined with wheelchairs holding gaunt-faced men and women with expressionless mouths and vacant eyes. Broad sashes tied many into their chairs to keep them from sliding out. Age and apathy had blotted out their features to the point where the only visible difference between many of them was in the names printed on their plastic ID wristbands. Some of the names were familiar. On one wristband Karen recognized the name of a male swimming star of the jungle movies of the thirties. Another held the name of a sultry blond dancer in the Ziegfeld extravaganzas.

The recreation room cast a pall of depression over Karen as she went from one creature to another. Why did life have to end this way? How many lives had she herself struggled to save so that they could finish their years like this?

From the recreation room, Wagoner led the way to the patients' rooms. Most were doubles. She frowned each time she found a patient still in bed. "I insist on getting them up at least once every morning," she said, writing briefly in a small notebook she carried. Karen felt sorry for the poor nurse's aide whose name she'd jotted.

Not all the patients were quiet and apathetic. From some rooms came the rattling of siderails or the cackling of laughter. Or eerie calls. In one room a woman sat upright in a siderailed bed. She came to life when Karen and Wagoner opened the door. "Help me . . . Help me . . . Help me . . .", she cried. Her eyes were wide with terror. Her lower legs were bent twigs.

Karen felt a fresh wave of concern for this job she'd agreed to take on. Could she ever get used to working day after day with patients like this one? She reached a hand over the siderail and placed it on the woman's sweating hand. "How can I help you?"

The woman quieted for a moment and stared at her. Her tongue ran over her lips. Spittle dripped down her chin. Then she looked away toward Wagoner and again began her refrain. "Help me . . . Help me . . . Help me. . . ."

As they returned to the hallway, a dark-haired man who appeared significantly younger than the rest shuffled toward them, eyes on the floor. He stopped in front of them and looked up with dull eyes.

"Good morning, Mr. Brammer," Wagoner said.

"All right," he said. His eyes fell back to the floor.

Karen reached a hand toward him. "I'm Dr. Formaker," she said.

This time the man didn't lift his eyes. "All right," he said.

Karen's hand stayed untouched in midair until she pulled it back.

As they walked off, Karen shook her head. "He seems so young."

"Fifty-five, doctor."

"How long has he been this way?"

"He was working as an X-ray technician in this hospital until two months ago."

Karen's eyes widened. "You mean he got this way in just two months?"

"That is correct, doctor."

The image of Duane suddenly sprang up in Karen's mind. Sitting befuddled in the emergency room, asking for Susan.

That's ridiculous—Duane's only forty!

She must have slowed down. Wagoner was several long strides ahead. Karen quickened her pace to catch up.

At the far end of the third wing, Wagoner opened the door to room C-31, and Karen gave a start as she heard the swooshing sigh of a ventilator. She'd never seen a case requiring a ventilator in a convalescent hospital.

The room was a single, filled with equipment—ventilator, suction apparatus, small refrigerator, IV regulator, EKG monitor screen. By the bedside, a paperback book on her lap, sat a woman in nurse's uniform.

"Good morning," Karen said.

The nurse looked up and down Karen with eyes that registered little interest. Her round face appeared young for her pure gray hair. Unlike Wagoner, her white uniform was wrinkled. She gave a bare nod and turned back to her book.

"Miss Lipton is the day-shift private on the case," Wagoner said.

Karen walked up to the bedside and looked down at the shriveled creature on the bed. Her hair had disappeared except for a few ragged strings of dusty gray. Parchment skin hung loose over sunken cheeks. Her fingers were two piles of frozen, caved-in matchsticks.

The woman might have been dead, except for the rhythmic expansion and collapse of her chest twelve times per minute with each puff from the ventilator. A tube protruded through an opening in her neck. Another tube led from the upper abdomen to a bottle that dripped creamy tube-feeding formula. A third tube snaked from beneath the sheets and drained urine into a plastic bag at the bedside. The EKG monitor registered a sinus rhythm, rate eighty-four.

Karen was quite familiar with ventilators and tracheostomies—she'd rotated through enough of them during her residency services on ICU and CCU. But there was something terribly disturbing about seeing one in this setting. "I didn't realize we had any ventilator cases," she said.

"She is Henrietta Lee, doctor," Wagoner said, as if that explained it.

The name wasn't lost on Karen. The star of the thirties was a legend. Twice, Karen had seen the velvet-voiced, golden-haired beauty in revivals of the classic film *Lost Love*. She felt a twisting in her belly as she stared at the skeleton on the bed. She turned to the round-faced private nurse seated in a straight chair near the foot of the bed. "Have you been with her long, Ms. Lipton?"

The nurse continued reading the paperback.

Karen spoke louder. "Have you specialed Henrietta Lee long, Ms. Lipton?"

Without looking up from the book, Clara Lipton answered in an expressionless voice. "Seven years."

Karen felt a smoldering anger. What the hell had she done to merit so rude a response? Clearly, the warm relations she'd enjoyed with nursing staffs at other hospitals didn't hold for this place.

She took one last look at the cadaverlike figure on the bed before leaving the room. "How long has Henrietta Lee been that way?" she asked Sybil Wagoner when they were out in the hallway.

"We've had her since we opened seven years ago, doctor. She's been on the respirator for the past year and a half."

"But . . . why?"

"I'm not certain I understand your question."

"What's the point in keeping her going like that?"

Wagoner stopped walking and turned to her with eyes flashing. "What's the *point*? This is a hospital in Cinema Acres, doctor. Henrietta Lee is one of the great names of the cinema."

Karen's arms dropped to her sides. "I mean—would she want to live this way?"

Wagoner made no attempt to hide the scorn in her voice. "She has her own funds. Her private nurse is not at the institution's expense."

"Certainly she's not scheduled to be in the study?"

"You mean the CRH analogs, doctor?"

"Yes."

"She will be entered in it."

Karen felt a helpless dismay. "But . . . she's too far gone."

From her rigid five feet eleven, Wagoner looked down at her with cold eyes. "May I point out, doctor, that you have been here less than twenty-four hours. Perhaps you should allow time to become better acquainted with us before starting to criticize."

Karen's mouth fell open. She struggled to find words.

Before she could, Wagoner turned away. "Shall we continue rounds, doctor?"

Karen drove home along Olympic Boulevard, jaw set, eyes squinting against the oncoming headlights. The rock beat on the radio was turned high to drown out her thoughts. She badly needed someone to talk to. She hoped Hank would be waiting.

The door opened to an empty apartment.

She kicked off her shoes, tore off the gray wool outfit she'd carefully chosen that morning, and threw them onto the closet floor. In bra and pantyhose, she padded into the kitchen and opened the refrigerator. The miserable assortment hadn't changed from the last time: a drying slab of cheese, an end of salami, an open jar of dill pickles, a darkening half of an avocado that had been divided three days before, a half carton of skimmed milk, six eggs, two instant puddings. She grabbed a can of Michelob, slammed the refrigerator door shut, tore open the flip-tab, and stalked off into the living room.

By the time Hank opened the door to the apartment, Karen had started her second beer and worked herself into a still blacker mood. Hank took one look at her, dropped his briefcase onto the floor, and plopped next to her on the couch. "Let me guess. Your appointment book was screwed up. You were actually scheduled to start at Cinema Acres yesterday."

She stared glumly at the beer can clutched in her hand and shook her head.

"You were a day early. You were supposed to start tomorrow."

She again shook her head. "Today was the day. I'm officially chief of medicine."

"You farted just as you were being introduced to the gathering of staff doctors."

"Worse than that."

He scratched behind his ear. "My imagination obviously pales before the true facts. What happened?"

She took a long swig of beer. "Breakfast was terrible. And then she destroyed what was left of me." Karen sank farther into the couch. "She fucking destroyed me."

"Just a minute." Hank rose wearily, disappeared into the kitchen, reappeared with a beer in hand, dropped back down. "Who?"

Karen poured out her story. "Hank, by the time that bitch of a chief nurse finished with me, I was twelve years old again. She had me feeling that I was meddling somewhere I didn't belong."

Hank took a drink. "Look, you gotta remember. You're the chief of medicine. She works under you. Even if she'd been there a hundred years, you're still the boss."

Karen pursed her lips sourly. "I *know* all that. But when Wagoner looks down that long pointed nose at me, it doesn't seem to make any difference. Look, she's run the damned hospital since it started seven years ago. It's her place. I'm an intruder."

Hank nodded. "Listen, I see the problem—and what you've got to do to handle it. It simply needs a little self-hypnosis, Henry Merrill style. Just before you talk to her the next time, psych yourself up by saying to yourself six times, 'I'm the boss, I'm the boss, I'm the boss.'"

Karen tried to avoid a smile. "You guarantee it will work?"

"Absolutely. Money back."

"Okay. Here goes." She set her face sternly. "I'm the boss," she intoned. "I'm the boss. I'm the boss."

Then she pictured the stern image of Sybil Wagoner towering over her, and her shoulders slumped. "I'm the boss. I'm a little girl three feet tall, and I'm the goddamned boss."

Hank rubbed his chin. "I see this is going to be tougher than I expected." He put down his beer, took her by both shoulders, and turned her to face him. "Tell you what. Next time you see her, just look into Nurse Wagoner's eyes and think of the fact that I'm taking Nurse Francie Davis out Saturday for a tennis lesson."

Karen sat straight up and shoved his hands off her. "What? You're fooling around with that little fake-eyelash-batting slut again?"

Hank nodded approvingly. "That's it! That's the barracuda look that'll put her in her place. Just think of Francie every time you look at Ms. Wagoner."

Karen stared at him a moment longer, then sank back into the couch. "Damn you, Hank Merrill! Someday you'll end up with a purple eye before I realize you're putting me on."

She looked up at him again. "But maybe it's worth a try."

8

Karen was grateful that she was scheduled to start the next morning at University Medical Center rather than at Collier Hospital. Eventually, she'd have to settle her role with Nurse Wagoner—but she wasn't ready yet.

She was at her office on the eighth floor of the medical school before seven, attacking the stack of journals and mail on her desk. Funny, she reflected—a couple weeks ago she'd worked out of a small metal desk in a house staff room in the basement. Now she had two spacious offices: one here as Dr. Berkholt's associate, the other as chief of medicine at Collier Hospital in Cinema Acres, three miles away.

By eight fifteen, she'd downed two cups of coffee and a buttermilk doughnut in the staff dining room and was back in the office to check with Sigrid Higheagle, Dr. Berkholt's secretary. Sigrid was blond and forty, with pink cheeks and blue eyes. Her maiden name had been Svensen before her ten-day marriage to Rafe Higheagle, a Havasupai Indian who'd turned out to have a fondness for bourbon and young men. Twenty years later the name was still an amusing conversation piece, and she held on to it.

Sigrid handed her the morning's list of new appointments. "Better oil your roller skates." She smiled brightly.

Karen eyed the neatly typed sheet. Six patients. Two for followup, and four new consults. The new ones were what slowed things down. With examination, review of past records, and the talks with relatives, she'd need an hour and a half each. But if she was to make it to Collier Hospital by one, she'd have to somehow cut them short. After word had leaked out that Dr. Berkholt was planning to try a new treatment for Alzheimer's, the applicant list had grown into the hundreds, but there was room at Collier Hospital for only a pitiful few. At Dr. Berkholt's instructions, preference was given to patients with a screen background because of the working arrangements with Cinema Acres. Still, politicians pulled their weight with the administration of the state-supported medical school, and names of prominent people unaffiliated with cinema or TV were sometimes on the appointment list.

She reviewed the chart of the first patient on her list. He'd already spent five days in the hospital. An eighty-six-year-old former high school principal, he'd been referred to University Medical Center by his outside doctor because of sudden personality deterioration. Treated for lung cancer six months earlier, he had been admitted as a suspected metastatic brain tumor. Studies had quickly ruled this out, and interviews with the family established that his deterioration had begun long before his lung surgery. The rest of the workup showed only brain atrophy on MRI scan. Diagnosis by exclusion was Alzheimer's.

The examination itself didn't take long. A few minutes trying to speak with the patient convinced Karen that the attending physician's diagnosis was correct. What threw her behind was the wrenching interview with the family afterward: the mentally clear but despair-ridden eighty-two-year-old wife who still couldn't accept what was happening to her husband of fifty-eight years; the two middle-age children with somber faces who pleaded for a spot for their father in Dr. Berkholt's upcoming CRH program. All were reaching for a hope, any hope.

When Karen left them, she was already behind in her schedule. The second name on her list was Cynthia Frame. She'd just been admitted to the NPI, the prestigious Neuropsychiatric Institute of the University Medical Center.

As Karen walked through the labyrinthine corridors that connected the main hospital to the NPI, the patient's name reverberated in her thoughts. *Cynthia Frame.* Somewhere, she'd heard it before.

She stopped at the nurses' desk on Seven East and picked up the chart. Without taking time to review the records, she knocked on the door of room 761. After waiting for an answer that didn't come, she opened it.

And stood there in stunned silence.

In front of the sink stood a beautiful woman—statuesque, with flowing golden-brown hair and skin the texture of brushed silk. The shapeless white hospital gown with its ties torn off in back looked particularly out of place on her tall, graceful body.

Karen knew this woman. Cynthia Frame was the thirty-nine-year-old nursing supervisor on Obstetrics at University Hospital. She and Susan had worked closely together for several years. They'd become good friends. Karen had met her at a Christmas party at Susan's house almost a year ago.

She tried to hide her surprise and keep her voice light. "Hello, Cynthia."

"Hello?" Cynthia Frame turned toward her. A worried smile crossed her face. She gave no sign of recognition.

Karen held out her hand. "I'm Karen. Karen Formaker, Susan's sister."

The beautiful woman looked at Karen's hand uneasily before taking it. Her hand was cool and limp. "I'm Cynthia."

"We met last Christmas," Karen said. "At Susan's."

Cynthia Frame studied Karen hard. Her forehead wrinkled. "Susan?"

"Susan Formaker. She's one of the obstetricians here." Karen's gut twisted as she heard her own words. She'd spoken as if Susan were still alive. "I mean—" She stopped herself. "I'll be one of your doctors while you're here."

Cynthia twisted the ends of the sash to her gown in her hands. "I know you?"

"You were—you are a good friend of my sister."

Cynthia's lower lip quivered. "I'm scared. I don't know what they're doing to me."

"You've had a lot of tests. You're probably through with most of them."

"Do you know why I'm here?"

Karen realized she should have reviewed the chart before coming in. "Why don't you sit down and get comfortable while I go over your records?" Karen herself sat in a chair against the wall and opened the chart.

She pressed her lips together as she read.

It had started with forgetting. Showing up either late or early for work. Showing up on a Sunday when she wasn't on duty. Missing the turnoff as she drove home. Stopping at a phone booth to call home because she couldn't recall how to get there, then not remembering her phone number. As the memory loss grew worse, her family doctor had referred her for neurology consultation to Michael Werner on the medical school faculty. Werner's studies were all normal. Assessment: dementia, manifested by loss of cognitive and memory functions. Consistent with Alzheimer's disease. Werner had placed her on the application list for Dr. Berkholt's CRH project.

Karen stopped reading and stared blindly at the chart. Cynthia Frame had worked until two months ago. Had supervised the obstetrics day shift at University Hospital.

Mr. Brammer, the X-ray technician at Collier Hospital, had worked until two months ago.

Consistent with Alzheimer's disease.

Duane had made flawless teaching rounds a month before he drove the wrong way down the freeway.

But he's only forty. . . .

Cynthia Frame was thirty-nine.

Karen looked again at Cynthia. She sat in a straight-backed chair at the foot of the bed. Her hands were clasped tight on her lap. Her eyes were fixed on Karen, waiting.

Karen spoke softly. "You started having trouble with your memory, and it made it hard for you in your work. Your husband talked to Dr. Werner, and they both thought it would be wise for you to come here for examination and some tests."

Cynthia ran her tongue over her lip. "Have you found out what's wrong with me?"

Karen moved her chair closer. "First, can I ask you some questions?"

"All right."

"Tell me about your family."

"What—what do you want to know?"

"You're married?"

Cynthia nodded.

"What's your husband's name?"

"Bill. His name is Bill."

"Do you have children?"

"A daughter. Her name is Karen."

Karen smiled. "That's the same as mine."

Cynthia's brow wrinkled. "What's your name?"

"Karen. Just like your daughter's."

Cynthia Frame bit her lip. "Oh."

"How long have you been here?" Karen asked.

Cynthia's eyes took on the look of a trapped animal. "A—a month?"

"I'm sorry. I meant here in the hospital. Actually, you've only been here three days."

Cynthia's beautiful face became desperate. She gazed wildly around the room. "Is this where I work?"

"It's part of the same medical center. You work in the Obstetrics section." She'd better stop trying to take a history. Her questions were only making Cynthia frantic. She stood up. "I'll examine you now, if that's okay."

Cynthia's tight face eased slightly. "All right."

Karen pulled a stethoscope and pocket flashlight from her bag. Cynthia's gown had slipped from one shoulder. Karen walked behind her, straightened the gown, and knotted the stubs of the torn ties together.

She reached for the wall blood pressure cuff and wrapped it around Cynthia's arm.

"I used to do that," Cynthia said as Karen inflated the cuff.

Karen smiled at her and let the air slowly escape. "One forty over ninety." She replaced the cuff in its wall basket. "That's the upper limit of normal, but normal."

"I think it was lower before," Cynthia Frame said.

"Oh. What do you usually run?"

"It's fifty over—I mean it's . . . I mean . . ." Her eyes suddenly glistened with tears, her lovely face became distorted, and she gave a low-pitched cry. She held her closed hand to her mouth. "What's happening to me? For God's sake, what's wrong with me?"

Karen opened her mouth, but words wouldn't come. She stared at Cynthia. Her eyes blurred. Suddenly she realized that tears were trickling down her cheeks. With a muffled sob of her own, she spread her arms and wrapped them around Cynthia.

Cynthia rested her face in Karen's hair. Her body shook as she cried in short, gasping breaths.

Karen closed her eyes and held Cynthia tighter. Her hand rubbed slowly over her back.

Seated at the Seven East nurses' desk, Karen wrote in Cynthia Frame's chart. The terror in Cynthia's eyes as she struggled to remember kept breaking into her thoughts and making her pause.

Of course she'd find a bed for her at Collier's. But oh God, thirty-nine . . .

"Hello, Karen."

She spun around with a gasp.

Mike Werner stood over her. "I didn't mean to startle you."

She shook her head. "I was somewhere else."

"Cynthia Frame?"

Karen nodded. "I know her."

"She worked with Susan, didn't she?"

Karen nodded. "Mike, it's so terrible!"

He said nothing.

"Isn't there anything else?" she said. "Any other possibility?" She heard in her own voice the plea she'd heard from so many patients' relatives.

Werner sat down wearily at the desk. "How can I answer that? I can't say there are no other possibilities. In the final analysis, Alzheimer's is an autopsy diagnosis—we don't have a reliable test for it on a patient who's still living. We make the diagnosis by inference only after excluding everything else it could be. And so far, every test for another possible cause of Cynthia's dementia has been negative."

Karen bit her lip. "She just came in yesterday."

"She had quite a workup before coming here. I'm repeating all the studies. But . . ." He shrugged grimly.

"She's only thirty-nine."

"It doesn't happen often. In the twelve years I've been in neurology, I've had two in their thirties. They tear your guts out."

She fought against the tears building up behind her eyes. She laid her pen on the desk and slowly closed the chart.

Mike studied her for a moment before speaking. "Have you seen Duane, Karen?"

Karen's shoulders sagged under an added weight. "Not since the emergency room."

"You still blame him?"

She gave a tight-lipped shrug. "I don't know, Mike. Every time I even talk about him, something inside me seems to die again. I see Susan on that ER table." She stared out into the distance before turning back to him. "Have you come up with anything?"

"No."

"He's worse?"

"It's as if someone's taking an eraser and wiping out a billion more neurons from his cortex every day."

She didn't want to hear any more. She didn't want to talk about it. "Like Cynthia Frame?" she said.

Werner nodded. "She's following exactly in his footsteps."

Karen's throat had a lump so big, she couldn't swallow. Her voice was a whisper. "When I saw her, I thought of Duane."

9

Karen arrived at the Cinema Acres campus shortly after two that afternoon. She parked in the visitors' lot outside Collier Hospital. As she hurried past the gated staff parking lot, she noted that an empty parking space next to the hospital entrance had a sign, RESERVED FOR MEDICAL DIRECTOR. That must be for me, she realized with a faint sense of wonder. But she didn't have a card key to let her into the lot so she could park in it.

She lugged a briefcase in one hand and her medical bag in the other. The briefcase bulged with her notes on CRH analogs. Later, she and Hank would rent a U-Haul trailer and move her books and files over, but first she had to see that the desk was emptied of Duane's belongings.

Outside the chief of medicine's office she shifted her two bags to one arm and tried the door. It was locked, and she didn't have a key. She left her bags outside the door and headed down the hallway to the director of nurses office. The door was open. Sybil Wagoner sat behind the desk. She looked up but didn't rise. "Good afternoon, doctor. It was my understanding that you would be here at one."

The muscles between Karen's shoulder blades tightened. "I was held up at the medical school, Ms. Wagoner." The moment she said it, she felt chagrined that she was explaining like a little girl making an excuse for being late to school. "The door to my office is locked. Do you have a key to it?"

"I shall let you in." Wagoner rose from her chair, reached for a key from a desk drawer, and without looking at Karen walked down the hall.

She opened the door to Karen's office. "Will there be anything else you need?"

"I would like my own key."

Wagoner looked down at her. The muscles at the sides of her jaw moved up and down for a moment before she spoke. "I shall arrange to have one made, doctor." She turned abruptly and headed back toward her office.

Until a few weeks ago, Duane had occupied this office.

Karen sat at the desk that had been Duane's desk and stared blankly at bookshelves lined with Duane's books. Her feet dangled above the floor. The leather desk chair had been adjusted for Duane's five feet ten— she'd have to lower it. Absently, she opened a drawer. Duane's pens, paper clips, notes. It was as if she were sitting here with his ghost.

She thought of her talk with Mike Werner that morning. Cynthia Frame and Duane—thirty-nine and forty years old. Maybe in a lifetime you could expect to see one person in that age group with Alzheimer's disease. But not two in the span of a week.

She remembered Duane's almost childlike face as he looked at her with bewilderment from his chair in the emergency room. That was the last time she'd seen him. She could no longer hold on to her hatred. Susan had loved him. Dr. Berkholt grieved over his illness as if he were his son. *I'm heartsick, Karen,* he'd said. She remembered the pain in his voice.

"Hi, chief."

She turned.

The handsome athletic figure of Ron Olsen stood in the doorway. He wore an open white lab coat over a fitted canary-yellow shirt, brown-and-green-striped tie, and pleated tan gabardine slacks. His tan lizard cowboy boots were brightly shined. He smiled. "How's it coming?"

She shrugged. "It'll take a few days, I suppose."

"Nurse Wagoner getting to you?"

"Well, she's not exactly your typical neighborhood welcoming committee."

He sat in the chair across from her desk, leaned back, crossed his legs. "You'll get used to her. She considers every nook and cranny of this place her own private domain. She was probably no better when Duane started here a couple years ago."

Karen felt her tension let up slightly. So far, Olsen was the only person at this place who'd tried to make her feel comfortable. "Once I know the patients and we start Dr. Berkholt's project, I might feel like I belong. But right now, I'm strictly the new kid on the block."

"In that case," Ron Olsen said, "the first thing to do is get to know one of the other kids better. How about dinner with me tonight?"

Hank probably wouldn't give a damn, she thought. "Thanks, Ron, I appreciate the offer. I'm meeting someone else."

He glanced down at her fingers. "Married?"

"No."

"Boyfriend?"

She gave a slight smile. "Yep."

He sighed. "Ahh, another sad case of one-on-one fixation. Obviously, unresolved Oedipus feelings are at play. But at least it's a curable disease. I was married until three years ago. Then I took the cure, and now I'm free for dinner at the drop of a hat." He stood up. "Perhaps some psychotherapy—you can stretch out on my couch, and we'll try to get to the roots of your fixation."

She laughed. "Thanks again for the offer."

He shrugged. "In that case, let me go get a few boxes. We'll get that desk cleaned out."

Karen was reviewing charts when Hank appeared in her doorway.

He nodded approvingly as he looked around her spacious oak-paneled office. "Two of my offices could fit into this one."

She looked at her watch, then at the pile of charts on her desk. "What are you doing here this early? We're not meeting for dinner until eight. I've got this whole workload in front of me."

He shook his head. "I come to offer not food but news."

Karen clicked off the cassette player she'd been dictating into, leaned back in her chair, and sighed. "Shoot."

Hank pulled up a straight-backed chair and straddled it. "Karen, my love, for a while you'll have to contend with me not only nights, but part of the day as well."

"Quit talking in riddles."

"No riddles. I'm now part of Project Alzheimer."

She sat up straight. "What are you talking about?"

"Berkholt wants me to set up a computer model for your project."

"What?"

"The VCR analogs."

"You mean CRH!"

He waved a hand impatiently. "Whatever. He told me you'd fill me in on the medical part."

She felt a momentary qualm. She and Hank had never worked together on anything professional. "What'll be involved?"

His face grew intent. "I've just begun to think about it. We'll start with the simple stuff. Double-blind protocol. Hundreds of input factors—birthplace, birth weight, every area lived in, every remote item of family history, every medicine ever taken, smoking, alcohol, illnesses, school level, exposures to paint fumes, metals—you name it. Add the current material—exam findings, blood chemistries, imaging studies. Then the treatment—what do you call it, an analog, or the placebo—everything coded so that nobody will know who's getting what. Not until Berkholt gives the signal to break the code."

"That's the *simple* stuff?"

"That's standard record keeping. If you had a test population of ten thousand, it might be all that's necessary. But to get significant statistics from just a hundred fifty, we need to sort the patients into subgroups with similar background factors and be sure that within each group some get placebo and some get the analogs."

Karen frowned. "Wait a minute. Once we start placing patients in subgroups, we'll have introduced exactly the kind of bias we're using a double-blind study to get away from."

Hank leaned forward. "Only if a human makes the decisions. Not if the computer makes them."

Karen slowly shook her head. "You're talking about a computer *thinking*?"

He nodded emphatically. "Exactly. We use logical and mathematical modeling to tell the computer all it needs to know to make decisions. It's called an expert system."

"And you've seen this work?"

"More than that. I designed one for a three-month cancer epidemiology project for the Oncology Department. I did it by writing some extensions to the Novar-3 program that runs on the university's mainframe. It'll adapt beautifully to your protocol, Karen. All you'll have to do is feed me the material."

Karen rose from her chair and kissed him lightly on the lips. "It's going to be good having you aboard."

She smiled to herself as she sat in thought at her desk. It would be interesting to work with Hank. But they'd have to learn to leave the problems at the med center.

Much of Hank's research for his Ph.D. dissertation had been conducted at University Medical Center. After his degree, the medical school had offered him a cubbyhole office in the basement to open a new Department of Biostatistics. It had started as a trial venture, but suddenly no department in the hospital or the medical school could manage without the skills of this intense, innovative young man. Now, three years later, the demand for his services had increased dramatically.

She slipped the cassette from her dictating equipment and headed down the corridor to leave it with the secretarial pool. Lost in thought, she almost crashed head-on into Sybil Wagoner as she stepped from the nursing director's office. Karen barely stopped in time.

Nurse Wagoner readjusted her glasses and glared coldly down at her. "Do you require my assistance, doctor?"

Karen reflexively started to make a denial. Then she recalled Hank's advice and pictured Francie Davis with her long fake eyelashes batting like the wings of a hummingbird. All five feet quarter-inch of her became totally erect as she looked up at Wagoner. "When I need you, you can rest assured that I shall call you, Ms. Wagoncr."

She nodded crisply and resumed her march down the hallway.

10

Word spread rapidly that Dr. Berkholt was close to beginning his CRH project. Karen's workload grew heavier as desperate families struggled to get a parent, husband, or wife into the program. On top of that, the normal attrition rate of two or four monthly deaths at Collier Hospital had leaped to eight, then ten, over the past two months, opening more beds for new patients.

Karen spent every morning at University Hospital, where she was responsible for final evaluation of candidates for admission. On her fourth day after starting at Collier Hospital, she didn't finish at the medical center until four-thirty. She drove the three miles to Cinema Acres, stopping on the way to pick up a Big Mac to munch on while she attacked her workload. By the time she finished at Collier with the pile of mail, charts, forms to be signed, and last-minute calls to be made, it was after eight.

The corridor lights had already been dimmed when she locked her office door and headed toward the exit. She noticed that the door to the basement was ajar. She'd never been down to the basement.

In curiosity, she opened the door. A light came from the foot of the stairs. After slight hesitation, she started down.

The long basement hallway was dimly lit and silent as a tomb. As she walked, her feet sounded like hammers striking the vinyl floor covering. The sounds echoed between the bare plaster walls.

She passed doors marked MAIL ROOM, HEATING AND ELECTRICAL, and LAUNDRY, and paused at a door marked MICROBIOLOGY. From inside, she heard a whirring sound, like a centrifuge spinning.

She checked her watch. Something told her to turn around and leave. She could check things out in the morning.

She knocked.

No answer. The whirring continued. She rested her hand on the door-knob and debated whether to turn it.

She gasped as the knob turned under her hand.

The door opened, and Alberto Ruiz gazed at her with a grave face. "You are working late, Doctora Karen."

"Dr. Ruiz! I hadn't expected to find anyone down here."

"I often work late." He stepped to the side. "You have never seen my laboratory? Please. Come in."

Uneasily, Karen entered.

She looked around in surprise. She stood in a well-lit, modern labora-tory that rivaled many she'd worked in at the medical center. The large room was meticulous. A counter divided it down the center, and counters lined each wall. One held a row of incubators, several of which were padlocked. On another counter rested a floor-to-ceiling rack that held cages of white rats. Above the remaining two wall counters, shelves held test tubes, petri dishes, flasks. Two large refrigerators book-ended the central counter.

Karen turned to Ruiz. "I didn't even know there was a lab down here." Routine blood tests on patients were sent to the small laboratory in the acute care hospital at Cinema Acres, where the more complex studies were rerouted to University Hospital.

Ruiz gave a slight smile. "This ees, Doctora Karen, the inducement that brought me here."

"I still don't understand how you ended up at Collier Hospital."

"You perhaps have heard of the Brazilian economy? Of the Third World debt failures? Government funding ended, and my grant at the *universidade* was cut off." He gestured expansively around the lab. "In this wealthy country, there ees much interest in dementia—specifically, in Alzheimer's. Here, the work ees well funded. The university offered me a grant."

"I see." She looked around the elaborately equipped room. "I knew you worked with virus studies in Brazil. I never asked what research you were doing here."

Ruiz rested a hand on the countertop. He stood only an inch taller than Karen. "You have heard of kuru?"

"Not for some time," Karen said. "It's a rare infectious dementia that was discovered in the highlands of New Guinea in a native tribe that ate the brains of dead relatives in funeral rituals. Tribal members came down with brain deterioration that's been compared with Alzheimer's. It could be spread to monkeys by injecting them with spinal fluid or brain tissue from victims. The current concept is that kuru involves a slow virus, one that takes its toll over months rather than days."

Ruiz answered softly. "Now, I understand why Dr. Berkholt appointed *la doctora* in charge."

A disturbing thought struck her. "Surely you're not working with the kuru virus in this laboratory?"

He smiled. His smile was awkward, had a forced quality. "Even if I wanted to, your government regulations would keep me from doing so. No, I have no access to kuru."

"Then you're working with . . . ?"

He shrugged. "Can there be a virus behind the disease we call Alzheimer's? To answer that question ees my mission. I work only with body fluids from your patients."

"You work alone?"

He nodded.

"It sounds like a large job for one man."

"Dr. Berkholt has been considerate. He has seen that I have all the funds I need. I have my tissue cultures and my animals. I have the freedom from heavy clinical work—Drs. Terhune and Eisenberg are kind enough to take care of most of the patient load." Ruiz walked over to a tray holding syringes and a rack of vials. He repeated his forced smile. "Now I must inoculate my little patients"—he nodded toward the cages of rats—"with spinal fluid and blood samples from your big patients. Please, you will observe?"

Karen could think of many places she would rather be late at night than with this strange little man in an isolated basement laboratory. "It's late, Dr. Ruiz. Perhaps another time."

At the nurses' desk on Seven East of the NPI the next morning, Karen studied Cynthia Frame's chart.

Reports of most of the studies had filtered in. Karen's disappointment grew as she read off one normal value after another. What she was desperately searching for was any abnormality that would give a lead toward a correctable component to Cynthia's illness. The search was futile: blood count, electrolytes, and blood chemistry panel normal; endocrine screen for pituitary, thyroid, and adrenal function normal; MRI brain scan normal; spinal fluid chemistries and serologies normal. The only equivocal study was the PET scan—positron emission tomography —which showed a spotty decrease in temporal lobe glucose metabolism. Karen's lips tightened. This solitary abnormality had been reported as one of the few positive findings sometimes seen in early Alzheimer's.

She closed the chart and walked into the room.

Cynthia Frame's face lit up as she rose from her chair. "You're—" Her smile faded. "Do I know you?"

"I'm Karen." She saw the worried look on Cynthia's face and took both of her hands. "I'm Susan's sister."

Cynthia Frame ran her tongue over her lower lip. The cornered-animal look returned to her eyes. "Susan?"

Speaking as if Susan were still there brought back Karen's loss acutely. For a moment she was back in the emergency room staring at the straight line crossing the EKG monitor screen. "She's your close friend. Dr. Susan Formaker."

Cynthia gave a weak smile, but no sign of understanding crossed her face. "Oh."

Karen let go of Cynthia's hands. They fell away slowly, as if reluctant to break the contact. "How are you feeling?" Karen asked.

"All right. But—" She stopped.

Karen spoke softly. "Are you still frightened?"

Cynthia nodded.

"Can you tell me about it?"

Cynthia bit her lip and looked toward the door. "I thought I heard my baby crying."

Karen winced. She knew from her review of the chart that Cynthia's "baby" was eighteen. "Your daughter's fine. But you've been ill, Cynthia."

"I'm sick?"

"That's why you're here."

"What—what's the matter with me?"

Exactly where was the border between truthfulness and cruelty? "You've had some memory problems. You've been having tests to try to find an answer."

Cynthia studied her for a moment, then slowly shook her head. "You don't want to tell me. It's my brain, isn't it?"

Karen wished she could stop talking, could just reach out and hold Cynthia as she had done when she first saw her three days ago, and let Cynthia cry away some of her pain. *Cynthia, what can I say to you? Yes, it's your brain, but what good does it do you to know? Why can't you be blind to it like the others?* "There are some neurologic problems," she said. "But we're working on a treatment. So it will get better." *Liar!* "You will get better, Cynthia."

Cynthia's eyes had grown wet. They glistened with an anguish that shut Karen out. "It's my brain," she said. "Something is wrong with my brain." She continued slowly shaking her head. "Something terrible is wrong with my brain."

*   *   *

After she finished her consults at University Hospital, Karen drove to the Cinema Acres complex. She parked now in the chief of medicine's spot outside Collier Hospital.

Sybil Wagoner stopped her as she walked in. Her face was expressionless. "Dr. Berkholt is waiting to see you."

Dr. Berkholt—here? Although they discussed their cases together almost daily at University Hospital, she'd never seen him at Collier. "Where is he?"

"In the chief of medicine's office, doctor." Karen noted Wagoner's phrasing: "the chief of medicine's office," not "your office."

Dr. Berkholt was standing by the window looking out on the Cinema Acres campus. In late fall the rolling west-side hills had browned, and the sycamores and coral trees wore a cover of gold.

"Hello, Dr. Berkholt," Karen said.

He turned toward her.

His face was sober. He wasted no time. "Karen, I'm afraid we can no longer avoid talking about something that's been on both of our minds."

She knew at once what he meant. "You mean Duane."

He nodded. "At the rate he's deteriorating, he'll be dead or on life support in less than a month."

She took in a deep breath. "That soon."

"I'm having him brought over to Collier Hospital."

Her mouth fell open. She stared at him. *No! Not under my care!*

Berkholt continued. "We know that the younger the person with Alzheimer's—and I have no choice but to call it that—the faster it tends to progress. But I've never seen the disease move this fast."

Her voice was hoarse. "Will he get CRH?"

"We have nothing else to offer. He'll be part of the protocol."

Sweat plastered her blouse to her back. She answered in a rush of words: "This is no place for him, Dr. Berkholt. He was medical director here! I'm just a substitute for him. It would be too bizarre to have him here among nurses who worked for him and people who were his patients. Why can't his treatment be given at the NPI?"

Dr. Berkholt spoke patiently. "Karen, you can't possibly be aware of the difficulties I've already had in getting the program through the Ethics in Research Committee. At times I've despaired that I'd ever get a go-ahead to conduct the studies on humans. The final language of the approval is explicit. It permits a rigid protocol here at Collier Hospital in Cinema Acres—and *only* here at Collier Hospital." He took a deep breath. "I don't know if I've ever fully expressed how important this project is to me. Its success means more to me than even the Nobel prize did. We're dealing not with theory and abstractions but with the possibility of sparing millions of people a degrading, terrible end to their lives."

Duane here. The thought was a heavy weight that pressed down on her shoulders.

Dr. Berkholt continued. "The pace of Duane's deterioration forces our hand. Hank Merrill tells me we can have the protocol ready by Monday. That gives him—and you—three days."

She nodded numbly.

"We'll give the analogs as weekly injections, divided between placebo and Analogs Nine, Fifteen, and Twenty-seven—the ones that have shown the greatest penetration into brain tissue in our animal trials. I've asked Hank to insure that the double-blind provisions of the protocol will be inviolable."

Karen swallowed. "What about Duane . . . and Cynthia Frame?"

"Of course they're in the program." Berkholt's eyes remained steadily on her. "But neither you nor I—nor anyone—will know what they get."

She gripped the sides of her chair. "But if Duane or Cynthia gets the placebo, then they won't have a chance."

He smiled sadly. "We have but one shot at this, Karen. I could count on my fingers the number of times in the past twenty years that a major biologic experiment has been permitted on humans after so limited an animal model. If we squander this chance—if our work is flawed—then the millions we hope to spare may pay before another opportunity comes along. Until the code is broken at the end of the project, no one can know what any patient gets. To protect us from ourselves, all vials of CRH analogs have already had their labels removed and been coded by the computer. Even if I tried, I myself couldn't identify them."

A feeling of hopelessness ate at her. "They're so young, Dr. Berkholt."

"Everyone in the program is part of the protocol," he said.

She stared at him a moment longer, then rested her forehead in her hand. "I see."

He walked over and laid a hand gently on her shoulder. "It's hard, I know."

She lifted her head and looked at him. "I guess there were a few twists I didn't anticipate."

11

Saturday morning Karen skipped going to University Medical Center and drove directly from her West Los Angeles apartment to Cinema Acres.

The temperature was reaching into the seventies on this mid-December day. A breeze from the ocean had cleared away the smog, and the first rains of the season had already greened the mountains. As she drove west on San Vicente, the Santa Monicas stood out clean and crisp above Pacific Palisades, with the ocean sparkling clear turquoise beyond.

Somewhere else, they'd call it Indian summer. But here such days were common enough to cause nostalgic transplants from the east to grumble over the lack of seasons. It was on this kind of day that Karen and Hank might have packed their dome tent into the trunk of one of their Toyotas and headed for a desert campsite in Anza-Borrego or Joshua Tree. But in two days the protocol would start. Karen had mounds of records to complete at Collier Hospital, and Hank was spending night and day with the computer mainframe at the university.

The hospital on Saturday morning was as it was on any weekday. Aged patients scraping aluminum walkers or four-legged canes shuffled down the hallway. The day staff of nurses and attendants smiled and nodded at her as she passed them. Sybil Wagoner sat behind her desk in the nursing director's office as she apparently did seven days a week. From the corner of her eye, Karen caught Wagoner's brief glance as she passed by her open door.

In her office, Karen planted herself at her desk behind a pile of patients' charts. One by one, she checked off names as she filed through them. She could have simply used the nursing census at Collier. One hundred twenty-four of the total 135 beds were currently filled. All were on the protocol.

On each chart she ordered pretreatment baseline laboratory tests: CBC, SMAC chemistry panel, and the special endocrine studies—free thyroxine, TSH, ACTH, cortisol, somatostatin.

When she flipped through the pile for Henrietta Lee's chart, it was missing. Karen asked the charge nurse for it.

"Her private keeps it in the room," the nurse said.

Karen walked slowly down the hallway toward room C-31. She didn't like going to that room. She couldn't rid herself of the feeling that there was something disturbing, almost sinister about it. Like digging up a grave and opening the coffin.

She turned the knob and pushed the door open.

The round-faced, gray-haired nurse sat in the same position she'd last seen her. The paperback on her lap might have been on the same page. The ventilator whooshed at twelve per minute, the EKG line on the overhead monitor bleeped at eighty-four. The nurse barely moved her head to look at Karen. "You looking for something?"

This woman was deliberately trying to be rude. Karen's voice hardened. "I'm Dr. Formaker, Ms. Lipton."

"I'm aware of who you are."

"I need the chart on Henrietta Lee."

The nurse nodded nonchalantly toward the sink. "You'll find it there."

Karen's irritation grew. She picked up the thick chart and thumbed through it. The current material covered the past three months. The entries under the "Doctor's Notes" section were scanty, about one or two weekly. All were signed by Bernard Eisenberg. The last entry was three days ago: "Lungs clear. Heart regular. No edema. Continues to show signs of pain when Dilaudid wears off."

Karen frowned and skimmed back through earlier notes. There it was again: "Continues to show signs of pain." She looked up with surprise at Clara Lipton. "She's in pain?"

Lipton's eyes were back on her paperback. "At times she is."

Karen looked at the curled-up, corpselike figure on the bed, its chest regularly rising and falling to the rhythm of the respirator. "She doesn't seem conscious enough to be suffering."

"I don't see how you can tell unless you're here with her every hour like I am."

Karen slowly shook her head as she gazed at Henrietta Lee. "It's hard to believe."

"She looks comfortable to you because she had her last Dilaudid an hour ago, doctor." Lipton said the word *doctor* as if she were chewing on something distasteful.

Karen returned to the graphic sheet in the front of the chart. "Where's this morning's temperature and blood pressure?"

The nurse placed a marker in her book and yawned. "Rectal temperature ninety-eight point two. Blood pressure one thirty-six over seventy-four."

"What time was that?"

"Nine this morning."

"That's five hours ago. Isn't it common, Ms. Lipton, to record these values in the chart?"

"Dr. Eisenberg has never required it. But if that's your wish, doctor, I'll start the practice."

"I shall certainly expect customary nursing procedures to be followed," Karen snapped.

Lipton sighed. "Very well." She reached for the chart.

Karen held on to it. "You can fill in your notes later. I need to write orders for tomorrow's lab."

The nurse smiled a mocking smile. "CBC, chem panel, thyroxine, TSH, ACTH, cortisol, somatostatin?"

Karen felt a twinge of alarm along with her surprise. "How did you know?"

"I'm acquainted with your protocol, doctor." She turned back to her book. "Don't worry, I'll see that your tests are ordered."

Karen felt a sense of relief when she left the room.

As she closed the door, she came face to face with a Huckleberry Finn look-alike. He was older, perhaps forty or so, lanky, and had tousled reddish-brown hair. He wore a white jacket and white pants but could just as easily have been wearing overalls and a straw hat, with a strand of hay in his mouth in place of the toothpick dangling from it. His angular frame leaned against the hallway wall. Both hands were in his pockets. His face was freckled, eyes bright blue, shirt collar open. He wore a grin, perhaps the first grin she'd seen in this place. "Howdy," he said.

After the somberness of the room she'd just left, she found herself laughing. "Howdy."

"You're the new doc?"

"That's what they tell me. Who're you?"

"Will Hayes. I'm the physical therapist."

She held out her hand. "Glad to meet you, Will." She nodded toward the room she'd just left. "You're working with Henrietta Lee?"

"I'm doing something with her, but I haven't figured out what to call it. Three times a day I go in there and move her arms and legs back and forth and try not to break them."

Karen pressed her lips together thoughtfully. "Does she act as if she's in pain?"

"Pain?" He shrugged. "Beats me. When you look at the skull of a skeleton, can you tell whether it's grinning or grimacing?"

"Do you think she knows you, Will?"

"Shoot, Henrietta doesn't know anybody. She probably died a year ago, and Clara Lipton in there hasn't worked up the energy to unhook her from the ventilator."

At least there was one person who worked here that she could talk to. "I'm glad I'm not the only one Nurse Lipton won't get up from her chair for. How many physical therapists have they got here, Will?"

"You're looking at half the department, doc."

"You must keep pretty busy."

He jammed his hands back into his pockets. "Shucks, no. After a new patient's been here awhile, nobody seems to care whether he walks or moves his arms or wiggles his tail. Joanne and I—Joanne's the other therapist—don't get many orders after the first couple weeks."

"But—" Karen looked again toward C-31.

"Henrietta? She's my one certain patient. Three times a day for the past seven years. Orders straight from the top."

"You mean Dr. Berkholt?"

"Okay, not quite the top. Laughing-Girl Lipton writes the orders and scribbles Eisenberg's initials next to 'em." He pulled a hand from his pocket and plucked the toothpick from his mouth. "I don't question who writes the orders—I figger it's part of the job. Shoot, if I didn't do it, I'd just get stuck with more nursing chores."

"Nursing?"

He grinned. "Got my RN in 'seventy-two at St. Vincent's. Male nurses are getting more common now, but back a few years ago too many guys rolled their eyes at me as Nurse Hayes, so I went back into training in PT. They still call on me to fill in when a night supervisor's off sick, or Doc Ruiz holds his immunization clinics, or Wagoner's off at a fellow zombie meeting."

Karen smiled. "I'm looking forward to getting to know you better, Will."

"Sounds like a good idea, doc." He rolled back his sleeves. "Well, back to the Tinker Toys." He opened the door and disappeared into the room.

12

The CRH protocol began on schedule Monday morning.

The usual deliberate pace of Collier Hospital gave way to a ferment of activity. Additional nursing staff was recruited from the other two hospitals of Cinema Acres. Coded vials of CRH analogs, which had been stored over the weekend in the refrigerators in Dr. Ruiz's lab, were brought up to the patient wings with elaborate precautions. Hank Merrill was at Collier to make sure that the coded material was correctly recorded for entry into the protocol. Will Hayes moved from wing to wing to supervise the giving of the analogs. He'd been in charge of the flu vaccine clinics at Cinema Acres for the past two years and was experienced in mass-inoculation techniques. Dr. Berkholt showed up and checked with Hank to see how the data entry was going.

In spite of her position as chief of medicine at Collier Hospital—or perhaps because of it—Karen felt that she was the only one there at loose ends. She couldn't figure out what her role should be. Her heavy work would begin soon with the early clinical evaluations, but for today people asked their questions of Hank, or Will, or Sybil Wagoner. Finally, she gave up shuttling aimlessly from nurses' station to nurses' station and headed for University Hospital.

She had only two patients to see. Both awaited her final transfer order before they could be moved to Collier the next day to start the CRH protocol. The patients were Cynthia Frame and Duane Dreyer.

She forced herself to go see Duane first. She still hadn't seen him since that day of horror when she had been called to the emergency room to find Susan dead. By now, he'd been studied by so many members of the attending faculty that she could have waited until he was at Collier. But she didn't want to see him for the first time in the setting of decay that permeated Collier Hospital.

She stopped outside the door and held her hand on the knob for a moment before she turned it. She remembered her burning-white hatred for him as she'd stared at Susan's lifeless body. This would be easier if she could have held on to the feeling.

He lay in bed. Someone had combed his light brown hair straight back, slicking it with an oily dressing that left it plastered to his skull. Perhaps that same someone had shaved him, an imperfect shave with stubble lining the rounded angle of his jaw like a picket fence. His mouth hung partway open, drooling from the left corner. He looked at her with vacant, unblinking eyes.

"Duane."

His eyes found her as she moved to the bedside.

She rested her hands on the siderails. "I'm Karen."

"Yeah," he said.

"Can you remember me, Duane?"

"Yeah," he said.

Her voice rose. "I'm Karen, Susan's sister."

He looked at her blankly.

"Susan was your wife, Duane!" Now she was shouting.

"Yeah," he said.

With a feeling that a lead weight had encased her heart, she bent down and looked more closely into his eyes. She felt she was looking through a round airplane window into black space. She remembered holding Cynthia Frame in her arms while her body shook with grief and terror.

Duane, how long did it take you to go through the phase Cynthia's in now? How long did you feel the panic of knowing something terrible was happening to your brain? Did Susan hold you in her arms while you cried for your loss?

Karen closed her eyes and tried to picture him as she should remember him. As Susan would have wanted her to remember him. Immaculately dressed, eyes sparkling, standing proud and erect at the lecture podium as he spoke with his incisive voice and wonderfully rich vocabulary. For a moment she held on to the image.

She opened her eyes. His gaze had turned away from her and had fixed on a wall lamp.

She set her lips and began to examine him. The findings ticked off mechanically in her mind: Pupils react equally. Tongue midline. Neck supple. Lungs clear. Heart regular, no murmurs. She pulled back the sheet to examine his abdomen, and for a moment she could go no further.

He wore soiled diapers.

*   *   *

Karen wearily walked the long corridors connecting the main hospital to Seven East in the NPI, where Cynthia Frame had been admitted. At the nurses' desk she reviewed Mike Werner's notes on the chart. Workup was complete. Diagnosis: dementia consistent with Alzheimer's disease.

Before going into the room, she wrote orders for Cynthia's transfer to Collier Hospital in the morning. Both she and Duane would arrive there in time to enter the CRH protocol a day after it started.

As she walked slowly down the hallway to Cynthia's room, she thought grimly of moving that beautiful, regal woman into the Collier Hospital setting of aged crones. How would she put it to her? *We're taking you to Collier Hospital for treatment, Cynthia. So you'll get well.* She frowned. It wasn't a lie. She'd worked with CRH—it was clearly deficient in Alzheimer's. If one of the CRH analogs could force its way into Cynthia's brain and take over the function of her own natural CRH, there was a chance it would help. Cynthia's disease was still early—it wasn't just an empty exercise. Of course there was a chance.

As long as she doesn't get the placebo.

She opened the door and stared around. Cynthia's room was empty. What further studies could she have been taken for?

She'd check at the nurses' desk. She started to leave, but stopped. Maybe she was in the bathroom.

She opened the door.

Not since her first day with the cadaver in freshman anatomy lab had Karen felt sickness like this.

Extending from the center of the shower ceiling, an L-shaped steel fixture fed pipe to the wall that held the showerhead. Cynthia Frame, her face a mottled purple, hung from that ceiling fixture by a thin brown leather belt. Her toes barely scraped the floor.

"Call a code!" Karen shouted as she lurched forward. Her shins struck the overturned chair Cynthia had kicked from under her. She straightened the chair, leaped on it, ripped the knotted belt loose from the fixture, and struggled to slow the slide of Cynthia's body as it dropped to the floor.

She jumped down, kicked the chair the rest of the way into the shower stall, and dragged the crumpled body partway through the bathroom door to straighten it. She gasped for breath as her fingers fumbled furiously at the tightened slipknot around Cynthia's neck, finally tearing it loose. She probed futilely for the carotid pulse at the angle of the jaw, then crouched down, clamped shut her nose, fitted her mouth over Cynthia's, and blew in.

Cynthia's mouth was cool, dry putty. Karen blew twice with all the force she could muster, then shifted position and jammed both palms into Cynthia's breastbone. She gave fifteen compressions, her body jerking up and down with every push, each of her own breaths starting with a sharp gasping sob. Then she went back to the cold mouth. Blow out twice, fifteen compressions.

She felt a hand on her shoulder. She hadn't been aware of the room and the doorway filling with people. "It's all right, Karen. I'll take over." The anesthesiology resident shifted his hand under her arm to help her up.

She moved numbly aside as he bent down with his glistening chrome tracheal intubation tool. A grim-faced nurse pushed by and crouched over Cynthia's chest to take over the cardiac compression. Another squeezed in to attach electrodes from the monitor on the crash cart.

Karen slumped back against the wall and stared ahead while the tumult raged around her. She barely noted the straight unblipping white line on the monitor screen. She'd stood by and watched an identical scene in the ER just over two weeks ago.

It was even the same anesthesiology resident. "She's been dead for a while, Karen," he said quietly.

Karen nodded dumbly. The image of Susan lying on the table, her skull shattered, blotted out the room. Shards of ice spread from her belly into her chest and throat. Her limbs had lost all feeling. Only the wall held her up.

The anesthesiologist's brow wrinkled. "Are you all right?"

She pushed herself away from the wall. "I'll go write a note on her chart."

Karen opened the door to the apartment shortly after ten o'clock that night. The living-room lights were off.

"Hank!" she called, with little hope that he'd be there.

He wasn't. She trudged in, threw her coat onto the back of the maple rocker, kicked off her shoes, and collapsed onto the couch. She was too tired and down to change clothes or go to the refrigerator or turn on the television. She sat and stared at an empty gray TV screen.

Shortly before eleven, Hank walked in. He brimmed over with energy. "What a day!" He threw his briefcase onto the couch and gave her a quick peck. "The first goddamned day of the protocol. A hundred hitches, but everyone's entered. We're rolling!"

She looked up at him from the couch. "Hank, one of my patients hung herself today."

He paced. "Every analog is cross-referenced and coded. Nobody will be able to get through the double-blind until the final go-ahead."

"If I'd have spent more time with her, if I'd only realized she was suicidal—"

"And Berkholt—I tell you, Karen, he was right with me every inch of the way. Each time I started explaining where I was in the programming, he instantly understood. I felt as if I were talking to another computer expert."

A feeling of desperation grew. He hadn't heard a word she'd said. Her voice rose. "It was Cynthia Frame. She was a friend of Susan's. She was in terror, Hank. The same thing was happening to her that had already happened to Duane. She killed herself while she was still aware enough to realize it."

Hank stopped pacing to look at her. "God, Karen, that must have been rough."

At last he had heard her. She sat forward on the couch. She wanted him to take her in his arms more than anything.

But the intent expression never left his face. He started pacing again. "Everything fell into place. It'll be the most elaborately protected double-blind program written."

She leaped up from the couch. "For God's sake, can't you understand? A patient of mine—a young woman—killed herself! She was Susan's friend. I was taking care of her, and she killed herself! I'm hurting, God damn it! Don't you care?"

His face sobered. "I didn't understand. I—I'm sorry." He reached for her.

She buried her face against his shoulder. The tears finally broke through. "She was only thirty-nine. She was beautiful. If I'd have known, maybe I could have done something. I'd just seen Duane—I couldn't believe what had happened to him. And Susan. It's so dreadful." She gave a wrenching sob.

"I'm sorry, Karen." His hand stroked her back. "What a nightmare this day must have been for you."

She sobbed again and pressed her face harder against him. Then she felt him pull away. She lifted her tear-stained face and looked at him.

His face had become animated again. "But our program is finally under way. It's just a matter of time now. There are answers to be found, and we'll find them."

She stared at him in disbelief. With a cry, she shoved him away from her and ran into the bedroom.

13

On the second day of the protocol, a late autumn storm swept into Southern California.

Winds of fifty miles an hour gusted through the Santa Monicas, stripping the birch and sycamores of their last leaves from summer. Palm trees lining the streets of Cinema Acres bent and swayed, their fronds swiping at the ground like large brooms sweeping the pavement. Through wind-driven needles of rain, Karen made a dash from the parking lot into Collier Hospital.

As she walked through the corridors, moans and cries came from open doors of patients' rooms. Siderails rattled. It was as if the howl of the wind had awakened dormant, turbulent centers in crumbling brains. A gnarled skeletonlike figure, already tied for the morning in her wheelchair, gibbered frantically as she stared at Karen with wide bloodshot eyes. Another patient with a long white beard stood starkly still in the middle of the hallway, his body bent crookedly over his aluminum walker, his face twisted toward the ceiling with his lips moving wordlessly.

Karen was reviewing charts at the nursing station on Wing C when the lights suddenly went out. The only remaining light in the windowless corridor was what daylight could filter in from opened doors of patients' rooms. The power supply to the entire hospital must have been disrupted. As Karen stood up, she was relieved that the initial analog injections had been completed the day before.

The level of cries and banging of siderails from the rooms increased. The floor nurse closed the medicine cabinet. "I'd better check the supply of flashlights." She sighed.

A clatter came from the direction of the central hallway. Karen turned. Far down the corridor she witnessed the remarkable scene of Sybil Wagoner running at full tilt. Behind her labored two attendants, pushing a cart that held a bulky portable generator, the type she'd seen in the operating room of the community hospital at which she'd clerked during her senior year of medical school.

In the dim light, Wagoner's face was gray and covered with beads of sweat. She appeared not to notice Karen as she ran by and disappeared into the doorway of room C-31. The two attendants followed her through the door with the portable generator. Karen strode in after them.

The private nurse, Clara Lipton, was squeezing and releasing a rubber bag attached to the disconnected end of the tube from the now-silent ventilator. Lipton moved with a businesslike competence that Karen wouldn't have thought possible from the nurse's indolent behavior she'd seen before. Breathing hard, Wagoner flipped a switch. The generator putt-putted into action. She pulled the ventilator plug from the wall socket and plugged it into the generator. Air swooshed from the ventilator. Silently, as if the two of them had rehearsed the scenario before, Lipton separated the hose to the tracheostomy tube from the ventilator bag and handed the end to Wagoner. Wagoner jammed it into the ventilator opening. The chest of the figure on the bed began to rise and fall rhythmically, one cycle every five seconds.

Lipton wrapped a blood pressure cuff around Henrietta Lee's arm, inflated it, studied the wall manometer as the column of mercury fell. "One thirty over seventy," she said, the first words spoken in the room since Karen had entered.

Wagoner wiped the sweat off her forehead and nodded. Her face looked haggard as she stared at the figure on the bed.

Then she turned and noticed Karen for the first time. Her already bloodless lips tightened. "I believe everything is under control, doctor." She straightened and, looking straight ahead, left the room.

Karen started to follow. As she reached the door, her way was blocked by the gaunt figure of Bernard Eisenberg. He was breathing hard, each exhalation starting with a short grunt. His face was pale. The right side of his mouth drooped more than she remembered. He looked past her.

Clara Lipton turned to him, and Karen thought she saw a glint of scorn on her face. "She's all right," Lipton said.

Eisenberg chewed at his lip. Then his eyes turned to Karen as if he were seeing her for the first time. He looked as if he were going to say something, then caught himself. The left side of his face gave a slight twitch. He turned and limped away.

As Karen left, she paused to look back into the room. The respirator was whooshing twelve times per minute. The white line on the monitor screen blipped in a regular pattern. Lipton was again sitting by the bedside, her eyes on the paperback on her lap. Only a barely perceptible increase in the depth of her breathing suggested that anything out of the ordinary had happened.

That afternoon, Duane Dreyer was transferred by ambulance from University Medical Center to Collier Hospital. Wagoner assigned him a private room on Wing B where it joined the main corridor. Karen was aware that he was only two doors down the hall from her own office—his office just a few weeks before.

She was in his room when Will Hayes carried in a tray with a syringe and a coded vial. As Hayes gave the injection, Karen said a silent prayer. *Please. Let it be a CRH analog, not the placebo.*

Hayes capped the needle and entered the number of the vial into a notebook. He looked at Karen with his head tilted to the side and gave a slight grin. "Well, doc, we're started."

With no more fanfare than that, Duane Dreyer became part of the CRH protocol at Collier Hospital.

By the time the program was into its fourth day, Karen thought she might be seeing small changes in a few patients. Mr. Brammer, the fifty four-year-old X-ray technician from Collier Hospital, seemed slightly better. He asked for cream with his breakfast coffee and addressed Karen as "nurse." Two patients who'd recently been moved over from the board-and-care section brightened.

But most of the patients showed no clinical change.

A few seemed to worsen at a rate faster than the usual deterioration of Alzheimer's patients. Three who'd been able to feed themselves now required hand feeding from one of the nurses or attendants. Two of them aspirated food and were transferred to the acute care hospital at Cinema Acres with pneumonia. But the patients involved were already so far advanced that it was difficult to judge how much they'd actually worsened.

Not so Duane Dreyer. Within three days of his transfer to Collier and his first injection, he lost all speech and was unable to stand or sit. He wouldn't swallow food placed in his mouth.

In her eighth-floor office at the medical school, Karen spilled out some of her fears to Percy Barnes, who'd come by to pick up a folder for endocrine service. "He's practically terminal," she said. "He simply can't go any further without having to be placed on life-support systems."

Percy Barnes looked at her with his magnified owl eyes. "That must be pretty tough on you, Karen."

She swallowed. "Nothing about his illness makes sense. Alzheimer's usually has a hereditary factor, but both of Duane's parents died in their eighties without a trace of senility. For God's sake, Percy, a galloping form of Alzheimer's doesn't just come out of the blue and destroy a forty-year-old!"

"What are you getting at?"

Karen struggled to put into words something that had been eating at her since her visit to Alberto Ruiz's lab. "I can't get the thought out of my mind that something infectious is involved."

"A slow virus? Like Creutzfeldt–Jakob disease—or kuru?"

She nodded, and her words came faster. "It's not too far out. I know that once in a while you'll come across a young Alzheimer's—but damn it, in less than a month's time, I've seen three, two of them forty and under."

"You're talking about Duane and Cynthia Frame, aren't you?" Barnes said.

"And a fifty-four-year-old X-ray technician who was still working at Collier Hospital until two months ago."

Percy nodded soberly. The overhead fluorescent light glinted off the prisms of his thick glasses. "It's probably only coincidental. But I think I'd start washing my hands pretty good if I worked at Collier."

Late that night Karen paced the floor of the living room. Hank sat on the couch, thumbing through pages of spreadsheet data.

"I thought there'd be more time," Karen said desolately. "Even if Duane received nothing but the placebo, he shouldn't have plummeted downhill this fast. Could something we're not recognizing be making him worse?"

Hank shrugged. "That's one of the multivariant factors to determine in the study."

She stopped pacing and glowered at him. All of a sudden, she was sick to death of the goddamned computerized program and the goddamned data entries and the goddamned lists and cross-lists. Her fists tightened. "Look, this isn't a fucking academic exercise with laboratory rats! I'm talking about one of the brightest men I've ever known. I'm talking about the only family I have left."

He shook his head sadly. "I'm sorry, Karen. I didn't mean to sound callous. But there really isn't much more you can do now. The program's already started."

Her hands loosened. "Hank, I'm very familiar with the analogs we're using. More than anyone except Dr. Berkholt, I was involved in their development. Only six are feasible—they're the ones that cross over from the bloodstream into the brain. Of the six, three are in the protocol.

Analog Fifteen lasts the longest in rat brains. If it works in humans, it would be Duane's best chance."

"If you're making a point, I'm not sure what it is."

She crouched in front of him. "What if you made an exception. What if—what if you broke the code just a wee bit?" When he rose, she jumped up and barely stopped herself from pushing him back down. Her words came faster. "Oh, I don't mean you should tell me. I'm part of the clinical team, the observer—it wouldn't be necessary for me to break the double-blind. But you, Hank, you could do it without interfering with the project. It wouldn't be just for Duane—it would be for Susan. All you'd have to do would be to change the matching number of the vial he's due to get so it lines up with Analog Fifteen."

Deep lines creased his forehead. He reached for her hands. "You don't understand, Karen."

She backed away from him. Her voice took on a pleading quality. "I'm not asking you to break any confidences. Just to manipulate one number. It wouldn't alter the outcome. He's almost dead now, don't you see, Hank? For all practical purposes, he's already dead. It wouldn't change anything."

"Karen, you still don't understand. Even if I agreed to, I couldn't."

"Damn it, you could if you wanted to!"

"I don't have the code!"

She blinked. Her legs felt weak. "What—what do you mean?"

"I've been trying to tell you. Berkholt himself foresaw this. That's why he insisted on a foolproof program. For the analogs, he gave me only code numbers to enter into the program. And then he asked me to protect the entire protocol against himself as well as me. I programmed the Novar-3 to reassign the codes on its own. There's no way anyone can determine which preparation any patient will get."

She reached for the arm of the couch and lowered herself into it. "I don't understand."

"Look. All of us who work with the program have our own user log-on password. That's standard for any major computer program. It lets us enter our data and keep track of each patient and the code number for each injection. But it doesn't let us know what material any of the code numbers represents. To access that information, the protocol has two security passwords. The computer gave one to Berkholt and one to me. Neither of us knows the other's." He paused. "Do you follow, so far?"

She nodded numbly.

He continued. "Okay. The computer won't allow anyone to break into the codes that identify what each vial contains—and what each patient's been given—unless it's fed back both security passwords. To keep these passwords from getting out, Berkholt and I have agreed that neither will be written—each would remain only in memory." He took in a deep breath. "So you see, if you want to break into the basic code of the protocol and find the analog you want Duane to get, you'd have to get Berkholt to agree to it as well."

Her throat was dry. She remembered Berkholt's steel gray eyes: *"We have but one shot at this. . . . Duane is part of the protocol."* She suddenly felt overwhelmingly tired. She wanted to close her eyes.

"We do have a failsafe," Hank said. "I told you that the password hasn't been written down. That's not quite correct. Dr. Berkholt and I each jotted our password on a three-by-four index card and sealed it in an envelope. Both envelopes are stored in a safe-deposit drawer in the West L.A. Bank of America vault. The only key to the vault is in the safe in the dean's office. Dean Patterson is committed to not release the key as long as both Dr. Berkholt and I are alive."

"You mean there's nothing you can do?"

"That's exactly what I'm saying."

She closed her eyes and sank back into the couch.

A feeling of utter hopelessness blanketed her. No one was in control. The protocol had developed a life of its own. It was a spider weaving a continually expanding web that had already ensnared Cynthia and Duane. And now it was reaching out to envelop Hank, Dr. Berkholt, and herself.

14

Among Susan's papers, Karen found living wills, one each for Susan and Duane: "If at such a time the situation should arise in which there is no reasonable expectation of my recovery from extreme physical or mental disability, I direct that I be allowed to die and not be kept alive by medications, artificial means, or heroic measures."

Karen discussed the living will at a meeting with Dr. Berkholt and Mike Werner.

"I don't disagree with Duane's philosophy," Dr. Berkholt said, "and I think no one has the right to deny him his directive. But the circumstances are so extraordinary that I think we should play for more time. I'd favor moving him back to University Hospital where we have the resources to keep him alive—and if he's no better after a period of time, then abandon the extraordinary life-support systems." He turned to Werner. "How do you feel about it, Mike?"

Werner nodded. "I just can't see letting go yet, either. Although I honestly don't know what else we have to offer."

Dr. Berkholt took a deep breath. "What if we agree to use every measure we can to keep him alive for three weeks?" He turned to Karen and asked gently, "Could you feel comfortable with that approach?"

Earlier, she'd thought of his rigid insistence on the protocol as scientific callousness. Now she could see only the terrible sadness in his eyes. "I think that's what Susan would want," she said.

"I don't think your boss *purposely* intended a slap in my face," Frank Terhune said. "But it's not the first time he's managed to achieve that result." In the two weeks Karen had been at Collier, Terhune had rarely referred to Dr. Berkholt by name, only as "*your* boss." Karen was sure that Terhune, more than any of the others, resented her appointment. He was in charge at Cinema Acres' small acute care hospital, and she suspected he felt he should have been appointed chief of medicine at Collier Hospital as well.

"From everything I've heard Dr. Berkholt say," Karen said, "he has the highest regard for you, Frank."

"He had a strange way of showing it when the two of you blithely went straight over my head."

"What are you talking about?"

"You know damned well what I'm talking about! Moving Duane directly to University rather than the acute care hospital here. In the past, the procedure has always been for these decisions to be made by me."

"For Christ's sake, Duane's no ordinary patient. He's a professor of medicine at the medical school."

"And I'm just an associate professor, is that it?"

"It has nothing to do with your rank!"

"Then why is this the first time in the two years since I've had my appointment here that I haven't at least been consulted in an acute care situation?"

Karen's voice grew hard. "How many times have you treated a forty-year-old who's progressed from brilliant intellect to preterminal brain deterioration in less than three months?"

Terhune stiffened. "Duane is no stranger to me, and I am as interested in his care as anyone. I have full access at the acute care hospital to every member of the medical school faculty. And if I thought that his care required special facilities at University Hospital, I'd be the first to recommend his transfer there. I simply think that I should be entitled to participate in the decision."

Her hands clenched into white fists by her sides. She bit off each word: "Duane will be moved this afternoon to University Hospital."

Still fuming over Frank Terhune's behavior, Karen collided head-on with Ron Olsen as she tore from her office.

"Whoa!" His arms wrapped around her. "Do you carry liability insurance?"

She pushed away from him. He had an unsettling way of showing up when she was at her most upset. "That pompous son of a bitch!"

He stroked his chin and frowned. "That describes too many people I know. Which pompous son of a bitch?"

She let out her breath. "Terhune."

"Oh, *that* pompous son of a bitch." He took her by the arm. "Come on, it's time to take a few minutes' break. Let's get some coffee."

They sat across from each other in the staff dining room. Ron Olsen stirred sugar and milk into his coffee with a plastic spoon. Karen sipped hers black from a Styrofoam cup.

She hadn't fully cooled down. "I keep getting the message that everywhere I turn here, I'm usurping someone else's private territory."

"Do I detect a trace of paranoia?" he asked with a smile.

She put down her cup. Her eyes narrowed. "Look, you invited me to coffee. Keep your psychiatric observations in the patients' rooms, where they belong."

His face reddened—then suddenly relaxed again. "I guess I did it again."

"Did *what* again?" she snapped.

He shook his head and grinned. "Sometimes I revert to talking in psychoanaleeze without realizing it. You'll have to let me know when I get started."

Her tight muscles loosened. He *could* have a disarming smile when he wasn't posing. "If I'm going to be working with you, you're damned right I'll let you know."

"It's a deal." He raised a hand protectively. "But be gentle about it. Don't forget that a footnote to your Hippocratic Oath requires you to show a little compassion for a troubled child."

She smiled in spite of herself. "You're no child."

"But I am troubled!"

She sighed. "That, I may learn to accept."

"Since you won't let me work on your problems, maybe we could get together to work on mine instead." He gestured palms up. "After all, they're not really my fault."

"Then whose are they?" She regretted the question the moment she asked it.

His eyes brightened. "Ah, I'll explain. I'm sure it's all because I came along late in a family of eight kids. With five older brothers, I had to work extra hard at impressing my folks to get any attention from them. That's probably the underlying reason I went into psychiatry. And if you wanted to be particularly hard on me, you might even suspect that that's what I'm doing with you here. You see, I'm still going through a narcissistic reaction formation that I never fully worked out in my training analysis. . . ."

Karen groaned, and slowly shook her head.

He stopped. "I'm at it again?"

"Yep," she said.

He stirred his coffee. Then he looked up at her with a grin. "I know a place to pick up some great Dungeness crab. How about working on it at my place tonight with a bottle of Chardonnay?"

She paused longer than she'd intended. "Thanks, Ron. I don't think so."

Deciding on a date to cut off Duane's life-support systems was unnecessary. By his second day at University Hospital, he stopped breathing and had to be connected to a respirator. On the fourth day, his blood pressure plummeted.

Karen stood at the bedside. How many times had she worked here in the intensive care unit surrounded by this electronic kaleidoscope of blinking lights, digital readouts, and monitor screens, barely taking time to note the grief-muddled eyes of relatives as they gazed in helpless bewilderment at the awesome array of equipment. Today, she was seeing the ICU through eyes that were blurred by her own grief.

Mike Werner and the cardiologist, Roger Harriman, were at the bedside with her. Roger had stood by Susan's inert body when Karen burst into the emergency room two and a half weeks ago. With them this time was Dr. Berkholt.

Duane's chest rose and fell twelve times per minute in sequence with the whoosh of the respirator. Just like Henrietta Lee, Karen thought grimly as she gazed at his placid face, from which all lines had been erased. The digital readout from the arterial pressure line read twenty over zero. The overhead EKG monitor screen showed atrial fibrillation with a sequence of bizarre ventricular complexes.

"He's getting a maximum IV drip of norepinephrine," Harriman said. "We can't give any more plasma—his central venous pressure's already above twenty-five. He's had no urine output for twenty-four hours."

"Then that's it," Karen said in a quiet voice.

"I'm afraid so," Harriman said. "What it boils down to is that nothing will keep his blood pressure up any longer. Whatever terrible process it is that's destroying his brain has reached the basic autonomic centers that support life."

Dr. Berkholt's face was heavily lined. His usually ramrod-erect figure sagged with fatigue. "Roger, are you saying it's time to disconnect?"

"I'm saying that he's already dead as far as his cardiovascular system is concerned, Dr. Berkholt. He doesn't have enough circulation to support his brain or kidneys." His lips tight, he gave a shrug and glanced at Karen. "As to the decision to disconnect, I can't make that by myself."

Berkholt turned toward Werner. "What are your thoughts, Mike?"

Werner looked as haggard as Dr. Berkholt. His voice had dropped an octave from its usual low pitch. "His last two EEGs showed no significant activity."

"He's brain dead, then?" Berkholt asked.

Werner nodded.

All eyes turned to Karen.

Dr. Berkholt spoke softly. "It's wrong to ask you this so soon after the last time. If you wish, I'll take the responsibility."

She looked from him to the body on the bed. For a terrible moment she was back in the unearthly quiet of the emergency room and Susan lay on the table.

"Disconnect him," she said.

She felt Dr. Berkholt's hand on her shoulder. She turned and looked into his eyes. She'd never seen tears in them before.

With a sob, she lurched forward and buried her face against him. She felt his chest rise and fall.

15

As Karen again sat in the front row of the mortuary chapel, it was as if time had stood still. The gold-paneled clock on the wall registered two thirty, just as it had at the beginning of Susan's memorial service three weeks before. The room was filled with the same doctors and staff workers from University Hospital. Men wore the same suits of navy blue or gray, women the same unadorned dresses or somber two-piece outfits. Behind the podium hung the same black velvet drapes.

She turned to Hank, seated in the same place next to her. He was looking straight ahead at the podium, his face still. She thought that this might be the second time she'd ever seen him in coat and tie. Hank, who'd renounced all family ties of his own, had lived with her through the loss of all that was left of her own family.

He sensed her gaze and turned to face her. He gave a slight smile and reached for her hand. She felt a sense of reassurance at his grip and squeezed back. Okay, she thought, he's got his own screwed-up background to deal with—but he's trying.

Two of the eulogies were delivered by new voices, but otherwise it was the same people. Some of them tried for eloquence, but this time it didn't catch fire. Even Dr. Berkholt's words were short and resigned. "The magnitude of our loss is too great, and the losses themselves too close upon each other, for me to try to give meaning to them. Perhaps distance will lend perspective. But right now—" His voice dropped. If the chapel had been less hushed, Karen might not have heard him finish. "Right now the pain is too much." He looked at Karen as he stepped down from the podium.

It would have been better if the ceremony had ended there. But Dr. Brigham Patterson, patrician dean of the medical school, followed: ". . . a man of greatness and of vision, a man who was a shining light to everyone around him." His words faded out of Karen's consciousness. This would be the fourth family requiem she'd sat through—there were no more to await. She had been five when her mother died. Mist-shrouded memories brought back a scene very different from these last two. The black-garbed, white-tallithed rabbi chanted his dirge over her mother in a foreign language that dripped anguish. Night after night for an entire week afterward, she sat fidgeting and miserable in the living room through the kaddish ceremony while grim-faced mourners intoned that same strange language of grief, until finally she'd fall asleep in Susan's arms.

When it was all over two girls remained, children of a lost, over-whelmed barber. Nine-year-old Susan became five-year-old Karen's mother. Susan cleared the path—high school valedictory, scholarship at UCLA, Phi Beta Kappa, student loans and scholarships through medical school. Karen followed in almost an exact replay. Who would have expected it? Two doctors forged from a defeated barber's daughters.

Their father didn't live to see it. He lasted twelve years after his wife died. He cut hair six days a week, rarely leaving the house except for the short drive to the shop. He never missed work until the day Karen returned home in her junior year at high school to find him still and cold in bed.

". . . and we pledge ourselves to carry on Dr. Dreyer's great work." Continuing his eulogy, Dean Patterson announced the establishment of the Duane Dreyer chair in the Department of Endocrinology. His voice drifted in and out of Karen's awareness as she stared at the closed velvet drapes.

A wave of anger suddenly struck her. It made no sense. Nothing any of them said made any sense. Duane was gone and her sister was gone—both destroyed as the result of a grotesque illness, a bizarre, freakish twist of the life cycle that was unexplained by the countless tests and surmises and theories and platitudes. For this funeral ceremony she no longer felt the threat of tears—only a growing, rending, directionless anger.

There has to be an answer, Susan.

Karen's beeper had started flashing during the ceremony. After Dean Patterson's eulogy was finished, she found a phone in the mortuary office.

It was Sigrid Higheagle from the eighth-floor office in the medical school. "I hope I didn't pull you out of services, but I thought you'd want to know—today's Alzheimer inpatient consults have grown to six."

"I'll be there by four thirty and get the list from you then," Karen said.

"One of them"—Sigrid paused meaningfully—"is Lauryn Hart."

"Who is Lauryn Hart?"

Sigrid's voice took on an incredulous quality. "Are you putting me on?"

Karen sighed. "I'm not putting anybody on today, Sigrid."

"Dr. Formaker, you *have* been working too hard. Lauryn Hart—she's the star of *Empire.* She's the hottest sex symbol on TV this season."

A vacuum suddenly opened in the center of Karen's chest. "Surely she's not for Collier Hospital?"

"They want to get her on the protocol."

She paused a moment before asking, "How old is she?"

"She's thirty-one," Sigrid said.

Karen had trouble holding on to the phone.

"Are you still there, Dr. Formaker?" Sigrid asked.

"Yes." Her throat was so dry that her voice caught.

Sigrid's voice took on a curious tone. "How old are you, Dr. Formaker?"

"I'm thirty-one."

"Well, I hope for your sake it isn't catching," Sigrid said lightly.

16

A collection of people clustered loosely outside room 812 in the Neuropsychiatric Institute of University Medical Center.

As Karen walked through them to enter the room, a uniformed private guard stopped her and asked for identification. He checked her faculty card and motioned toward a man in a rumpled white shirt and loosened tie. The man spoke to a woman next to him. She nodded and walked over.

She didn't look at the card. "Dr. Karen Formaker?"

"Yes."

She was in her early forties, of medium build, with square jaw and square shoulders. Her two-piece navy suit was smartly tailored. Her short dark hair was peppered with gray. "You're from Collier—with Dr. Berkholt."

"That's right."

The woman held out her hand. "I'm Bev Millar." Her grip was steel. "Lauryn Hart's agent. I have power of attorney for her." She nodded toward the room. "The neurologist, Dr. Michael Werner, is examining her now."

"I've worked with Dr. Werner before," Karen said.

"I'll expect to discuss your recommendations with you after you're through with your examination."

"Yes."

Millar looked at her with steady eyes. "As far as the press is concerned, Lauryn has been hospitalized for treatment of a viral fatigue syndrome. It is imperative to her interests that no information regarding her medical status be released through anyone but me."

"I'm comfortable with that," Karen said.

Millar glanced toward some of the people standing around the hallway. "Part of what you see is the contingent from Five Star Studios trying to figure out how to guard their interests." For the first time she permitted herself a slight smile. "Don't let them—or the press—make you feel pressured, Dr. Formaker. I'll be doing enough of that myself."

Mike Werner appeared, looking grim. "Do you have a few minutes to talk before you see her?"

"I think that would be a good idea, Mike." The two of them had suddenly started sharing an unusual number of cases together. "Let's go somewhere private." She turned to Millar. "Will you excuse us?"

"Sure." Millar turned and walked away.

Karen walked with Werner to the small conference room next to the nurses' station. Werner closed the door behind them and pulled up a folding chair so that he could face her. "I wonder if I'm losing my grip on reality, Karen."

"Another Alzheimer's?" she said.

"Thirty-one years old. She's already had a full workup at Cedars. She was admitted there under another name, but you can't hide looks like she has. The press got wind, and the people at Cedars came up with this viral fatigue syndrome shit."

"What do you find, Mike?"

"Neurologically, not a thing. Intellectually, she's someone who can't remember what day it is, how many husbands she's had, or how to subtract three from seven. But she still radiates so damned much sex that I don't think I'd have the courage to try to describe her to my wife."

"And Cedars?"

"They did everything short of a brain biopsy."

"And found nothing," she said.

"They tried her twelve days on the Hopkins acetylcholine protocol. Then they dripped bethanechol directly into her spinal fluid."

"Yes. There've been trials with that in the eastern centers."

"According to their notes, she continued to get worse through both treatment programs."

"At a rate faster than usually seen in Alzheimer's," she said quietly.

"Those are almost their exact words." Werner pursed his lips. "Karen, you're taking this bit of Alice-in-Horrorland as if I were giving you a straightforward case history on a stroke."

She pressed her lips together. "Mike, in addition to Duane, you and I have had a thirty-nine-year-old nursing supervisor who hung herself and a fifty-four-year-old X-ray technician. And now"—she let out a heavy breath—"I'm getting ready to go see an Alzheimer's who's the same age as I am." She looked up into his eyes and shook her head. "If you're losing your grip on reality, I've surely already lost mine."

*   *   *

Karen wasn't quite prepared for what she found.

The beautiful woman lying on the bed would need little change to pose for the cover of *TV Guide, Glamour,* or *Playboy.* Her glistening blond hair, curled with planned haphazardness, covered one side of a perfect forehead. Velvet-soft eye shadow accentuated large green eyes. Her lips were a rich and moist red. She wore a green satin robe.

Her eyes were on the wall television when Karen walked in. She turned, and Karen's heart fell as she saw the empty expression in her eyes. It looked as if this woman had already gone beyond the stage Cynthia Frame had reached.

Karen held out her hand. "I'm Karen. Dr. Karen Formaker."

"It's good to see you again," Lauryn Hart said.

"Actually, I don't believe we've met before," Karen said.

For a second the eyes clouded, then the vacancy returned. "No, of course not." She pushed herself up in bed. "I don't know why I'm lying around all day like this." She swung her long, shapely legs over the side of the bed and stood up. She looked around the room as if she'd just wandered into unfamiliar territory.

"If you don't mind, I'll turn off the TV so we can talk," Karen said. She punched buttons on the bedside console, then sat in a side chair and motioned to a chair across from her. "Why don't you sit, too, Lauryn?"

"Yes, thank you." Lauryn Hart's body seemed to have a volition of its own. It didn't just sit, it molded itself into the chair with a sensuous, uncoiling motion. "What did you say your name was?"

"I'm Karen."

"Oh. It's good to see you again."

Karen bit her lip. She pulled a pen and notepad from her lab coat. "Do you understand why you're here?"

"It's for a checkup?"

"That's right. How do you feel?"

One leg carefully crossed the other. "All right."

"You've had some tests done?"

"Yes, I think so."

"Where were they done?"

Lauryn looked around the room. "You know . . ." Her eyes caught the mirror, and she got up from the chair to walk over to it. She picked up a brush and began teasing her hair.

"Your hair looks very nice, Lauryn," Karen said.

"Thank you." She concentrated hard on the reflection in the mirror as she brushed.

"Could you tell me about your family?"

"Family?"

"Your mother and father?"

"Oh. Mama."

"Where does your mother live?"

Lauryn stopped brushing and turned back toward her. A puzzled look crossed her face. "Are you from the studio?"

"I'm a doctor here at the medical center."

"It's good to see you again."

When Karen left the room, only Bev Millar and the security guard waited outside. "I got rid of the studio and the press at the same time by convincing both that there'd be no medical pronouncements tonight." She nodded toward the door to room 812. "I want a drink, but for the sake of company I'm willing to chase it with some food. You hungry?"

"I've got another consult to see."

"I'll wait."

Karen looked at her watch. "I'll meet you down in the lobby at seven thirty."

At Pepito's Restaurant on San Vicente, a mile from the medical center, Millar sipped a double margarita, Karen a California Chardonnay.

"She got halfway through the season's filming," Millar said. "Then suddenly she started forgetting her lines."

"How long ago did you first notice it?"

"It happened so fast that within a week everybody knew something was bad. I'd estimate"—she put the straw to her lips and took a deep draw from the margarita—"seven weeks ago." She held up the straw like a baton, to make a point. "In fact, I'd place it exactly four days before November fourth the day we stopped filming."

"I understand the show's still on the air," Karen said.

"They've got two original episodes that haven't aired. The studio brass is shitting sour pickles about what to do with their contracts after that."

"Reruns?"

Millar laughed grimly. "Sure. The minute they announce their first rerun before the end of the season, a million dollars in sponsors' revenue flies right out the window." Her face sobered. "Before they get to reruns, they'll play for time by trying to work around her role. They're already shooting one episode in which she's away on a trip, and they've hassled up another script in which she'll be hospitalized after an accident. They'll get away with it maybe for a couple episodes, no more. That million's only the first installment—another twenty million or so depends on what's going on in that hospital room we just left." She took a long sip of her drink. "What do you think about what you found?"

Karen frowned. "She's farther advanced than I expected. And if she was okay six weeks ago and all this only happened since then . . ." She shrugged.

"That's what I figure." Millar pursed her lips. "You calling it Alzheimer's?"

Karen nodded.

"Isn't she young for it?"

"You're damned right she's young. But at this stage we can't find anything else to call it." Karen tapped her fingers restlessly on the tablecloth. "Alzheimer's disease is an autopsy diagnosis. Outside of a microscope slide of brain tissue, there's no test that says, 'Aha! This is the Big A.' But when you find a muddied intellect and loss of memory for what happened just a few minutes ago—while a lot of the social graces hang on—that is the classic picture of the early disease."

"You saw the way she was dressed," Millar said. "You saw her eye makeup, her lipstick, her hairstyle. Every morning she still spends a couple hours putting on makeup and combing and arranging her hair. How can you fit that behavior with her diagnosis?"

"For Lauryn, those are behavior patterns that have become part of her. They're the social graces I spoke of that hang on long after the intellect slips. As the disease progresses, they'll eventually be lost, too." She took a deep breath. "And at the rate it's moving, that may not be very long from now."

When Millar spoke, her voice was surprisingly soft. "Will it be very rough on her?"

Karen thought of Cynthia Frame. "I suspect that the most painful stage is when the victim's still with it enough to realize what she's losing. Later, when the disease is further along, maybe it gets easier." She let out a deep breath and gazed soberly at Millar. "Lauryn may already be past that terrible stage."

The muscles of Bev Millar's jaw worked up and down before she spoke. "I think I know what you mean. At Cedars one night, Lauryn panicked. She screamed over and over that her mind was crumbling. I spent the next couple nights in her room holding her until she could fall asleep."

Karen finished her wine, ignoring the salad plate the waiter had just set on the table. The wine was beginning to slow her sensation of hurtling downhill on a crowded street in a car without brakes. "Doesn't she have anyone?"

Millar shook her head slowly. "The sex bitch of *Empire,* second and now first in Nielsen ratings the last two years? No." She took in a deep breath. "Deserted by her mother when she was five, raised by a grand-mother, three busted marriages by thirty-one. I guess it goes with the turf." She disposed of the rest of her margarita with the next deep sip from the straw. "Okay if I call you Karen?"

"It's fine . . . Bev."

"Karen, do you think you can help her?"

Karen studied her untouched salad plate. "It's an experimental treat-ment, never used on humans. We don't even have an animal model to refer back to. All previous approaches—like the acetylcholine one they used on her at Cedars—have been dismal failures. We're trying a new approach—that's the only thing really going for it. Theoretically there's a basis." She shrugged. "What else can I say?"

Millar's glass was empty. She signaled for the waiter and turned back to Karen. "I've seen Collier Hospital. It looks like a holding tank for a graveyard. Is there a chance she could get the treatment at home?"

"Not a prayer. Dr. Berkholt turned over heaven and earth to get an okay for experimenting with humans by agreeing to limit the project to a strictly designed and controlled protocol at Collier." She sat forward on her chair. "Bev, even when Lauryn's at Collier, there's no assurance she'll get an active CRH analog. The protocol calls for a quarter of the subjects to receive placebo, at least in the beginning."

Bev Millar took in a deep breath. "I know that," she said heavily. "I had to sign permission before she could get into the project."

"If she should start in the placebo group," Karen said more gently, "once the computer gives us the word that we're seeing a statistically significant difference in the treated patients, she could then cross over into the analog group."

The waiter appeared, and Millar ordered two more drinks. Karen smiled. "Until this moment, I had some crazy thoughts about getting back to the hospital tonight."

Bev's forehead wrinkled. "After nine at night? You've got a helluva job."

Karen shrugged. "I get trapped by habits."

Bev Millar was silent for a moment, her lips pursed, eyes trained on some distant spot. "Do you realize," she finally said, "that when the word gets out that Lauryn's entering a mental hospital—an *old-age* mental hospital at that—her career's ruined and Five Star Studios is in shambles. Even I won't be in the greatest shape financially."

"We could use a fake name again, if you want to try it," Karen said.

"That worked for exactly eight hours at Cedars," Millar said. "With the press already parked outside the door, it wouldn't work for thirty minutes now." She sucked on her lip. *"C'est la vie.* The stakes are a helluva lot bigger than Five Star Studios."

Karen realized that she felt comfortable talking to this straightforward woman sitting across from her. She had the strange feeling that she'd known her for years. Particularly since Cynthia Frame's death, Karen had had a desperate need to talk with *someone.* Before, she'd always had Susan. She was still angry with Hank's insensitivity, his complete obliviousness to everything outside the project. "Bev, in the past month I've seen more young people with Alzheimer's than I should. Lauryn's the youngest."

"An Alzheimer's epidemic?" Millar said wryly.

"Sometimes it feels like that." Karen paused. She remembered her conversation with Percy Barnes over Duane. "It's not entirely wild speculation. There are two diseases known to be transmitted by a virus that have caused dementia like what we see in Alzheimer's. They're both rare as hell—in fact, the most common one's only been found in a remote tribe in New Guinea. But at least there *is* a precedent."

Bev Millar looked at her incredulously. "A virus? You mean, like a brain flu?"

Karen shook her head. "It's not our usual concept of a virus. The diseases I'm referring to are classified as slow-virus diseases. The idea is that the viruses enter the body, and instead of causing an acute disease that reaches a peak and then clears up, they adjust to living in certain body cells and slowly alter their function. In the diseases I'm talking about, the viruses take up residence in the brain cells—and just stay there. Then, over months or years, they slowly affect and finally destroy their host cells."

Bev grimaced. "For chrissake, that sounds like an alien invader in a science fiction script."

Karen chewed thoughtfully on her lip. "It would almost fit, except for Lauryn. The others I've seen—I mean the younger ones—there've been three of them before Lauryn—worked at either Cinema Acres or University Hospital. I was beginning to think maybe we had some kind of virus spreading between the two campuses. But Lauryn doesn't fit into the mold."

Millar stared at Karen. "I'm afraid that she does."

Karen frowned. "What do you mean?"

"I told you that her grandmother raised her. Lauryn visited her every week." Bev took a deep breath. "For the last three years of her life, her grandmother has lived in the board-and-care section at Cinema Acres."

17

Karen frowned as she crept in morning rush-hour traffic toward the medical center. It was high time to talk over her suspicions with Dr. Berkholt.

The first couple of weeks working at Collier might have given her the false impression of an epidemic of Alzheimer's. After all, she reasoned, Collier *is* an Alzheimer's referral center. And the publicity from leaks about Berkholt's work could well be responsible for an increase in the patient load.

But this awful spread of the disease into the young?

She shook her head. No way could that be purely random occurrence. Something was wrong, terribly wrong. You might expect to find one out of every hundred Alzheimer's in their fifties, perhaps one in a thousand in their forties. But in their thirties?

What about kuru, the brain-eroding virus that had decimated an entire tribe in the highlands of New Guinea? Was there any way?

Of course not. Except in experiments that involved injecting primates, the kuru virus had been spread only by eating infected brains. How many people in West Los Angeles go around paying tribute to their dead relatives by eating their brains?

Still, she thought of the locked incubators in Ruiz's microbiology lab. How hard would it have been to bring a contraband virus into this country without the knowledge of the watchdog Centers for Disease Control? Ruiz was collecting blood and spinal fluid from patients for tissue cultures, he said. Could those tissue cultures support the virus of kuru?

Dr. Berkholt wasn't in his office. She asked Sigrid Higheagle to page her when he appeared. She was interviewing the children of an eighty-four-year-old star of thirties' Westerns when the call came.

Her level of tension dropped the moment she walked into his office. Once she shared her suspicions with him, the load wouldn't be as heavy.

He motioned for her to sit. "You've had some long days," he said.

Karen couldn't remember him ever looking so tired. "I suspect you have, too," she said.

His smile didn't have much behind it. "These are the dog days of an experiment—when you're waiting for the first signs to suggest you're past square one."

She leaned forward. "Dr. Berkholt, I just saw a new candidate for the protocol. She troubles me a great deal."

"A thirty-one-year-old television actress?"

She looked at him in surprise.

"For the past forty-eight hours, Karen, I've fielded calls about Miss Hart from the chairman of Five Star Studios, the president of the Screen Actors Guild, the chairman of the board of directors of the corporation that's the biggest contributor to Cinema Acres, and two members of the board of regents of the university."

"And I thought I was under pressure."

"We both are," he said. "There's no question that the unfortunate young woman is entitled to enter the program. The pressure has been for us to make an exception and ensure that she isn't in the placebo group. That, of course, would destroy the integrity of the entire project. And that's one place where your friend Hank's prowess has been put into use. He's made the program inviolable. This allows me to explain to each caller that all vials of CRH analog from my lab, as well as the placebo preparations, are so irretrievably coded that no one—and that includes both you and myself—can tell what any subject receives until the protocol is broken open at the end."

Yes, Hank's already made that very clear, she thought with a trace of bitterness. "What bothers me most"—she cleared her throat—"is that we're seeing too many young people with Alzheimer's."

"That's one of the tragedies of the disease, Karen."

"But the number of exceptionally young people we're seeing has got to be outside of the range of random occurrence."

He nodded slowly. "I try to tell myself that the dice have a way of coming up two and twelve several times in a row. In a grim sense we're fortunate that it's happening now. We may be able to better assess the clinical effect of treatment on younger people, purely because their preillness baseline is more distinct."

She persisted. "Still, in one month to have three new patients age forty or under? Don't we have to look for something out of the ordinary that's triggering this?"

He answered quietly. "You're thinking of a slow virus like kuru, aren't you?"

She swallowed. He managed to be a step ahead of her every time she talked to him. "Is that unreasonable?"

He fitted his fingertips together and slowly shook his head. "When you look at the age group you're describing—no, it's not unreasonable. Most of the fears you've had the courage to voice are identical to my own."

He rose, walked to the door, closed it, and returned once more to his desk. "You and I both use kuru as an example because, other than Creutzfeldt–Jakob disease, it's the only dementia in humans known to be caused by a virus. Still, that so rare a virus could skip halfway across the world from a remote tribe in New Guinea is almost beyond belief." He slowly tapped his finger on the desk. "On the other hand, another as yet unknown slow virus that can be passed from person to person is in the realm of possibility."

She bit her lip. That's exactly what she was getting at. "You mean a new disease?"

He frowned. "It's a heavy thought, but I don't see how we can dismiss it. You realize, however, that if we even hint that we're thinking in these terms, we risk an immediate panic at Cinema Acres, and perhaps here at the medical center. That could destroy our program, and we'd have thrown away our one chance."

"I understand." Her voice lacked conviction.

He continued. "It's important that those of us who are most intimately involved—you, myself, Mike Werner, Alberto Ruiz—discuss our concerns among ourselves. But until we have more to go on, I think it best that we limit the number of people privy to those concerns."

She remembered voicing her fears to Bev Millar last night. She'd have to be more careful. She fidgeted with the stethoscope earpiece protruding from her lab coat pocket. "If we're truly concerned about the possibility of a slow virus causing Alzheimer's at Cinema Acres, we have to look for a source."

"Go on," he said.

She shifted in her chair. "Dr. Berkholt, I wonder about Dr. Ruiz. I don't understand his role. He's been involved not only with the cases at Collier—but with most of those I've seen here at University, sometimes before I'm called to consult on them."

"Oh, I scc." He touched the ends of his fingers together on his desk. "That would be a way of explaining the appearance of the disease in the obstetrics nurse who worked only here at University Hospital. You've wondered if Alberto Ruiz could be a clandestine factor in the spread of the dementia?"

Her eyes stayed on him as she nodded.

He smiled gently. "I can see where you're coming from. And it's entirely my fault. I should have explained Alberto Ruiz's role to you earlier."

The moment she heard the patient, understanding note in his voice, her newfound confidence disappeared.

"Karen, what if all along the basic cause of Alzheimer's has been a kurulike virus, and we haven't focused on it because the disease was prevalent only in old age, when the immune system weakens? What if then that virus underwent a mutation that made it deadlier so that it spread to the young? A mutation such as happened to the AIDS virus, which probably lay dormant on the African continent for decades before it exploded on the world scene a few years ago."

"But," Karen argued, "if that were the case—if Alzheimer's is caused by a slow virus—our current work would be pointless."

"Would it? What if the slow-virus infection were the the underlying cause of the CRH deficiency we're trying to correct in Alzheimer's? Finding a way to replace CRH could still reverse the disease." The lines of fatigue left his face. "Don't misunderstand me, I don't think that's the probable scenario." His finger sliced the air in emphasis. "But it's not impossible. That's precisely why I fought to bring Alberto Ruiz to Cinema Acres after I took over as chairman of the board. His search for an infectious component lends balance to my neurotransmitter emphasis. Alberto Ruiz is a talented virologist who's done excellent work in slow-virus disease in his home country. It's at my request that he's obtained virus studies on every Alzheimer patient at both Collier and University Hospital."

Karen felt her face burning. "I didn't realize."

Berkholt rose and walked around the desk. "I hadn't anticipated how close to my analysis you would come on your own."

"I should have asked you about Dr. Ruiz earlier."

He smiled and rested a hand on her shoulder. "You've got a rough job, Karen, and you're handling it admirably. I can't tell you how highly I respect your opinions and your judgment."

"Thank you," Karen said in a subdued voice.

She tried to concentrate as she wrote orders on a new consult. But her thoughts kept drifting back to her talk with Dr. Berkholt. She'd made a fool of herself voicing suspicions she'd been too careless to check out. If only she'd first asked why Ruiz had been recruited for Collier Hospital, instead of coming empty-headedly to him full of wild surmises.

Oh, Dr. Berkholt had been kind enough about it. He'd done everything he could to try to keep her from feeling like an absolute fool. And more than that, he'd told her that he had his own concerns about what was happening.

Three cases forty or under. Another, fifty-four. All of them worked in two neighboring campuses.

She stopped writing and tightened her grip around the pen. Alberto Ruiz—she must learn more about him.

But before she went to Dr. Berkholt again with any suspicions, she'd make sure she knew what she was talking about first.

She skipped lunch and went to the medical school library before heading for Collier Hospital.

At the central reference section, she worked her way through the R's in the electronic *Indexus Medicus* on the computer screen. There it was: RUIZ, ALBERTO. Seven references were available on the six floors of journal stacks. She jotted the names of the journals and the English translations of the article titles.

She sat and looked at the list. "Immunofluorescent Stains for Herpes Simplex Types I and II"; "Tissue Culture for Epstein-Barr Virus"; "Adenovirus Antibodies in Aseptic Meningitis." She gave a resigned sigh. Well, what had she expected to find? She shouldn't have missed lunch; this was straightforward virology.

She crumpled the note sheet and threw it into a wastebasket. The pressure of the work was doing strange things to her imagination. That was what Dr. Berkholt had really been referring to when he'd said, "You've got a rough job." It *was* getting to her.

Hell, maybe she ought to check with Ron Olsen and see if he could suggest a psychotherapist she could talk to.

She headed for the library exit, stopped. She stood poised in indecision. Then, with her lips pressed tightly together, she spun around and marched back to the reference librarian's desk. She snatched up a request sheet and wrote: "Ruiz, Alberto. Any articles related to dementia, kuru, Creutzfeldt-Jakob disease." She handed the note to the research reference librarian. "Would you run a literature search on this?"

The librarian looked at the note. "Leave your daytime phone number on it. I'll notify you if I find anything."

Karen jotted her number and turned to leave. As she walked toward the door, she suddenly stopped short.

Carrying a large black leather briefcase, Alberto Ruiz headed for her. "Good afternoon, *doctora*."

Before she could collect herself to answer, he'd passed and was heading for the reference librarian's desk.

The back of Karen's neck crawled as she walked out of the library. She felt as if Ruiz's eyes were following her.

18

With Christmas four days off, the corridors of Collier Hospital bustled with activity. Volunteers climbed ladders and strung garlands and streamers from the ceilings. So many Christmas trees had been donated by local merchants, studios, and theater chains that the hallways ran out of room, and newly donated trees were set up in the patios between the wings.

Scout troops, church choirs, and Salvation Army contingents competed for hallway space to sing carols. Ancient bearded men with red eyes stared at plump, bearded Santas in red uniforms. Gnomes bent angular like matchstick figures struggled to push aluminum walkers through Christmas tree forests. Shriveled patients tied in wheelchairs grinned eerily at fresh young Girl Scouts, who sang still louder while trying to look everywhere but into their faces.

Over the past week three patients at Collier had died, and another had been transferred to the acute care hospital in Cinema Acres with aspiration pneumonia. Four new admissions, all of them screened and approved by Karen during their preadmission evaluation at University Hospital, had moved in. One, a kitchen worker at the restaurant for the board-and-care section of Cinema Acres, was forty-five years old.

Room A-17, a single, was being readied for another arrival: Lauryn Hart.

Frank Terhune stopped Karen as she left the nurses' station on Wing A. The expression on his face could only be described as a leer. "For the first time since I've been here, I'll be looking forward to doing an intake exam on a new patient."

"I don't understand," Karen said in a puzzled tone.

"What I mean is, we'll finally be getting someone worth looking at in this godforsaken geriatric outpost."

Karen didn't want to believe what she'd heard. "What are you talking about?"

He straightened his tie. "Lauryn Hart, who else? Tell me, Karen, is she really as good-looking in person as she is on TV?"

Karen stared at him. "For God's sake, Frank, you actually sound pleased that a young woman stands to lose sixty years of her life!"

He coughed and cleared his throat. "Of course I'm not happy about it. I'm just saying—well, the field of geriatrics has its rewards, but glamorous patients aren't exactly one of them."

She shook her head and walked off.

Ron Olsen, sporting a royal blue blazer, pink shirt with button-down collar, navy-and-maroon paisley tie, and tan slacks, joined her as she walked down the hallway. Ron was the one doctor at Collier she never saw in a white lab coat. "I got samples of a new antidepressant from Bristol Labs," he said. "You look like a good subject for my first clinical trial."

"You have a way of appearing right after I've just had to deal with that pompous horse's ass," Karen muttered.

He nodded thoughtfully. "It's amazing how well you capture Frank Terhune in just a few verbal brushstrokes."

She stopped just outside her office door. "I guess it does sound as if I'm stuck in one track."

"With Frank it's hard not to be." He nodded toward her door. "Okay if I come in?"

"Sure."

She dropped into her desk chair. Olsen sat across from her. "Is it getting to you?" he said.

"I'm more worried than I want to admit. I don't have any feel for where we're heading."

"It's only been eight days. What did you expect?"

She shrugged. "Since we started we've had four deaths, with one more waiting to die in the next few hours. I would've settled for just holding still."

"That's the nature of the clientèle here. Patients come to Collier in a car or an ambulance, but they all ultimately leave in a box."

"I guess you're right." Ron was the only doctor here she could talk to. Certainly she couldn't speak to Alberto Ruiz or Frank Terhune. And the fourth staff doctor, Bernard Eisenberg, seemed to be avoiding her. She thought of Dr. Berkholt's admonition to keep their fears from spreading. But surely Ron had some suspicions of his own. "How're your scores going?" she asked.

"The DMEs?" Olsen had adapted the dementia multiphasic evaluation screen from a Veterans Administration project. The test used oral and motor responses to measure levels of dementia—the lower the score, the worse the dementia. "Not much to show yet. Only fifteen percent showed a significant change. But it's just been a week."

"How many of those changes were for the better?"

"Three. The X-ray technician had the highest jump in score."

"Three improvements in a study population of a hundred thirty? That's not very impressive."

"True. Figures out to only two percent," he said. "Not much more than the expected variability of any test procedure."

"And the other side of the coin—the other thirteen percent? That would be"—she calculated quickly—"sixteen or so. They were all worse?"

"Well, as you pointed out, four of them died—I figured that would put their test scores pretty low. The rest of them showed drops up to twenty-two percent."

She sighed. "I see."

"What about your endocrine studies?" he asked. "Perhaps we can correlate them with the DME scores."

"I don't know the results."

He raised his brows.

"The Novar-3 won't tell me," she said.

"You're talking in riddles."

"I work in riddles. The computer takes the lab results I feed it and codes them before it reassigns them to the coded patient." She gave a grim laugh. "But you see, the computer doesn't trust me. It won't let me know which code represents which patient. It's afraid that otherwise I might be tempted to modify my clinical impressions to fit the lab results."

He made a short whistle. "Every time I hear a story like that, I appreciate being a computer illiterate."

"How can that be?" Karen asked. "You're part of the clinical team on the CRH project. Don't you have your own user ID for accessing the protocol?"

Olsen shrugged. "Sure, they gave me one. But I ignore it—I don't fool with computers, and they don't fool with me. I just feed my score sheets to Merrill. I guess I'm fortunate your Novar-3 lets me keep my DME results."

"That's because you do the testing yourself. If it could figure out a way to hide the results from you, it would."

"Is that your boyfriend's work?"

"Not in the long run. It's what Dr. Berkholt asked him to do."

Olsen tented his fingers together and studied them. "What's with Merrill, Karen?"

She felt suddenly guarded. "What do you mean?"

"Every time I see him around here," Olsen said, "he's hunched over a terminal to the central computer."

"Well, that *is* his project."

He leaned forward and tapped a finger on her desk. "It's more than that. I've worked with these computer types before. I know them. They make relationships with a machine more easily than they do with a person."

She sucked at her lip. "Oh, Hank's got feelings. He just gets carried away in a project sometimes."

Ron continued as if he hadn't heard her, "The relationship with the computer becomes a substitute for personal interaction. It serves as a defense against accepting the risk of emotional commitment. And let me tell you—it can grow into an impossible defense to penetrate."

She shook her head. "Now you're back on your psychoanalytic spiel."

After a few seconds, Ron nodded. "You're right. I'll stop right now."

"Thanks," she said wearily.

"Have you got any plans for tonight?"

"I'm working late. I want to be here when Lauryn Hart comes in."

"Tomorrow night?" he pressed.

"I'm afraid not, Ron."

"Speaking of defenses," he said, "you've got some mighty tough ones to break through."

She let out a deep breath. "I guess I'm just not willing to concede defeat to a computer."

Sybil Wagoner walked into her office. That, in itself, was unusual. Ordinarily, when she had something to say to Karen, she stood just outside the door and said it from the hallway. "I would like to have a word with you, doctor."

Karen motioned to a chair. "Have a seat, Ms. Wagoner."

The nurse continued standing. Her tall body was as starched as her white cap and uniform. "Is it quite definite that Miss Hart is coming here tomorrow?"

"Those are the plans."

"Her agent informs me that she will have a private nurse during the day."

"If she wants it, that's her prerogative," Karen said.

"I've arranged a private room for her. Beyond that, I do not think it is wise for her to be treated this differently from the rest of the patient population. It sets a poor example for the staff."

Karen looked up at her. "Henrietta Lee has had a private for seven years. I should think that would set enough of an example."

Wagoner's bloodless face showed a faint flush of color. "I would suggest to you that Miss Lee is an entirely different situation. She requires private nursing to be kept alive. Her expenses are paid by the Henrietta Lee Foundation."

"I can assure you," Karen said coldly, "that Miss Hart's private duty expenses will be fully paid from her own funds."

Wagoner looked at her a moment longer. Only the tiny movements of her jaw muscles broke the still of her face. "Very well, doctor." She turned and left the room.

Karen picked up a pizza and camped out in her office to attack her burgeoning load of paperwork while awaiting Lauryn Hart's appearance. To thwart the press, the transfer from University Hospital to Collier was scheduled for eleven o'clock at night.

At eleven thirty, Lauryn arrived.

She was dressed in a one-piece skin-tight outfit of glistening pink. Her long legs accounted for more than half of her spectacular figure as she walked in slowly and regally next to Bev Millar. The jumpsuit's throat-to-crotch zipper, more than slightly open at her breasts, displayed a generous cleavage. And again, that hair—angel blond, probably bleached. L'Oréal perfect.

As Karen walked up to meet the star in the foyer of the main entrance, she couldn't help thinking of her own plain-cut, bobbed, drab brown hair, her ordinary legs and hips that were a little too wide. "Hello, Lauryn," she said.

"Hello." Lauryn's face was blank. Karen would have liked it better if she'd at least register concern or fear.

"I'm Karen. We spent some time together at University Hospital."

Lauryn's eyes moved slowly over her. "Are you here to do my hair?"

Karen swallowed. "It's late now. We'll see that your hairdresser comes by during the day." She turned to Bev Millar. "Everything's ready for her."

Millar nodded and took Lauryn's hand. "Come on, Lauryn. Let's go to your room."

Although the arrival was carefully unheralded, two-thirds of Collier Hospital's night staff—certainly a hundred percent of the *male* night staff —was waiting at the entrance to Wing A. With Lauryn positioned between her and Bev, Karen felt as if she were walking a gauntlet through the staring crowd of night workers. She wished she could shield Lauryn with drawn curtains, as in movies in which Cleopatra entered a grand hall on a curtain-shielded chair borne by hundreds of slaves. Well, maybe it's just as well this way, she thought. Lauryn's spent most of her life in the glare of publicity—she's not only accustomed to it, she probably craves it.

Karen looked around. Each time her gaze caught an attendant or orderly, his eyes would move away from her and he'd change position, or back away, or turn to laugh uncomfortably with someone next to him.

But this wasn't just the lure of glamour, the excitement of seeing a star. These onlookers with their wide, curious eyes weren't here to watch the arrival of a fabled sex queen. They were here to witness the entrance of a freak—to gape at a young body and beautiful face that masked a mind that was crumbling into a premature and grotesque senility.

Karen set her jaw and took Lauryn's hand. She held herself straight and her head high as the three of them marched past the onlookers into room A-17 and closed the door behind them.

It was after one in the morning when Karen finally parked her car at the apartment and trudged through the dimly lit underground garage to the elevator. She couldn't rid her mind of the image of the statuesque figure of Lauryn Hart walking through the leering crowd—and then the sight of Lauryn's name already imprinted on the doorplate of room A-17. That room was to be the home, in all likelihood the final home, of a woman only three weeks older than herself.

Her gut twisted as she remembered the gibberish sounds coming from the crone in the room next door. They started as a low babble, built in volume into coarse cries, and finally peaked in an ear-piercing scream—then abruptly died, only to begin a new cycle seconds later. When Karen plied the halls of Collier Hospital during the daytime, she became so accustomed to the background cries, pleas, moans, and cackles from patients' rooms that she no longer noticed them. Tonight, they were curdling. When the first screams broke through the thin wall after Lauryn arrived, Lauryn had looked around with a glint of fear in her eyes. Then the glint faded, and the vacant depths returned.

Bev Millar, who'd been unloading a suitcase, had turned pale. She looked wordlessly at Karen.

Karen had reached out to take Bev's arm. Her voice caught. "I'm sorry," she said. "I'll see if I can do something about it in the morning."

Hank was still working at his desk in the living room when she walked into the apartment. He didn't notice her until she slammed the door behind her.

He looked up from the computer screen and gave a tired grin. "You managed to get home even later than me." He stood.

"Yes, for a change I won the competition," she said stiffly, and walked past him.

He sucked at his lip. "It was a rough day?"

"I don't want to talk about it."

He walked up to her, took her by the elbow, and tried to pull her to him. She shook loose.

"Are you still pissed off with me about Duane?" he asked.

Her eyes felt suddenly warm and moist. God damn it, she wasn't going to break down in front of him. "Yes, I'm still pissed off with you. And right now I'm pissed off with the whole damned world."

He stood quietly.

She snatched a Kleenex from the box on the coffee table. "Oh shit, I'm going to bed."

He blocked her path. "Karen, I've told you before that I'm genuinely sorry about Duane. I wish he could have gotten special treatment. But from what you've said, it was probably too late for him no matter what anyone could have done."

She looked at him for a moment. Her eyes blurred. With a muffled sob, she pressed her face against his shoulder. "Oh, Hank, I'm so fucking miserable. Duane hasn't been the only one. I feel helpless—I don't have control over anything anymore."

He held her against him. "Come on, look at it with a little perspective. You're Berkholt's right hand. He may set the overall policy, but you're the one really in charge."

She shook her head, and her eyes rubbed against his sweatshirt. "I'm not talking about Dr. Berkholt. The goddamned computer's taken over. I feel like a robot. It's taken everything out of my hands." She swallowed to rid herself of the lump stuck in her throat. "And now I've just had admitted to the hospital a beautiful thirty-one-year-old woman whose fate is under the same rotten, shitty, impersonal control."

Hank rubbed his cheek against her hair. "Try to get some sleep. Things will make more sense when you can see them from a little distance."

She pushed back and looked up at him through tearful eyes. "How can they make sense, Hank? How can there be any sense to Susan's death? To Duane being reduced to a code number on a computer program? To a woman my own age who's destined to spend her last days in an old-age hospital?"

He took her by the shoulders. "You've got to realize that Duane's fate was determined before he ever entered any computer program. We don't yet know what determined it. And I doubt that right now you have the least idea what's determined the fate of your young woman. Nor does anyone else. That's why you and Berkholt and I are working so hard on this project—to find some of these answers. But if we don't keep a statistically valid program, none of us will learn a thing."

It was too much. Something exploded inside her. Maybe it was the patient tone in his voice—or the condescending logic. Duane's empty eyes. The screams from the room next to Lauryn Hart's. Cynthia Frame's purple face as she hung by the belt looped around her neck. She shoved him away from her and spat out her words through clenched teeth. "Don't pontificate with me about statistically valid programs, you bastard! I've wallowed in so much of your statistical shit, I'm going to drown in it!"

The lines of weariness in his face dissolved into a stunned expression of pain. His voice grew constricted. "Statistical shit? Is that all you think I'm doing? Is that what you think of the program?"

"Yes!"

He stared at her a moment longer, then turned back to his computer screen. "Don't bother to leave a light on. I'll sleep in the living room when I'm finished."

She fought to catch her breath. "You can sleep with your computer, as far as I care!"

His jaw set tight, he began typing on the keyboard.

19

At University Medical Center the waiting list of patients approved for admission to Collier Hospital had grown to thirty-eight. The three-day University Hospital workups were fully funded by one of the many generous grants awarded to Dr. Berkholt. The initial grant of a million dollars had been donated by the Screen Actors Guild and had quickly been supplemented by matching funds from two major studios and a Southern California aerospace corporation. By now, there was no shortage of funds for the CRH protocol; there was only a shortage of beds at Collier Hospital to handle the growing number of would-be patients.

The burden of deciding who was to be placed on the admission waiting list rested on Karen.

Each time Sigrid Higheagle handed her a new list of consults to be seen, she quickly scanned the charts for their ages. To her distress, the demand for beds for younger patients continued to increase. By the eleventh day of the protocol the census of cases under age sixty had grown to eight. All but one of this younger group were from the staff of Cinema Acres. The average age of Collier Hospital's patients was now seventy-six, down from eighty-four only six months earlier.

The statistics hid the human tragedies: Lauryn Hart, Cynthia Frame, Duane Dreyer . . .

Susan.

When she arrived at Collier, Karen headed directly for Lauryn Hart's room.

Will Hayes was just leaving when she walked up. He wore a short white lab coat over a light blue polo shirt, white slacks, basket-weave beige oxfords. In his hands was a tray holding a used syringe, empty vial, and pocket-size loose-leaf notebook.

To assure uniformity, the protocol called for Hayes to personally give the first injection to each new patient. The vials had been coded under elaborate formalities. Initially prepared in Dr. Berkholt's lab in the medical school, each was labeled only by a code number given by the computer. The vials were then transferred to Dr. Ruiz's lab at Collier Hospital, where the computer assigned them another randomized set of code numbers. By the time a new patient received the first injection it had been recorded three times, and the only sequence that could identify what the patient received was hidden in the double-password-protected program of the computer itself.

Will looked dejected. Even in the dismal atmosphere of Collier Hospital, that was unusual. He rarely let go of his amiable, easygoing exterior. He nodded toward the door he'd just left. "Pretty rough one, huh, Doc?"

"It's a rough one all right, Will."

His face stayed sober, and he made a clicking sound with his tongue. "You wonder if she'd want to keep going if she could know what's happening to her." He studied the tray in his hands for a moment, then looked up at Karen with a forced, freckled-face grin.

When Karen walked into the room, Lauryn was sitting before the mirror, carefully applying eye shadow. She seemed to be concentrating hard, her tongue between her teeth. She didn't notice Karen.

Bev Millar rose from a chair and gestured toward a plump, white-haired woman of about sixty, dressed in a traditional white nurse's uniform. "Karen, I want you to meet Felice Matthews, Lauryn's aide. Felice, Dr. Karen Formaker."

Karen shook her hand. "Glad to meet you, Ms. Matthews."

"Call me Felice," the nurse's aide said in a deep, hearty voice. "I'm glad to see a lady doc here. I think you'll be able to understand our little darlin's feelings better than a man."

Karen studied the woman. "Haven't I met you before?"

Bev Millar laughed. "You probably started seeing Felice in movies and TV when you were five. She must have played a nurse in more than a hundred roles."

"There aren't many roles now for fat sixty-year-old nurses," Felice said, "so I fill in my time on private duty. I don't have any degrees, but I sure know my way around a hospital."

Lauryn had turned from the mirror. She wore a bright green square-neck tank top, harem-style baggy slacks of silver parachute cloth, and silver, high-heeled slippers. Her eyes found Karen.

"Hello, Lauryn," Karen said.

"Are you from the studio?"

"No. I'm a doctor here at the hospital."

Lauryn reached down and rubbed her butt. "It hurts."

That must have been where Will had given her the shot. "It'll get better," Karen said.

Lauryn turned back to the mirror and began combing her hair.

Karen had rounds to make, as well as a noon meeting with Dr. Berkholt and the Cinema Acres administrator. "I'll drop back later." She turned toward the nurse's aide. "And I'll look forward to seeing more of you, Felice."

"That shouldn't be hard. There's a lot of me to see."

As Karen started to leave, she looked at Bev Millar.

Bev's eyes were fixed on her as if she were trying hard to read something from her face. It took a moment before Bev seemed to realize that Karen had returned her gaze.

Bev gave a tight-lipped smile and shrugged. "Well, we're finally started."

"Yes," Karen said. "We're started."

It was seven thirty that night when she finished entering clinical notes and lab results into the computer protocol. She looked dully at the correspondence and forms piled up on her desk. She couldn't tackle them now. But she didn't want to go home.

Last night Hank had slept on the living-room couch. In the morning, neither of them had spoken. She'd barely nodded to him as she swept into the kitchen for coffee. He'd dressed and left without a word.

Hank had the infuriating ability to detach himself. No, *ability* wasn't the right word—*need* was more like it. Hank fled from personal involvement. She hadn't wanted to tell Ron how on target he was when he classified Hank as a "computer type." Hank and the computer did make an ideal pair. The CRH protocol was a perfect example—the computer program had turned into a buffer that separated Hank's feelings from the tragic people who were the subjects of the experiment. Hank and the Novar-3 were a match made in heaven.

Oh, he could break the pattern occasionally. Like when she'd been sick with *Borrelia*. For two weeks he'd been as attentive as any worried parent. He'd hovered over her, brought her meals, checked her temperature, kept track of her medications.

And he'd been crazy about Susan. Hell, he'd felt freer to show his feelings with Susan than with her.

"I thought I saw a light coming from your office."

She looked up to see the handsome figure of Ron Olsen in the open doorway. He wore a stonewashed denim jacket with matching slacks and a striped blue-and-gray open-collar shirt. "I guess I was lost somewhere. Hello, Ron."

"You're working late hours," he said.

She shrugged. "It's getting common. The material's beginning to pour in now. But I'm not accustomed to seeing you here so late."

"You're right, it's against my principles. Ever since I got out of residency, I've been a firm believer in the eight-hour work day. But somehow I got stuck analyzing my latest batch of DME scores."

"Anything new?"

He shook his head. "The same trends I told you about yesterday." He leaned forward. "Look, why don't we leave this crap behind us and work at forgetting it together?"

"What've you got in mind?"

"Remember I told you about a great little place to pick up fresh dungeness crab? They've got a sign in the window that it's back in season. I've got a bottle of champagne already chilled in the refrig in my condo."

She started to refuse, then thought of coming home to find Hank sitting in front of his computer screen.

What the hell. "Sounds good," she said.

Ron Olsen's two bedroom condominium perched on the twelfth floor of an oceanfront highrise. The living room had a broad central window facing out over Santa Monica Bay. Furniture was modern plush—an L-shaped low-backed couch cushioned in royal blue velvet nylon, two cushioned maroon armchairs of matching material, clear glass coffee table, soft powder-blue carpet. Two abstract Miro posters hung on adjoining walls.

At the kitchen sink, Ron unloaded a white paper bag of its contents of deli-wrapped cracked dungeness, a loaf of sourdough French, and a pint of coleslaw.

"Can I help?" Karen asked.

"Just make yourself comfortable. I need a minute to rummage up paper plates and plastic forks."

She wandered over to the living-room window. Below, a line of headlights crawled along Ocean Avenue. Brightly lit Santa Monica Pier made a glistening sword that projected out into the ocean. In the distance, lights of small boats flickered and bobbed in Santa Monica Bay.

"Ron, what do you think about Alberto Ruiz?" she called out.

He answered from the kitchen. "He's not my closest buddy, if that's what you mean."

To the south, the lights lining the channels of Marina del Rey were jeweled fingers of a black glove that reached into Venice and Mar Vista. "I mean—do you trust him?"

Ron approached from the kitchen carrying a tray. He set a dish heaped with cracked crab, sourdough bread, the carton of coleslaw, paper plates, napkins, and nutcrackers on the table. "He seems to know what he's doing."

"You and he have worked together at Collier a couple years. Haven't you gotten to know him?"

Ron headed back for the kitchen. "He's not exactly the talkative kind. He mostly keeps to himself down in the basement."

"Isn't that a little strange?"

She heard a refrigerator door close. "From what I understand, that's what he's here for. He leaves the clinical stuff to Terhune and Eisenberg."

"What about Bernard Eisenberg?" she asked.

He returned to the dining room carrying a bottle of champagne and two crystal tulip glasses. "Bernie? I suppose he's okay. He's another guy who keeps to himself. He and I share the same office at Collier, but I don't see him often. He does his job and not much more. It's hard to believe, but on the shelves behind his desk are five books on rheumatology and immunology that he's authored."

She turned from the window. "Something about him bothers me, Ron. And it's not just the aftereffects of the stroke. I get the feeling he tries to avoid me."

He probed a knifeblade under the foil that sealed the champagne cork and peeled it back. "As long as you're analyzing weirdos, what about Frank Terhune?"

"Nah, I've dealt with Frank's type a hundred times before. He's a pompous ass, but at least I understand him." She paused. "There's a fourth staff doctor we haven't talked about. I thought I had him figured out, but I'm beginning to realize I don't understand him as well as I'd thought."

Ron broke into a grin. "I was sure you could read me like an open book. Haven't I confided my inferiority complexes? Haven't I bared my array of defensive reaction formations?"

Karen shook her head. "Just when I think I have you nicely categorized as a one-dimensional nerd hiding behind your shield of psychoanalytic prattle, you come up with something that makes me suspect there's more."

For a moment his face grew serious, and she had a feeling that she'd broken through the surface. Then his white-toothed smile returned. "I'm still a simple boy displaced from a Wisconsin farm, Karen." He twisted the champagne cork. It came out with a resounding *pop!* Mist spewed up from the bottle. "Someday, you'll accept that." He raised his glass. "In the meantime—cheers."

Finished, Karen scraped the crabshell into a plastic bag. She carried it and the empty champagne bottle into the kitchen.

She felt a pleasant glow. "I can't believe we drank the *whole* thing," she said as she deposited the bottle in the sink. She pronounced each word carefully to keep it from slurring.

"Mumm's 'eighty-five. Would've been a crime to leave any." Ron stuffed the bag of crabshell along with the paper plates into the trash compactor.

Karen walked back into the living room and gazed out the wide picture window. The floor rocked gently to and fro beneath her feet as she gazed at the reflection of moonlight on Santa Monica Bay. She had the illusion that she was looking out the window of an ocean liner far, far away from Collier Hospital.

Ron reappeared and handed her a brandy goblet. "I hope you like cognac."

She took a sip and felt its velvet warmth slowly descend beneath her breastbone. "Right now I like everything."

He took her arm. "I hope that includes me."

She smiled. For the first time in days, the headlong pace had slowed. "That includes you," she said.

His eyes stayed on the window. He pointed into the distance. "See the tiny cluster of lights way out there? That's Avalon."

She peered out. "That far?"

"You can only see it on the clearest of nights," he said.

She took another sip of cognac and looked at him. His eyes were still on the window. He pointed north. "They don't have enough lights to see at night, but some days when the Santa Anas have cleared the air, you can see one or two of the Channel Islands."

In profile, his face was unlined. He had a crisp, almost sparkling hand-someness. His hair and neatly trimmed beard were a golden red. The outlines of his forehead, brow, cheekbones, and chin were smooth and sharp. His nose was a straight brushstroke above a thin red moustache.

He sensed her looking at him and turned to her. His eyes were a mountain-lake blue. His smile was no longer a white toothpaste ad but had an appealing warmth.

"I'm not sure why we're here, Ron."

He thought for a moment. "We're here to celebrate."

"Celebrate what?"

"Let's see, how about winter solstice a day late? Christmas Eve a day early?"

Her eyes still on his, she lifted her goblet to her lips. "And Lauryn Hart's first shot," she said softly.

"What?"

Karen stared out the window. "She's following Duane's course almost to a T."

Ron frowned. "I can see that we've really got our work cut out for us." He took her brandy goblet from her hand and rested it on the sill. "Karen, we're here to get away from all that."

She turned to him. "I forgot."

He held her by both shoulders. "Tonight, Collier Hospital belongs to another world."

"You're right. To hell with Collier Hospital."

"That's better."

She nodded.

His arms circled her waist and pulled her toward him. His voice was low and resonant. "I don't think you fully realize how desirable you are."

She ran her tongue over her lips. She'd come here to forget the damned protocol, forget Hank and Lauryn Hart, not think about Susan and Cynthia Frame.

It was a mistake. She'd tell him she was sorry. She'd leave now.

Her head lifted.

Up close, his face blurred. His arms felt firm and secure. They stopped the wavering of the floor beneath her.

Their lips met.

She placed her hands against his chest to push away, but his lips were moist and warm. She felt his tongue against her lips.

Her hands left his chest and reached around him.

One hand moved slowly down the back of her neck. Her spine tingled.

He stroked her cheek, letting his hand run beneath her ear and under her hair. "You are the most desirable woman I've ever known," he whispered.

She was still going to tell him it was a mistake. But her voice wouldn't come.

His hand slid down her back and onto her thigh. Their lips pressed together again. This time hers opened. Their tongues probed. Her body strained. Her pelvis ground against him.

"Let's go to bed," he said.

"Yes," she said.

20

The following morning, Karen awakened before six with a hammer beating inside her skull. She remembered the empty champagne bottle and groaned as she turned over and saw Ron sleeping soundly next to her.

Painfully, she climbed out of bed and dressed. He was still asleep when she left.

She headed for her apartment to change clothes before starting the day at University Medical Center. The first light of dawn had blanketed the beachfront streets in a misty gray. A cold, moist breeze blew in from the ocean. Her light cardigan sweater was too flimsy, and she shivered until the engine heat warmed the heater air.

She stopped at a Winchell's Do-Nut shop for coffee to ease the throbbing in her head. Outside rested a shopping cart filled with sooty blankets and bloated plastic bags. The only customer in the shop was a dull-eyed woman whose head was swathed in shawls and whose blotchy cheeks were the texture of cantaloupe skin. Her body was hidden inside a soiled coat of black, furry material, and black long-johns covered her thick legs. Swollen feet were jammed into unlaced oxfords that bulged out at the sides. On the table in front of her sat a half-full cup of cream-diluted coffee. During Karen's residency rotation through one of the county hospitals, she'd cared for hundreds of such people on the wards.

She returned to the car, where she sat with the heater running and sipped coffee while gazing dully at the early morning traffic on Pico Boulevard.

She'd made a mistake in going to Ron's apartment.

Not that she had a fixed set of rules to follow. But she'd always been a one-man woman. There *was* such a thing as commitment.

The pounding in her head eased as the level of coffee in the sixteen-ounce cup inched lower. Were there really commitments? Hank had long ago given her the message loud and clear that there were none for him. "I already screwed up two lives, Kare. I don't want to screw up yours. If you see me start to get possessive, just slap me down."

For six months they'd shared an apartment, that was all. Well, more than an apartment—they'd shared a bed. Her hand tightened around the coffee cup as she recalled the details of last night. Ron had been a totally different experience in bed from Hank. He was confident, sure of himself. She sighed. Let's face it, he was *skilled.*

With Hank, she'd always had the feeling that the two of them were still learning together. She swallowed. What was wrong with that? Right now, it sounded great. She thought of falling asleep with her head in the crook of Hank's arm, his firm, slim body warm against her, his leg thrown over her thighs.

Ahhh, to hell with it. She rolled down the window and dumped the rest of the coffee onto the asphalt. She gunned the engine as she drove off.

The apartment was empty. She checked her desk and the kitchen table for a note. None.

As she started to leave, her eyes caught the tiny, tinsel Christmas tree in the corner of the living room. At its foot sat a small, thin box, its silver wrapping patched with Scotch tape.

Only now did she recall that tonight was Christmas Eve.

With a hollow feeling in the pit of her stomach, she stared at the box. It was from Hank, all right. No one could do as rotten a job of wrapping a package as Hank. She bit her lip and headed for the bedroom. From her closet she pulled the gift-wrapped cashmere pullover sweater she'd bought for him. She knelt by the small Christmas tree and laid it next to the silver-wrapped box.

Then she remembered the card. She ran to her desk and pulled out the card she'd bought two days ago. She sat at the desk and wrote: "Merry Christmas, Hank. Love, Karen."

She slowly folded the card and fitted it in the envelope. *Love, Karen.* By unspoken agreement, the word *love* was reserved for cards. It was a word she and Hank otherwise never used. He'd never said it in so many words, but well before they moved in together it was clear that the word made him uncomfortable. She avoided it.

Except on cards or gifts.

Even gifts hadn't been easy. Last Christmas she'd given him a wallet and tie. He'd thanked her weakly and looked so uncomfortable that she seethed.

"Look, if you can't use them, you can exchange them," she said stiffly.

"It's not that."

"Then what's eating you?"

"I didn't get you anything."

"Well, for chrissake, that's no crime!"

He looked down at his feet. His lips were set tight. "If we're going to give gifts, it ought to be mutual. Not just one of us."

A couple days later, Karen came to appreciate the full extent of Hank's distrust of gifts.

They'd left the hospital together and dropped by his apartment. He'd become unusually quiet from the moment he picked up his mail. In the living room he dropped all but one envelope onto the coffee table. Fingering the paper, he looked at the return address and slowly opened it.

From the envelope he pulled out a Christmas card with a check folded inside. "Shit!" he muttered.

He seemed to have forgotten Karen was with him as he read the card. When he finished, he tore the check into small pieces, crumpled them, and stuffed them into his pocket. He grabbed the phone on the divider bar between the kitchen and living room. As he dialed, he struck each push-button ferociously.

Karen picked up a copy of *PC World* that lay on the table and thumbed idly through it while he spoke. "Hello, Mom." His voice was strained, controlled.

"Merry Christmas to you, too."

"I got the check. I tore it up. Tell Dad." Karen glanced at him. His lips were tight and bloodless.

"I'm doing fine, Mom. I don't need any help."

A longer pause.

"I love you, too. But I don't need it."

His voice rose the next time he spoke. "Mom, there's no point in my talking to him—"

He shut his eyes tightly and clenched his hand around the phone receiver as if trying to crush it. When he next spoke, his voice sounded so constricted that Karen wouldn't have recognized it. "Dad, I don't need it. Can't you understand? I—don't—want it."

Pause.

"If you send another, I'll tear it up, too."

"I'm sorry I disappoint you, Dad. But that's an old story, isn't it?" He slammed down the receiver.

He stood quietly for a moment, hand still resting on the phone, head bowed.

When he turned, he looked at Karen as if seeing her for the first time.

"I didn't intend to eavesdrop," Karen said. "I should have gone into the bedroom."

Hank dropped onto the couch. "It made no difference. When I saw that check, I could have been a teenager back in Dallas."

"I don't understand." She sat next to him on the couch and rested a hand on his arm.

He gazed grimly across the room. "Gifts—and money—they've always been his way of controlling me. 'Follow my path, son. I've got a spot waiting for you in the Merrill Clinic. We'll start a dynasty.' When I married Terri, he supported us through our senior year at SMU. He would've kept supporting us while I went through med school. 'It's my pleasure, son,' he'd say each time he handed me a check. 'After all, what are parents for?' But when I cracked up—when I couldn't continue any longer—everything changed. He told me I was disinherited. I'd wrecked his hopes. I'd destroyed him the same as if I'd pulled out a gun and shot him."

"And Terri?"

He sucked at his lip for a moment before answering. "She was in no better shape than I was. She was just as programmed. The eternal home-town belle of the ball." He gave a short, grim laugh. "You know what she told me? I mean, after the checks from my folks quit coming in. She said that if she hadn't married me, she would've been a shoo-in for homecoming queen. That was her first thought when the money stopped."

Karen didn't speak. Her hand stayed on his arm.

He continued. "A couple weeks later, she told me she was in love with a bandleader."

"Did you love her?"

"I don't know, Karen. I don't think I even know what that means." He stared at the telephone. "At the time it tore me apart."

"I'm sorry," Karen said.

He shrugged. "It wasn't her fault. Both of us were trapped. We didn't have a chance."

"I guess you don't keep much contact with your folks."

"It's eight years since I left Dallas. I haven't been back. Every once in a while, Mom calls. She probably picks a time when Dad isn't home. She's —I guess she's okay. But he keeps her on a leash. Just as he did me and my sister."

"Your sister? You've never spoken about her."

"Ruthie. She's three years older than me. A good daughter. Lives seven blocks from the folks. Married a stockbroker, has two sons. Dad's already started college trust funds for both of them. Showers them with gifts. They're already programmed to take the place of the son who failed him."

Hank's voice took on urgency. "That Christmas check was the first word I've heard from him in eight years. And you know what it was?" She felt his fist clench under her hand. "It was for five thousand dollars. A little Christmas gift for five thousand dollars. The first trial outreach of his tentacles in eight years. To see if he can retrieve any of his losses."

"Hank—he might be feeling some guilt. That's all the check might mean."

He laughed bitterly. "Guilt? A five-thousand-dollar advance on the price of absolution? Bullshit. That check had so many strings attached that I should have used scissors to cut it up."

She'd never before seen his eyes moist. She reached out to hold him For a moment he let himself be drawn close. Then he stiffened.

He stood up and walked to the window and stared out.

At University Hospital, she checked the lab results and MRI reports on the three new consults left over from Wednesday. The waiting list for Collier Hospital had grown so long that candidates were now limited entirely to screen or TV workers. The only exceptions were employees at Cinema Acres. At Dr. Berkholt's advice, Karen gave first choice to those who had the greatest chance of improvement. In practice, this meant patients below the age of eighty. The others had to return to their family's care or to private convalescent hospitals scattered throughout the area.

She dropped by her office in the medical school, checked the notes from Sigrid, then drove to Collier Hospital.

She made quick rounds of the nurses' stations and visited a few patients on whom changes had been reported. The changes were rarely for the better. One exception was the fifty-four-year-old X-ray technician, who was now able to remember Karen's name. The charge nurse on the floor said that in the three years she'd worked at Collier, she'd never seen an Alzheimer's turn around to the degree he had.

With Christmas Eve only hours off, the carolers clogged the hallways. Groups were so close together that their voices merged—it sounded as if "Silent Night," "Jingle Bells," and "Oh Tannenbaum" had been joined together in one chaotic rondo. Karen shut the door to her office to block the sound.

Almost immediately, a knock sounded. The door opened before she could answer.

"I tried earlier," Ron Olsen said.

The pounding in her head had almost cleared. Now it returned in a fresh wave. "I had to see a few people at University. Come on in."

He wore a cream-colored sport coat over a canary yellow open-collar shirt. "You didn't even give me a chance to fix coffee this morning," he said.

"I had to get to the hospital early, Ron."

He smiled. He was back to his old toothpaste ad smile. "Well, I dropped by to let you know that you've got the greatest body of any chief of medicine I've ever worked under."

She didn't feel like fielding his bullshit. "That's sweet of you." She pulled up a folder and began thumbing through it.

"It's Christmas Eve. What're your plans?"

She continued looking at the folder. "I'm busy."

"Oh my. Was I that bad?"

Her head pounded harder. She looked up at him. His face was as handsome as ever, but with its bright smile and trim red beard, it had taken on a diabolic quality. "You were fine. But I've got other commitments."

His smile faded. "The boyfriend again?"

She sighed. "Ron, I need time to put things into place. Last night was a mistake. Again, you were fine, the mistake was mine. I can't even blame it on the champagne. The work here has taken a bigger toll than I expected. I need time to put the pieces together."

He continued standing. How could his eyes be so crystal clear when hers felt as if they must be bloodred? "Very well," he said. "But I'll give you fair warning, Karen. I'm going to crowd you. When you put those pieces together, I want to be part of them."

His smile returned. He gave a slight salute. "I'll be back."

21

A knock sounded on the door.

She stopped dictating. "Door's open."

Hank walked in.

Her hand holding the tape recorder dropped to the desk. In a sudden wave of self-reproach that felt close to panic, she had all she could do to keep sitting.

He wore khaki slacks, a loose-fitting brown-striped sport shirt, sneakers. He looked tired. "You okay?" he asked.

She felt more miserable by the moment. "I'm fine, Hank. How about you?"

"I'm fine, too."

"Good." She wished she could keep the quaver from her voice.

"You didn't come home last night," he said.

"I got tied up late."

"Oh."

The tape recorder in her hand suddenly whirred in fast forward. She must have pushed a button. She fumbled with it, turned it off, pushed it away. "I was by the apartment this morning. You must have left real early."

"I got a call from Wagoner. The first analog shot on one of the new admits from yesterday had been entered twice, and the computer was raising hell about it."

She gave a weak laugh. "Oh."

After a pause: "Got any plans for tonight?" he asked.

Her words came out before she was even aware she was speaking. "Afraid so. I'm busy." She tightened her hands. *Why did I say that?*

"I see." He studied the floor.

The awkward pause that followed was interminable.

She cleared her throat.

He cleared his throat.

They both spoke at the same time. "There's a package under the tree—"

They both laughed.

"I hope you like it," she said.

"You too." He shifted feet again. "Karen—I guess I do come across as kind of unfeeling."

She tried to smile. "Ah, I sometimes overreact. I think the job gets to me."

He ran his tongue over his lips. "A lot of times I don't understand myself. I talk this big line about being objective—and deep inside, I feel like something else."

She swallowed. "I guess I don't always realize that, Hank."

His dark blue eyes seemed to melt. He moved as if to come toward her, but his feet were glued to the carpet.

All of a sudden she realized that she wanted more than anything else for him to take her in his arms. She started to take a step forward.

Before she could, he took in a deep breath, and his eyes grew clear again. "I suppose we'll see each other Sunday."

"Guess so," she said in a suddenly quiet voice.

The last of the carolers had left Collier Hospital by six. Karen finished a McDonald's Quarter Pounder and French fries in her office. The halls were quiet now, and she left the door open. Occasionally a passing nurse or attendant would look in at her in surprise and call out, "Merry Christmas, Dr. Formaker."

"Merry Christmas," she'd answer bleakly.

A little after nine she wandered down the hallway to A-17. Lauryn was in front of the mirror carefully stroking her long eyelashes with a tiny brush. Bev Millar sat watching television.

"Hi, Bev."

"Merry Christmas, Karen."

"You too. And Merry Christmas to you, Lauryn."

At her name, Lauryn turned and looked at Karen without sign of recognition. "It's good to see you again." She turned back to the mirror.

"You feel like going out for a drink after Lauryn goes to bed?" Karen said.

Bev nodded. She walked over to Lauryn and laid a hand on her shoulder. "Are you sleepy, Lauryn?"

Lauryn put down her eyelash brush. "I'm sleepy."

Bev turned to Karen. "I'll pick you up in your office."

* * *

Karen thumbed vacantly through journals until Bev came. "Half the restaurants will be closed," Bev said. "My place is fifteen minutes away in Santa Monica. It's got a fireplace. The logs are fake, but I've got an unopened bottle of twelve-year-old Metaxas brandy that might make 'em look real."

"Sounds like the best deal in town." Karen closed the folder she was working on and went to the closet for her jacket. "We'd better take separate cars."

"You'd have a devil of a time parking. Let me drive. I'll get you back here by morning."

Bev's condo was on the top floor of a modern three-story building four blocks from the beach. From the living-room window a slot between two highrises gave a narrow view of the ocean.

The living room was furnished in warmly upholstered French Provincial. An original Miro and two Picasso prints hung on the walls. A granite fireplace occupied one corner. Bev dumped her car coat on the couch and turned on the gas. Flames sprang up around ersatz logs. She gestured to the grouping of chairs around an incidental table. "Pull up a couple while I get the brandy and some chips."

Karen sat and stared at the flames.

Bev returned with a tall bottle of brandy. She unfolded the legs of a TV table and set it between them, placed snifters on the table, and poured generously.

Karen lifted her glass. "Cheers."

Bev touched her glass to Karen's. "Sure."

The brandy burned soothingly on the way down. Karen smiled. "I think this is gonna help."

"Is it all getting to you?"

Karen nodded. "The job. And Hank."

"He's your guy?"

"I don't know if you'd even call it that. We've been living together the past five months. But we're modern—we don't make commitments."

Bev nodded soberly. "Oh."

Karen took a larger swallow of brandy. "We've been fighting a lot." She told Bev about Hank's role with the program. "We had a big fight over it two nights ago. Weren't talking. I got pretty far down." She shrugged. "I spent the next night with another guy."

Bev nodded again. "I've been there, too."

Karen finished her glass with a single swallow and looked at Bev. "Really?"

Bev poured more brandy into both glasses. "His name was Leonard. He was a doc—a hematology resident at Mt. Sinai. I was a graduate student in English lit." She frowned. "Let's see, I was twenty-five then. Hell, that's seventeen years ago."

Karen took another drink.

"Leonard and I lived together a little over a year. Same damned thing you were talking about—don't get tied down, two careers and all that shit. I thought that was okay with me until I dropped by the hospital one night he was on call and found he wasn't on call." She lifted her glass and took a big swallow. "Her name was Marcie."

Karen pursed her lips pensively. "Hank had a Francie Davis."

"Anyway, all that nonpossessive crap went by the boards. I told him I was through. He could live with that little bitch if he wanted to. I moved out. Took a two-month sabbatical and went to Athens and found me a Greek named Pedros and slept in a fisherman's shack."

Karen nodded. "That showed Leonard."

"Right." Bev held up the brandy bottle. "See this?"

Karen looked. "Metaxas?"

"Don't know what I've been saving it for. Damned stuff's got to be twenty-nine years old now." She refilled both snifters. "I came back from Greece with two souvenirs: this bottle of Metaxas, and a good case of trichomonas. Took me a week to get rid of the trichomonas. I figure we'll get rid of the Metaxas tonight."

"What happened to Leonard?"

"He married Marcie."

Karen looked sadly into her glass. "I'm sorry."

Bev shrugged. "It was no loss. Last I heard, Leonard was working on his third wife." She took another drink. "I got my master's and could've taught literature at starvation wages at a community college. Instead I fell into a job at one of the agencies. Lauryn Hart was a newcomer then, and she became my client. I've taken care of her since, through three divorces and more affairs than I can count. I thought I was immune, and then this goddamned disease you're working with came along."

Bev stared at her glass a moment longer, then looked up at Karen. "I'm sorry. It must be the Metaxas—hell, I haven't spilled off like this since high school. I didn't give you a chance to finish telling me about Hank."

22

After Karen woke up, it took her a moment to remember where she was.

As she stared around the spare bedroom of Bev's apartment, the memory of last night's decimated bottle of brandy returned. Reflexively, she reached for her forehead to test for the whopping hangover she'd awakened to the day before in Ron's apartment. She grinned sheepishly as she realized her head was clear.

She climbed out of bed and looked around. Sunlight barely filtered through thick royal blue drapes. A broad dressing table with a large mirror covered most of one wall. The array of makeup material gave the table the look of a pharmacist's shelf.

Lauryn's green silk pajamas dragged on the floor as Karen walked to the closet. In it she found a dressing gown with a chinchilla fur collar, a parachute cloth jumpsuit, gold and silver lamé jackets, a red satin robe, an array of blouses, and several pairs of slacks that would choke off Karen's breath if she tried to squeeze into them. There was no question who'd used this room before her.

Karen put on the red satin robe and padded barefoot out to the kitchen.

Monday was analog-administration day at Collier Hospital. Karen stayed until the injections were completed and fed into the computer, then headed for University Medical Center.

When she arrived there late that afternoon, Sigrid Higheagle handed her a faxed report that had been sent up from the medical library. It consisted of three short paragraphs from the November 1986 edition of the *Buletin de Universidade de São Paulo*. She could read it no better than Sigrid, but she noted the name at the bottom: Alberto Ruiz.

She took the copy down to the third floor where Carlos Rodriguez worked as fellow in nephrology.

Carlos glanced over the report. "It's Portuguese—taken from the 'Ongoing Projects' section of the university bulletin. Want me to read it?"

"I sure would appreciate it."

Carlos read:

The author spent four months with the Apuruana tribe in the Carauari section of the Amazon basin. A number of members of this remote tribe have been afflicted with a dementing illness—its name translates from the native language to *Loucuras do Diabo*.

The afflicted individuals manifest a relentlessly downhill dementia that fits the clinical description of the disease kuru, which previously has been found only in the highlands of New Guinea. The similarity goes further—Apuruana natives practice ritual eating of brains of deceased relatives and tribal leaders, just as did the New Guinea natives.

Tissue cultures in primate brain medium were obtained from the brains of three deceased tribal members who died with clinical manifestations of the disease. It remains to be determined whether the cultures themselves will transmit the disease to higher primates. After suitable primate subjects are obtained and inoculated, the author plans to return to the Apuruanas to further study this unique disease.

> Alberto Ruiz
> August 1987

Karen spoke in a hushed tone. "August 1987. That would be four months before he came to Cinema Acres."

"What?" Carlos Rodriguez said.

"It's—I was just drifting." She bit her lip. "Carlos, what does the name mean?"

He looked at her quizzically. *"Loucuras do Diabo?"*

She nodded.

"Madness of the devil," he said.

Her thoughts spun as she drove back to Cinema Acres that evening. *Kuru. Loucuras do Diabo.* The words became a refrain in her mind. What about those tissue cultures? Had he brought them with him? Had he finally found his supply of "suitable primate subjects" here at Cinema Acres?"

At Collier she tried to concentrate on the pile of charts and letters and

computer protocol forms in front of her. She couldn't again approach
Dr. Berkholt with her suspicions, not until she had more information.
She'd already lost credibility with him over Ruiz. The last thing she
wanted was to lose his confidence.

She looked at the wall clock. A quarter to twelve.

Kuru. Loucuras do Diabo.

She took her ring of hospital keys from her purse and headed down
the hallway.

She opened the door to the staircase leading to the basement and
fumbled for the light switch without finding it. Carefully probing one foot
ahead of the other, she made her way down the dark stairway.

She emerged into the dimly lit corridor. The only sound in the entire
basement was the squeak of her crepe soles on the cement floor. As she
passed by each wall light fixture, her shadow loomed suddenly at her
side, then drifted behind her and disappeared.

She tried the door to microbiology. Locked.

She reached for the key ring and fitted the master key into the lock.

The door gave a single ratchety creak as it opened.

She found the switch, and in an instant the laboratory was flooded with
light. She lifted a hand to shield her eyes.

The room looked different from the time Alberto Ruiz had escorted
her to it. More sinister. As if something menacing lurked behind the
closed cabinet doors.

She was aware of a pounding in her chest as she checked the two large
refrigerators at each end of the central work counter. On the top two
shelves of one she recognized coded vials of analogs and placebo. The
rest of the refrigerator space was devoted to standard stuff: bacteriologic
stains, chemicals, fixatives, flu vaccines, pneumonia vaccine, tetanus tox-
oid.

She heard a sudden scratching noise behind her and spun around.

Nothing moved.

The pounding in her chest crept up into her throat.

The scratching increased. She looked at the animal cages and gave a
weak laugh. The lights had awakened the rats. Some were running from
side to side in their wire cages and banging frantically on the mesh sides.

Her skin prickled as a wave of cold air struck her. She spun back. The
refrigerator door had swung fully open. She took a deep breath and
closed it.

She looked around.

Her eyes fixed on the two shelves of incubators that extended from
countertop to ceiling. Twelve in each row, lined up in precise pairs, one

above the other. Surely an unusual number of incubators, even for a microbiology lab.

She walked to one wall of incubators and began to open doors, one after another. Agar plates, culture broths, blood media—again, nothing out of the ordinary.

She came to the far wall. Here, the incubators all had locks. This would be where he kept the cultures. She thought of what she might find inside. The pounding in her throat wouldn't let up.

She tried the first door. Locked. Another. Then a third. All locked.

Would one of her keys work on these locks? She fumbled in her coat pocket for the ring.

She tried a smaller key. It didn't fit. She sorted out a second key, tried it.

As she worked on the locks, she could hear the scratching of the rats in the cages behind her, the ticking of the wall clock, the slow drip of a faucet in a lab sink. From the hallway she heard the distant sound of elevator gears.

The scratching seemed to grow louder, closer. Were the rats infected with the virus? Could one have gotten loose?

Before she again tried the lock, her eyes once more scanned the rat cages, Formica counters, and vinyl floors.

She selected a third key.

Her ears picked up that single ratchety creak of the corridor door.

She whirled around and faced straight into the barrel of a gun in the hand of Sybil Wagoner.

Wagoner's thin face grew even whiter. Her eyes widened. The gun shook in her hand.

Karen tried to speak, tried to swallow, but her throat was too dry.

The gun must have remained fixed on her for only seconds, but it seemed an eternity.

Slowly, the hand that held it dropped.

Sweat glistened on Wagoner's forehead. Her voice was so low that Karen could barely hear it. "What are you doing here?"

Karen's eyes fell to the gun dangling in Wagoner's hand. She couldn't squelch the tremor in her voice. "I work here. What the hell were you doing pointing a gun at me?"

The overhead fluorescent light glinted in the black of Wagoner's eyes. When she spoke again, her voice came out chillingly clear. "I would suggest that from now on, doctor, you limit your inspections to more conventional hours."

Wagoner turned and walked out of the room.

* * *

She had to get home and talk to Hank. If he were asleep, she'd wake him. She had to talk.

She closed the laboratory door behind her and headed down the dim hallway. The sound of her heels striking the floor echoed as if someone were following. She didn't look back.

She took the stairs, although her thighs felt so weak, she had to hold on to the railing to drag herself up. She wouldn't take the elevator. Wagoner might be on the elevator.

In the main corridor she headed for the exit. She'd get her briefcase tomorrow. Tonight she wanted only to get home.

The night air was cool. She started to shiver the moment she stepped outside.

By the time she reached her car she was trembling so violently that she sat with her hands resting on the steering wheel. When the pounding of her heart finally began to ease, she reached for the ignition. And stopped.

A movement caught the corner of her eye. Someone else had just left the hospital entrance.

She held stark still.

Whoever was leaving the hospital at one-thirty in the morning wasn't interested in looking around. With a lopsided gait, he headed directly across the parking lot. One foot dragged along the cement, with a sound like the scrape of sandpaper.

In the parking lot lights she recognized the gaunt, angular figure of Bernard Eisenberg.

23

Headlights coming at her in the sparse early morning traffic grew into wide, gleaming eyes before veering past. She gripped the steering wheel tightly, as if by clutching it harder she could stop the trembling.

Hank would be home. She'd been too hard on him the other night when she tore into him. She'd tell him so. If he were asleep, she'd wake him up and tell him what an absolute bitch she'd been. She struggled to hold back the tears that kept wanting to burst out. She'd hold them until she saw Hank and told him how sorry she was. Then she could let herself cry.

She parked in the car stall, ran up the stairs to the second-floor apartment, jammed the key in the lock, and threw the door open.

The couch was empty. At least he'd forgiven her enough to go back to using the bed. She ran through the hallway and pushed open the bedroom door, but the room was empty.

She stared dumbly at the bed. The covers were thrown back on only her side. The pillow was bunched up into the same narrow-waisted mold as the last time she'd clutched it in restless sleep.

She sat on the edge of the bed and slowly pushed off her shoes as she stared out the open bedroom door into the narrow hallway.

In her stockinged feet she padded into the kitchen. The sink was empty. The morning coffee cups had been put away. Her eyes caught the phone answering machine. A sheet of note paper rested on it. The red light of a waiting message was blinking.

She picked up the note.

Karen,
    The work has piled up. I'll be staying nights at my office. I've taken a few of my things with me.
    There's a message for you on the answering machine.
                    Hank

She turned on the machine and heard the voice of Ron Olsen. The message ended with: "In case I didn't tell you, you've got the most exciting body of any chief of medicine I've ever slept with."

She sat on the living-room couch and gazed numbly at the empty computer screen on Hank's desk. It gazed back at her like a giant gray eye.

After an hour lying sleepless, she got up and reread Hank's message. Numbness gave way to anger. What right had he to treat her as if she'd cheated on him? He had no claims on her. When they'd moved in together five months ago, it was he who'd made a point of insisting they had no commitments. Hank's only commitments were to the protocol and the statistics and the methodology and all that shit he expounded.

She returned to bed. When she closed her eyes, she again saw the locked incubator doors, the gun pointed at her, Wagoner's widened eyes and white, sweating face.

At five she gave up, got out of bed, and went into the kitchen.

Her hand shook as she poured water for instant coffee. She couldn't go to work like this—she had to have someone to talk to about what happened last night in that basement lab.

She could forget about Hank, that was clear. He'd had her tried, convicted, and sentenced without giving her a chance. She wouldn't crawl to him.

Ron? She took a deep breath as a fresh wave of guilt struck. He offered a handsome face, a well-built body, and glib banter, that was all. She frowned. Two nights ago, those attributes seemed to be enough.

She'd simply slipped up. After the fight with Hank, she'd drifted into self-pity and rotten judgment. No, Ron wasn't the one to talk to now.

Bev Millar? Excluding Susan, Karen hadn't felt as comfortable with any woman as she did with Bev. In Lauryn, they shared some of the same pain. But the medical aspects of the project were foreign territory to her. And if she learned of Karen's fears, it would increase her concern over Lauryn.

Besides, Karen had agreed with Dr. Berkholt not to let their fears spread.

Dr. Berkholt . . . ?

She'd dialed his home number once before, when she called after Susan's funeral to tell him she'd take the job at Cinema Acres. Only when the phone was already ringing did she glance at the kitchen clock and note that it was 6:10 A.M.

She almost hung up.

He answered as if he'd been awake for hours.

"Dr. Berkholt." Her voice caught.

"Karen?"

"Dr. Berkholt, I'm—I need to talk to you."

His voice registered neither surprise nor hesitancy. "Are you able to drive, Karen?"

"Yes."

"Can you come to my place?"

"I—I don't know where you live."

"Do you have a pen?"

"Yes."

"Take down the directions."

As Karen drove west on Sunset Boulevard into the suburb of Pacific Palisades, she was plagued by second thoughts. She'd been determined she wouldn't let herself go off half-cocked with Dr. Berkholt again. And here she was, doing exactly what she wanted to avoid.

Yet the moment Dr. Berkholt answered the phone, she'd felt calmed. With that prescient empathy he'd shown many times in the past, he somehow sensed what she was feeling. She sucked at her lip. What would it have been like to grow up with a father like him to turn to?

He might think she was mad. That was okay, she'd been worried about her sanity, too. Perhaps the isolation of her work had driven her over the brink. Perhaps Susan's death was too much to handle. Dr. Berkholt would help her get back on course.

She turned right on Amalfi Drive, pulled over to the curb to recheck the directions, then resumed the curving drive as it led deeper into the Santa Monica Mountains. She turned right again, then angled left onto Mountainview Road. The street dead-ended at the beginning of a fire road. There it was, 3320—the last number on the street.

She parked at the curb and climbed a long, steep driveway. The house came into view.

Arnold Berkholt's house wasn't huge, not by affluent Pacific Palisades standards, but it was a jewel tucked into a wooded niche in the Santa Monicas. The one-level wood-and-brick structure appeared to merge into the forestlike surrounds. Except for a small front lawn and a flower-bordered entrance atrium, the landscape consisted entirely of native trees and shrubs. A thick-trunked canyon oak spread from the center of the lawn, one branch soaring through an opening in the redwood-slatted roof of the atrium. A grove of manzanita with twisted trunks and shiny red-brown bark screened off the yard from the vacant hillside lot to one side. On the other side, a steeply terraced sandstone cliff formed a natural wall.

She walked into the atrium. The door opened before she reached it.

Dr. Berkholt took her hand.

She tried to smile.

"Everything will be all right, Karen," he said gently.

She did the one thing she hadn't prepared for. She buried her head against his chest and cried.

"I can imagine what a terrifying feeling it was when you faced her gun," he said.

"When I looked in her eyes, Dr. Berkholt, I felt she wanted to kill me. I had the feeling that it took a superhuman effort of will for her not to pull the trigger."

"Miss Wagoner even at her most cheerful is formidable-looking. When you were facing into a gun barrel, it would've been easy to overread what you saw in her eyes."

"But why—why was she there with a gun in the first place?"

"At midnight, when she investigated a noise in the basement, I suspect that she was asking herself the same question about you."

For the first time since she'd opened the door of the microbiology lab, Karen felt herself let loose. She gave a weak smile. "I see what you mean."

"Try to picture in your own mind where Sybil Wagoner was coming from," Berkholt said. "She's been with Collier Hospital the seven years since its inception. Her first years there it was little more than a medical swamp, run mostly by tired, jaded doctors looking only for a place to draw a salary and work the fewest hours possible. She's seen Collier through the turbulent two years since we linked it to the medical school and turned it into what promises to become the most prominent research-oriented geriatric institution in the country. I can assure you that this wasn't the first night she was still working at the hospital at midnight. Sybil Wagoner, to my knowledge, lives alone—has no family, no children. Collier Hospital is her baby. She guards its turf like a mother bear guards her cubs."

Karen wiped her eyes and smiled. "I'm not certain that makes me feel any safer."

Berkholt laughed. "I may have overdone the analogy. But keep hanging on, Karen, she's bound to eventually recognize the talent and vitality you bring to what she considers *her* institution." His face sobered. "I think, however, that we should also talk about Alberto Ruiz."

Her eyes were dry now. Wordlessly, she pulled the translated reprint from the journal of the Brazilian medical school from her purse and handed it to him.

He nodded thoughtfully as he finished reading. "I see. You suspect that the increased incidence of Alzheimer's at Cinema Acres may be due to an imported strain of *Loucuras do Diabo*?"

The fear had passed. Her voice was strong now. "I know it sounds crazy—but as of this moment, it's the only explanation I can think of."

He continued to gaze at the reprint sheet. "I'm familiar with Alberto Ruiz's work on *Loucuras do Diabo*. I'd be derelict if I minimized your suspicions. I'll speak to him."

She felt a wave of relief. "Thank you."

He handed back the reprint. "Where were you planning to have breakfast?"

"At the medical center, I guess."

"I smell coffee coming from the kitchen. I suspect that my housekeeper, Marta, is poised there waiting to see who my visitor is—and more important, whether she can fix her something to eat. Would you make Marta a happy woman and join me for breakfast?"

"An hour ago I thought I'd never be hungry again," she said. "But that sounds good."

They sat across from each other at the table in the breakfast nook. Broad French windows overlooked the wooded canyon. A gravel walk led between canyon oaks into a chaparral forest. The canyon view was blocked by a grove of manzanita interspersed with laurel, toyon, and wild lilac. From the window view they might have been on the borders of a remote wilderness area.

As Karen stirred artificial sweetener into her coffee, she realized that she'd been so involved in her tale of facing Sybil Wagoner's gun in Ruiz's lab that she'd forgotten to mention seeing Bernard Eisenberg leave the hospital at two in the morning. By now, it had paled in importance, and she was sure Dr. Berkholt would make light of it.

Instead, his face clouded. "Are you sure it was him?" he said.

"He was outlined clearly in the parking lot lights. At the moment, the last thing I wanted to do was have an encounter with anyone else." She laid down her spoon. "Does it bother you?"

Dr. Berkholt toyed with the spoon by his coffee mug. "I'm not sure what to make of it."

She said nothing.

"Do you know much about the background of Bernard Eisenberg, Karen?"

She shook her head. "Only that he's got full professorship status at the medical school. And he's been at Cinema Acres a long time."

"He's retired from active teaching. He was one of the original staff doctors at Collier Hospital when it was organized seven years ago. When

I arranged Cinema Acres' affiliation as geriatric teaching branch of the medical school two years ago, he was the only physician member of the staff that I kept on. That was in deference to his prestige—and his past accomplishments, which were considerable."

Marta bustled over carrying Karen's breakfast plate. She was an olive-skinned, dark-haired woman in her late thirties. She had rosy, round cheeks and wore a colorful apron over her plump belly. "Here, Meeses Doctor. I hope the eggs are right." She deposited scrambled eggs, crisp bacon, and rye toast on the table.

"Everything looks perfect, Marta. Thank you very much."

Marta smiled a wide, white-toothed smile and scurried for Dr. Berkholt's cold cereal and tomato juice.

"I knew Eisenberg when I was at University of Chicago," Berkholt continued. "He was one of the prominent rheumatologists in the country. A quick, facile mind. Until he had the stroke. He recovered physically to a large extent, but I don't think he recovered emotionally. His marriage dissolved. His interest in medicine appeared to collapse. Probably he should have retired, but he took the job out here. It was undemanding, gave him an income, a place to go to every day."

Karen took a bite of bacon. "You're worried about him, aren't you, Dr. Berkholt?"

"I'm afraid so." Berkholt poured milk into the cereal and stirred much longer than was necessary. "Things don't generally work out as simply as you'd think they should on paper."

She took a sip of coffee without taking her eyes from him.

He gazed for a moment at his cereal, then looked up. "What does Hank Merrill think about what's going on?"

She felt a sudden pang. "You mean about last night in Dr. Ruiz's lab?"

He nodded.

"I haven't talked to him."

"Oh?"

"He—well, we haven't exactly been seeing eye to eye. He's moved out for a while."

Dr. Berkholt nodded as if he'd expected it. "Does that make the strain worse on you?"

She tried to sound matter-of-fact. "I don't know. We never had too clear a commitment."

"There's still time," he said gently.

Tears suddenly welled up. She blinked to hold them back. "Sure," she said, and stuffed a bite of toast into her mouth.

He studied her for a moment, then spoke slowly. "Karen, as you may have surmised, I'm a somewhat private person. I've never asked anyone to become my associate before. Since I've saddled you with that role, perhaps it's only fair to tell you something of myself."

She swallowed the dry toast and looked at him in surprise.

"I've lived alone for the past twenty-six years," he said. "I'd been married three years when my wife left me. That was shortly after I finished my residency. She was an actress—at least, she strove toward it, but never made the top ranks. At the time, I blamed her leaving me on her career. But I suspect it actually was more my fault. I was too immersed in my own work to understand, or even be aware of, her needs." He toyed with his cup, but his eyes stayed on Karen. "If I was bad about getting lost in my work before she left me, I became monomaniacal about it afterward. It paid off with some recognition, as you know. There was a heavy price, however, and I paid it in terms of loneliness."

Karen felt a fresh wave of pain. Dr. Berkholt could be telling Hank's story. Once more, the thought of Hank returned, sore and acute like a raw burn that had been left undressed.

He laid down his spoon and smiled. "I haven't told anyone about this for many years." There was a poignant sadness behind his smile. She had an urge to reach out and touch his arm, as if it were he who needed comforting rather than she.

His eyes left her, and he gazed at his cup.

Then he looked up, and his voice became businesslike. "All right, let's talk now about the protocol."

24

Before going to her office at Collier Hospital, Karen stopped by the nurses' station on Wing C to deliver a folder. It contained the clinical records on a fifty-three-year-old volunteer worker at Cinema Acres who'd been admitted three days earlier to University Hospital and was now being transferred to Collier.

When she left the nurses' desk, she slowed when she saw Sybil Wagoner step from Henrietta Lee's room. Her heart skipped a beat as she recalled last night. At first Wagoner didn't notice her. She was speaking in hushed tones to Clara Lipton, Lee's private nurse. As she started down the hall her eyes caught Karen. Her face turned expressionless. "Good afternoon, doctor."

"Good afternoon, Ms. Wagoner." Her voice matched the chill in Wagoner's.

Karen brooded as she continued on to her office. To look at the nurse, nothing had changed. Her demeanor had been no different from the way it had been every day since Karen had taken over as chief of medicine.

And yet everything had changed last night when she faced the gun in Sybil Wagoner's hand. Something sinister was going on in that basement lab that Wagoner was covetously guarding.

What was the connection between Ruiz and Wagoner? What devil's pact had thrown them together? Karen gave a short bitter laugh: devil's pact—*Loucuras do Diabo*. This time Dr. Berkholt hadn't tried to explain away her concerns. He'd said he would talk to Ruiz. At least she had him on her side.

She recalled the power failure, when Wagoner had torn into Henrietta Lee's room with the portable generator, and she remembered how often she'd observed Wagoner leaving that same musty, tomblike room, speak-

ing in a low voice to Lipton. What was behind the strange relationship
between Wagoner, Lipton, and that corpselike figure on the bed?

And where did Bernard Eisenberg fit into the picture? Dr. Berkholt's
face had clouded when she told him she'd seen Eisenberg leave the
hospital at two in the morning. When he'd spoken to her about Eisenberg's background, she had had the feeling that he was leaving much
unsaid. What concerns had run through his mind?

She sat at her desk and gazed blankly out the window.

An overpowering sense of futility struck her. What difference did it
make, anyway?

She closed her eyes as the pain of Susan's loss swept over her in a fresh
wave.

When Karen stopped by University Medical Center, Sigrid Higheagle
handed her a folder. Her usually impassive face was troubled. "Another
preadmission workup," she said.

"Leave it on the desk, Sigrid. I just dropped by to pick up some charts.
I've got to get back to Collier."

"You might want to check this one out before you leave."

Karen sighed. "What's special about this one?"

"He's twenty-eight."

"Oh, no," Karen groaned.

She reached wearily for the chart.

Pete Paritski had been in the Neuropsychiatric Institute of University
Medical Center for the past six days after being referred there by student
health with a diagnosis of suspected brain tumor. Working part time as a
lab technician in the acute care hospital at Cinema Acres, he was supporting himself through his third year of premed. A month ago he'd
suddenly become forgetful. An A-minus student until then, he flunked an
organic chemistry final a week later with an abysmal twenty points out of
a hundred. Within the next few days he became unable to function in the
lab.

MRI brain scan had been normal, effectively ruling out brain tumor.
Metabolic studies had come up with nothing. Multiple spinal fluid studies, HIV testing for AIDS, EEG, evoked potentials, PET scan were all
negative. The psychiatrist found depression and anxiety but nothing to
explain his sudden intellectual deterioration. The psychologist ran him
through two batteries of psychological tests. The computerized conclusion on both was organic dementia.

Karen closed the chart and walked into room 522 of the NPI.

A young man stood at the window, gazing out.

"Pete?"

He turned.

Her heart sank. *How am I going to protect myself against this one?* He was beautiful—the word *handsome* wouldn't fit the fine, delicate beauty of his face. He was slim, five feet ten, with soft blond hair, azure blue eyes, slightly upturned nose, and a flawlessly smooth complexion. His eyes registered fear, perhaps terror. She was relieved to see this. Any expression was better than the empty eyes that accompanied the later stages of the disease.

"I'm Dr. Karen Formaker." She held out her hand.

His hand was cold and wet. "What—what are you going to do?" His voice had a slight tremor.

"I know you've been through a lot of tests, Pete. I won't put you through any more, but I'd like to talk to you, then examine you."

"I don't know what's happening," he said.

As if I did. "I'll try to explain as much as I can. But first, let's sit down." She pointed to a chair next to the window and pulled up another for herself. "Have you been here long?"

"About . . . about . . ." His eyes widened, and he twisted his hands together. "I don't know. I just don't know."

"You're in the hospital, Pete. You've been here six days. What kind of work do you usually do?"

"I—I work with blood. In a hospital, too, I think." The fear in his eyes tore at her.

She took both of his hands in hers. "You're frightened?"

His hands clutched hers as if he were drowning and she could pull him up. "I'm scared. I'm real scared. I don't know what's happening to me."

"You'll be all right, Pete. You'll be getting treatment. And I'm going to help take care of you."

"What's your name?"

"I'm Karen."

"You're a doctor?"

"That's right."

"I'm in a hospital?"

"Yes. But you'll be moving soon to another hospital, where I can take care of you more closely."

His hands loosened. She released them, and they settled on his knees. He tried to smile.

"What's your name?" he said.

* * *

The nurse caught her as she started to take a seat at the nurses' desk. "Paritski's mother is in the waiting room. I thought you might want to talk to her."

"Thanks, Helen." Karen headed down the hall.

Mrs. Paritski was a thin woman with braided gray hair, reddened eyelids, colorless lips. Looking at her face, Karen suspected that she'd had more than her share of pain in a lifetime. She sat across from Karen at the small writing table in the corner of the waiting room.

"He's been such a good boy. Didn't get into drugs like the younger ones. They never had a father—he ran off when Petey was eight. I did the best I could—it wasn't good enough for the other two. But Petey—when I had my stomach operation and couldn't work, he got a job as an orderly at the hospital. Since he's been in college, he's worked nights and weekends in the lab. His adviser told him he was on his way to a scholarship for medical school. And now . . ." She shook her head as she bit her lip and looked away from Karen.

"When did you first notice anything wrong?"

"About three weeks ago. He started staying up studying until three and four in the morning. Acted scared, like I never saw him before—said he couldn't remember anything. One morning at four, I saw the light on in the living room and went there to find him pacing back and forth. When he saw me he broke down. I held him in my arms like when he was a baby, and he cried and cried like his heart would break." She swallowed. "Mine did break. I tried to comfort him, but it didn't do no good, and soon I was crying, too."

"Do you remember anything unusual that happened around then? Did he ever say anything about sticking himself with a needle in the lab?"

"No." Her eyes widened. "Do you think he could have picked anything up in the lab?"

"These are just routine questions, Mrs. Paritski. Had Pete been anywhere unusual? Maybe out of the country?"

She shook her head.

"Does he have a girlfriend?"

"June. They went together since high school, but she left him. The two kids were crazy about each other, but she wouldn't wait any longer. He wanted to finish medical school." Eyes brimming with tears bored into Karen. "I've already signed permission for Petey to get the new treatment. Do you think it will help him, Dr. Formaker?"

It was all Karen could do to keep from crying out that she was groping in the dark, foundering. That she too was frightened. She wanted to take the woman in her arms and weep with her.

But this woman had already had more crushing news than a person should have to bear. This was no time to pour out her own doubts and fears. "I think the treatment may help, Mrs. Paritski."

As Karen drove back to Collier Hospital, the image of Pete Paritski wouldn't leave her. Tears welled up suddenly, and she reached for a Kleenex. She had the feeling that she was rushing back and forth from one nightmare to another.

Twenty-eight years old. Oh, God!

By the time she walked into Collier, the day staff had left. On her desk Will Hayes had left the current list of injections. She sat down and forced herself to go over it. By each name she recorded the grade number of the patient's status from the last staff review and Ron's latest DME score. She got halfway through and could go no further.

She laid down her pen and dropped her head onto her arms.

She sobbed. She had to get away from here.

And yet the prospect of returning again to her empty apartment was crushing. Never had she been weighed down with so much that she needed to share—and been so alone.

First she'd lost Susan. Now Hank.

She felt a hand on her shoulder and looked up at Bev Millar.

"Are you all right?" Bev said.

Karen stared desolately at her through tear-filled eyes. "I've never had to face anything like this." She shook her head. "I don't know if I can."

"What happened?"

Karen poured out how she had found Hank's note in the empty apartment. Her voice broke as she went on to tell about Pete Paritski. She noted the wince of pain in Bev's eyes as she described the twenty-eight-year-old boy. Too late, she thought of Lauryn.

"Put on your coat," Bev said. "We're going by your place to pick up your stuff. You're staying with me."

Karen wiped her eyes. "No. No, I'm fine now."

Bev faced her firmly. "Like I said, I've been there before. You're not going back to that empty apartment." ·

Karen shook her head. "Bev. Really, I'll be okay. I just needed to pour some of it out."

"Look. Lauryn spent the night in my extra room whenever she was in trouble—which was half the time. With her in the hospital, I miss having someone there."

Karen stared at her.

"Hell, it's sure no intrusion," Bev said. "I'm not the best company—

I've got to spend most of my weekends in New York. But it beats an empty apartment that's booby-trapped with memories."

Karen bit her lip and nodded. "Only till I get my act together."

"Sure," Bev said.

25

At Collier Hospital the next morning she had four new admissions to see. One was eighty-four—he'd been a working screenwriter until a year ago. Two were in their seventies and had played supporting roles in movies and TV programs over four decades. One was forty-nine—she'd been a desk clerk in the admissions office of Cinema Acres. Karen no longer developed quite the same stunned, sick feeling each time she checked the consult list and found a new patient in so young an age group—there'd already been too many of them.

She checked the clinical records of the new admissions. The full files of their studies at University Hospital had been transferred to their charts at Collier. Family permits for them to be entered in the protocol were displayed on the front of the charts. Of the 135 beds at Collier Hospital, 132 were now filled. All were registered in the program.

With the addition of the forty-nine-year-old desk clerk, the number of patients under the age of sixty had grown to ten.

Eighteen days had passed since the protocol began. Those who'd been started on the first day had already received their third weekly injection. It was far too short a time to draw conclusions, but some of the patterns that had been hinted at a week ago were more evident. The great majority of patients still showed no change. A few—perhaps seven in all—showed improvement. Since Alzheimer's was a one-way downhill street, this in itself would be promising.

If it weren't for the larger number—between fifteen and twenty—who were measurably worse.

During the intervening week, one more patient had been transferred to the acute care hospital and died. The death itself wasn't unusual. In fact, this week's toll was actually below Collier Hospital's average attrition rate of 1.2 deaths per week. Neither was it unusual for patients to get worse; but the rate at which some had worsened—that was what was disturbing. Were such sudden increases in downhill momentum common in the disease? Until she'd taken the job as Dr. Berkholt's assistant, Karen had never observed and followed a cohort of Alzheimer's. She needed to talk with someone who'd been around the hospital for a while.

Mentally, she ran through the four regular staff doctors:

Ron Olsen? A deep breath escaped her. She'd already made one big mistake letting her private life get entangled with his.

Frank Terhune? No way. The less contact she had with him, the better.

Bernard Eisenberg? She shook her head. She was too uneasy with him. And he seemed to try to avoid her as well.

Alberto Ruiz? She gave a quick shudder.

Her thoughts returned to Ron Olsen. What the hell, all she wanted to do was talk to him, not go to bed with him.

Why *not* Ron Olsen?

At Collier Hospital, Ron shared an office with Bernard Eisenberg.

When Karen appeared in the doorway, Ron was talking on the phone, his chair tilted back and his feet propped on the desk. His wavy red hair was combed casually back, with a strand falling loosely over his forehead. She pictured him with his moustache and his trim, red beard shaved off —he'd be a Robert Redford look-alike.

Karen was relieved to find him there alone. She cleared her throat.

He looked up. His light blue eyes sparkled in surprise. He dropped his feet, stood up, and spoke hurriedly into the receiver. "Oh-oh, gotta go, Evie. I'm being paged for an emergency."

As he walked up to her he nodded toward the phone. "A convenient emergency in time saves nine minutes of explanation."

"I need to pick your brain," she said.

He took her by both shoulders, and his voice dropped to a deep, modulated baritone. "Karen, my love, you can pick any part of my anatomy you're in the mood for."

She sighed. "Ron, believe it or not, right now I'm not interested in your anatomy." She lifted his hands from her shoulders, firmly deposited them at his sides, and took a chair by his desk. "I'm troubled by the rapid deterioration in a few of the patients. I always thought of Alzheimer's as a disease that progressed more slowly. You've been here over a year. Does what's happening seem out of the ordinary to you?"

He smiled tolerantly. "You complained about me talking psychoanalytic. *Now* look who's getting clinical."

"For God's sake, Ron, this *is* clinical! That's why I'm here."

He sighed. "Ah, how quickly you forget." He raised his eyes to the ceiling. "Sharper than a serpent's tooth is a lovely woman's rejection."

She folded her arms. "Do you think you're ready yet to dispense with the bullshit and answer my question?"

He dropped into his desk chair. The springs creaked as he leaned back. "Karen, someday you must learn to release this tight, constricting grip of your superego and give your magnificent id a chance to express itself. But in answer to your question, I've been here two and a half years, to be exact. I've seen abrupt steplike spurts of deterioration with most of our Alzheimer patients, but I don't think I've ever seen so many spurt downhill at the same time. Four have dropped more than twenty-five on the MPE scores since your protocol started."

"And yet," she said, "a few have improved."

"Yes," he said, "a few have improved."

"Alzheimer's patients don't improve, Ron."

He waggled his hand. "Well, there's a little natural day-to-day variability. And the MPE tests aren't perfect—they too have a range of variation."

"A natural variation as great as what we're seeing in the few who improved?"

He slowly shook his head. "Nooo. . . . There are six, maybe seven of them who seem to have improved beyond the error range of the test."

"That's what I thought." She paused. "Have you drawn any correlations?"

"You're referring, I take it, to the fact that three out of the seven who improved were under the age of sixty?"

Sometimes Ron surprised her with his astuteness. That's exactly what she'd meant. "Yes."

"How do you account then for the remaining four who were in the usual older age group?"

"Everyone who improved—and that includes those in their seventies—had recent onset of the disease. All were newcomers to Collier."

"True." He pursed his lips. "What you're getting at is that those who improved had been afflicted for a relatively short period of time."

"Not just relatively short, Ron. None of them had shown evidence of Alzheimer's longer than three months before they entered the program. The X-ray technician had been working here until two months before he was admitted as a patient."

He nodded. "I'll accept that. But I could find a still larger number of cases of equally recent onset that have gotten worse faster than average."

She nodded slowly. "Like Duane?"

"Like Duane."

She let out a deep breath. "Okay, thanks for the input." She turned to leave.

"What about tomorrow night?" he said.

"What *about* tomorrow night?"

"New Year's Eve."

"Oh. Tomorrow's New Year's Eve?"

"My God, Karen, you *are* working too hard." He rose from the chair and came around the desk to her. "Look, you already wounded me bitterly when you wrote me off for Christmas Eve. Now you can make amends. Just say the word, and I'll phone back my casual friend Evie and tell her the emergency looks as if it'll last through the rest of the year."

"Don't bother to cancel Evie. I'm busy tomorrow night."

"Not your friend Hank?"

"No, I'm not busy tomorrow night with Hank."

He smiled. "Are you two finally on the outs?"

His message on her answering machine replayed itself in her mind. A connection clicked.

She stared at him. "You son of a bitch—you knew damned well what you were doing when you left that message on the answering machine!"

"What message?"

"Your idiotic crap about us sleeping together. You knew Hank might pick it up."

Ron's smile faded. He answered carefully, deliberately. "The answering machine's message was in your voice. I had no way of knowing you and Merrill shared the same phone number and answering machine. I'll admit that if I had known—or even thought about it—I would have said the same thing." He intertwined his fingers together on his desk. "Besides, from what you told me, I thought Merrill wasn't possessive."

She stared at him a moment longer, then rested her forehead on her hand.

"Karen, my love, I have but one interest—and that's to help you break your regressive fixation on a compulsive character who has an emotional block for anything that doesn't operate on microchips."

She shook her head. "I'm getting out of here. Go find a patient to hand your bullshit to."

The afternoon before New Year's Eve, the staff at Collier Hospital had been cut to a skeleton crew. The atmosphere of decay seemed heavier than ever.

Bev was in New York. She wouldn't be back for two days.

Karen wandered into Lauryn's room. Lauryn sat at a new dressing table that had been brought in for her. She wore a taupe silk mousseline robe over a low-cut gown of black chiffon. With her lips slightly puck-ered, she concentrated hard on the mirror as she applied silver-pink lipstick.

"Doesn't my little darlin' look pretty?" the nurse's aide, Felice Mat-thews, said in a booming voice.

"Yes, she does," Karen said.

At the sound of Karen's voice, Lauryn turned and gave a faint smile.

"How are you, Lauryn?" Karen said.

"I'm all right."

"Have you heard from Bev?" Karen asked.

"Bev?"

Remember her, Goddamn it! Show me some sign of improvement! "Your friend Bev."

"Oh." Lauryn's brow grew wrinkled. She bit her lip, then turned back to the mirror.

The medical school was no better than Collier. Saturday night its laby-rinthine corridors were empty. Karen occupied the entire eighth floor suite of offices by herself. She sat at her desk and thumbed through papers and articles, futilely trying to concentrate. Every time she stepped out of the suite, her footsteps echoed in the eerie silence of the long hallways. She thought of a science fiction novel she'd read years ago in which the heroine emerges from a subterranean trip to find herself in a post-nuclear holocaust city where the buildings remained but all living beings had disappeared.

She wanted desperately to talk to Dr. Berkholt, but yesterday Sigrid had told her he'd been called away on a rush trip to Washington.

She hadn't yet found out if he'd talked to Ruiz.

Around eleven, she locked the main door to the eighth-floor suite of offices, walked out to her car, and drove off. She didn't realize until she was already a block away that she was heading for her old apartment.

She slowed at the next corner in preparation to turn around. Then she tightened her lips. Why not? So what if Hank was there. They still shared the rent. It wasn't as if she were crawling back.

She drove to the apartment.

She opened the door to a living room as dark and deserted as an underground tomb.

She looked around for a moment. Then she carefully closed and locked the door and headed back down the stairs.

She drove toward Bev's. Along the way, homes were filled with lights. Cars lined the curbs. Inside the homes crowds of party-goers would be warmly chatting with relatives and friends, drinking, laughing, dancing—waiting to welcome in the new year together.

Last year she and Hank had gone to a party at the home of Susan and Duane. They'd rented awnings and gas heaters for the patio and bathed it with extra floodlights. At a minute before midnight, the crowd refilled their fluted, disposable champagne glasses. Then the horns sounded, and Hank had lifted her off her feet, hugged her, and said, "Happy New Year, Karen!" Susan grabbed her and cried out, "Happy New Year, little sister," and Duane put his arm around her as he bellowed "Auld Lang Syne."

They had stayed behind when the rest of the guests were gone. She and Susan had finished loading dishes into the dishwasher and sat at the kitchen table over a final cup of coffee.

"It was a good evening," Karen said.

"Yep, the best," Susan said. "Start the new year with your closest friends—what more could you ask?" She took a sip of coffee. "You and Hank getting serious?"

Karen still felt a warm glow from the drinks and the camaraderie. "I guess we like each other a lot."

"*Like?* Kare, I've seen the way he looks at you. The guy's in love."

Karen grinned self-consciously. "The L word? That's *verboten*. It's not in Hank's vocabulary."

"It might not be in his vocabulary," Susan said, "but it's sure in his eyes. What's the hangup?"

"He got burned before. Bad. I think he'd panic if he thought he was in danger of losing his freedom." Karen shrugged. "That's fine with me. I'm not ready to let myself get tied down, either."

Susan looked at her with soft eyes. "Don't wait too long, Karen. We've still got our biological clocks to deal with."

"You're talking about having a kid?" Karen laughed. "Before I use that word around Hank, I'd have to see him a lot more plastered than he is tonight."

Susan's face grew sober. "I don't know. There's sometimes not as much time as we think. I'm not certain I didn't wait too long."

Karen sensed the wave of concern that came from Susan. She laid down her cup and looked at her sister.

"We've been trying for over a year," Susan continued. "Duane's tested out okay. I guess I'll go in for testing."

"I'm sorry." Karen reached out a hand to take Susan's. "But a year isn't that long."

Her face still sober, Susan nodded slowly. Then she smiled. Her hand tightened on Karen's.

* * *

Karen stopped at a liquor store along the way.

"Do you have Metaxas brandy?" she asked the clerk.

He shook his head. "How about Courvoisier?"

"All right."

Two hours later she sat by herself before the fireplace in Bev's living room. She took a swallow of brandy. It was larger than she'd intended, and she coughed. Her eyes watered.

No, this wasn't the time to think of last year when she had been with Hank and Susan and Duane. This was the time to stare into the fire and forget about Pete Paritski and Lauryn Hart and Cynthia Frame. This was the time to sit here and sip her brandy.

The pendulum clock rang—twelve strikes, the sound of each not quite gone before the next one started. As the ring of the twelfth stroke died into the night, she lifted her glass and said bitingly, "Happy New Year, Formaker."

PART TWO

26

January second marked the beginning of the fourth week of the protocol. The full list of patients who'd started on Monday Day One were due for their weekly injection. Even though Karen had little function in the actual procedure, she still arrived early at Collier each Monday. There was a sense of drama to the giving of the analogs, and she felt it was her place to be there.

As she approached the nurses' desk on Wing B, she came to an abrupt stop.

Hank was just snapping shut his briefcase. She barely stopped herself from calling out his name and running to him.

He straightened up suddenly when he saw her. "Hello . . . Karen."

"Hello, Hank."

He looked tired. His hair was long, actually shaggy. It had been a while since he'd had a haircut. She'd always called it to his attention before, reminding him when he needed one. "Happy New Year," he said.

"Happy New Year to you, too."

He shifted his briefcase to his left hand. "How're you getting along?"

"Oh, pretty good. I'm keeping busy." If only he'd say he missed her, she'd be in his arms in a second, telling him how sorry she was, how lonely she felt.

"Yeah," he said. "I guess the program keeps us both busy."

"Right." She studied her feet. "Where're you staying?"

"I've got a fairly good setup in a room across from my med school office. Not much of a view from the basement, but I don't have to do any cooking."

She laughed weakly. "No, you've got that delicious cafeteria food upstairs."

"That's right." He shifted his briefcase back to his right hand, seemed undecided what to do with it, set it on the desk. "I've been back to the apartment a few times for things."

"Oh," she said.

"It looked like you hadn't slept there for a while."

"I'm staying over at Bev Millar's. We've—well, we've become good friends."

Was that a look of relief she saw on his face?

She caught her breath. *He thought I moved in with Ron Olsen!*

"I didn't know that," he said.

Her face felt flushed. She'd never dreamed he'd get that idea. "It's a nice place."

He nodded. "That's nice."

She brushed back a strand of hair that had fallen over one eye. "Right. Bev is a nice person."

He stuffed his hands into his pockets. "It's funny," he said. "Just a month ago, we were getting ready to start the project."

"And now, it feels like the project's gone on forever." She smiled sadly. "Sometimes it feels like the protocol's taken us over."

He ran his tongue over his lip. "Karen, I . . ."

She held her breath. If only he'd talk about what happened, just bring it up.

He closed his eyes for a moment. When he opened them, they were harder. "I guess I better get back to work."

She stiffened. "Me, too."

Sigrid's voice caught her as she headed for her office at the medical center. "The boss wants to see you."

"Dr. Berkholt? He's back?"

Sigrid's eyes moved like a pointer toward his office.

The door was open. Karen stopped in the doorway.

Dr. Berkholt was dictating. When he saw Karen, he clicked off his cassette player and laid it on the desk. "Come in, Karen." He gestured toward the chair across from him.

She set her briefcase on the floor next to the chair and sat. "I didn't know you'd returned from Washington, Dr. Berkholt. I've been anxious to talk to you."

"I've spoken to Alberto Ruiz," he said.

She was again startled by how attuned he was. She sat forward.

"He said that he brought no virus cultures with him from Brazil."

"Oh," she said, suddenly deflated. She'd thought he'd at least investigate Ruiz. She tried to hide her disappointment. "I see."

"But you have questions, don't you?"

"Dr. Berkholt, six days ago I saw a new consult with classic Alzheimer's. He started work at Cinema Acres six months ago. He's twenty-eight years old."

Dr. Berkholt winced. "I hadn't heard."

"I still think we're dealing with more than a random incidence of Alzheimer's at Cinema Acres."

His forehead wrinkled as he nodded slowly. "What you just saw certainly reinforces those suspicions."

She plowed on. "You yourself indicated concern over an infectious component. Dr. Ruiz interrupted his work with a virus-caused dementia when he came here less than two years ago. To our knowledge, no one other than he has worked with the virus strain the Brazilian medical journal called *Loucuras do Diabo*. His lab has more locked incubators than any three microbiology departments I've ever been in." She became aware that her words were rushing out, and she forced herself to slow down. "I realize that we haven't found a direct connection between Dr. Ruiz and the patients outside of Collier who came down with Alzheimer's, but they've all worked in health care in the same four-mile radius. There's just too much circumstantial evidence for me to feel reassured."

"Have you asked Dr. Ruiz to show you the contents of his incubators?"

She blinked. "No."

"The incubators were set up with my knowledge. They contain cultures in sheep brain media from the blood and spinal fluid of every patient in Collier Hospital, as well as everyone who's been admitted to University Medical Center for Alzheimer's evaluation."

"But as far as I could find, no tissue cultures were listed in the protocol."

"They couldn't be," he said. "Since the cultures are identified by patient name, not code number, they had to be kept outside the protocol. I couldn't risk programming the cultures on a double-blind basis. If a virus grows out on any one of them, we need to know which patient was involved without having to tear open the entire protocol."

Everything led to a dead end. "I see," she said heavily.

"Look, Karen, I'm in no way writing off your concerns. Something strange and worrisome is troubling the program. The questions you've posed have to be faced."

She nodded mechanically. He was simply trying to mollify her.

He sat silently for a moment, lost in thought. Again, he spoke. "We should get as detailed a picture as we can of where we stand in the program now. I'll ask Hank Merrill to prepare a full statistical age and demographic rundown."

She swallowed. Then he *was* serious about investigating.

And Hank would probably have to call her for her clinical input. They'd have a chance to talk.

Dr. Berkholt continued. "We have to ask whether the disease is behaving like classic Alzheimer's in all cases. I've already spoken about it with Mike Werner. I'll ask Olsen to program a computerized analysis combining his psychological testing with Werner's studies."

Karen jarred to attention. "Ron Olsen?"

Berkholt lifted his brows. "Yes."

"Not Ron," she said. "He has no computer experience."

Berkholt smiled. "We're not speaking about the same person. Other than Hank Merrill, Olsen probably has more computer expertise than anyone on the medical school faculty."

"But," she sputtered, "he told me he didn't—"

He leaned back in his chair. "You're familiar with the dementia multiphasic evaluation testing?"

"Sure. Ron does the clinical DME testing. He says he just feeds the results to Hank to be entered in the protocol."

Berkholt patiently shook his head. "Ron Olsen not only adapted the DME procedure for our protocol, but he was one of the two men who programmed the initial DME for the Veterans Administration."

She stared at Berkholt disbelievingly.

"Olsen had an undergraduate degree in computer science before he started medical school."

Her face burned. She recalled Ron Olsen's glib disclaimer: *"I don't fool with computers, and they don't fool with me. I just feed my score sheets to Merrill."*

She realized Dr. Berkholt was looking at her quizzically.

"Somewhere I must have picked up the wrong impression," she said.

27

The line of traffic crawled as Karen headed west on San Vicente toward Cinema Acres.

She kept rehashing her talk with Dr. Berkholt. Why had Ron hidden his computer background?

Were he and Eisenberg tied in? They'd shared an office for more than two years. What had Eisenberg been doing at the hospital at one thirty in the morning last week?

She shrugged. What difference did it make, anyway? The big problem was still Ruiz. Even though Dr. Berkholt hadn't totally agreed with her suspicions, at least he hadn't belittled them. If he thought she was mad, her isolation would be complete.

Dr. Berkholt had a logical explanation for everything she'd brought up regarding Ruiz. But it was too pat. There were simply too many incubators. Why did they have to be locked? Who would tamper with tissue cultures?

No, those incubators held more than just the blood and spinal fluid cultures of patients at Collier Hospital. It was up to her now. She'd have to come up with evidence on her own. The time had come for confrontation. She would demand to see for herself what was in the locked incubators.

She found Ruiz in the hallway, carrying his tray of syringes and vials. "Dr. Ruiz, I'd like to talk to you."

"Certainly, Doctora Karen. Should I come to your office?"

Face to face, he stood barely an inch taller than she. "No. In your lab."

"I have my spinal fluid specimens. I was going to inoculate them in the tissue cultures."

"I'll go with you," she said.

She followed him into the laboratory. He placed several containers of vials in the refrigerator. "They will keep here until we finish." He waved a hand around the laboratory and gave a knowing smile. "Does it look different during daylight hours?"

She ignored his thinly veiled reference to her midnight visit. "Last week," she said, "I saw a new consult at University. A twenty-eight-year-old premedical student whom I'll be transferring here. He has classic Alzheimer's."

Ruiz shook his head. "Ah, the tragedy!"

She studied him, but his face was a mask. "Alzheimer's shouldn't strike twenty-eight-year-olds, Dr. Ruiz."

"You are making a point, *doctora?*"

She pulled the reprint from the *Buletin de Universidade de São Paulo* from the pocket of her lab coat. "Are we seeing cases of *Loucuras do Diabo* at Cinema Acres?"

He stared at her with disbelieving eyes. "I cannot believe you suggest this!"

"What have you done with your tissue cultures of brains from the Amazonian tribe?"

"Do you think the Public Health Service would have let me bring them in?"

"Dr. Berkholt advised that I take a look at what's in your locked incubators. I wish to do that now."

His face grew livid. "Very well." He jerked a key ring from his pocket and rustled through the keys. His lips were a tight line. His hand shook as he stuck one in the first locked incubator door and pulled it open. He went down the line of incubators, throwing open each door. "Go on! Search!"

Karen followed him. Each incubator held rows of neatly stacked petri dishes and clear glass narrow-necked flasks.

Ruiz's voice rose. "Check the medium on all of them! See if anything grows."

One after another she pulled out flasks of clear amber liquid and dishes of smooth, transparent pink gel, all of them unmarked by furrow or turbulence. On each was a name she recognized as that of a patient at Collier. She went from incubator to incubator, repeating the procedure. She pulled up a stepstool to reach the top row.

Finally, with a feeling of futility she climbed down from the stepstool, backed away, and stared at the rows of incubators.

Her eyes wandered slowly from one end of the long room to the other. Her hands opened and closed in frustration at her sides. *Something* was different from the last time she'd been down here.

"Ees there anything else, *doctora?*" His voice was icy.

She let out a deep breath. "No. I'm sorry I disturbed you."

A troubled feeling accompanied her as she left the lab. She was certain that she'd have to come down here again.

Next time, she'd be better prepared.

She started right away.

"What numbah do you want?" asked the Atlanta operator.

"The CDC. Centers for Disease Control," Karen said. "It would be listed under U.S. Public Health Service."

"Thank you, honey. Heah's your numbah."

The next voice was a computer's. Karen jotted the number and dialed.

"Dr. William Horlich," she told the operator at the CDC.

She waited.

"No one answers in Dr. Horlich's office. Do you want to leave a message?"

She glanced at her watch. Three fifteen. It would be six fifteen in Georgia. "Ask him to call Dr. Karen Formaker." She left her medical school number with the operator.

Karen's beeper went off while she was driving to Cinema Acres. She phoned her answering service on the car phone. It was the central switchboard number for Collier Hospital.

She finished her short drive to the hospital and parked. She walked briskly into the entrance.

"There's a crisis of some sort or other on Wing C," the volunteer manning the desk told her.

When she reached Wing C, there was no question where the crisis was centered. A crowd of white-garbed nurses and attendants milled in and out of C-31, Henrietta Lee's room. As Karen approached, a red-faced Frank Terhune burst from the room. He didn't notice her as he grabbed for a phone at the nurses' station. He shouted into the phone, "Who's the on-call surgeon?" He listened breathlessly, then shouted, "Get him to Collier, stat! We need an emergency cut-down!"

He slammed down the receiver, looked up, saw Karen. "That goddamned bitch!" he said.

"What are you talking about?" Karen said, bewildered.

"Wagoner." He gestured toward room C-31. "Henrietta's tracheostomy tube pulled loose, and a bronchus plugged up before we could get it back in. She managed to suction it clear, but the bottom's dropped out of the blood pressure."

"Are you giving her dopamine?"

Terhune wiped his forehead. "I tried, but there's not a vein left in her miserable body to give anything in. We gotta get a surgeon to cut-down on a vein." He clenched his fist. "She belongs in the acute care hospital, but Wagoner won't let me move her."

Karen headed grimly for C-31.

Four people were working on the corpselike figure on the bed. A respiratory technician turned knobs on the ventilator. The private nurse, Clara Lipton, inflated a blood pressure cuff on the left arm. Sybil Wagoner had tied a tourniquet around the matchstick right arm and was slapping the arm as if she could beat a vein into making an appearance. Her face, whiter than ever, was covered with sweat. A third nurse stood next to Wagoner, holding up a needle on the end of IV tubing.

Wagoner lifted her eyes and saw Karen. "I can't find a vein for an IV," she said hoarsely.

Karen stepped in and felt for the femoral pulse in the groin. A weak, thready beat matched each of the 124-per-minute blips on the overhead monitor screen. "Dr. Terhune wants to transfer her to the acute hospital," Karen said.

Wagoner's voice registered contempt. "She's got a systolic pressure of twenty-five. She wouldn't make it through the trip there."

Why in God's name are you trying to keep her alive? And what the hell am I doing here? Karen wanted to turn around and run from the hospital. She took a deep breath. "I'll put in a jugular line." She turned to the standby nurse. Her voice turned crisp. "Get me a venous catheter setup."

The nurse nodded and dashed off.

Karen twisted Henrietta Lee's head to the side. "Keep an eye on the tracheostomy tube," she snapped at the respiratory technician. The jugular vein on the side of the neck bulged but was knotted upon itself. She looked at Wagoner. "I need something under her neck."

Wagoner grabbed a thick towel from the rack below the basin, rolled it, lifted Henrietta's head, and positioned the towel-roll beneath her neck. With the head bent sideways over the roll, the jugular vein stretched out into something close to a straight line.

The third nurse returned with a Veno-Cath set. Karen's throat was dry. Skills erode when you don't use them; the last time she'd put in a jugular line was during her service on intensive care unit two and a half years ago. Could she still do it? She tightened her lips. She'd find out soon enough.

Without taking time to put on sterile gloves, she swiped the side of the neck with Betadine antiseptic, took the Veno-Cath outer needle by the hub to avoid contaminating the shaft, and stretched the vein between her thumb and index finger. With a single jab, she plunged the needle into the side of the neck.

Nothing happened. The thin catheter tubing stayed empty.

She fingered the needle through the parchment skin and felt its tip slide along the side of the jugular vein. The room had grown still. She heard only the swooshing sound of the ventilator. She felt every eye in the room on her.

She pulled the needle back a fraction, tightened the jugular further between her fingers, and gave another quick, hard jab. She felt the sharp *plunk* of the needle tip going through blood vessel wall.

Purple-red blood shot upward into the thin catheter tubing. Karen let out a deep breath. Now she had time to get sterile. She glanced at Wagoner. "Hold it in place while I put on gloves."

She slid her hands into sterile gloves while Wagoner held the needle hub. Then Karen slipped the vinyl covering off the catheter and threaded the narrow plastic tube through the shaft of the needle until she estimated it was deep enough to be in the vena cava. She turned to the standby nurse. "Got the IV ready?"

The nurse held up the needle at the end of the tubing.

"Get rid of the needle."

The nurse fumbled with the needle, finally pried it from the plastic connector.

"Be ready to hand me the tubing." Karen pulled the plug from the end of the venous catheter. Blood gushed over her hand and onto the sheets. She plucked the IV connector from the nurse's fingers and jammed it into the hub at the end of the plastic catheter. "Open it wide!"

Dextrose in saline poured into the jugular catheter.

Karen backed away and looked at Wagoner. "Start the dopamine drip at seventy-five micrograms."

A trace of color appeared on Sybil Wagoner's face. "Yes, doctor." Her voice was barely audible.

As Karen headed for the door, she tore off the bloody gloves and threw them into the waste container, wishing that she could as easily rid herself of her feeling of absolute futility.

It was worse than futility. In keeping Henrietta Lee alive, she felt that she'd done something degrading.

28

By the next morning Henrietta Lee was somewhat better. With the dopamine drip down to fifty micrograms per minute, her blood pressure still held above one hundred. Another two hours, and she'd be off blood pressure support measures entirely. In the meantime, Karen's presence was hardly necessary. Henrietta was now being followed by a cardiologist and a pulmonary man from the medical school faculty. Both had agreed that the ventilator setup in the patient's room at Collier was as good as could be arranged at University Hospital, and there was no compelling reason for transfer.

Ron Olsen sauntered into Karen's office, smiling broadly. "The word's around that you saved Henrietta yesterday."

Karen closed the folder she was reviewing and looked up at him sourly. "Ron, why was it so important for you to hide your computer background from me?"

His smile faded. "What do you mean?"

"Dr. Berkholt told me about your work on the DME."

"Oh."

"Look," she said, "I don't give a damn if you worked on the Manhattan Project, but I don't appreciate being deliberately misled."

He took the chair across from her desk, sat back, crossed his legs. "Karen, my love, 'deliberate misleading' is putting it harshly. Perhaps 'selective unveiling' would be a little more appropriate."

"I seem to remember hearing someone describe computer types 'who can't relate to anything that doesn't operate on microchips.'"

His smile returned, something of a little-boy smile. It was amazing how quickly his face could change expression. "I think I got carried away. It's part of my slavish determination to distance you from your archaically

determined, misguided involvement with an obsessive-compulsive character disorder—like Merrill, to be specific."

She sighed. "Okay, you win. I'd rather be deliberately misled than
listen to your psychoanalytic bullshit."

His brows lifted in pain. "I am deeply wounded." Then he shrugged.
"Nonetheless, I'll try to soothe my damaged feelings by recognizing the
stress that yesterday's heroics placed on you. Your dramatic saving of
Henrietta Lee has already become a legend in the halls of Collier Hospital."

She grimaced. "My big mistake was showing up here in the first place."

"No way," Ron said. "It was worth everything just to hear about Frank
Terhune's face when he came running into the room dragging the sur-
geon to do a cut-down and found your IV already dripping in the jugular.
Some people are saying that you even tamed Miss Wagoner."

"There must be better ways of doing it." She gave a deep breath. "I
feel like a charlatan, Ron. I had no business helping keep that pitiful
creature alive."

He waggled a finger. "Do I detect a counterphobic reaction to an
unresolved child-parent guilt formula?"

"I can't believe it," she groaned. "You're at it again!"

He smiled. "I regress when my libido isn't humored." He walked
around her desk and reached for her hands. She pulled them away.
"Look, Karen, it's not your fault that some foundation with money dripping from its coffers insists on keeping Henrietta hooked up to the hard-
ware."

"Is that what's behind it? A goddamned foundation demands these
absurd measures?"

"That's what I understand. The Henrietta Lee Foundation. I guess the
old crone's still a legend to a passel of old-timers."

"Even so, it's plenty weird." Karen pursed her lips. "I think I'd better
drop by the library and see if I can find out more about Henrietta Lee."

"Not a bad idea," Ron said. "But first let's work on your transference
to me. When am I going to get you back in bed?"

In spite of herself, Karen smiled. "Get outta here so I can get to
work."

After he left, she reopened the folder in front of her and began filling
in evaluation forms.

Two sheets were all she finished. She stopped and slowly fingered her
pen while gazing at the closed door.

She still had no idea why Ron had lied about his background in computers. Had he diverted her on purpose?

She shrugged. What did it matter?

She went back to the folder, but after reading the same sentence three times, she gave up.

The Henrietta Lee Foundation.

She closed the folder and stood up. She might as well see what she could find out about the old girl.

The library at Cinema Acres was a brick and stucco building in the cluster of cottages that constituted the board-and-care section. The elderly volunteer librarian didn't look up from the book on her desk when Karen walked in.

The biography section took up two-thirds of the shelf space. Karen had seen some of the names on wristbands at Collier—she suspected that the census of the other two divisions of Cinema Acres held many more of these famous names from films and early TV.

The books were alphabetized by last names of the stars. She paused in the L's.

On the third shelf she found a book titled *Henrietta, the Blond Siren.* She pulled it down, sat at a table, and began to read.

"How can they call it life?" Karen sat across the table from Bev Millar following lunch. It had become a common sight to see the two of them together in the staff dining room. "There's no way I can reconcile the gorgeous creature on the book jacket with that"—she shuddered—"that ghastly sight on the bed."

"Is there any chance your CRH will help her?" Bev asked.

Karen dumped a packet of sugar into her coffee. "She's too far gone. She's a skeleton, Bev—a shriveled mummy. If she opened her eyes and looked at me, I'd scream."

"Maybe you ought to try to talk to her family about turning off the juice."

Karen shook her head. "Dead end. There's no one listed on the chart —just a foundation that pays her bills. That's why I looked up her biography. She had a kid when she was twenty-two, a few years before she did *Lost Love.* Her husband died five years later. The book was published in 'forty-six. I figure"—Karen counted on her fingers—"she had to be thirty-nine then. As of that time she hadn't remarried."

"What about the kid?"

"He was in a prep school at the time the book was written. There's no mention of a son on the info sheet on her chart." She paused and sucked thoughtfully on her lip. "Bev, want to hear something peculiar? Her husband was a doctor. A neurologist just out of residency. He put a bullet through his head when he was thirty-six. He developed what was then called Pick's disease, a form of presenile dementia. We know now that it's just a rare Alzheimer's occurring in the young. He must have been at that nether stage when he was still lucid enough to realize something was happening to his brain." Her voice slowed. "Like Cynthia Frame."

"Is there anything to this heredity stuff?" Bev asked.

"There's a lot to it. The younger the parent when Alzheimer's strikes, the more chance of it being passed on to the child. And when it's on both sides of the family, the risk becomes huge."

"Christ," Bev said, "what a scenario! Father's brain scrambled in his thirties, mother's in her sixties." She shook her head. "I wouldn't want to have that kid's heredity."

"Nor would I," Karen said.

Karen answered her phone.

"Atlanta phoned," Sigrid Higheagle said. "Were you expecting a call from the Seedy Sea?"

"CDC. That's the Centers for Disease Control." Karen chuckled. "Yes, I'm expecting it, Sigrid."

Sigrid sputtered. "I thought you were getting a call from a bar! Here's the number."

Karen dialed.

"Karen?"

"Bill. I'm so glad to hear your voice."

"I've missed yours, too. How're things at the old training grounds?"

"A little too active. But I see you're making your mark in Atlanta. I read your paper on Lyme disease in the *Annals.*"

"I'm afraid it was a bit premature, but you know what it's like in academia. If you don't publish, you get passed over when the next grants are handed out. What about you? Are you holding up? You're still involved in that project with Dr. Berkholt?"

"I'm over my head in it. Actually, that's why I called."

"What I don't know about Alzheimer's, Karen, could fill every textbook ever written on the subject."

"Bill, in a hospital of a hundred thirty-five Alzheimer's patients, I have twelve who are younger than sixty, four under forty. One is younger than me."

He paused before answering. "That *is* unusual."

"Are you familiar with kuru?"

"Sure—I've read about it as a subject of purely academic interest. Just as I've read about Cruetzfeldt–Jakob, the other slow virus that affects the brain."

"Have you ever heard of *Loucuras do Diabo?*" she asked.

"Can't say that I have."

She told him about Alberto Ruiz and read him the translation of the article in *Buletin de Universidade de São Paulo*.

He was silent for a long time. Then he gave a soft whistle. "I'll track down everything that's been published on *Loucuras* and get back to you."

29

The next morning, Karen was sitting in her office graphing results from the third week of the protocol when Sybil Wagoner walked in. "Peter Paritski is scheduled to transfer here tomorrow afternoon," she said. "Do you have any preference for room assignment?"

Karen hid her surprise. The chief nurse had never asked for her input before. "I think he should have a private room, Ms. Wagoner. He's too young to share one with any of the other patients."

"I shall arrange for A-19, doctor."

"That will be fine." Karen was aware that A-19 was the room next to Lauryn Hart's.

After Wagoner left her office, Karen slowly tapped her fingers on the desk. Wagoner had been as unsmiling as ever, but there'd been a difference. Her eyes weren't as cold. She hadn't said "doctor" with the same distasteful inflection.

The difference had to be what happened two days ago in Henrietta Lee's room. Why did it mean so much to Wagoner to keep her alive? If Karen could talk about Henrietta Lee with her, she might find an answer to some of the questions that hounded her.

She gave a short laugh. As if she could ever talk with Wagoner about anyone! She went back to her graphs.

At the medical school that afternoon, the sheaf of messages from Sigrid Higheagle included one from a pathologist, Herb Fogelson.

Karen dialed.

"I've got the final slides on Duane," Fogelson said. "Want to drop by?"

"I'll be right there, Herb."

"I'm in cytology lab."

Fogelson was a short, round-bellied man in his fifties, with smooth, pink cheeks and a wide circular bald spot covering the rear half of his head. He'd worked more closely with Arnold Berkholt from the early phases of Berkholt's CRH studies than had any other pathologist at the medical school. He'd also been a superb instructor to Karen during the year of fellowship she had spent in Berkholt's lab.

Fogelson waved her in and motioned to a stool in front of a microscope. "The slide's from the frontal lobe, but it's typical of the rest of the cortex."

She fiddled with the fine adjustment. From a blur, a familiar scene sprang into view: degenerating neurones filled with tangles of twisted intracellular fibrils; silver-staining plaques clustered around amyloid cores. She moved the slide from field to field—the same picture.

She lifted her head from the eyepiece. "It's classic Alzheimer's, Herb. The identical patterns you've shown me many times over."

"Yes," he said. "The slides are classic Alzheimer's."

As she rose to leave, she wondered why he'd bothered to call her. "Well, thanks for showing them to me."

Fogelson walked with her to the door. "There's more to it. Come with me."

He led her into his office. "Have a seat." He rummaged through a file drawer, found a thick folder with Duane's name on it, and handed her several sheets from it. "These are the results of the receptor studies."

"You'll have to explain them. The receptor project was completed before I joined the department. You never taught me to read the patterns."

"Something doesn't fit, Karen."

"Oh?"

"I know you're familiar with the unique CRH receptor situation in Alzheimer's."

"Sure. In Alzheimer's, CRH is the only neurotransmitter for which the supply of open receptors is increased."

"Duane's brain cells had no open receptors for CRH."

"You mean—they were decreased?"

"I mean there were none."

"But how is that possible?"

"The receptors were there—but were filled. Every one of them. Duane's neurones were probably intact until he died. But with no open receptors they had no chance of responding to CRH stimulation." He shook his head grimly. "Even his own CRH wouldn't be able to function."

"Herb, it makes no sense."

"Like you said, Karen, the pathology slides of Duane's brain tissue were classic Alzheimer's. But chemically, something was drastically different from the disease as we know it."

"What else could it be?"

"That's what you'll have to find out and tell me."

"What about others? Have you done receptor studies on any other patients from Collier?"

"No. But I reviewed our earlier data. Each study showed the increase in CRH receptors that's typical of Alzheimer's. What we found with Duane"—he gestured toward the folder—"is brand new."

"Have you checked any of the other recent deaths?"

"I haven't done any receptor studies since Arnold and I published our final paper on them in 1986. Setting up the procedure is no small job, and the earlier results were so conclusive that there seemed little reason to spend more time and funds."

"But you did on Duane."

He pursed his lips and nodded. "That's right. I did on Duane."

"Why?"

"I've occasionally seen a forty-year-old with Alzheimer's. But Duane . . ." He shook his head. "Something's very wrong, Karen."

"Have you told Dr. Berkholt about these findings?"

"He worked on the studies with me. Actually, he suggested we do them. We got our first results four days ago. Neither one of us could believe them until they were repeated."

"Herb, please check receptors on the other recent deaths."

"I plan to."

"Would you particularly check them on a patient named Cynthia Frame?"

As she entered the corridors of Collier Hospital, she waved absently at the volunteer manning the entrance desk. Her mind still whirled. What had these findings to do with kuru? Or *Loucuras do Diabo?* Had any receptor studies ever been done with the virus-caused dementias?

She stopped walking and bit her lip. The person who was most likely to know was Alberto Ruiz.

She had to talk to Dr. Berkholt.

"Karen?"

She blinked. Bev Millar was looking at her worriedly.

"Bev! When'd you get back?"

"Just this morning. I haven't even been by the apartment yet. Are you all right?"

"Sure, I'm okay."

"A second ago you looked as if you were carrying the world on your shoulders."

Karen gave a weak smile. "You're a good diagnostician."

"Is it something you can talk about?"

Karen looked around. A bent, white-haired man hobbled down the hallway toward them, pushing his aluminum walker in short jerks. Two shrunken, bony patients sat slumped against canvas restraints that tied them into their wheelchairs. They both wore white gowns wrapped double around them. One of them repeated over and over in a hoarse monotone, "Baby hurts, baby hurts, baby hurts." The only way Karen could tell the patient was a woman was by the absence of a beard. Far down the central hallway, she saw Sybil Wagoner come out from the corridor of Wing C.

"Let's take a walk," Karen said. "I need some air."

They strolled the cement and gravel paths of the gently rolling grounds of Cinema Acres, beneath broad-trunked oaks a century old, through terraced gardens of azaleas and camellias just springing into winter bloom. It was a warm, sunny day in Southern California, and the only hint of winter came when the air cleared and the snow-capped peak of Mount Baldy appeared far to the east.

"It's the pathology report from my brother-in-law's autopsy," Karen said. "The findings weren't what I expected."

"From the look on your face, they weren't very welcome either."

"That's right."

"Let's see how much I can understand."

"Okay, but you'll have to bear with me while I give you a little background." Karen's steps slowed. "The way the brain functions is through signals delivered from one neuron to another by special chemicals called neurotransmitters. Several of these neurotransmitters are in short supply in Alzheimer's disease. The whole purpose of what we're doing—in fact, our entire project—is to replace one of them."

"You're talking about CRH," Bev said. "That much I gathered from the brochure they gave me before I signed Lauryn into the project."

"Right. The neurotransmitter chemical we're working with is CRH. For it to work, it has to fit into molecules especially shaped to receive it on the surface of the target neurons. These molecules are called receptors—if they're not available, the target neuron won't function, no matter how much CRH is dumped onto it."

"You mean, like you gotta have a square hole to receive a square peg?"

"Exactly." They'd stopped walking. "Now, one of the reasons that replacing CRH has promise is that its receptor situation is unique. In

Alzheimer's, receptors for all of the other known neurotransmitters are decreased. CRH is the only one for which the receptors are actually increased. It's as if they're trying to make a bigger target for the shrunken supply of CRH to latch onto."

"I think I follow you. What's the hitch?"

"The pathologist found that the neurons in Duane's brain had no open receptors for CRH."

"And that's bad?"

Karen sucked at her lip. "It means that the analogs we gave him didn't have a chance of working. It means that even his own CRH couldn't work."

"I don't know if I still follow you," Bev said.

"Beverly, we're basing our whole protocol on the proven concept that although the Alzheimer's brain is low in CRH, it has plenty of receptors that can respond if we can only get it into the brain. Don't you see—that wasn't the case with Duane. He had no receptors open to accept the CRH we gave him. The treatment was absolutely useless. Without open receptors, nothing we gave him could have helped."

The muscles of Bev's jaw moved up and down for a moment before she spoke. "What about Lauryn?"

"I'm speaking of only one case. It's too soon to make any generalizations, and it may be a freak finding. We can't test Lauryn—there's no way of testing for receptors short of an autopsy. But we have brain tissue from six more deaths since the protocol started. Those specimens will be tested."

Bev stared hard at her a moment longer. Finally, she let out a deep breath.

30

Sigrid wasn't yet at her desk when Karen walked into the eighth-floor suite early the next morning. As she headed for her office, she noticed that Dr. Berkholt's door was open. She felt a wave of relief when she saw him at his desk.

He looked up with a welcoming smile. "We're both keeping early hours. Come in."

She took the chair across the desk from him. "Dr. Berkholt, there's something I need to discuss."

"Certainly."

"I spoke to Herb Fogelson yesterday."

"About Duane?"

"Yes."

"I'm glad he filled you in," he said. "I'd been waiting until he repeated the receptor studies."

"It makes you question whether we were dealing with true Alzheimer's with Duane."

"That's a very real question that you and I have both been racking ourselves over, Karen."

"He said that you're testing receptors on the other recent deaths."

"Right. But it looks as though it'll be another week before we can get enough monoclonal antibodies to go ahead."

"What if you find that the CRH receptors on those were also filled?"

He looked at her strangely. "Go on."

"Would that end the protocol?"

A look of pain crossed his face as if she'd struck him. "Why? Why would you ask?"

She felt suddenly insecure. "I only meant if everyone else showed the same findings as Duane."

He leaned forward. "Karen, on your last report you observed that seven patients had improved. How often do you think anyone has seen seven Alzheimer's patients improve?"

"But if there are no open receptors on the brain cells, how can we expect the CRH analogs to work?"

"That would certainly leave us more to explain. But it wouldn't alter the fact that *some patients have improved!*" To Karen's stunned surprise, his voice quavered as he emphasized the last words. Then the familiar, firm resonance returned. "So far, the percentage is small, but I'm certain that you don't need to be reminded that twenty-five percent received placebo. And do we know what analog was given to those who improved?"

She sat silently. His question was rhetorical.

He answered himself. "We won't know until we break the code. But I'll tell you this—when we do, I'll be well satisfied even if we learn it was but one out of the three analogs in the program."

She nodded slowly.

He rubbed his chin as he gazed at her. Then he rose. "We still have a lot of work ahead of us, Karen."

She swallowed.

"It's a painful disease to deal with," he said gently.

"It's very painful," she said.

He rested a hand on her shoulder. "The early weeks are always the worst. The program is sound. It will work out."

"Yes," she said softly.

At Collier she started rounds on Wing A.

She began with A-17. Lauryn Hart sat with her back to her at the dressing table, applying makeup with thin cotton pads. Bev Millar was in an armchair, reading.

Bev looked up. "You must've woken at an ungodly hour. You were long gone when I got out of bed at six thirty." She slipped a bookmark in place and closed the book. "I'm getting spoiled waking up to find coffee already brewed every morning."

Karen smiled. "I've been getting up early these days."

"You weren't at your office when I got here."

"I started at the med center," Karen said.

"I figured. I was planning to come look you up again after Felice got back. I'm keeping an eye on the store while she goes to Burger King for some 'filling food.'" She shrugged. "She thinks the hospital menu doesn't qualify."

"The hospital chef will be crushed to hear it." Karen walked across the room. "Hi, Lauryn."

Lauryn turned. Her tossed blond hair had more gold tint to it than yesterday. She wore shiny black Charmeuse lounging pajamas, just transparent enough for the outline of her figure to show through. A light of recognition came into her eyes when she saw Karen. She slipped her feet out of her high-heeled silver-fur slippers and held out both hands. Her toenails and fingernails were a glistening green.

"Her manicurist was just in," Bev said.

"The color matches my eyes," Lauryn said.

It did. "It looks very nice," Karen said.

Lauryn smiled. "Thank you. Bev likes it, too."

Karen caught her breath and turned quickly to look at Bev. She was putting items in her purse and didn't seem to notice anything.

Karen tried to keep her excitement from showing in her voice. "Let's go to the cafeteria when Felice comes back. I need a coffee break real bad."

They sat at a table in the staff cafeteria.

"For God's sake, Bev, didn't you notice anything different?"

Bev dumped a packet of Sweet'n Low into her coffee and swirled the cup. "Well, I've gotta admit the green polish was a bit farther out than I like, but her manicurist thought it might cheer her up."

"I'm not talking about the nail polish! I'm talking about what she said."

Bev looked at her peculiarly. "What did she say?"

"She called you Bev. She said, 'Bev likes it, too.' "

Bev's eyes widened. "I didn't pick it up."

"That's the first time I've heard her remember a name."

In her excitement Bev sloshed coffee from her cup. "What the hell does it mean?"

Karen bit her lip. "I don't know. Maybe nothing. But still, it's the first time."

Bev took a napkin and slowly wiped at the spilled coffee. She took a moment before looking back at Karen. Her eyes were moist. "Wouldn't it be something?"

Karen answered the page from the nurses' desk on Wing C.

"The new patient arrived," the volunteer at the entrance desk said. "He's with his mother. They won't come in any farther. She says she wants you."

Karen took off at a run. She found them where Wing A joined the central corridor.

Pete Paritski's eyes were filled with terror. A half-foot taller than his mother, he seemed to be trying to shrink down to hide behind her.

Mrs. Paritski stood stolid and firm, lips set, head swiveling from side to side. Standing nervously behind them was a woman in the tan uniform of the Medical Center Volunteers who'd driven them over. Milling around the new diversion was a smattering of the ambulatory patients at Collier Hospital.

Mrs. Paritski's eyes lit with recognition when she saw Karen. Breathing hard, she held onto Pete's arm tightly. "This is an old-age home! I'm not letting my boy stay here."

Nearby, a bent, gnarled old man, one side of his face twisted from total facial nerve palsy, leaned forward on his walker, staring at them. At the mother's look he made a blowing sound through his loose, askew lips and backed up a step. Someone with matted white hair hobbled up, clumping a quad cane before her. Spittle dripped from the side of her mouth as she peered at the boy. She reached out to touch him. Karen quickly stepped between them. The woman's claw touched Karen's breast, fingered it.

Karen gently grasped the woman's wrist and moved her hand back to her side. "It's time to go back to your room, Hortense."

The woman looked at Karen dully, then turned around and hobbled off.

Karen took Pete's hand. He clutched hers, as he'd done when he first met her in the NPI. She rested her other hand on the mother's arm. "He has a private room, Mrs. Paritski. And not everyone here is as old as the people you see."

Mrs. Paritski continued staring around. "No," she said in little more than a whisper.

"If he doesn't stay here," Karen said softly, "I can't give him the treatment."

Mrs. Paritski looked at Karen with wet, pleading eyes. The muscles around the sides of her mouth made little twitchlike movements.

Suddenly, she gave a deep, wrenching sob. She clutched Pete to her.

"He will be all right," Karen said, desperately trying to hide the despair in her own voice. "I'll take care of him."

She returned to her office, closed the door, and collapsed into her desk chair. For a long period of time, she sat motionless, numb. The phone had finished seven rings before she reached for it.

"Atlanta calling," the hospital operator said.

Karen felt a slight reawakening as she answered. "Bill?"

"Is that you, Karen?"

"I'm so glad you called."

"Have you got a cold?"

She forced tone back into her voice. "I just admitted a twenty-eight-year-old to the Alzheimer's hospital."

He was silent for a moment. "I see."

"Did you learn anything?"

"I did a computer search, and sure enough, I found *Loucuras do Diabo.* But only one reference—and that's the blurb in the São Paulo med school's bulletin."

"Then it's the same as the reprint I read to you."

"Right. I checked with every ID specialist in the Center to see if anyone was familiar with *Loucuras* and finally came to the conclusion that you and I—and your friend Alberto Ruiz—are the only people in this entire country who've ever heard of the disease."

"Do you have any suggestions, Bill?"

"As far as I can tell, we have no legal recourse unless he's brought classified biologically active material into the country without clearing it through our people at customs."

"Well?"

"There's no action we can take unless that substance—in this case, the culture—is in hand. Karen, it isn't."

She let out a deep breath. There was nothing left to say.

He continued. "I spoke to the assistant director in charge of CDC's Office of Biosafety and wangled permission to farm out my current project. I'm to fly to L.A. to unofficially check out a possible infectious focus at a hospital a dear friend runs."

She grasped the phone disbelievingly and practically shouted, "You mean you're coming?"

"I'll be there a week from Monday."

Her surge of reassurance was similar to when he'd shown her the *Borrelia* on the blood smear. "Oh, Bill . . . thanks."

She slipped on her lab coat and was heading for the door when her pager beeped.

The LED readout flashed the code number for emergency. She picked up the phone at the reception desk and dialed operator.

"It's a Code Blue in C-31!" the switchboard operator said.

Shit, it's Henrietta again! She took off on a run.

Others had arrived before her. A nurse waved her into the room. "Cardiac arrest," she said breathlessly.

The scene was even wilder than when she started the jugular IV line in this same room four days earlier. At the head of the bed the respiratory therapy technician was triggering respirations under manual control. Nurse Clara Lipton had climbed onto the bed, her lips pressed into a tight line as she pumped the skeletal chest with the heel of both hands: five compressions, a pause to allow the respiratory technician to inflate the chest, another five compressions. Another nurse was emptying a syringe into the IV tubing.

At the side of the bed stood Sybil Wagoner, holding defibrillator paddles wired to a crash cart. She looked at Karen. "Two hundred watts did nothing," she said breathlessly. "I'm giving her three hundred!"

Karen looked up at the overhead monitor. Between the artificial gyrations produced by Clara Lipton's chest compressions, the jagged sawtooth pattern of ventricular fibrillation marched across the screen.

Wagoner clutched the two paddles so hard that all trace of blood left her fingers. "Stand back!" she said. Clara Lipton crawled down from the mattress. The crowd faded from around the bed. Red burn circles already stood out on Henrietta Lee's chest from the previous jolt. Over these Wagoner applied the paddles. She pressed both buttons at the same time.

A terse *thunk!* broke the quiet of the room. The emaciated body arched above the bed like a hooked fish taking a last gasp, then fell limp. Two new red circles gradually materialized on her chest wall, like a Polaroid picture developing. They overlapped the first red circles. Overhead, the monitor showed a straight line followed by a scatter of complexes. Then, the sawtooth of ventricular fibrillation returned.

Paralyzed, Karen watched.

Wagoner, face paler than ever, nodded at Clara Lipton. Lipton frowned, climbed back onto the bed, crouched over the body, jammed the heels of her hands onto the breastbone. As Lipton began pumping, Karen heard the sharp *crack!* of a rib breaking. The rhythm resumed: five compressions, pause for breath, five compressions . . .

"Another vial of bicarb," Wagoner ordered.

The third nurse probed the needle of the syringe through the IV tubing and fed a vial of bicarbonate into the reservoir.

Wagoner's voice had a tremor. Sweat poured down her face. "Four hundred watts. Stand back." She jammed the paddles against the chest.

"Wait until I get down!" Lipton shouted. "You want to kill me?" She jumped from the bed.

Thunk!

The corpselike figure once more flopped on the bed. The smell of cooked flesh reached Karen's nostrils. Her eyes rose to the monitor. A straight line. Then the jagged, irregular sawtooth returned.

"Get back to the heart massage!" Wagoner's voice took on a shrill quality. "Give another bolus of seventy-five milligrams lidocaine!" Her hands clutched the paddles convulsively.

Lipton's eyes showed fear. She started to climb back onto the bed.

Karen could stand no more. "Stop. That's enough. She's dead."

As if she'd pulled a switch, the scene froze. It seemed moments before anyone moved. Then Lipton wiped her arm across her face and slowly climbed down from the bed. The respiratory technician pulled the ventilator tubing from the tracheostomy tube. The third nurse shut off the IV drip.

Henrietta Lee's ravaged body lay still on the bed.

Wagoner stared at Karen. For a moment, Karen expected her to shout out new orders. Then Wagoner's shoulders dropped. She herself seemed to stop breathing. She mechanically deposited the electrode paddles, one at a time, onto the crash cart. Eyes staring blankly ahead, she walked from the room.

Karen took in a deep breath. "All of you did a fine job," she said.

The remaining nurses and attendants filed from the room, until only Karen and Clara Lipton remained.

"I'll write a note on the chart," Karen said.

Lipton, looking drawn and haggard, handed her the chart. "Thank you for intervening." She ran her tongue beneath her cheek as if she were going to say something more. But she simply gave a slight nod and walked out of the room.

Alone now, Karen gazed at Henrietta's corpse. The left side of her chest was caved in where her brittle ribs had cracked loose from her breastbone. Her eyes were wide open. Dilated pupils stared at the ceiling. A *risus sardonicus* grin had frozen across her skull-like face.

Karen glanced at the monitor. A wavering line still crawled across the screen. She reached for the monitor switch, flipped it off. The screen went gray.

Carefully, she pulled down Henrietta's eyelids. When she lifted her fingers, the lids slowly crept back up. The skull-face of Henrietta, the blond siren, grinned at her with half-open eyes.

Karen sat by the side of the bed and wrote: "January 7. Onset of ventricular fibrillation. Expired 3:10 P.M. CPR abandoned after approximately 20 minutes with no response."

She closed the chart, rose to leave.

And stopped.

In the doorway stood Bernard Eisenberg.

His twisted face dripped with sweat. His one fully open eye stared past her.

With an animallike groan, he turned around. As he started away, his foot caught on the carpet and he stumbled. He righted himself and continued on, walking faster and faster, his left foot scraping the carpet with a dull rasping sound.

31

Karen lay sleepless in her room in Bev's apartment, unable to rid herself of the image of Bernard Eisenberg's eyes, Henrietta's grin, Pete Paritski's beautiful, frightened face. When the first sunlight came through the drawn curtains Sunday morning, she was relieved to get out of bed. She showered, dressed, and sat in the kitchen over coffee and toast.

Today was Sunday, and Bev was again in New York. Karen's feeling of isolation had never been greater.

Why couldn't she phone Hank? There came a point where pride was crippling. She'd reached that point.

Sure—call him where? If she phoned the apartment, she'd get her own message on the answering machine. Sunday she wouldn't be able to reach him at the medical school.

As she sipped coffee, she recalled her excitement yesterday when Lauryn had remembered Bev's name. It was such a small change, but it was a change.

She gazed out the window. She hadn't told Dr. Berkholt. He needed the encouragement as much as she did.

She also hadn't told him about Henrietta Lee's death. He'd told her to call him for any new developments. She should let him know about Lauryn and Henrietta. She picked up the phone and dialed.

The line was busy. She returned to her coffee.

She dialed again. Still busy.

She went to the window and looked out. A blue sliver of the Pacific gleamed between two highrises.

What the hell, she wouldn't spend the day here. She went to her room and pulled a lightweight jacket from the closet. With Bev gone, the apartment was as lonely as the one she'd shared with Hank. She'd drive somewhere. Perhaps into the hills. Anywhere but Cinema Acres or the medical center.

Impatiently she dialed once more. Busy.

She dialed the operator. "Would you see if his phone is out of order?"

The operator returned. "It's off the hook. I get no response to the signal."

Karen sat at the table a moment longer, then put on her jacket and headed for the door.

She'd go by his house.

She was relieved to see his car in the carport.

She checked her watch. Eight-thirty. He said he was an early riser. He'd probably long been up. She headed up the front path.

She rang the bell and waited.

Should she also tell him about Bill Horlich?

Bill was going to check with authorities at the Center about the legalities of bringing an alien virus strain into the country. A new concern struck her: What if a CDC investigation interfered with the protocol? Or blocked it? Perhaps she should have thought that out more clearly before she'd called Bill. It was obvious how important this program was to Dr. Berkholt. She'd be devastated if he felt she were responsible for obstructing it.

But Bill had said his visit would be unofficial.

She rang the bell again.

If he wasn't home, what was his car doing in the driveway?

She stood there a moment longer, then turned to leave. She caught herself, turned back, tried the door.

Locked.

As she disappointedly walked away, she wondered why she'd even tried the door. What if it had been unlocked? She certainly wouldn't have gone in. It would be like spying, intruding into a forbidden place.

Forbidden place. She thought of the basement laboratory and shuddered as the memory returned of facing the gun in Wagoner's hand.

And yet somehow, she'd have to get herself to return to that lab. She bit her lip. Next time, hopefully, it would be with Bill Horlich.

As she walked back to her car, she passed the gate to the fire road and stopped.

It would be a good day for a walk, as she and Hank used to do on weekends. After spending sixteen hours every day in the crowded corridors of University Medical Center and the stagnant halls of Collier Hospital, the cool, green hills looked inviting.

She went back to her car, pulled sneakers from the trunk, and changed shoes. Then she started up the clay fireroad, picking her way between sharp ruts left over from the recent rain's runoff.

As she walked, her thoughts returned to the macabre scene in room C-31. What had driven Sybil Wagoner to maintain her fanatic, unswerving mission to keep Henrietta alive? And what horror was Bernard Eisenberg seeing when he looked blindly past her into Henrietta's room?

She stopped abruptly. A memory returned with a jolt.

The order sheet on Henrietta Lee's chart! *"Dilaudid 3 mgm prn for pain."*

Signed by Lipton with Eisenberg's name.

Henrietta wasn't being treated for pain. The narcotic was for Eisenberg!

Henrietta was his avenue for obtaining Dilaudid. Clara Lipton was his tool.

Each vial of Dilaudid ordered for Henrietta had been stored away until Eisenberg collected it. That's what he had been doing when Karen saw him in the parking lot at one thirty in the morning.

How long had it been going on? For the entire seven years Henrietta had been at Collier? Lipton had been there seven years, too.

She shook her head and started walking again, walking faster, as though if she walked fast enough and far enough, the labyrinthine puzzles of Collier Hospital would unravel.

Sunlight filtered through the fine morning haze and softened the chaparral, giving it a slightly out-of-focus look. The first rains of the season had left their mark. A green carpet of mustard and wild grasses showed through the dry brown vegetation. The leaves of the black sage, curled and shriveled to preserve their scanty moisture, had started to unfurl. Delicate reddish-orange blossoms of wild currant and the first buds on the manzanita announced the winter beginnings of the Southern California wildflower season.

Now the fire road climbed steeply. Gradually, the beauty of the canyon and the challenge of the steep grade worked their spell. The faces of Eisenberg, Lipton, Wagoner, Ruiz receded into the background. She relished the deep, air-hungry breaths that filled her chest with fresh, crisp mountain air.

She met no one as she continued through the chaparral forest of scrub oak, toyon, black sage, manzanita, mountain mahogany, and wild ceanothus. Overhead, jays and mockingbirds called for her attention. Below, a cricket announced her passage. A brown lizard scooted from her path. A gray squirrel stood on its hind legs and studied her.

She forgot that she only planned to explore a short distance as she lost track of time. Beyond a crest, the fire road narrowed to a trail that descended to a fast running creek. From there the trail followed the creek uphill.

Along the creek the dry chaparral was split by growth of sycamore, birch, and alder. A mile up, she came on the crumbling remains of a cluster of cottages, their wood gray and rotting, doors fallen, windows empty of glass. This must be the old Boy Scout camp she'd read about. It had been abandoned after it was flooded out sometime back in the twenties.

As Karen stood among the ruins, she realized that the calves of her legs ached from the unaccustomed activity. She had no idea how far she'd come, but her legs told her that this was far enough.

A bright sun warmed the clearing. She slipped off her jacket, sat by the edge of the creek, and leaned back against the trunk of an alder.

Sunlight glistened golden on the rippling surface of the water. A woodpecker tapped a soothing tattoo overhead. In front of her the stream cascaded down a jumbled granite rockfall. She and Hank had camped last summer in a setting like this.

That was a year after the Idaho trip when Karen had returned with *Borrelia* relapsing fever. During her illness, Hank had been as solicitous as a worried parent. He'd been at Susan's daily during the five days Karen had spent there. While she was in the hospital, he had spent most of the day in her room or hovered outside while she had tests. When Bill Horlich told him the diagnosis was established and assured him she'd be cured, his feet left the floor as he hugged Bill's six-foot-four frame, then he backed off with a red face.

Three weeks after Karen left the hospital, she and Hank had slept together for the first time since they'd shared her tent at Cramer Lake. Afterward, she'd lain in the crook of his arm. She felt warm, glowing, as if she'd come out of a wintry blizzard into a cozy fireplace-lit room.

If she could have purred, she would have. "That was nice."

He rubbed his cheek against her hair.

"Sleepy?"

"Uh-huh."

"Me, too."

He stroked her arm softly. "Karen . . ."

She turned and snuggled against his chest. "What?"

"It's just—I'm so glad you're okay."

She could hear his heartbeat. "Were you worried?"

"Kind of."

"Oh."

Her eyes closed. But as she lay against him, she became aware of a vague, troubled feeling that prickled at her sense of well-being and kept her from falling asleep.

She realized what it was, but she felt foolish about it—why couldn't he say "I love you?"

Suddenly, she wanted to hear that more than anything in the world.

Why was she afraid of saying it herself? She felt strangely awkward. "Hank."

His breathing was slow and regular.

"Hank, are you awake?"

"Uh-unh."

"Yes, you are."

"Well, maybe I am," he mumbled.

"Hank, Susan likes you."

She thought his arm tensed slightly. "I like Susan," he said.

Karen's feeling of awkwardness gave way to an undercurrent of anger. "What about us?"

A moment passed before he answered. His voice was no longer sleepy. "I like you, too."

"Do you . . . think we're going to make it? I mean, together?"

"We're doing okay, aren't we?"

She lifted her head and pulled back from him. "No, we're not."

He lay completely still, eyes on the ceiling. "I guess you'll have to explain."

"How do you feel about me, Hank?"

He turned and faced her. "I told you, I like you. A lot."

She bit her lip. "Sometimes that's not enough."

He was silent a long time. Finally: "Karen, I'd rather you be lying here than anyone else in the world. But we're both free. I don't want to spoil that."

She stayed motionless, partially propped up with her elbow on the pillow. Her anger was an unwelcome intrusion. She couldn't suppress it. It ate at her.

She rolled away from him and got out of bed.

"Where are you going?" he asked.

"I'm not sleepy," she said tersely.

More time must have passed than she realized. A cool wind had sprung up. The shadows of the sycamore reached across the creekbed. She rose and stretched tall to loosen her stiff limbs. It was time to leave.

Still, the lonely tranquillity of the setting held her. Once the Boy Scout camp had been alive with children who'd climbed these same trees and slept in these same cottages. Now those children would be in their seventies or eighties. Or just as likely, dead. The ruins of the deserted camp were haunted by their ghosts. It was almost as if she could hear them now.

She spun and looked upstream. She *had* heard them. Or she'd heard something. Like a low-pitched sob, or a gasp.

Perhaps it had just been the wind, or the hoot of an owl. All was quiet now except for the gentle ripple of the creek.

She started to call out but thought better of it. She was here alone. Better find out what had made that noise upriver.

The trail ended at the campsite. Beyond was a bend where the walls of the canyon closed in on each side of the creek. To go any farther, she'd have to wade.

Instead, she climbed the rise next to the creek. Others had done so before. Rotting railroad ties set into the ground made a crude stairway.

At the top of the rise she made her way around a large granite boulder.

Below her, the stream widened into a broad pool, so clear that every rock or tuft of moss on the bottom stood out as if framed in glass. Surely this had been the old swimming hole. A meadow reached from the side of the pool to the edge of the invading forest thirty yards away. A huge oak rose from the meadow. From a branch extending above the pool a strand of rope dangled. It might have once held a board or tire that children had used to swing back and forth over the water.

Underneath the oak, his head in his hands, sat Arnold Berkholt.

Berkholt's shoulders shook. That hadn't been the wind or an owl she'd heard earlier—that had been his sob.

She couldn't move. But she shouldn't be standing here, silently eyeing him when he thought he was alone. She felt like a trespasser, a voyeur.

She thought again of calling out to him, but the words stuck in her dry throat.

Slowly, she backed away until she was hidden behind the boulder. She stood stone still, trying to quiet her breathing. Overhead, a red-tailed hawk, its serrated wings widespread, soared upward on a silent draft of wind. Pine needles rustled by her feet, and a marmot, gray with beadlike black eyes, scurried behind a scrubby yellow pine. Below, hidden by the boulder, the creek rustled and sighed like the whoosh of a respirator.

With a feeling of strangeness that bordered on the surreal, she turned and began to make her way downstream.

Halfway back, at the crest of the trail that led out of the creekbed, a cool breeze reminded her that she'd left her jacket at the ruins of the abandoned campsite. She thought about heading back to get it, but she'd already intruded enough. She'd return another time.

She continued down the fireroad and out of the hills.

32

As usual for Monday morning, Will Hayes brought coded vials up from refrigerators in the basement microbiology lab. Routine nursing care was suspended until the weekly injections of analog or placebo were completed.

Another three patients had died last week. One was an eighty-nine-year-old who'd been teetering for several months. Another was eighty-two. She'd been a long-term resident of Collier, drifting along in a state of affable confusion for the past two years, when suddenly she had plummeted downhill, losing the ability to swallow food, then to breathe. The third was a sixty-two-year-old admissions officer from the Cinema Acres administration building who'd been working until two and a half months earlier. Every Collier Hospital bed was now filled, and the waiting list numbered eighty-nine. The nurses complained that when a patient died, the bed didn't have time to cool off before another patient filled it.

There was no question that a few had improved. Mr. Brammer, the fifty-four-year-old X-ray technician, couldn't in all conscience be kept hospitalized. Two days last week he'd filled in for a sick X-ray tech at the acute care hospital and handled the job well. At the Friday staff meeting, all had agreed that he was ready to be discharged from the program. He'd leave later today after his final injection. Two more old-time board-and-care residents at Cinema Acres, one in her nineties, the other eighty-eight, seemed to have improved back to the stage where they had been a few months ago. But with people so old—even with Ron Olsen's dementia multiphasic evaluation tests—it was hard to judge fine shades of improvement.

Then there was Lauryn.

Bev said she'd complained about breakfast because she'd wanted rye toast and gotten white. She'd complained because the hairdresser hadn't come yesterday. (She hadn't.) She'd complained because her toothpaste was green and she was used to white. "Damn," Bev said, "it's so good to hear her *complain*!"

When Karen walked in, Lauryn was alone in her room. A light of recognition flickered in her eyes. "I know you," she said.

"Yes, you do. I'm Karen."

Lauryn's beautiful face scrunched up in concentration. "You're not the nurse."

"I'm a doctor."

"Why aren't you wearing one of those things around your neck?"

"I only wear a stethoscope when I'm going to examine someone."

Lauryn nodded soberly. "The other doctor was in here. He listened to my chest with one of those things."

"Did he wear big black-rimmed glasses?"

Lauryn frowned. "I don't know." Then suddenly, she giggled. Karen had never seen her laugh. "He listened for a long time."

Yes, that definitely had been Frank. "Where's Felice?" Karen asked.

"Who?"

"Felice. Your nurse's aide."

"Is she the big fat one?"

"Well, she is built kind of generous."

"Generous my ass!" boomed Felice's voice from the door. "The little darlin' had it right, doc. I'm the big fat one." She marched in, set a white bag labeled HARRY'S DELI on the table, and pulled from it three sandwich cartons, two bags of French fries, two shakes. "She needs a break from hospital food." She tucked in her lower lip. "Lucky I figured we might have company, so I brought an extra sandwich. Patty-melt okay?" She looked at the table and shook her head. "Of course I goofed getting only two shakes and fries, but we can split 'em up."

"Thanks, Felice, I already ate. You two go ahead. I've got to get back to work." Karen started to leave.

"Doctor."

Karen spun around.

Lauryn was gazing at her. "I want to go for a ride. Bev will take me for a ride if I ask her."

There it was again! She'd called Bev by name! Karen's elation was tempered only by the realization that as Lauryn continued to improve, it would be harder to hold her here. "I'm sorry, Lauryn. The treatment program you're under doesn't permit patients to leave the hospital grounds."

Lauryn's lips tightened in a pout. It quickly passed over. She looked at the table. "I'm hungry. Give me a sandwich."

* * *

When Karen left Lauryn's room, she stopped by Ron Olsen's office.

"How did you know I was daydreaming about you?" He smiled and came around from his desk. His arms reached for hers.

She ignored them. "Have you tested Lauryn recently?"

He shook his head reprovingly. "Always repressing. You never want to face your emotions, do you?"

"If I faced my emotions, I'd clobber you. Will you answer my question?"

He sighed. "I last tested her a week ago. She's on a biweekly schedule."

"I'd appreciate your retesting soon, Ron."

"Is she worse?"

"Just the opposite. She looks better."

"I'll see her this afternoon."

"Thanks." She looked around the room. "Have you seen Bernard Eisenberg today?"

Olsen shook his head. "He must have been here over the weekend." He glanced over at Eisenberg's desk. It was piled with papers, journals, small boxes, and desk drawer paraphernalia. "His desk looks like a hurricane hit it. Do you want to leave a message?"

She thought of Eisenberg's twisted face, his animallike groan as he stood in the doorway after Henrietta's death. Did Ron realize Eisenberg was on narcotics? Sharing the same office, how could he have avoided it?

It would help to talk it over with Ron.

Something stopped her. A feeling—an inner warning—that Ron wasn't the person to confide in. Perhaps it was simply because he'd lied to her about his computer background. She wasn't sure why that still ate at her. "No message," she said. "It's just that I thought he's looked sort of bad lately."

"Bernie's looked like hell the entire two years I've known him," Ron said.

Karen finished rounds at Pete Paritski's room. She steeled herself before walking in.

Pete sat half bent over, the back of his chair to the window.

"Hello, Pete."

He lifted his eyes. They were red, as if he'd been crying. He cringed back in his chair as she approached. "What are you going to do to me?"

"I just want to visit."

"Who—who are you?"

"I'm Karen. I'm one of your doctors."

He looked fearfully around the room. "Where's my ma?"

She was appalled by how much worse he looked. *He got his first shot today. Please, dear God, let it not be the placebo.* "She'll be here later, Pete. Is there anything I can do?"

He looked up at her with wide eyes. "I have to use the toilet."

"The bathroom's here in your room. I'll show you." She held out her hand.

He hesitated for a second, then took her hand and got up from the chair. His feet shuffled like an old man's as he walked beside her.

She held open the bathroom door.

"Wait for me," he said, and clutched her hand harder. "I'm scared."

"I'll wait," she said.

She arrived at the medical school late that afternoon.

"The boss wants to see you." Sigrid Higheagle motioned toward his door.

Karen hesitated before heading for his office. She had an unreasonable fear that her face would show that she'd seen him at the Boy Scout camp.

"Have a seat, Karen." He leaned back in his chair. "Have you been bothered much by the press?"

"The press? No, I don't believe I've spoken to any reporters since Lauryn Hart came into the hospital."

"Good. I'd left strict instructions with administration to route any calls and inquiries through my office."

She felt a shock of surprise. "I guess I simply hadn't thought about it. I'm grateful."

"I did it to spare the project conflicting voices. Public interest in our work has increased greatly since the program started. And with the arrival of Ms. Hart and the death of Henrietta Lee, the pressure for information is becoming even more demanding."

"Then you did hear about Henrietta Lee's death," she said, relieved.

He nodded sadly. "Ms. Wagoner notified me."

"Are you getting a lot of calls from the press?"

"I've managed to put most of them off with the promise of a full press conference at the end of the program's first month." He folded his hands together on the desk. "I don't know if it's as great a surprise to you as it was to me to be reminded that the month is up three days from now, on Thursday."

"It is hard to believe," she said.

"I wish we could operate more anonymously, but it's not possible. Because of the nature of its population, Cinema Acres has always had a high degree of exposure. On top of that, the institution depends heavily on public grants, and our CRH project is feasible only because of generous corporate and public endowments." He gave a deep breath. "I'm afraid that the Thursday press conference has escalated. All three daily papers and one of the news services will attend. And I understand that at least two of the networks will be filming."

Karen smiled. "I'll look forward to seeing you on television."

"You'll do more than see me, Karen. I'd like you to participate in the press conference."

She sat forward on her chair. "What?"

"I'll need your help. Like no one else, you've had your finger on the pulse of the project."

She shook her head. "I won't know how to act at a press conference."

"I've seen your podium presence on grand rounds. You'll have no problems. Besides, I'll field most of the questions. I used to feel just as apprehensive as I'm sure you do, but"—he shrugged—"in recent years I've spent a fair amount of time in front of the cameras, and it's become almost old hat."

Her mind raced. "What if I'm asked questions about the young ones?"

"I'm not sure what you're referring to."

"I mean—we've talked about it before—the fact that we've had so many young patients."

"I'm certain you'll handle the questions openly and honestly, as you always do. The young ones are the greatest tragedy of the disease." He paused, and his eyes rested quietly on her. "I think you should particularly be prepared to field questions about Lauryn Hart. She naturally excites a great deal of media interest. That's where I'll almost certainly call on you."

Karen remembered Bev's admonitions when they first met about speaking to the press. She'd have to talk it over with Bev before the conference. "I think Lauryn may have shown some improvement."

"Oh?"

"Little things. Not much to hang your hat on. Like remembering her agent's name. Or remembering what kind of toast she wants for breakfast."

"That's encouraging. It could be very helpful at the interview."

Karen bit her lip. "You mentioned Henrietta Lee, Dr. Berkholt. What about her?"

"Yes, questions are bound to come up, aren't they?" He touched the fingertips of both hands together and studied them before once again lifting his eyes to her. "Her stay at Cinema Acres was mostly before your time. I'll handle all the questions about her myself."

He seemed to go off into a reverie, gazing out the window.

Karen shifted in her chair. There was something about the distant look in his eyes that kept her from interrupting.

After a minute or two, he turned back to her. He smiled.

His smile carried a feeling of sadness. "Let's go over our statistics now," he said in a quiet voice.

Sybil Wagoner hadn't shown up at Collier Hospital on Monday. One of the old-time nurses who'd been with the hospital from its beginning commented that this was the first time she'd ever known Wagoner to miss a day's work.

Tuesday, when Karen saw her in the hallway, Wagoner appeared to have aged several years. Her usual tight, rigid face was drawn and sagging. She didn't seem to see Karen.

"Good morning, Ms. Wagoner."

Wagoner stopped. It took a moment for her eyes to focus. "Good morning, doctor." The crisp disdain was missing from her voice. She gave a slight nod and walked on.

Karen continued down the hall to Wing A. Just as she came up to Lauryn's room, Frank Terhune walked out. He wore a light blue ultrasuede sport jacket, pink shirt, blue-and-maroon-striped tie. At Collier Hospital, she'd never seen Frank in anything but a white lab coat.

He also wore a big smile. "Good morning, Karen!" he sang out.

"Hello, Frank." She thought she heard him whistling after he sauntered by. She shook her head.

Bev was in Lauryn's room. Felice had gone to buy doughnuts.

Lauryn looked spectacular. Her blond locks fell over her forehead with a haphazardness that must have taken hours to achieve. Deep purple eye shadow set off her green eyes. Her lips were red. Her nails had changed from Saturday's green to the identical red of her lips. She wore a leggy gold lamé jumpsuit that faithfully followed every curve of her body.

Karen couldn't recall ever seeing Lauryn in the same outfit twice. "Where on earth do you find room here for all her clothes?" she asked Bev.

"Felice and I rotate her wardrobe. She's got four walk-in closets that are full in her Bel-Air home, plus what you see in the closet at my condo."

Lauryn's brows lifted in concern. "Don't I look all right?"

"Lauryn," Karen said, "I'd trade all my degrees to look like you."

Lauryn looked puzzled for a moment, then smiled.

"Dr. Marcus Welby was just in," Bev Millar said.

"Oh. Frank."

"Does he always wear that shit-eating grin?"

"Not with me. But he hadn't had a chance to wipe it off before I saw him in the hallway a minute ago."

Bev chuckled. "I wonder if all the other patients get a daily physical exam."

"I don't think it's a required part of the protocol." Karen turned to Lauryn. "What'd you have for lunch?"

Lauryn's forehead crinkled. "I didn't like the hospital food. The fat nurse brought in some fried chicken."

Bev nodded in approval. "That's right, fried chicken."

Karen pulled up a chair and faced Bev. "Dr. Berkholt's going to have a press conference in two days. He wants me there."

"I see," Bev said slowly. "I've wondered how you've been keeping the press from pestering you."

"That's because they haven't. Berkholt's kept them in tow by promising them this conference." She paused. "They're bound to ask about Lauryn."

Bev gave a brief nod.

"When we met, you told me to release no information unless it came through you. Does that still hold?"

"Hell, no," Bev said. "There are a lot bigger issues now than Five Star Studios. Say whatever you want."

"Thanks. That makes it easier."

Karen started to leave, then turned back. "She's better, Bev."

"I know," Bev said.

33

"Have you thought about what you'll wear at the news conference tomorrow morning?" Bev sat across from Karen in the staff dining room the next day. Most of the lunch crowd had already left.

Karen took a bite of tuna salad and chased it with diet Coke. "I've saved a gray flannel suit fresh from the cleaners for just such an event. I figure for a news conference I'd better look professional." The last time she'd worn that suit was for the breakfast meeting when she'd met the four staff doctors at Collier Hospital as the new chief of medicine. It was hard to believe that was only five and a half weeks ago.

Bev polished off the last bite of her turkey sandwich and shook her head. "Uh-unh. When you get in front of TV cameras, you're in my line of business. And you're not going to wear a gray flannel suit."

"Bev, I don't have anything else. I can't go in slacks or jeans."

Bev wiped her lips, crumpled her napkin into a ball, and deposited it firmly on her plate. "I've got just the thing for you."

The next morning Karen was grateful when the alarm rang. In her dream she'd been climbing a rocky hill and something was wrong with her legs. They didn't move right. She had to concentrate hard on lifting her feet for every step. Someone was after her, or perhaps it was some kind of animal chasing her, something very threatening. She couldn't get her legs to move fast enough—it would be upon her any minute. Then the alarm went off.

She sat up with a jolt as she remembered that this was the morning of the press conference. She rushed to the bathroom and checked herself in the mirror. She gave a breath of relief. With a little brushing, her plain brown hair would be back to the way the studio hairdresser had fixed it yesterday afternoon. And the eye shadow was still intact. It was too heavy to suit her, but Bev had said that the TV cameraman's lights would bleach out her eyes and that the extra accent was needed.

Yesterday afternoon Bev had taken her to Ferillo's, an elegant boutique in Beverly Hills. Every salesperson had greeted Bev and asked about Lauryn. Bev latched onto a tall, slim woman of about fifty with smooth, jet black hair, heavily mascaraed eyebrows, penetrating dark eyes, and a complexion of milk. Her name was Marguerite. She wore a tailored knee-length dress of black taffeta with a slit at the side. She still carried an accent from her earlier years in Buenos Aires, where she'd modeled in the fashionable stores of the Florida Street district.

Marguerite studied Karen carefully. "The doctor has potential," she said thoughtfully. "The eyes particularly strike one. They sparkle. We'll use a color that will call attention to them." She ran her hands over Karen's shoulders, down her sides to her waist. "Perhaps a mild accentuation of the bust. And a narrow belt to slim the waist." Her eyes moved down to Karen's legs. She frowned. "The calves are more difficult."

"It's a press conference, not a beauty pageant," Karen said stiffly. She always knew her calves were too thick. They looked natural under a hiker's khaki shorts, but the one time she looked in a mirror while wearing dancer's tights, she realized she'd never make it on the stage.

Marguerite gave a perfunctory smile. "The hemline at midcalf should help." She looked at Karen's flat-heeled sandals and shook her head. "With high heels. High heels are a must."

Karen left Ferillo's carrying black snakeskin pumps, a dark green gabardine jacket, a silk blouse in a lighter shade of green, and a pleated calflength black skirt—all the while protesting that there was no way she could get everything altered in time. Bev ushered her into Five Star Studios, where Lauryn's dressmaker loosened the jacket, adjusted the hem, and tightened the waist. Lauryn's hairdresser set her hair, darkened her eyelashes, and meticulously applied the eye shadow. "Ahh!" she said. "The beautiful sparkle in the eyes must be enhanced and emphasized."

Now Karen studied her eyes in the bathroom mirror. Whatever sparkle that hairdresser had seen in them yesterday afternoon was certainly absent this morning.

She checked the bathroom clock. Seven fifteen. The press conference would start in less than three hours. She showered, carefully avoiding getting water on her hair or face. She touched up the eye makeup and slipped into a robe.

When she walked into the kitchen Bev was starting the coffee. She looked at Karen and nodded approvingly. "You look fine," she said.

"You don't think there's too much eye shadow?"

"You need it for TV." She gestured with a movement of her head toward the refrigerator. "Breakfast's on me this morning. How 'bout scrambled and bacon?"

"No way. My stomach's got enough butterflies to fill it for the rest of the day."

"English muffin then," Bev said. "Nothing settles butterflies better than an English muffin."

The press conference was housed in the generous Cinema Acres theater. The auditorium was empty except for the first four rows, which accommodated reporters from three national TV networks, the Associated Press, Station KFWB, TV Channel 5, and three local newspapers. Cameramen prowled behind freshly set-up stagelights.

Carrying a folder with sheets of statistics, Karen entered with Dr. Berkholt. As they walked to the podium, she tugged self-consciously downward on the back of the jacket. The studio dressmaker had made it too tight in the waist. And she felt she was walking on stilts as the high heels threatened to pitch her forward.

Dr. Berkholt was speaking now. He introduced her: "My associate, Dr. Karen Formaker." She tried to smile, but the bright lights made her squint, and she was sure it came out more like a grimace.

She felt less nervous as Dr. Berkholt's rich, clear voice filled the auditorium. If she could speak like that, she wouldn't have butterflies in her stomach. She noticed that he glanced periodically at the notes in his hand—she didn't remember him speaking from notes before. "Alzheimer's now ranks as the fifth leading cause of death in the country," he said. "But those statistics, which are based solely on the diagnoses listed on death certificates, fail to reveal the true extent of the disease. Alzheimer's destroys the intellectual centers of the brain long before it causes the neurologic damage that leads to death. The death certificate often reads 'pneumonia' or 'heart failure,' while the true underlying cause of death is Alzheimer's."

The lights dimmed, and the slide projections started. The slide Dr. Berkholt was now discussing showed the incidence of age of onset of Alzheimer's in the general population. The graph line began with the appearance of a tiny number of cases in the twenties, stayed just barely above the zero mark into the forties, then began creeping upward in a gradually steepening curve through the fifties, still steeper in sixties and seventies, and leveled off at its highest incidence in the eighties. "Current evidence indicates that the incidence here"—he tapped the pointer over the eighties—"reaches forty to fifty percent of the population. But the personal tragedy of the disease becomes more poignant as we move down the curve into the young." He slowly slid the pointer down into the sixties, fifties, forties.

As the pointer moved down, Karen pictured the fearful young face of Pete Paritski. Her hands tightened at her sides.

Dr. Berkholt moved on to the graphs of the patient population at Collier. "Where do we stand one month into our project? In a disease that may have its beginnings years before it first becomes evident, one month is a short time." He pointed to the graph bars representing the nine patients who'd improved. "We can, however, see that a reversal of the usual relentless progression of the disease has been made in a few." His eyes scanned the audience. "A pitiful few. And yet with Alzheimer's, there are no precedents for even this small a percentage of patients improving.

"Once we are confident that a certain number of patients have defied the usual downhill course of Alzheimer's, then, and only then, can we break the protocol to evaluate our results. Let's say we end up with fifteen—or even our present nine—in the improved category. If, when we break the protocol, we find that they are equally divided between those who received the analog and those who received placebo, we'll know that our results are but a pitiless, random twist of nature, and that our experiment—like all preceding Alzheimer's experiments—has led to a dead end." His voice grew more commanding: "On the other hand, should we find that all fifteen, or twelve, or nine subjects who've improved have received only the analog—be it one, or several—then we shall know that we're on the right track. For, ladies and gentlemen, even if we have just *one*—one single analog that alters the course of this cruel, soul-destroying disease—then we've made an inroad into Alzheimer's." He paused. The room was dead silent. "It may only be a small inroad—but with God's help, it will be a beginning."

One of the younger reporters started to applaud, caught himself, flushed.

Berkholt laid down his notes. "Now, can we answer any questions?"

Several hands went up. Dr. Berkholt pointed to a middle-age woman wearing a gray wool suit—the kind Karen wished she'd worn. "There's been a virtual blackout of news regarding Henrietta Lee's death, doctor. Could you elaborate on this?"

Berkholt nodded. "Henrietta Lee died five days ago. Her death was long expected." The timbre of his voice deepened. "What died, however, was only her body. What did *not* die was her soul, her legend. The unique talent of Miss Lee may have been snuffed out by this terrible disease, but her legend is as alive now as it ever was. Her death only emphasizes the urgency of our job."

The woman looked unsatisfied, but before she could question him further, Berkholt pointed to a stocky, bald-headed man whose hand was raised.

"Can you give us a progress report on Lauryn Hart?" the reporter asked.

Berkholt nodded. "First, I'd like to mention that Five Star Studio has just presented me with a hundred-thousand-dollar check toward the endowment of our project."

Karen looked toward him in surprise. She'd heard nothing of this.

He continued. "We can quote statistics that from four to seven million people in this country are now afflicted with Alzheimer's. Yet those statistics cannot convey the terrible and indiscriminate cruelty of the disease nearly so poignantly as this single case of a beautiful woman who was struck down at the zenith of her career. Even from this tragedy, however, hope arises like the legendary Phoenix from the pyre of its ashes. It's far too early to draw conclusions, but Lauryn Hart is one of the nine cases who so far have shown promise of a reversal of the disease."

He turned to Karen. "For specific details as to Miss Hart's progress, I'll turn you over to my associate, who's been intimately involved in her day-to-day management." He turned back to the assembled reporters. "Ladies and gentlemen, I give you my colleague, Dr.—" He stopped and looked back at Karen. "I give you—" His fingers fumbled at the podium. A flash of fear crossed his eyes.

He's forgotten my name!

The realization hit her like a fist in the belly. She scribbled on the outside of her folder, slid it onto the podium.

"Dr. Formaker," he said. "I give you Dr. Formaker."

Karen stepped in front of the microphone and started to speak rapidly. "Lauryn Hart has been with us three and a half weeks now." She cleared her throat, and her speech slowed. "When Lauryn first entered the hospital, she . . ."

34

Karen didn't get out of the press conference until half past noon. She skipped lunch and began hurried rounds at Collier.

She hardly had time to puzzle over Dr. Berkholt's performance. Another old-timer on Wing C had gone bad, and she checked with members of the family to confirm that they wanted no life-support measures. Pete Paritski had been found wandering the hallway, opening one door after another, trying to find his bedroom at home. The latest admission, a seventy-two-year-old former song-and-dance actor from the board-and-care section of Cinema Acres, had developed a high fever with a flulike illness. The fear of influenza sweeping through a closed hospital community was ever present—aged patients had poor immune responses. The next scheduled flu vaccine clinic for the hospital staff was moved up.

She checked her watch. A new outpatient consult was due at the medical school at two; she'd have to come back and finish rounds later. She returned to her office and loaded papers from her desk into her briefcase.

"Maybe we ought to make another trip to the makeup room." Bev Millar stood in the doorway.

Karen stopped. "I look that bad?"

"Nah, you look fine. Just harried. How'd it go?"

"All right, I guess," Karen said in a distracted tone. "Right now, I'm late for an appointment at the med school."

"I'll walk out with you. I'm leaving, too. It may be hard to believe, but I still have a few other clients."

As they walked down the hallway, Karen told Bev of the hundred-thousand-dollar check from Five Star Studios.

"Very interesting," Bev said thoughtfully. "Looks like they gave up trying to hide that she's ill and decided to milk it for all the publicity they can get. They must figure the pathos will increase the value of her reruns."

"That's what it looks like." Karen nodded at the volunteer manning the entrance desk as she opened the door. "What if Lauryn keeps improving?"

"Karen, if through some miracle Lauryn ever gets back on the set, she'll be the hottest property on TV."

They walked into the parking lot. Karen had intended to avoid talking about Dr. Berkholt, but she had to. "Bev, something strange happened during the conference."

"Oh?"

"Dr. Berkholt called on me to answer questions about Lauryn. When he tried to introduce me, he couldn't remember my name."

Bev chuckled. "Well, I'm glad to hear that Dr. God Almighty has a human streak after all."

"I don't see what's funny about it," Karen said stiffly.

"For Christ's sake, Karen, I forget my own name at times! You've been living with Alzheimer's too long."

They stopped before Karen's car. "You think that's all there is to it?" Karen asked.

"Of course that's all. What else?"

Karen shrugged.

Her first consult at Collier was forty-nine years old.

She'd been the superintendent of supplies for Cinema Acres' three hospitals. She'd last worked two months ago.

When Karen finished the exam, she helped the husband guide his wife's wheelchair out of the examining room. She felt sick. The woman had deep, foul-smelling bedsores on her heels and buttocks. She must have sat in a chair or lain in bed without moving for days. It wasn't that she was paralyzed—she'd simply lost the will to move. How could she have regressed so far in barely two months?

Karen closed the door to her private office and dropped heavily into her desk chair. She knew now that she'd never get used to it: the terrible fear on the faces of the patients—and later, the apathy. The childlike hope in the eyes of the husbands or wives that accompanied the unspoken plea for help. She felt like a fraud, that if only she were honest, she'd confess to them that she was as helpless as they were.

What was she doing here anyway, going from one consult to another as if hopelessly senile patients in their forties were routine? The world around Cinema Acres had gone berserk.

Loucuras do Diabo.

She recalled the flash of fear in Berkholt's eyes this morning at the press conference.

What if he were coming down with it?

She tightened her hands. No! It was just the stress. Like Bev said, he'd simply blocked on a name.

If Ruiz had brought his deadly culture with him from Brazil, had the virus escaped, gone beyond his control?

What's to prevent me from coming down with it?

She pressed the side of her hand against her mouth and bit on it. She was letting herself get carried away. How could Ruiz's virus have spot-hopped from Cinema Acres to University Medical Center to infect Cynthia Frame?

She desperately needed someone knowledgeable to talk to. Bill Horlich would arrive on Monday.

She hadn't told Bill about the receptors.

The receptors!

She jerked open her desk calendar. It was January 5th, seven days ago, that Fogelson had told her about the blocked receptors found on Duane's autopsy. He'd never gotten back to her.

She practically ran through the hallways to the cytology lab.

Fogelson looked up from the microscope.

"Herb, you haven't told me about the receptor studies."

"Arnold and I just finished them. Hasn't he had a chance to discuss them with you?"

"No."

He straightened up on his stool, slipped his glasses on, and looked closely at her. "Duane wasn't an exception, Karen. On eleven of the last thirteen autopsies, every CRH receptor site was filled."

Her shoulders fell. "I was afraid of that."

"Arnold was hit hard by it, too."

She let out a deep breath. "Thanks, Herb." She turned to leave.

"Karen?"

She turned back.

"Has Arnold been acting any different lately?"

Her pulse quickened. "What've you noticed?"

"I don't know. A distance. Sort of an absent-mindedness. A feeling that we're not talking on the same plane." He shook his head. "Ah, I'm making mountains out of molehills. I think I'm just getting tired."

She didn't tell him about the look on Berkholt's face when he had forgotten her name at the press conference. "I think perhaps the project's got him bothered, Herb. The number of people who've grown worse."

He sighed. "I guess you're right."

"Herb—you haven't done any brain virus tissue cultures on the recent deaths, have you?"

"No," he said, as much a question as an answer.

"Could you start doing them?"

"It's feasible. I could enlist Alberto Ruiz over at your place. Arnold tells me he's expert in brain virus cultures."

"No! This has to be independent of Ruiz!"

He studied her. "I have a feeling that something I don't know about's got you worried."

She nodded.

"Not kuru?" He started to smile, stopped.

"Something like it."

"Do you have anything to go on?"

"Not much."

"I'll set up your brain tissue cultures." He frowned. "Too bad we didn't start them earlier—it might take a while to accumulate data."

"I'm afraid I can promise you an ample supply of autopsy material, Herb."

35

"I want to go home! Why can't I go home?" Her lips tightened in an angry pout.

"You will, Lauryn. But right now, you have to stay here for treatment. When you're through, you'll go home."

"I explained that to the little darlin'," Felice said.

"Where am I?"

"You're in a hospital," Karen said. "A hospital for a special form of treatment."

Lauryn's beautiful face wrinkled. "Something's wrong with me, isn't it? Something's wrong with my mind."

Karen wanted to take her by the hands and cry out how happy she was just to hear Lauryn able to express those concerns. "Something has been wrong, but it's getting better. Much better."

Lauryn shook her head back and forth. "I can't remember anything. I try, but I can't remember."

"You will."

"You're my doctor, aren't you?"

"That's right."

"What's your name?"

"Karen."

The door opened. Frank Terhune walked in.

He carried a gift-wrapped package. His broad smile faded when he saw Karen. He reached up and straightened his tie. "Oh. I just came by to check up on our patient."

A smile came over Lauryn's lips. She crossed one leg over the other. "There's my other doctor."

"That's right." Frank regained his composure. "I'm your other doctor." He cleared his throat with a harrumph, and his voice dropped to a resonant baritone. "And how is my little patient today?"

"Are you going to examine me again, doctor?" Karen could have sworn that there was a trace of slyness in Lauryn's inflection when she said "doctor."

Frank cleared his throat again. "Well, I wanted to make sure everything's progressing—" He turned to Karen. "I can come back when you're through."

"I'm leaving now, Frank." Karen rose.

"What did you bring me today?" Lauryn pointed to the package in his hands.

"Oh, nothing much. Just a little candy." He gave a weak laugh.

"The boss wants to see you," Sigrid said when Karen walked into the eighth-floor suite.

Karen hadn't spoken to him since the press conference yesterday. He'd left the auditorium grim-faced, without a word. "He wants to see me now?"

Sigrid shrugged. "Whatever."

How would he react after his slipup at the conference? She knocked on the door.

"Come in," he called.

He was on the phone: "I won't be able to get the chapter to you before the end of the month." When he looked up and saw it was she, he smiled and motioned her to have a seat across from him. "I've been tied down by the CRH Alzheimer's project, Stan. It's slowed everything else up."

She sat down. The tense muscles between her shoulder blades began to relax. She'd forgotten the reassuring warmth of his smile.

"Thanks, Stan. And give my regards to Mariellen."

He hung up. "That was Stan Moser at Yale. I'm writing the pituitary chapter for the upcoming nineteenth edition of Cecil's *Textbook of Medicine,* and the publisher's pressing him for the final galleys." He fit his pen back into its desk holder. "I've been in Stan's position before, and he's got my sympathy. It's an impossible job getting a hundred or so prima donnas to send in their work on time."

Bev was right, she thought with relief. His slip at the press conference had meant nothing. "I thought your chapter in the eighteenth edition was great," Karen said.

"Thank you." He leaned forward with his arms on the desk. "Well, Karen, we're into our second month. What're your reactions?"

She cleared her throat. "They're mixed, Dr. Berkholt. I'm impatient for more signs of favorable response."

"Understandable. Yet from the excellent ongoing reports you're send-ing me, as well as what I glean from the staff conferences, a few have continued to improve."

"Eight, definitely. Possibly as many as eleven. The clearest results are still in the younger ones."

"Yes," he said. "Although the tragedy of the disease is greatest among the young, that's where we also have the rare opportunity to witness, as you say, the clearest results."

"I guess so." She wasn't sure that *opportunity* was the right word.

"I'm afraid I was ambiguous when I asked about your reactions, Karen. I'm aware of your clinical assessment of the program—I was referring more to your personal reactions. I've put a heavy load on you," he said gently, "heavier than I suspect either of us anticipated when we started the program. How are you holding up?"

"I'm doing okay, Dr. Berkholt. It's just that—well, a few of the cases have hit me harder than I expected."

"Like?"

"There's that twenty-eight-year-old I told you about before, Pete Parit-ski. He was getting ready to start medical school. He's pretty bad."

Berkholt nodded slowly. "I see."

Karen swallowed. "Is there a chance—I mean, could we separate him from the protocol because of his age? You see, if we could give him whatever we're giving Lauryn, we wouldn't have to break any codes—and then we could be sure we were giving him every chance."

Dr. Berkholt folded his hands on his desk. "I never expected to say this —but I wish we could, too. However, I must repeat that we set up the protocol so that this decision couldn't be in our hands. Only the Novar-3 program knows what each vial contains, and every week it furnishes only a single newly coded vial to pair up with each patient's entry code. Until Hank Merrill and I both join our passwords to break the code and termi-nate the entire program, no one can have access to it."

He smiled sadly. "I know that at times you must think me callous. I don't mean to be intrusive, but I suspect you may have felt the same about Hank." He unfolded his hands. "Don't think that sometimes I haven't thought about terminating. But if we did—then we'd blow our single shot. For a gesture toward helping one person—a gesture that's uncertain at best—we'd lose our chance for helping millions."

Suddenly she had to struggle to restrain tears. There was nothing she could say in answer. If she had reasoned it out earlier, she might not have screwed things up so badly with Hank.

And yet if it were in her hands, she wondered if she wouldn't still shelve the whole protocol if it increased Pete's chances.

Dr. Berkholt stood up, walked around the desk, and rested a hand on her shoulder. "It's rough."

"Sometimes I feel that I'm not doing the job"—her voice caught—"that I'm doing a rotten job of holding up my end of the load."

"You know, Karen, I've felt that way many times about myself."

She looked up at him. "You?"

"I can't tell you how often." He lifted his hand from her shoulder, walked over to the window, and gazed out onto the campus below. "I spent my childhood in this area—actually, not far from my present house. I grew up without a father—he died when I was five. I can't remember a time during my childhood when I didn't think it was my job to be the man in the house." He paused. "And I can't remember a time when I didn't feel I was botching it."

He turned from the window. She didn't recall getting up, but she was standing, too.

"Behind my house," he said, "a fire road leads down canyon to an old Boy Scout camp that had been abandoned to fire and floods around the time I was born. Many times when I felt most like a failure, I'd hike there and pretend I was lord of the mountains, or Tarzan, or Robin Hood in Sherwood Forest. People sometimes hiked into it on the weekends. I avoided it then because I didn't want to share it with anyone. But weekdays I had it all to myself. Sometimes I'd skip school and head for it."

His eyes had a distant look, as if he were seeing it now. "A stream went through the old campsite. It widened into a swimming hole. From a big oak tree a rope hung over it with an old tire tied at its end. I guess it was left over from the Boy Scout days. I used to swing back and forth across the water. I hope no one ever heard me call out my Tarzan cry." He broke into a short laugh. "My early teen voice wouldn't stop changing.

"One day the rope broke, and both the tire and I tumbled into the pool. It was early spring and the creek was full. I was swept down on the tire to a small waterfall, where finally the tire and I parted company. When I got home all scratched and bruised, I had to make up a story about falling down in the schoolyard because my mother had made me promise I wouldn't go into the mountains alone."

Karen listened, transfixed. She felt like an imposter. She felt she should interrupt before he went further. How would he feel if he knew she'd been there and seen him?

He continued. "I suspect that's why I bought the house at the entrance to the canyon. It was as if I'd filed a claim to my own special private place." He paused for a moment and smiled. "I know I'm getting old when I call you in to ask about your reactions and do nothing but talk about myself."

"I'm awfully glad you did," she said. "It helps me put a few of my own feelings into place."

He rested a hand on her shoulder. "That's kind of you. Somehow it makes me feel more comfortable about prattling on like I have." He accompanied her to the doorway.

She was already in her own office when she realized she hadn't asked him anything about Dr. Ruiz—or the receptors.

36

Monday morning the routines of Collier Hospital were again suspended until the giving of analogs was completed.

The great majority of the patients had been with the protocol from its beginning, and today marked the sixth weekly injection. Extra nursing personnel were recruited from the other two Cinema Acres hospitals. Will Hayes roamed from nurses' station to nurses' station dispensing the vials. Sybil Wagoner showed up at eight-thirty and disappeared into her office.

Karen was at the hospital even before the day shift started. Repeatedly, she checked the hospital administrator's office where the main computer terminal was located. Hank always showed up on Mondays.

The fifth time she checked, she found him sitting there.

She cleared her throat.

He looked up from the computer screen and gave an uncertain smile. "Hello, Karen."

She was sure he'd lost weight. She wondered how often he took time to go to the cafeteria for meals. "Hello, Hank."

He waved at the stack of data on the desk. "Looks like you've kept busy."

"I imagine you have, as well."

"How've you been?"

"I've been better at times," she said. "How 'bout you?"

"That pretty well holds for me, too."

With a sudden rush of feeling, she again realized how sorely she missed him. "Sometimes the program gets kind of discouraging."

"From what I can see, you're doing a good job," he said.

"Thanks." She took the stethoscope from around her neck and slipped it into the pocket of her lab coat.

He ran his tongue over his lip. "I've been back to our place a few nights. The little room across from my office is getting small."

He'd said "our place"! She swallowed. "Hank—what about taking a few minutes to break for coffee?"

"Dr. Formaker?"

She turned.

The charge nurse from Wing C stood in the doorway. "The new admit from the med center came over without a signed permit. Will Hayes says he can't give her the shot unless a permit's on the chart."

She turned back to Hank and shrugged sadly. "Her husband's a lawyer. I'd better get busy."

"Sure," he said. "Monday's always a rough day."

She bit her lip. "Hank, I've missed you."

"I've missed you, too."

"Maybe you'll give me a call. We could take a rain check on that coffee."

"I'd like that, Karen."

When she returned to Collier Hospital from a noontime faculty meeting at the medical school, she stopped first in Lauryn Hart's room.

Lauryn wore a royal blue tank top and body-hugging denim jeans. Silver bangle bracelets adorned both her wrists, and large silver hoops hung from her ears. Her long nails were painted wet-look pink. She stopped applying her makeup and turned to Karen. "Hello." Her forehead wrinkled. "You're my other doctor, aren't you?"

"I'm one of them, Lauryn. You look beautiful."

Lauryn's face lit up. "Do you like my hair?" she asked, swinging it away from her shoulders. "I'm wearing it softer."

"It looks great." Karen turned to the private nurse, who sat in an armchair munching a piece of chocolate. "How're you, Felice?"

"I think I've gained another four pounds since our little darlin' told Dr. Terhune that she likes candy," Felice said. She lifted a box of chocolates. "Have a piece. The ones with the cherry centers are real good."

"Thanks, but I think I'll pass this time."

"Our main visitor these days is Dr. Terhune." She replaced the lid on the box of chocolates. "Do you think you could suggest to our little darlin' that she tell him she's tired of candy before I get too fat to get through the door?"

"What about suggesting flowers?"

Felice nodded toward the window, where a bouquet of red roses rested on the sill.

Karen glanced back at Lauryn. This time she was certain she saw a touch of slyness in her answering smile.

She left Lauryn's room to continue rounds. As she turned into the central corridor, Ron Olsen was just stepping out of her office. He saw her, and in a few long rapid strides he was at her side.

"Well, do your observations on Hart agree with my DME scores?" he asked.

"There's no question about it, Ron. She's getting better."

He stroked his beard slowly. "You'd like to know which preparation she's getting, wouldn't you?"

"Yep." She pressed her lips together. "But I guess we'd screw up the protocol if we broke it open before we have statistically significant patterns."

He lifted his brows. "Hey, what's going on? You sound like your ex-boyfriend."

She stiffened. "If you wish to refer to Hank Merrill, I would appreciate your doing so by name. And while you're at it, try to remember that this is my program as well as Dr. Berkholt's. It's the main reason he appointed me here. It means a great deal to me to see it succeed."

He raised his hands. "Okay, okay, I retreat." He held her by both shoulders. "How about letting me apologize over dinner at my place tonight?"

"No."

"I replenished the champagne."

"I've sworn off champagne."

They had reached her office. He stopped at the door and smiled. "Karen, my love, if you think you can discourage me, you're dead wrong. I'm going to break through your defenses yet." He turned to leave.

She thought of Dr. Berkholt's words about his computer expertise. Had Ron been hinting? "Ron—"

He turned back.

"When you said that I'd like to know what Lauryn Hart was getting, were you suggesting you could find out?"

He folded his arms. "I understand your ex"—he stopped and gave a brief disclaimer smile—"Merrill, that is, did an elaborate job of protecting the code."

It was a stupid question for her to have asked in the first place. "Right. I was just speculating."

"In that case," he said, "as long as we're speculating, I don't think a foolproof protocol has ever been programmed."

She bit her lip. She wished she'd never brought up the subject. "Are you intimating that you could get around the code?"

He smiled artfully. "Me? Why, Karen, I'm just a simple farm boy from Wisconsin who got involved in Freudian circles by way of convoluted, misguided reaction formations."

She sighed.

"On the other hand," he said, "when you're satisfied that you've got your statistically significant patterns, you can give me a try." He gave a casual little salute and walked off.

Karen stared after him. Her hands opened and closed at her sides. She took in a deep breath and continued on rounds.

Pete Paritski's mother had been sleeping in the armchair. She jumped up when Karen walked in.

Pete was curled in bed in a fetal position. Diapers showed through the break in his hospital gown. Milky white liquid dripped from an overhead plastic bag into a feeding tube that disappeared into his nose.

He'd deteriorated rapidly. Yesterday the nurses had reported that he was taking nothing by mouth—when either the nurses or his mother had tried to spoon-feed him, he had choked. Unless they started some form of artificial feeding, Karen had explained to Mrs. Paritski, he wouldn't live. Ordinarily, with far-advanced Alzheimer's she'd never recommend it, but in view of Pete's age and rapid downhill course, she saw no alternative. Mrs. Paritski had agreed.

Karen examined Pete. Blood pressure holding normal at 105/70. Pulse eighty-four. Lungs clear. Heart regular. Neurologic: no response to verbal stimuli; withdrawal response from painful stimuli; pupils equal and slightly reactive; tendon reflexes absent. An ominous development was a change in his respiration to a pattern of fast, deep breaths alternating with long pauses, indicating spread of nerve cell damage from the brain cortex to the basic life-function centers of the midbrain.

Mrs. Paritski looked as if she'd aged ten years since Karen saw her yesterday. "He's worse, isn't he?"

"I'm afraid so," Karen said.

"I tried putting a spoonful of water in his mouth, and he turned blue until he coughed it up."

"He's getting enough liquids through the stomach tube, Mrs. Paritski."

"I don't understand. They told me this was a slow disease. Petey looks like he's going to"—she swallowed—"going to die."

Karen rested a hand on Mrs. Paritski's arm. "It's an unpredictable disease—none of us understands why he's getting worse so fast."

"Is there anything else you can do?"

At that moment, Karen became aware of a deadly silence in the room.

Pete was in the nonbreathing phase of his cycle. She checked her watch —in the fourteen seconds before he started breathing again, his face turned blue. "Unless he improves soon, he'll need to be placed on a ventilator," she said.

"What—what's that?"

"A tube is fitted through his mouth into his windpipe, Mrs. Paritski. It's connected to a machine that blows air and oxygen into his lungs."

"Does it hurt?"

"If a person is wide awake, it may cause something like a choking sensation." She looked again at Pete. "It's hard to know how awake he actually is, but I don't think he'd feel much."

"Are you going to do it?"

"We'll do nothing without your permission. But if we put him on the ventilator, he'll have to be moved over to University Hospital where we have acute care facilities."

She looked back and forth from Pete to Karen. "What do you think?"

"I think we ought to go ahead with it. At least for a while."

Mrs. Paritski nodded. "All right." Her eyes fixed on Karen's. "It won't really make any difference, will it? Nothing will make any difference."

Karen stared at Mrs. Paritski. Her lips moved, but no words came out.

Suddenly, her breath caught. She reached out and wrapped her arms around the woman.

Mrs. Paritski didn't cry, didn't move. She just stood there, breathing softly, in Karen's arms.

37

The sun had disappeared by the time Karen parked outside the Delta Airlines baggage counter. Bill Horlich wasn't hard to spot—six feet four, broad-shouldered, bare-headed, and ebony black, he stood out above the crowd. He wore a navy-and-gray plaid sport jacket and pleated navy blue slacks. A lightweight topcoat dangled from his arm. Karen pulled over to the curb, jumped from the car, and waved. "Bill!"

His eyes caught her, and he broke into a wide smile. He lifted a fair-size suitcase as if it weighed an ounce and reached her in a few strides. "Karen, it's good of you to pick me up." He dropped his bag and held out his hand.

She ignored his outstretched hand and gave him a hug. "I can't tell you how happy I am to see you."

"It's hard to believe a year's already passed." He smiled gently. "I'm still sad that I couldn't be with you for Susan's funeral."

"It helped a great deal when you called after you got back from Sweden, Bill. Susan always thought you were special." She took his arm. "Come on, let's go fight the traffic."

She drove at a crawl along the departure level circle. "I hope you haven't paid a deposit on a hotel. I wish I'd have thought of suggesting it earlier, but neither Hank nor I are staying at our apartment, and you've got a perfectly good base there."

"I have a sister in Culver City—she'd be pissed if I didn't stay with her. Have you and Hank got a new place?"

She swung around a hotel pickup bus and drove onto the airport exit road. "We didn't exactly move together. We're both staying at different places."

"Oh, I see," he said, as if he really did.

"Let's get something to eat." She turned to him. She felt as if a weight had been lifted off her. "Oh Bill, it's so good to have you here."

At Knight's Coffee Shop on Sepulveda Boulevard, they sat over coffee while waiting for their order. "Tell me about the program," Bill said.

Karen reviewed the CRH protocol. When she finished her description, he whistled softly. "That," he said, "is one helluva computer protocol."

Karen shrugged.

"Hank, huh?" He pursed his lips. "Is the rift between you two pretty serious?"

"I don't know, Bill. At this point, I don't even know whose fault it is."

He took a sip of coffee. "Did the CRH program have anything to do with it?"

"I guess so."

"Is this the first time you two have worked together on a program?" She bit her lip and nodded.

"It's got to be tough," he said. "Two strong-minded people sharing a home and working together day and night. That's bound to be an emotional drain."

She picked up her spoon and slowly turned it between her thumb and forefinger. "I kind of think that, if I had another chance, I could be a little less strong-minded."

He smiled softly. "If there's a way I can help, I'd be honored to have the chance."

She reached a hand across the table and took his. "Thanks."

The next morning Bill Horlich joined Karen in her office at Collier Hospital. He nodded toward the computer terminal on the table next to her desk. "Let me get a firsthand look at the protocol. Okay if I use your ID number?"

"It's 93404. And my log-on password is SILVER.BROOM."

Before Karen could explain anything more, Bill's fingers were on the keyboard. The main menu lit up. He ran through several screens until he stopped at the statistical breakdown summary of the enrolled patients.

Karen shook her head. "You seem right at home."

Bill smiled. "I'm working with an IBM 3090 mainframe at the CDC— the same as the one running your Novar-3 program." He scrolled the screen. "Nineteen dead in thirty-six days. Those are brutal figures."

"With the usual age group of Alzheimer's patients, the predicted mortality would have been ten. The additional nine deaths calculate out to be statistically valid, even at only five weeks. But what's more brutal is their age—three of the deaths were under fifty."

"I noticed that." He scrolled further. "Twenty-five percent get placebo. What analogs are in the other seventy-five percent?"

"We've tested thirty-two analogs on rats, but only three of the most active—nine, fifteen, and twenty-seven—are being used in the protocol. The full supply, though, has been coded in the Novar-3 program, so that it's impossible to tell which is which."

"What about simply getting fresh analogs from endocrine lab?" Bill asked.

She shook her head. "Endocrine lab's production of them was shut down four months ago. Dr. Berkholt didn't want any uncoded ones on hand to tempt unauthorized use."

"I see." He scrolled through more screens. "Sometimes it's hard to remember that there are real people behind the code numbers in so intricate a program."

Karen's voice dropped. "That's part of what happened between Hank and me."

He turned from the computer screen and silently looked at her. His eyes were warm and sad.

She gave a tight-lipped smile and stood up. "Come on. Let me show you a few of the patients."

They stopped at Pete Paritski's room.

His intervals without breathing extended up to twenty seconds now. Karen felt a fresh sense of alarm. "He's slowed down even more. I'll arrange for an ambulance to take him to University."

Bill stared at the boy. "You can hear all the descriptions in the world, but it doesn't really hit you until you see it, does it?"

"That's one of the reasons I'm so glad you're here, Bill."

"I'll get blood and spinal fluid for tissue cultures and air express them to our virology lab at the CDC," he said. "As long as he's transferring to University Hospital, I can wait and use the microbiology laboratory there to prepare them."

Karen ran her tongue underneath her lip. "Why don't you use the lab here? Ruiz has an elaborate microbiology setup, as well as a supply of primate brain mediums for culture. I don't think he could refuse you without feeling that he's throwing heavy suspicion on himself."

Bill pursed his lips. "It might be a good way to get to know Dr. Ruiz." He nodded. "And that way I can start cultures on a number of your cases."

They continued rounds.

Karen selected the younger patients. As they left the room of the eighth one, Bill shook his head. "I've got a pretty good idea of what you're dealing with. It must be like waking up every day to face a night-mare."

Karen nodded grimly. She took him by the arm. "Enough of rounds for now. One of the unique experiences of Collier Hospital awaits you. It's time to meet our chief nurse."

The door to Sybil Wagoner's office was closed. Karen knocked.

"Come in."

Bill followed her in. "Ms. Wagoner," Karen said, "this is Dr. William Horlich. He's visiting us from the CDC—that's the Centers for Disease Control in Atlanta. It incorporates the old Communicable Disease Center of the Public Health Service—"

Wagoner interrupted. "I'm perfectly familiar with the CDC," she said starchily.

Karen gritted her teeth. Whatever had happened to soften Wagoner with Henrietta Lee's death, she seemed to have fully recovered. "Dr. Horlich, Ms. Wagoner."

Wagoner nodded. Bill made no attempt to extend his hand.

"Dr. Horlich will assess the feasibility of further virus studies on some of our patients," Karen said.

Wagoner's face stayed expressionless. Her eyes moved up and down Bill. "Have you informed Dr. Berkholt of Dr. Horlich's involvement?"

Karen's voice turned to steel. "I'm informing you, Ms. Wagoner. I am chief of medicine at Collier Hospital, and Dr. Horlich is here at my invitation."

Sybil Wagoner's eyes narrowed. "Very well, doctor." She turned back to the correspondence on her desk.

As they walked down the hall, Bill swooshed out a breath. "I can see you've got your hands full with that one."

"She's not your typical Florence Nightingale." Karen chuckled as she opened the door to the basement stairway. "And you'll find that Alberto Ruiz isn't your typical Young Dr. Kildare."

She knocked on the door to the microbiology lab.

"Wait a meenute."

They waited several minutes before the lock clicked and the door opened.

Ruiz kicked the door catch to prop the door. "I was plating spinal fluid cultures. The medium ees tricky. I didn't want an open door to let in air until I finished."

"Dr. Ruiz, I want you to meet Dr. Bill Horlich."

Ruiz's nose barely reached above the level of Bill's belt. His gaze climbed up to his face. "How do you do."

Ruiz's hand disappeared in Bill's grip. Bill looked around the lab and nodded approvingly. "It's an impressive setup."

"Dr. Horlich used to be here at the medical center," Karen said. "He's now in Infectious Disease at the CDC. He works there in Virology."

"The CDC." Ruiz turned to her with tightened lips. He nodded slowly. "Yes, I begin to see, Doctora Karen."

"Dr. Formaker feels that there's an unusual concentration of patients with Alzheimer's who don't fit into the accepted age curve for the disease," Bill said. "One of her understandable concerns is the possibility of an infectious element."

"Like one of the slow viruses," Ruiz said softly.

"Precisely," Bill said. "Like kuru, or Creutzfeldt–Jakob."

"Or *Loucuras do Diabo*. Ees that perhaps also your interest?" He looked again at Karen.

"As a matter of fact," Bill answered, "I would be honored to have the opportunity to learn something of that disease from you."

Ruiz scrunched his lips together and moved them side to side. "I will tell you what I can."

"Thank you. It is a rare opportunity for me."

While the two men talked, Karen was looking around the lab. The countertops were meticulous. The white rats scurried in the animal cages. The incubators were lined up in two rows on shelves traversing a full wall.

Suddenly, what was different dawned on her—the change from the terrible night she'd inspected the lab after midnight. She'd been impressed then by the military precision of the way the incubators were lined up in pairs, one above the other.

Now, they weren't lined up at all!

Quickly, she counted. Bottom row, twelve. Top row, eleven.

Last time there'd been twelve incubators on each shelf.

He'd removed one of them between the time she'd faced Sybil Wagoner's gun, and her next time in the lab, when Ruiz had stood behind her while she fruitlessly inspected the incubators.

Bill was still speaking. "I shall also impose on you for the use of your facilities in collecting virus cultures on a few cases. And I invite you to reciprocate—in our new virology building at the CDC, we have some very sophisticated facilities I'd be happy to make available to you."

"You are exceptionally kind, Dr. Horlich," Ruiz said in a low voice.

Karen escorted Bill Horlich to her office and closed the door behind them. "Bill, he changed things. One of the incubators is missing."

Bill looked at her and pursed his lips.

She continued. "He even made a point of rearranging the eleven incubators that were left on the top shelf so it wouldn't be obvious that one had been removed."

"You're sure?"

"I clearly counted them the first time. Twelve on each row. I remembered how precisely lined up they were."

He nodded slowly. "I'd certainly like to check the contents of that twelfth incubator."

Karen gripped his arm. "At least now we know. Let's not waste time, Bill. Let's get a warrant to search his house."

He smiled patiently. "Karen, there's a long distance between a suspicion and the evidence required to get a search warrant. We're not there yet."

Her hand fell.

"Give me time," he said.

38

Lauryn wore a bare-backed halter dress of red silk with an embroidered serpent belt. She was concentrating on spraying perfume behind her ears when Karen walked in.

"Hello, Lauryn."

Lauryn turned from the mirror. She laid down the atomizer and stood up. She seemed to study Karen hard. "Hello, Dr. Karen."

Karen gasped. She grabbed Lauryn and hugged her. "You called me by name! You remembered my name!" She ran over to Bev and hugged her next.

Bev stayed seated. She tried to posture a frown but didn't succeed. "What's so big about remembering a name?"

"Don't try to put on a Miss Nonchalant act with me—you're as excited as I am!"

Lauryn had broken out into a smile of relief. "Before you came, I practiced with Bev."

"It's the nicest present you could have given me," Karen said.

Bev folded her hands on her lap. "When I got back yesterday, she knew mine, too."

"You didn't tell me," Karen said. "You kept it to yourself."

"When did I have a chance to tell you, doctor?" Bev said. "You didn't get in until after eleven last night, and you were already gone when I got into the kitchen this morning."

Karen let out a deep breath. "I'm bogged down in consults at University. Dr. Berkholt's out of town again." She looked again at Lauryn. "But this makes up for everything."

Bev nodded matter-of-factly, but the corners of her eyes crinkled.

"Where's Felice?" Karen asked.

"She took off early," Bev said. "Made me promise to take the boxes of chocolate away before she returned."

Karen glanced around the room. In addition to the red roses on the windowsill, a vase of orchids and fern rested on the corner table, and another vase of yellow roses was on the floor next to the bathroom door. "Frank's been here?"

"Is he the doctor who always wears the thing hanging from his neck?" Lauryn asked.

"That sounds like him."

Lauryn's eyes twinkled for a second. "Yes, he's been here."

Minutes later, Karen sat with Bev over coffee in the staff dining room. She still felt exuberant about Lauryn. "Oh Bev," she said, "I'm so delighted with the changes in her!"

"She told you that we practiced."

"I know, I know," Karen said. "She's still got a long way to go. But she's on her way back."

Bev nodded soberly. "That she is."

Karen blew on her coffee before sipping. "Do you think I ought to say something to Frank?"

"Whaddaya mean?"

"He's married. He's a doctor in a hospital where Lauryn's a patient. I'm uncomfortable seeing him take advantage of that situation. I think you're perfectly aware that his attentions go beyond the strictly professional."

Bev laughed. "Karen, if I were you, I'd worry about your doctor, not Lauryn."

"Huh?"

"When it comes to men, Lauryn's in about as much danger as a lioness around a deer. I can assure you that the risk is all his."

Karen couldn't suppress a smile as she thought of Frank's pink shirt, yellow tie, and silly grin. "You think so?"

Bev nodded. "Try to think of your Dr. Terhune as a form of occupational therapy for Lauryn. To help her resharpen her claws."

In contrast to Lauryn and a pitifully few others, the DME scores continued to plummet for many patients. The death toll for the past week had reached four. Worriedly, Karen walked the paved pathways outside of Collier Hospital with Bill Horlich. "Have you learned anything, Bill?"

"I've only been here a day," he said, "but that's long enough to convince me that Ruiz knows his stuff. I've already learned a few things from him about fluorescent antibody staining."

"Do you believe him when he says he hasn't brought the *Loucuras do Diabo* strain with him?"

"No."

She nodded thoughtfully. "I suppose I'm glad to hear you say that. I've got mixed feelings. I wouldn't want to think I'm going paranoid, but it scares the hell out of me."

"With good reason," Bill said. "You realize that every vial—analog or placebo—brought over here from the endocrine lab goes into that refrigerator in his lab? He has access to everything before it's taken up to the floor to give to a patient."

"Even so," Karen said, "his access is limited. The vials are fully sealed and coded by the computer program before they get here. To know what each one contains, he'd have to break into the security code of the protocol."

"Karen, I sat with Ruiz while he entered some of his data into the program. The man is highly computer literate. What's to prevent him from tampering with the code? He's got his own log-on ID and password, just as you do."

She sighed. "I'm beginning to think everyone at Collier Hospital is a computer expert except me." She stopped walking and turned to Bill. "Look, Hank tried to fix the program so no one could break the double blind protocol until he and Dr. Berkholt were ready." She described to him the setup with the two special security passwords.

"If Hank programmed it that way, it would certainly be difficult to sabotage. But there's no such thing as a foolproof security program—they've drummed that into us at the CDC." He frowned. "I'm still impressed with how thoroughly Ruiz knows his way around the protocol."

"I might as well muddy the waters further," she said. "Ron Olsen's designed some major computer programs on his own."

Bill raised his brows. "The psychiatrist? The bearded Robert Redford?"

So he'd noticed, too. "He has an undergraduate degree in computer science."

Bill slowly shook his head. "This is one helluva geriatric hospital. Do either one of them supervise the giving of the injections?"

"That part's up to Will Hayes. He's both a registered nurse and a physical therapist at Collier."

"That can't be the young freckle-faced lad who looks as if he came straight out of a Mark Twain novel?"

Karen smiled. "That young freckle-faced lad is thirty-nine years old."

Bill whistled. "I'd like to learn his secret." He smiled dryly. "Not the freckles, mind you." They started walking again. "Is there anything connecting him and Ruiz?"

"Not that I know of, except that he picks up the vials in Ruiz's lab every Monday. Will's an awfully nice guy, but he's pretty private. He's in charge of all the immunization programs here. I think that's the reasoning behind his supervising the giving of the analogs."

"Does he have access to the protocol?"

"Same as I do—through his own individual ID number and log-on password. But that doesn't include the security code. It still seems to me that our best bet would be to find Ruiz's missing incubator. Do you think we could get a warrant to search his house?"

"When I said I didn't believe Ruiz, I was talking about a gut feeling that he's holding something back. Gut feelings don't mean much in court when you're requesting a search warrant. We need something more substantial."

"What if we prove that some of our patients are harboring a brain virus?"

"That might be a different matter."

"How long will it take to get the results on your cultures?"

"Five days at the earliest," he said. "But they're on blood and spinal fluid. If we're talking about a relative of the kuru or Creutzfeldt–Jakob virus, don't forget that neither has been transmitted other than from brain tissue itself."

"Herb Fogelson in pathology agreed to make brain tissue cultures on all the new deaths. I asked him six days ago, and we've had four deaths since."

"I'll speak to Herb." Bill rubbed his chin thoughtfully. "And while I'm sending material to the CDC, I might as well see if they can grow anything from that stuff in the fridge."

She struggled awake and reached for the phone.

"Medical ICU, University Hospital," the answering-service operator said.

"It's Paritski," said the nurse. "Blood pressure's fallen to seventy over fifty."

Karen fought the rest of the way into consciousness. "Get a dopamine drip started."

"The ICU resident already ordered it," the nurse said. "He thought we'd better notify you anyway."

"I'll be there."

Five minutes later, she was speeding down the dark, curving streets of Pacific Palisades toward the medical center.

A solitary figure occupied the waiting room outside of Medical ICU. Mrs. Paritski huddled in a corner of the couch. Her eyes rose to Karen's.

"I'll be back after I see him," Karen said.

Pete Paritski lay flat in the ICU bed. Tubes sprouted from him like tendrils from a climbing plant. The ventilator swooshed. The LED blood pressure readout registered ninety-four over seventy. She lifted his eyelids. Pupils were wide, black, empty. She shined her penlight in them. They didn't change.

The medical resident joined her. His lab coat was wrinkled. Stubble darkened his cheeks and chin. "Blood pressure's up some," he said.

"I saw."

"Urine output's zero. Central venous pressure's fifteen, so it looks like renal failure."

Karen nodded.

"Should he be a No Code?" the resident asked.

"We'll see."

She stopped again in the waiting room. Mrs. Paritski looked up. "Is he still alive?"

"Yes, he is," Karen said gently, "but it doesn't look good."

"I don't want him tortured," she said. "If God says I have to let go of him, I will."

"Let me get the neurologist to go over him again before we make any decisions."

Standing at the bedside of Pete Paritski, Mike Werner shook his head. "Pupils wide, doll's-eye fixation, every reflex gone. He's brain dead, Karen."

Karen ran her tongue over her dry lip. "No chance of any return?"

"None. The EEG shows no activity."

Karen let out a heavy breath. "That's what I thought."

"Are you going to talk to the family about disconnecting?"

"I'll present it to his mother. But it's almost academic. We're not able to keep his blood pressure up anymore, even with the IV wide open."

Werner gazed at the still figure on the bed. "He's got a young body— and except for the brain, young organs. The waiting list for donor organs is long." He shrugged. "At least we can salvage something out of this tragedy."

Karen shook her head grimly. "Mike, by now I've had three Alzheimer's cases under forty, thirteen under fifty. Out of maybe two hundred subjects, all but one of them were focused around Cinema Acres. There are no Alzheimer dementia percentages like that anywhere in the world—unless you want to include the highlands of New Guinea."

He stared at her. "Are you suggesting that you're dealing with something contagious?"

She nodded.

"My God," he said, "do you know what you're saying? Even if there's the least question of transmissibility, organ donations are out."

"I know. We don't even have that solace to fall back on," she said heavily.

His voice dropped. "I'd like to think you've gone off your rocker, but" —he looked again at Pete—"I'm afraid I don't. What are you doing about it?"

"I've got Bill Horlich from the CDC here to help me. We're culturing everything in sight."

"What about your own Alberto Ruiz?"

"That's a large part of what I'm worried about."

Mrs. Paritski hadn't moved from the corner of the waiting-room couch. Karen told her of Werner's findings.

Mrs. Paritski slowly stood up. "I want to see my boy."

Karen led her into Pete's ICU cubicle. She signaled to one of the ICU nurses to join them.

The mother stood by the bedside. Karen lowered the siderails.

"So many tubes coming from him," Mrs. Paritski said.

"I know," Karen said.

"Take the tubes out."

"You understand that he will die then, Mrs. Paritski," Karen said gently.

"He dies no matter. He shouldn't die like that, not with the tubes coming from everywhere. He should die in his mother's arms."

Karen nodded. She undid the tape that anchored the stomach feeding tube to Pete's nose and slowly drew out the long vinyl tube. She clamped shut the IV and nodded to the nurse to remove the needle from the vein in Pete's neck. Then she turned off the ventilator, released the pressure from the balloon cuff fixing the tracheostomy tube, and carefully withdrew the tube from Pete's throat. With the distortion from the tube removed, Pete's mouth returned to a peaceful position.

His chest didn't move. The overhead monitor still showed a regular heartbeat.

Mrs. Paritski bent over the bed, cradled her son's head in her arms, rested her face against it. She moaned softly.

Pete Paritski gave a single breath. Then, no more.

His mother rocked slowly, holding his head against her, her soft moan returning over and over like a low-pitched lullaby.

The heartbeat on the monitor slowed, stopped.

Karen stood next to her, without a word, without moving. She had to remember to breathe.

39

Karen put off phoning Sigrid when she returned to Collier Hospital Friday morning. If any new appointments awaited her at the medical school, she wasn't ready to hear about them. With each new consult the waiting list for admission to the program stretched longer. It was at a hundred ten now. Its order was constantly being reshuffled to accommodate the younger ones. What good had it done Pete Paritski to be moved up to the head of the list? It was cruel to let others build up their pitiful hopes.

She suddenly had a terrible fear that Lauryn's improvement had been but a passing phase. That the next time she walked into her room, Lauryn would look at her with vacant eyes.

She couldn't wait. She'd see Lauryn now.

Before she could leave her office, Sybil Wagoner appeared.

Wagoner looked strange. Her face was as white as ever, but a look of uncertainty shrouded it. The only time Karen had ever before seen uncertainty on that cheerless face was immediately after Henrietta Lee's death. "Doctor," Wagoner said, "could I talk to you?"

Puzzled, Karen returned to her desk and motioned to Wagoner to take a chair.

Wagoner stood for a moment, hands fidgeting at her sides, before sitting. Her lips moved wordlessly before her voice finally came. "The night I came across you in Dr. Ruiz's lab, doctor, I didn't know who I would find. I was as surprised to see you as you were me." She ran her tongue over her dry lips. "Why were you there?"

Karen felt her anger rise. "Why do you ask now?"

"You brought Dr. Horlich in."

"You commented on that earlier, Ms. Wagoner," Karen said coldly.

Wagoner's fingers worried a button on the lap of her starched white uniform while her eyes stayed fixed on Karen's. "I understand you're looking for a brain virus."

Karen stared at the rigid, white-faced woman. There *had* to be a connection between her and Ruiz. She nodded.

"Have you isolated it?"

"No." Something was very strange about the direction of this conversation.

"If there is such a virus," Wagoner swallowed, "is there a cure?"

Karen was more confused than ever. "Look, Ms. Wagoner, when we're talking about dementia viruses, we're talking about very rare disorders."

Wagoner sat forward. Her voice grew sharper. "Do not patronize me, doctor. They are rare, but they exist." The muscles of Wagoner's jaw moved up and down. "Those that have been discovered. Is there a cure?"

Karen shook her head.

Wagoner's tall, rigid frame seemed to slump in the chair.

Karen caught her breath as it suddenly dawned on her. *She thinks she's got the disease!*

Wagoner's eyes fell. For a moment she studied the floor. Then, her shoulders straightened, and she stood up. "Thank you, doctor." She turned.

Karen stood up. "Ms. Wagoner. Wait!"

If Wagoner heard her, she gave no signal as she walked stiffly from the room.

Karen's concern that she'd only imagined Lauryn's improvement disappeared the moment she walked into Lauryn's room and saw Frank Terhune sitting by the bedside.

Terhune jumped up as if called to attention. He'd developed a chameleonlike capacity to change to an instant red each time Karen found him there. He cleared his throat. "Well, if it isn't our lady doctor!"

Lauryn lounged on the bed. She wore a low-cut tiger-stripe negligee. Her long nails were bright orange. "Hello, Dr. Karen."

Karen heaved a breath of relief. "Hello, Lauryn." She turned to Terhune. "How are you, Frank?"

"I was making rounds." He cleared his throat again. "Our little patient is doing very well, isn't she?"

Lauryn sat up and slid from the bed. She reached over and pinched Frank's cheek. "I don't know what I'd do without my Dr. Frankie."

It was hard to believe that Frank's face could have grown redder, but it did.

Lauryn lifted her hand to the thin gold chain around her neck and smiled knowingly at Karen. "This is what my doctor brought me."

Karen tried to look serious as she fingered it. "It's very pretty, Lauryn." Her side vision caught Frank straightening his tie. Sweat had appeared on his forehead. "Where are Bev and Felice?"

"I think Bev's working," Lauryn answered. "And I told Felice to go get something to eat while my doctor takes care of me."

"I'm glad you're doing so well. Tell Bev to buzz me when she comes in." Karen headed for the door.

"I've gotta finish making my rounds, too." Frank's words trailed behind Karen as she walked out.

She answered the phone.

"Karen?"

She spoke stiffly. After their last meeting at Collier, she'd expected him to call before now. "Hello, Hank."

"Karen, I—I'd like to talk to you."

She felt a sudden sense of alarm. She'd never heard that note of fear in his voice before. "What's wrong?"

"I think it would be better to wait until I see you."

"Here?"

"Can you come to Palisades Park?"

"Give me twenty minutes."

"I'll wait for you off Montana Avenue."

She saw him pacing the sidewalk. By the time she dropped two quarters into the parking meter, he'd reached her.

"How are you, Karen?" He looked gaunt. His face was lined, hair disheveled, eyes red. He wore a wrinkled short-sleeve shirt, jeans, faded blue sneakers.

"I'm okay. What's happened, Hank?"

"Let's find a seat," he said.

They took a bench facing the ocean. A light breeze wafted in from the ocean and blew his hair, which still hadn't been cut, loosely over his forehead. His hands moved constantly. She wanted to reach out and take them, hold them still.

In spite of the winter month, it was a clear, warm afternoon. Joggers puffed and panted along the gravel paths. The sparse weekday picnic crowd had anchored blankets and sheets with Thermos bottles and spread out coleslaw, potato salad, fried chicken, and cans of pop. Only four months ago she and Hank had picnicked on the same grass with Susan and Duane.

His eyes held a mixture of concern, longing, and fear. "I—I've been wanting to see you."

His fear was contagious. It twisted at her belly as she waited.

"It's about the program," he said. "I waited to tell you until I was more certain. I still don't know what it means."

"What's going on, Hank?"

"Someone's accessed the protocol."

"A number of us have data-entry access."

He shook his head. "I mean the security codes—the ones that identify the analogs and placebo."

She drew in her breath sharply. "But I thought that was impossible. At least, without both passwords."

"I tried to set it up that way, but there's no such thing as a foolproof program."

She'd heard those same damned words from Bill Horlich. "How can you be sure the codes have been accessed?"

"Remember I told you about a computer virus that infected some PCs earlier this year?"

"Vaguely. Something was planted in a program, and it spread to every other program used in the same system. Didn't it do a lot of damage?"

"That's the general idea. It's much harder to infect a mainframe such as the one we're using than a PC, so I figured the risk was remote. Still, I didn't want to take any chances, so I installed a virus monitor in the Novar-3 when I first programmed it."

"Now I'm lost," she said.

"It's a program to detect unauthorized access. If a virus were trying to invade the system, it would have to go through the security code. The monitor should pick that up."

"I think I follow. Go on."

His lips were dry. He ran his tongue over them. "I really wasn't very concerned—I figured it's just one of those precautions a compulsive like me puts in. For a while after the protocol started, I checked the monitor every day. But so much else was going on that pretty soon I forgot about it."

He turned his head and looked out toward the ocean. "Might have been eight or nine days that went by before I rechecked it. When I did, at first I doubted my own interpretation. It appeared that the database containing the code had been accessed a week earlier, December thirtieth."

"What does that mean?"

He turned toward her. "I don't know. I ran a complete systems check and found nothing to suggest a virus. I figured maybe it was a glitch and did nothing. But from then on, I went back to checking the monitor daily."

His fingers continued to weave restlessly on his lap. "It was twelve days ago when I first discovered the break-in. There were no more attempts at access until a week later. Then the same thing. The security module that held the codes had been entered again."

"Had the codes for either placebo or analogs been altered?"

He lifted both hands in a gesture of futility. "Again, I don't know. I can't find out until I can access the security code myself. Which I can't, without Berkholt's password."

She let out a deep breath. "Shit!"

"I did use one precaution to protect the protocol against tampering. A week ago I froze the codes. Without security access I may not be able to read the codes, but as the Novar-3's systems operator, I can freeze them. After that, even if a virus—or a person—broke into the program, the codes couldn't be altered."

She thought of the expression of pain on Dr. Berkholt's face when she'd brought up the possibility of the program being interrupted. "Won't that stop the program?"

"No. Every patient will keep getting the same stuff he's been getting. All it means is that no new analogs can be given. Until the code's un-frozen, only the placebo or the three analogs already entered will be available." The lines in his forehead deepened. "Whatever happened is still going on, Karen. The security database has been entered the past three days in a row." He slowly shook his head. "This type of access pattern isn't the way a virus could function. It has to be a person."

She still wasn't certain she grasped the full significance, but his concern transmitted itself sharply to her. "Who could've done it, Hank?"

He shook his head helplessly. "Whoever did it would have needed some luck and a lot of computer expertise."

She pressed her lips together. "I'm afraid there's a lot of computer expertise running around the hospital."

His face became more troubled. "You're speaking of Dr. Berkholt?"

"More than him, I'm afraid." She repeated what Bill had said about Ruiz's expertness with the system. Then she took a deep breath. "Ron Olsen had a degree in computer science before he started medical school."

"Olsen?" Hank stiffened.

It took a moment for his eyes to soften. Then he smiled sadly. "I didn't realize I'd still react so much."

She gazed at him. How good it would be to sit again on the living-room couch and rest her head against his shoulder! "This protocol has been jinxed from the beginning, Hank."

"For us it has, Karen."

She stared out at the ocean. "Perhaps we gave up too quickly."

"I've wondered about that many times," he said.

She turned to face him. "You've lost too much weight. What do you say we meet at the apartment tonight and let me do some cooking?"

He didn't answer for a moment. "I'd like that," he said slowly.

His hesitation bothered her. "Eight o'clock?" she said.

"All right." His fingers wove patterns on his lap. "About the protocol?"

"Yes, about the protocol," she said.

"I wanted you to know about the break-in before I told anyone else. But I think we should go to Dr. Berkholt."

"That's not simple. I've already been trying to reach him. Sigrid hasn't seen him for the last three days."

"Oh," Hank said.

"I could contact Dean Patterson and ask him to check on both keys."

"Why Dean Patterson?"

"You told me both keys to the safe-deposit drawers that held the passwords were in his bank vault."

She saw a flash of fear cross his eyes before he answered. "I forgot," he said.

She shrugged. "His office would be closed this late on Friday afternoon, anyway."

He looked away from her. "I think we'd better wait, Karen."

"We'll have to wait until Monday."

"I mean, about us getting together at the apartment tonight."

"Oh. Maybe you're right. Maybe the apartment isn't a good idea. Why don't we just go out to dinner after we're both through work?"

"I'd forgotten. I'm tied up."

Her stomach knotted. "Is there someone else?"

His eyes widened. "No. There's no one else!"

"For God's sake, what's wrong, Hank? What's wrong that you haven't told me?"

"I—I can't explain yet."

Karen stood up and spoke coldly. "All right. It's your decision. Call me as soon as you feel you're ready to explain." She started walking toward her car.

He followed. She turned to face him when she reached her car. Her throat tightened. He looked terrible. His face was drawn, haggard. "Hank, please. What's the matter?"

He took both her hands. She felt his tremble. "Karen, I promise I'll explain—as soon as I can. But in the meantime, be careful. Something's going on that I don't understand. Something heavy." He swallowed. "Until we know more, don't trust anybody. Be careful. Please."

40

She'd turned onto the ramp and picked up speed as she entered the four-lane freeway. Only all the cars were coming *at* her! A warning bell sounded. Too late—she'd taken the wrong way up the offramp! She desperately twisted the steering wheel and headed for the safety lane in the center, but a truck hurtled down on her. The bell rang again, louder.

She sat up, gasping. The phone rang a third time. She grasped for it, knocked it off the hook, retrieved it from the floor.

"I would like to speak to Dr. Formaker."

Karen struggled to wake up and place the voice. "I am Dr. Formaker. Who is this?"

"Doctor, you must stop him. It is too late for me, but you must put an end to it."

"Ms. Wagoner! Are you ill?"

"Yes. I am ill." The resigned note in her voice was more chilling than its former icy disdain had been.

"I'll come by."

"There will be no point in that, doctor. My illness cannot be cured. I would like, however, to see that others are spared."

"What are you talking about?"

"The virus, doctor. The virus that you and the doctor from the government laboratory are looking for. The disease that is robbing me of my mind. You must stop Dr.—Dr.—" Her voice caught. "The foreign doctor who brought it here."

"Dr. Ruiz?"

"Yes, Dr. Ruiz. You must find the incubator that he took from his laboratory."

Karen caught her breath. "What did he do with it?"

"I don't know." She paused, then continued sadly. "If I once knew, I no longer remember. You must find it and stop him."

"Please, Ms. Wagoner, let me come over."

"No, doctor. But would you speak to Dr. Berkholt for me?"

"About what?"

"Tell him—tell him I tried. Tell him I did everything I could to save his mother."

"What?"

"I tried to keep her alive. He won't speak to me. He won't take my calls."

Karen knew without asking. She was aghast that she'd been so blind, but she had to hear it from Wagoner. "Who was his mother?"

Wagoner stammered. "She was—" She gave a low moan. "Oh God, I can't remember her name."

The name escaped Karen's lips as if someone else had said it: "Henrietta Lee." Her grip loosened on the phone, and it almost dropped. Once again she saw Dr. Berkholt sitting desolately with his head in his hands at the abandoned Boy Scout camp. That had been the day after her death.

"Yes, Henrietta Lee. But that's not why I'm giving up. I do not wish to become like the others. I cannot let myself become like the others."

Karen broke out of her daze. "Ms. Wagoner, wait! Wait until I get there!"

"Don't let him think ill of me, doctor. Tell him that I tried."

The receiver went dead.

Karen clicked it. The dial tone answered.

She grabbed her address book and dialed Wagoner's private number at the hospital.

No answer.

She hung up and dialed the switchboard. "Lillian, phone Ms. Wagoner at her home for me."

She paced the floor in front of the desk while she waited.

"No one answers," the operator said.

"Then get someone to check her office. She's sick."

"She hasn't been here since Friday," the operator said. "Dr. Formaker, it's barely seven Sunday morning."

Karen gritted her teeth. She hadn't thought to ask Wagoner where she was calling from. "Have someone check her office anyway." She hung up, changed from her house shoes, ran to her car.

Minutes later, she pulled to a stop outside Collier Hospital and dashed in the front entrance.

"Like I said, she's not here," the operator said.

Karen took time to catch her breath. "Maybe she left something in her office that'll help locate her. I'll take a look."

The Sunday supervisor had come up. "I checked it out. Miss Wagoner's office is locked."

"Oh, shit!" Karen groaned. She faced the nursing supervisor. "She never keeps it locked. She's there. We've got to break in."

The supervisor looked at her curiously. "You and she have the only master keys."

Karen took off at a run down the central corridor, threw open the door to her own office, unlocked her desk, fumbled in the side drawer, came out with a key ring. With the supervisor trailing behind her, she ran the short distance to Wagoner's office.

She fitted the key. The lock was stuck. She pushed hard, gave the key a wrench, and turned the knob.

She threw open the door and took only a couple of steps forward.

Sybil Wagoner lay stretched out on the floor. The lampshade had been removed from her desk lamp. Dangling from the lampshade post was an empty IV bottle. Its tubing ended in a needle in Wagoner's arm. Her face was a mottled blue-white. Her eyes, pupils wide and black, stared at the ceiling.

Numbly, Karen picked up one of six neatly arranged empty vials on the desktop: POTASSIUM CHLORIDE 20 MILLIEQUIVALENTS. She looked again at the empty IV. All six ampules had run in undiluted. Silently, she handed one of the ampules to the supervisor.

By rote, she reached for the stethoscope on Wagoner's bookcase and crouched down. She listened for a few seconds to the silent chest, then wearily stood up and replaced the stethoscope where she'd found it. She turned and faced the small gathering of stunned, open-mouthed staff who'd gathered outside the doorway.

While Karen awaited the arrival of the detective from West L.A. Homicide, her eyes scanned the walls of Wagoner's office. Diplomas: bachelor's from Occidental; RN from Queen of Angels; master's in nursing from USC. One painting—a still-life of a basket of oranges and grapes. No photographs.

She checked the desktop for a note. None. Everything was carefully arranged, as if Wagoner had tidied up for visitors. She opened the shallow top drawer of the desk. Two pens, four sharpened pencils, calipers, dental floss, measuring tape. Everything was perfectly in place.

She opened a side drawer to dividers that held rubber bands, paper clips, staples, small index cards. She pulled open the file drawer beneath.

In the back, behind the last carefully indexed file, was a notebook. She lifted it out.

It was a scrapbook. The black leather cover was cracked and weathered. She opened it and stared at the eight-by-ten color photograph on the first page.

Three people stood in the foyer of a building. The woman in the center was still beautiful, but there was something about her—the facial stiffness, the expressionless eyes, the subtle line of demarcation halfway down the neck—that suggested that the passage of years had been camouflaged by plastic surgery. There was no question that this was the same woman she'd seen on the jacket of the book *Henrietta, the Blond Siren.*

Of the two who stood on each side of Henrietta, one was a woman in a starched white nurse's uniform, the other a man in a three-piece, pinstripe navy suit. The man's face caught her immediately. Arnold Berkholt was erect and imposing. The same penetrating eyes gazed at her from the photo. Not a trace of gray showed in his carefully parted, dark brown hair.

Nor was there any question of the identity of the tall, raven-haired, stern-faced nurse.

A date was imprinted on the lower edge of the photo: AUGUST 17, 1973. *Dr. Berkholt and Wagoner go back fifteen years!*

She turned the page and thumbed through the scrapbook. It was filled with newspaper and magazine clippings: Arnold Berkholt's first isolation of CRH; his arrival at the medical school from his last post at the University of Chicago; his appointment as chairman of endocrinology; seven pages of photos and stories of him receiving the Nobel prize for his CRH work; his taking over as chairman of the board of Cinema Acres.

Karen closed the scrapbook and replaced it in the file drawer.

She stepped around the desk and gazed once more at the still body on the floor. She'd asked the staff not to move or alter anything until the detective arrived. Except for the bluish mottling, Wagoner in death looked little different from Wagoner in life.

Karen slowly shook her head as she thought of the loneliness in which this strange, rigid woman had spent her life. Had Dr. Berkholt known of her idolization of him? She doubted it. Wagoner was a private person. How could he possibly have been aware of her fervor?

Again, she picked up the scrapbook and gazed at the picture on the first page. Fervor alone wouldn't have been enough to keep her serving him these past fifteen years.

She'd been in love with him.

Karen rechecked the date beneath the picture. Nineteen seventy-three was the year he had returned to Southern California from the Midwest.

Already well started on his road to academic fame, he'd come back to his old home territory. Was it Henrietta Lee's illness that had brought him back? Henrietta had been eighty at her death—she'd have been sixty-five in this picture.

What about Wagoner? Again, she checked Wagoner's diplomas. Bachelor's; 1952. RN; 1954. Assuming she was twenty-one for her bachelor's, she'd have been forty-two in the picture.

Something bothered her about the photograph, and she studied it again.

She snapped her fingers. The eyes! That expression on Henrietta's face wasn't just from face-lifts. At sixty-five, she was already afflicted with Alzheimer's. That was when Sybil Wagoner had entered the picture—it was she who'd been charged to buffer the failing Henrietta from her adoring fans—and to preserve the identity of Henrietta's son from the rest of the world.

When Collier Hospital had opened seven years ago, Sybil Wagoner had been its chief nurse. Henrietta may have been the first patient.

Solemnly, she replaced the scrapbook in the file drawer. She sat quietly in Wagoner's chair. She heard the tick of the desk clock, the low-pitched hum of the heater vent, footsteps passing in the hallway outside the door.

She didn't like the feeling of being here. Ghosts had already invaded the room.

She'd wait for the detective in her own office. She rose and was just stepping around the body when a man appeared in the doorway.

He was short, a little pudgy, with the wide-based stance of someone who'd once been fat. He had sagging jowls and a spiky Einstein-like shock of gray hair. He wore a shapeless tweed sport jacket, and his thin navy-stripe tie was askew. "I was told to look for Dr. Formaker."

"I am Dr. Formaker."

"Pritchard," he said. "Frederick Pritchard, from Homicide." He took in Wagoner's body on the floor with all the affect of seeing a pair of shoes cluttering the carpet. He looked back at Karen, bemused.

"Thank you for coming out, detective. When I phoned the coroner, his deputy said I should call your office."

"On a Sunday, folks in the coroner's office will tell you to call the Joint Chiefs of Staff if they think it'll put off their doing any extra work." He made a sucking sound, sort of like the grating crackle of a poorly tuned-in FM station. Karen blinked as she watched his cheeks draw in and his jowls disappear. They reappeared when he spoke. "What'd she get in the IV?"

"Potassium chloride. The same stuff we add to regular IV's. Given straight, it stops the heart."

He sucked in his cheeks again, and Karen felt the fine hairs on the back of her neck stand up at the sound. "Couple years ago," he said, "I had a case of a surgeon in Torrance who knocked off his wife with IV potassium after her hysterectomy. Tough as hell to trace. If he hadn't seen the avenging Angel Gabriel next time he stepped in the operating room, he'd have gotten away with it." He crouched down and lifted Wagoner's hand. It slapped the floor loudly when he let loose. "Already stiff, huh?"

"She's been dead at least forty-five minutes."

He absently closed her eyelids with his fingers. "Who found her?"

"I did. The door was locked when I got here." She glanced at her watch. "That was about seven thirty. I had the key and was the first one in. The nursing supervisor was with me."

He half-sat on the edge of Wagoner's desk. "Whaddaya figure happened?"

Karen told Pritchard about Wagoner's phone call. She omitted telling him about the scrapbook in the file drawer. She'd been guilty of enough invasion of privacy—he could find the scrapbook for himself. "Her behavior had been strange the past few days. I believe she thought she'd picked up a form of dementing brain disease and that she wanted to take her own life before she became too far gone to carry it out."

"You'd better go slow for me, doc. What's this dementing brain business?"

Karen sat down in Wagoner's desk chair. Actually, she was relieved to have a chance to talk to someone from the police. It was too late to hold back on any suspicions now. Dr. Berkholt would understand.

Pritchard listened wordlessly as she told him of the young patients who'd come down with what to all appearances was Alzheimer's, and the apparent focus of cases here at Cinema Acres. She told him of the precedent of an infectious dementia in the forms of kuru, Creutzfeldt–Jacob, and *Loucuras do Diabo.*

He sat for a moment sucking in his jowls as he digested what she'd said. "You're saying you've got the same worry the nurse here had—that she's picked up a bug from somewhere?"

Karen nodded.

"I'll ask you to write some of this out. My spelling would break down at Alzheimer's."

"Sure."

He grunted as he stood stiffly and stretched. "Looks like the coroner's people got their work cut out for 'em. If she's got an infection, with enough warning they should be able to find it."

Karen shook her head. "The autopsy might show the standard pathology features of Alzheimer's, but as far as infection goes, their routine cultures would be useless. We're not talking about any kind of infection that you're accustomed to even thinking of. We're talking about a rare bird called a slow virus, one that can't be seen on any microscope—not even an electron microscope. If it can be grown at all, it has to be grown in a medium of brain tissue. And the only way its infectiousness can be proved is by injecting the culture growth into another primate, then examining slices of its brain after it's had time to take effect."

Pritchard gave a dry laugh. "Doesn't sound like a job for *our* coroner's office."

"I'll tell you what they could do," Karen said. "I understand it's not unusual for the coroner to arrange for complex autopsies to be performed at a medical center. Our Dr. Fogelson has done many autopsies on the disease. If he could do the work at University Hospital morgue, we'd be assured of getting adequate studies. And Dr. Horlich, who's here from the CDC, could express specimens there."

"Arranging the autopsy here's no sweat." Pritchard gazed at the corpse at his feet. "If you find a bug growing in her brain, doc—where would you figure it came from? I wouldn't think any of your patients have recently been swinging from vines in the Amazon or New Guinea."

She told him about Alberto Ruiz.

When she finished, he sucked in his jowls. "Not much to go on, is there?"

"We might have more if we could get a search warrant for Dr. Ruiz's residence."

"You find hard evidence one of your patients has got a virus, doc, and I'll get you a warrant."

41

Monday morning. Will Hayes brought up his cart of coded vials from the microbiology lab. Extra staff came over from the other two Cinema Acres hospitals. Routine activities of Collier Hospital were again suspended while the analogs and placebos were administered to patients, and their codes entered in the double-blind data system.

There was one notable difference. Whenever the swollen, bustling ranks of workers passed the office of the chief of nursing, a hush came over them. It was as if the ghost of Sybil Wagoner were standing tall and stern in the doorway, frowning upon everyone who passed.

Repeatedly Karen checked the small computer room in the business office. She hadn't spoken to Hank since their meeting in Palisades Park three days ago. Mondays Hank always showed up. This morning passed, and he still hadn't shown.

Lauryn was wonderful. For days now she'd taken to complaining every minute—about the food, the crowded quarters, the hard water that wrecked her shampoos, the skimpy mirrors, the lack of closets. Felice had returned Saturday afternoon with a pepperoni pizza when Lauryn insisted she'd asked for mushroom and meatball. She threw the pizza at Felice and sent Frank out for another.

The protocol that had been approved by the Human Experimentation Subcommittee of the university's Ethics in Research Committee specified that treatment could be carried out only on inpatients at Collier Hospital. If Lauryn were to continue getting the analog—and by now Karen was certain she wasn't receiving the placebo—she'd have to stay.

Two days ago, Saturday, under full press and television coverage, Five Star Studios had wheeled a giant production trailer onto the parking lot. The trailer contained a makeup room, a fully equipped hairdressing room, and two walk-in closets. Fortuitously, room A-17 faced onto the parking lot, and within twenty-four hours studio carpenters created a connecting passageway to the trailer.

Bill Horlich became Alberto Ruiz's frequent companion, asking questions, peering over him in the lab, accompanying him to patients' rooms as he drew specimens. The little man appeared smaller than ever next to Bill's giant frame. He plodded through his work, never smiled, answered Bill with short retorts. The times his path crossed Karen's, he didn't look at her.

Before she left for the medical school, she checked one last time in the business office. Hank still hadn't shown.

She didn't reach the medical school until after three. Sigrid Higheagle looked harassed as she handed her a stack of messages. "Where the hell is Dr. B hiding out?"

"I haven't seen him in over a week, Sigrid. I was going to ask you the same thing."

"Last time he showed his face here was six days ago. A thousand phone calls are waiting, the publisher of the *Journal of Endocrinology* is screaming for an editorial he was supposed to send, the editor of Cecil's *Textbook of Medicine* is yelling for a chapter that's holding up publication, the board of regents is hounding me for a proposal for a grant—" She sat down heavily in her chair. "I gave up a perfectly good job in Outpatient Urology for this fucking job."

"I'll call you if I hear from him. By the way, have you heard from Hank Merrill?"

"He hasn't been around for weeks. I thought you two were on the outs."

"We've had our problems. I've been trying to reach him."

"If he shows up, I'll tell him."

Karen phoned Hank's office. She gave up on the twelfth ring. The answering machine wasn't even turned on.

She checked with the hospital operator. He'd left no messages.

There was no one else she could call.

Perhaps she'd find a clue in his office.

She took the elevator to the basement, and knocked on a door labeled BIOSTATISTICS.

She tried the door. It was unlocked.

The room was certainly familiar to her. One entire wall was hidden by floor-to-ceiling file cabinets. The rest of the wall space was covered with shelves filled with books, journals, stationery supplies. On the desk a personal computer was surrounded by piles of books, folders, and loose papers. A terminal to the university mainframe sat on a table next to the desk. Both computer screens were gray.

She tried the next door down the hall. It opened to a small room that smelled stale and unaired. Bedcovers were piled in a heap on a cot flush against the wall. Journals and papers littered two small tables. From the floor next to the bed she picked up the front section of the *Los Angeles Times* and checked the date. January 23. He'd last been here two days ago—the day after she saw him in the park.

She sat on the edge of the cot and stared blankly at the calendar on the opposite wall. Something was terribly wrong. All the time they'd lived together, Hank had never let a weekend pass without using his office. And then to have missed the morning of the injections.

He'd reacted almost with panic when she'd suggested that they get together. Why?

Could he still be angry about her night with Ron Olsen?

That wasn't anger she'd seen in his eyes. That was fear.

When she'd reached out for his hands, he'd backed away.

She caught her breath as it struck her. She'd seen the same look in Wagoner's eyes.

He thinks he's got the disease! He's afraid of giving it to me!

A frantic feeling filled her. She had to find him.

Her hands opened and closed at her sides. She had to talk to someone. Bill! She'd get hold of Bill!

She wove in and out through the traffic on San Vicente as she headed back to Collier Hospital. By the time she arrived, the injections had been completed. She checked with the interim nursing supervisor.

"Last I saw of Dr. Horlich, he was in the microbiology lab," the supervisor said.

The door to the lab was open. Bill stood at a counter pipetting a clear solution into a culture flask. He signaled to Karen with a raised finger.

She straddled a lab stool and waited.

He finished pipetting. When he looked at her, his face sobered. "What's wrong?"

"I'm very worried about Hank. This is the first Monday he's failed to show."

"Maybe with the program established, he doesn't think he's needed for each new set of injections."

"I went down to his office. He hasn't been there for two days. I—I've got to find him."

"He probably had to go somewhere. I'm sure he's okay, Karen. Hank's resilient."

"Bill, I'm almost certain Hank thinks he has the disease."

Bill blinked. "What disease?"

"Alzheimer's. Or our own variety of it."

He sat on a stool and blew out a deep breath. "Why?"

She told him of their last meeting in Palisades Park last Friday. "It didn't dawn on me until I sat in the crummy, makeshift bedroom next to his office. I can't forgive myself for not recognizing what was going on with him at the time."

Bill's voice was soft. "Do you think he was right, Karen?"

"I don't know, Bill. I'm scared."

He stood up and rested a hand gently on her shoulder. "Give me a minute to finish plating these cultures. Then we'll talk about where we go from here."

"I was supposed to pick Bev up for dinner. Let me tell her to go without me."

She found Bev sitting by herself in room A-17. "Where's Lauryn?"

Bev gestured toward the passageway to the studio trailer. "She spends practically every minute there." She studied Karen and frowned. "What's the matter?"

"I'm worried about Hank." She told Bev about their last conversation at Palisades Park.

Bev's forehead creased. "I see."

"I'll have to pass on dinner tonight. I've got to talk with Bill about what we can do."

"Hell, don't worry about that. Is there anything I can do?"

Karen smiled. "Thanks, Bev. I'll sure let you know if there is."

Lauryn's voice sounded from the passageway. "Who's there?"

"Your doctor," Bev called out.

"You're back already, Frankie Boy?" Lauryn entered the room. "Ohhh. Hello, Karen."

"Hello, Lauryn. You look spectacular."

She did. Her hair had changed to strawberry blond. It curled over her forehead and fell in swirls down the back of her neck. Her long eyelashes were violet. She wore a dress of crimson silk organza draped with mauve silk chiffon at the bust and hips. A side slit extended almost to her waist. A half-month's paycheck from Karen's recent Endocrine fellowship couldn't have bought that dress. "The only thing I can do with myself here," Lauryn grumbled, "is try to keep looking presentable."

"I can understand how old it must get," Karen said.

Bev stood up. "I know it feels like more, but it's only been a month."

"Whaddaya mean, *only* a month? It feels like a lifetime! When the hell am I getting out?"

"Lauryn, you're in the home stretch," Karen said. "At the rate you're going, you'll soon need no more treatments. But you were very sick. Just a little while longer."

Tears had come to Lauryn's eyes. "Listen, Karen, I know you've done a lot for me. I remember how terrible I felt when I was losing my mind. But I want to do things, don't you understand? I want to be with people again. *Real* people."

"You can have visitors," Karen said. "You're not restricted as to who comes to see you."

Lauryn waved her arm toward the hallway. "Bring people here? You think I want people I know to come see me in this place for crazies?"

Karen sighed. "If I could give you the treatment outside the hospital, I would. All I can say is that it won't be long."

"That's what I've been telling you," Bev said.

Lauryn turned away abruptly. She sat on the stool in front of the dressing table and studied her face in the mirror. She reached for a Kleenex and carefully wiped at a streak in her mascara. "How many more shots?"

Karen counted on her fingers. "Let's see. On a once-a-week basis, today would've been your sixth. I'd have to talk it over with the other doctors involved in the program, but I'd guess maybe a total of ten or eleven shots altogether."

Lauryn turned back to her, and her face brightened. "You mean, from the first one?"

Karen shrugged. "That's what it looks like at this stage."

"Does that include the first shot that nerd gave me?"

"Nerd?"

"The funny-looking guy with red hair and freckles who looks like he shouldn't have left the farm."

Karen suppressed a smile. "You've got to be talking about Will Hayes. He's in charge of giving all the shots here in Collier Hospital."

"I know *that!* I'm not talking about here. I'm talking about the shot he gave me before I got here."

"Lauryn, when anyone's been real sick, it's easy to remember things that happened after getting sick as if they'd happened earlier. That's not unusual. It's nothing to worry about."

"I'm not worrying, for chrissake! I'm telling you what happened. He gave me the shot when I was visiting my grandma. I sure haven't seen my grandma since I became a patient in this lousy hospital!"

A prickly feeling began to gnaw deep inside Karen. Lauryn's grandmother was a resident in one of the Cinema Acres cottages. Karen tried to keep her voice calm. "What kind of shot was it, Lauryn? Try to remember."

"I remember very well. It was one of those clinics where they get people all lined up. They give the shots to everyone staying here. The nerd asked me if I wanted to get one, as long as I was there with Grandma. I thought maybe it would keep me from catching colds so easy. So I let him give me the flu vaccine."

42

$\mathbb{B}$ev stared at Karen. "I don't know what's going on—but *something* just happened."

"I'll get back to you!" Karen ran from the room, took the stairs to the basement two at a time, and ran gasping into the microbiology lab. "Bill, the flu vaccine! Lauryn got the goddamned flu vaccine!"

Bill Horlich looked at her strangely. "That's very nice."

"No! She got the flu vaccine before she ever came here—before she ever got sick! Ruiz runs the flu vaccine clinic at Cinema Acres. Hayes gave her the flu vaccine!"

"Christ!" Bill jumped up from the chair, ran to the large refrigerator at the end of the central counter, threw open the door. He waved at the top shelves. "All I could see were the analog vials!" He crouched down, pulled box after box of flu vaccine vials from the bottom shelf. "I barely noticed these bastards!"

Karen crouched beside him and pulled out more vials. "Don't you see? It's the perfect vehicle! Everyone who lives in any of the divisions of Cinema Acres gets it. Everyone who works here is required to take it. And the boosters are repeated every fall. They even offer it to the medical center employees who're willing to come here for it." Her eyes widened. "Good God—the staff secretary called me last Monday and reminded me I was due for it! A clinic was moved up to Tuesday." She swallowed. "And I'd have taken it—except I couldn't get away from University Hospital until too late." She stared with horror at the vials in her hand.

Bill read the labels on vial after vial. "Three manufacturers—Merck, Lederle, and Fieldstone. Almost equal numbers of each." He shoved the vials back onto the shelf and in a few long strides was over at the computer terminal. "Give me your log-on ID number and password!"

In his rush, he made a typo on the password and had to reenter. The main menu lit up on the screen. He impatiently flipped through screen after screen until he reached PATIENT PROFILES. He selected the category of IMMUNIZATIONS. "Now give me names!"

"Duane Dreyer."

"Flu vaccine September twenty-first."

"Cynthia Frame."

"October twenty-eighth."

"Lauryn Hart."

"October twenty-eighth."

"Pete Paritski."

"December first."

Karen sat. "The son of a bitch found his 'suitable primate subjects.' "

Bill continued staring at the computer screen.

"Bill, is Sybil Wagoner on the list?"

He scrolled through the W's on the IMMUNIZATIONS list and shook his head. "She isn't in the protocol. No one would be listed other than patients admitted to Collier, or at least scheduled for admission here."

Karen slowly stood up. "I guess the same thing applies to Dr. Berkholt?"

Bill's brow wrinkled. "What 'same thing' are you talking about?"

"Did he get the flu vaccine?"

He scrolled back through the database. "Not listed either." He pursed his lips. "Are you worried about Dr. Berkholt coming down with the disease?"

"He's shown some uncharacteristic forgetfulness lately."

Bill whistled softly. "You've just raised the ante." He swiveled his chair around and faced her. "Did Ruiz conduct the flu vaccine clinics?"

"Ruiz was in charge, although Will Hayes did the actual running of the clinics. The three drug companies gave Ruiz a grant to study the immune responses to it—checking antibody levels afterward."

"Then Hayes himself gave the shots?"

"For the flu vaccine clinics, he gave all of them. For the analog injections at Collier, he gave some, but mostly he supervised the other nurses."

"Do you think he was in on it with Ruiz?"

"If all he did was give the shots, he wouldn't have had to know some had been changed. Ruiz could've made the substitution anytime." Karen chewed at her lip. "What about confronting Will?"

Bill shook his head. "He might unintentionally give it away to Ruiz. I don't want that bastard to have any warning that might cause him to fly the coop before we're ready."

Karen started to answer but stopped when she heard the ratchety creak of the doorknob. She and Bill both spun around.

The door opened. Alberto Ruiz stepped in.

He stopped abruptly inside the doorway. He wore a gray dacron lab coat that reached to his ankles. His necktie was pulled down loosely beneath the open collar of his white shirt.

Karen must have turned pale. "Are you all right, *doctora?*" Ruiz said.

She stood up. "I'm perfectly fine. I was just leaving."

"In truth, I come to look for Dr. Horlich, but I am pleased you are here, *doctora.* It ees well that I speak to both of you."

Numbly, Karen sat.

Ruiz pulled up a lab stool. "Dr. Horlich, you told me when we first met that you would be willing to make the facilities of your lab at the Centers for Disease Control available to me."

"That's true."

Ruiz turned toward Karen. "You have made it very clear that you suspect something irregular goes on." He moved his pursed lips from side to side as he looked at her. "I, too, find something unusual. That ees why I wish to take Dr. Horlich up on his offer."

Neither Karen nor Bill spoke.

"Something I cannot explain ees happening with the influenza vaccine."

Karen gasped. "What?"

Ruiz's forehead was deeply creased. "I was placed in charge of the influenza vaccine program when I came to Cinema Acres. Three manufacturers give us matching grants to study the immune responses to their vaccines. On thees latest series I have started checking antibody responses. That ees where the strange findings have shown up." He looked from Bill to Karen.

"Go on," Karen said hoarsely.

"We began giving the current batches of vaccine early in September. Two months later and again four days ago, when I checked antibody levels, I obtained the same results. For both Lederle and Merck, ninety percent of patients showed a good rise. For Fieldstone, none of the patients showed any effect.

"I did not believe the first results, but after the second series, I phoned Fieldstone and told my findings to the production director. He checked with four other facilities that are doing field studies on the same batch. Ninety percent of cases showed good antibody response." He gestured with both hands palms up. "Our results are like no others."

Karen stared at him. "Will your immunization records show whether particular patients got Fieldstone?"

Ruiz nodded. He propped himself up on a stool in front of the computer. The menus changed rapidly as his fingers probed the keyboard. He stopped at a menu and looked at Karen.

"Check for Dreyer, Frame, Paritski," she said.

Ruiz's eyes widened. He turned back to the computer. "*Sí*. Dreyer, Frame, Paritski—all received Fieldstone."

Karen's hands tightened at her sides. "Does your vaccine program list even those who aren't in the protocol?"

"The influenza program ees independent of the protocol."

"Is Sybil Wagoner on it?"

Ruiz scrolled. "Fieldstone—January thirteenth."

Karen could no longer hold off the question that screamed at her. "Hank Merrill?"

Ruiz scrolled again. " 'Henry Merrill: Fieldstone—January thirteenth.' " When he turned back to Karen, his face became grave.

She'd known before she asked. Still, with his answer, she felt as if the floor had caved in beneath her feet. She dropped back into her chair.

Bill moved over and rested a hand on her shoulder. "Dr. Ruiz, have you handled the Fieldstone vials any differently from the others?"

"I store them all in the same refrigerator. I bring them all at the same time from Dr. Berkholt's lab."

"From Berkholt's lab? I thought the drug companies sent them to you."

"I do the studies, but the grant is to Dr. Berkholt. The shipments go to him. I bring them here from his laboratory."

Bill reached for the phone on Karen's desk. His face set, he dialed.

"Virology—extension 7223," he said.

The muscles above each side of Alberto Ruiz's jaw moved up and down as he watched.

"Horlich here. Let me speak to Brad." He pulled a ballpoint pen from his pocket and absently clicked the point. "Brad—about the batch of vials I sent from L.A. Do you remember some flu vaccines?"

His grip tightened on the phone. "Were you able to identify the viral material?"

As he listened, all expression left his face.

In a low voice he said, "Thanks. I guess we'd still better go ahead with a few primate inoculations, but see if Biochem can pin it down further."

Bill hung up, and looked from Ruiz to Karen. "Nothing out of the ordinary on Lederle or Merck. Fieldstone wasn't a vaccine."

"I still do not understand." Ruiz spoke even more slowly and cautiously than usual.

"We've just determined that every young patient who was struck with

Alzheimer's over the past three months had received the flu vaccine at your clinics. Friday I expressed samples of all the vials in your refrigerator to the CDC. The flu vaccines were among them."

Ruiz clutched the arms of his chair and stared at Bill. "What virus did they find?"

"They've already checked three blot electrophoretic patterns. There was no trace of RNA or DNA in any of the Fieldstone vials."

"Then it could not be a virus," Ruiz said bewilderedly. "A virus would leave some trace of RNA."

"They found a peptide," Bill said.

Karen leaped up from her chair. *"What?"*

Now, Bill looked bewildered. "A peptide. They found a peptide."

"What kind of peptide?"

"Biochemistry is working on it now. It has a 41-amino acid chain."

"Oh, no!" Karen groaned.

Both Bill and Ruiz stared at her.

"A forty-one-amino-acid peptide," she said in a hushed voice. "That's the basic CRH formula." She swallowed. "The Fieldstone vials don't contain flu vaccine. They contain a goddamned CRH analog."

43

The scene in the basement microbiology lab could have been a still photograph. Ruiz was the first to speak. "The flu clinics started in September."

"Then the first CRH analogs were injected three months before the protocol ever began," Bill Horlich said in an awe-filled voice. "They were the means for *spreading* the disease."

Ruiz shook his head. "I do not understand how it could happen."

"The vials must have left Fieldstone intact," Karen said, "because they're from the same batch that tested out normal in four other facilities. The substitution had to have taken place either at the endocrine lab at University, or here in this laboratory." She pressed her lips together. "Back in September, only three people involved in the program had unlimited access to the vaccines after they left Fieldstone labs. Here at Collier, only you, Dr. Ruiz."

His small, sharp features were pinched, his cheeks sunken. At that moment his white face brought to her mind one of the laboratory mice. "I have no experience with the analogs. That ees not my field."

Karen continued. "And at the endocrine lab, myself and Dr. Berkholt."

Ruiz stared from Karen to Bill. He wiped his hand across his forehead. "Dr. Berkholt," he said softly.

Bill repeated, "Berkholt."

Karen took in a deep breath. "I must find Hank."

She didn't recall leaving the laboratory or climbing the stairs. Bill Horlich followed her into her office.

He gazed out the window while she phoned Hank's medical school office, the hospital operator, their apartment.

She laid down the phone. "I'm going by the apartment," she said.

"There was no answer when you called."

"He might not have been able to answer."

"I'll go with you," Bill said.

Karen had last been to the apartment eight days ago to pick up a jacket to replace the one she'd left at the deserted Boy Scout camp. As she turned off the alley into the parking shed and saw Hank's two-door Tercel, she first felt a surge of relief. She cried out, "Bill, that's his car!"

Her relief was short-lived. His windshield was dusted over, as if the car hadn't been driven for days. She thought of the many times she'd phoned and heard only her own message on the answering machine. Why hadn't he answered the phone?

She didn't want to think of the answer. She parked in the nearest stall and took off at a run. Bill loped in long strides behind her. She ran up the stairs to the second floor, jammed her key into the lock, threw open the door.

The room smelled stale and musty. On a table against the far wall the screen to Hank's computer was lit. She stumbled as she ran to it and grabbed for the back of the couch to catch herself. When she reached the computer, she stared at the screen. Black letters on a green background spelled out the chilling message, YOUR ID NUMBER IS NOT RECOGNIZED.

Bill followed her into the short hallway. The bedroom door was open. "Hank!"

He lay on his back, sprawled loosely on top of a wrinkled blanket. He wore a grayish-white T-shirt and wrinkled khaki pants. His eyes were closed, mouth agape. His chest didn't move.

Her legs buckled. *I'm too late!*

Then he gave a deep, gasping breath, followed by a sequence of rapid breaths. She fell to her knees by the bed, wrapped her arms around him, pressed her face to his cheek. His skin was hot and dry. A sweet acetone-like odor came from his breath.

"Hank, say something! Please!"

His eyelids opened. Sunken eyes gazed vacantly at her before they closed again.

Bill crouched beside her. He lifted a fold of Hank's skin between two fingers—it wrinkled like parchment. "He's badly dehydrated," he said quietly.

Karen ran to the kitchen, returned with a glass of water. She cradled Hank's head in one arm, held the glass to his mouth. Water ran in. Hank choked, coughed feebly. The water trickled out.

Bill lifted him in his arms as if he were a rag doll and headed for the door. "Let's not waste time waiting for an ambulance," he said.

*   *   *

The first liter of IV fluids was poured in during the half hour after Hank arrived in the emergency room. By the time his gurney was wheeled into room 504 in University Hospital, he'd finished receiving his second liter and had awakened enough to take several swallows of apple juice and tapioca pudding.

Oxygen hissed through vinyl prongs into his nostrils at three liters per minute. Wires from electrodes on his chest led to a small transistor box that relayed each heartbeat to a telemetry monitor on the cardiac floor. Her eyes kept returning to the EKG monitor screen above his bed. His heart so far was behaving, but during the rapid electrolyte changes of rehydration, rhythm abnormalities could be life-threatening.

Whenever Hank's eyes opened they searched for Karen. They followed her around the room, settled on her when she sat on the side of the bed, closed briefly when she held his hand. Only for a moment was the grave expression on his face broken by a trace of a smile when she bent forward and kissed his parched lips.

He answered her in short phrases.

"Does anything hurt?"

"No."

"Are you thirsty?"

"Yeah."

"Hank, why didn't you call me?"

"I don't know."

"Do you know me?"

"Yeah."

"Please—what's my name?"

Wrinkles deepened in his forehead.

"I forgot," he said.

The medical resident on Five West had been Karen's intern during his two-month rotation through Endocrinology two years ago. Now he fell back into the same role, running all test results through her. When Hank had been brought in, his blood pH was down to 7.20, reflecting an acidosis from dehydration approaching the severity Karen had many times seen in impending diabetic coma.

The resident came to Karen with the second set of arterial blood studies. "His pH is only up to seven twenty-five. He got two ampules of bicarbonate in the ER. Should we give him two more?"

"Where are the last electrolytes?" Karen asked.

He handed her a computer readout.

Karen scanned the sheet. "His anion gap is improving. The big need is

still hydration. Correcting the pH in a hurry runs too much risk of cere-
bral edema."

"Should I keep up the half-normal saline, then?"

"You're handling it fine," she said. "Keep monitoring the potassium
hourly until he's out of it."

Hank had received his sixth liter of IV fluids in as many hours before
Karen left his room. By then, when he fell back asleep, his breathing was
slow and easy, no longer the deep, labored breath of acidosis.

Bill Horlich and Mike Werner waited for Karen in the small fifth-floor
conference room. The three of them sat at the round central table. "He
must not have gotten out of bed to get anything to eat or drink," Bill
said.

"It has to be at least thirty-six hours since he's taken any liquids,"
Karen said. "I'm sick at the thought of what we'd have found if we'd
gotten there a few hours later." She turned to Werner. "Mike, do you
think he recognized us?"

"He knew you, Karen. He wouldn't take his eyes off you. He might not
be able to remember your name, but at some basic brain level he responded to your presence as to no one else's." Werner frowned and
shook his head. "It still hasn't fully sunk in. Only a week and a half ago, I
consulted him about statistical methodology for my multiple sclerosis
paper. And he was his same clear, succinct self." He turned to Bill. "I
finally became convinced that Karen's suspicions were right—that whatever's been going on at Cinema Acres had to be in the line of an infectious dementia. There's simply no naturally occurring Alzheimer's that
could progress as fast as we've been seeing. And now you both tell me it's
not a virus?"

"I couldn't believe it either," Bill said. "But after analyzing Ruiz's
records, there's no question in my mind that the Fieldstone product was
the vehicle for introducing the disease. And my entire team at the CDC
assures me that the Fieldstone vials we sent them contain no virus breakdown products."

"Does that apply to the entire supply?"

"We sent them only eight vials of each company's product, but I'm
certain we'll find the same thing for all the rest. I've asked the local
health service to confiscate all vials of flu vaccine in the hospital until
they're checked out. A full team from Fieldstone Pharmaceuticals is ar-
riving tonight. If word of this leaks out, it will virtually shut down their
nationwide operation, even though flu vaccine is but a small part of their
product line."

Bill and Werner's words formed but a dim backdrop to the thoughts
that were racing through Karen's mind. Hank was out of immediate

danger from dehydration—but at the rate of his brain deterioration, in less than a week he'd be where Pete Paritski was when he had to go on the ventilator. A feeling that approached panic grew inside of her. She was running out of time.

She had to find Berkholt. Her heart told her that he couldn't have orchestrated the tragedies that had unfolded in the past few months. But her mind told her there was no other explanation.

"We've got to find Berkholt."

She sat straight up with a start. "What?"

Both Mike Werner and Bill were looking at her strangely. It was Werner's voice she'd heard. "I said we've got to get hold of Berkholt," Werner repeated.

"His secretary hasn't heard from him for six days," Karen said.

"He didn't leave any word about where he's gone?"

Karen shook her head.

"It's mind-boggling to think that he's behind this," Werner said. "Could he have gone mad?"

"It's possible that he has the disease," Karen said quietly.

Werner's mouth fell open. "What do you mean?"

She told him of Berkholt forgetting her name at the press conference, of the fear in his eyes, of Fogelson's questions about his behavior.

Werner slowly shook his head. "It grows more bizarre—and gruesome —as it unfolds."

"Where does all this leave us with Alberto Ruiz?" Bill said.

"Ruiz has never worked with the analogs," Karen said. "He was as surprised as we were at the contents of the Fieldstone vials. I don't think he would have come to us with the information if he'd tampered with them."

"I agree," Bill said reluctantly. "I'm still not convinced he doesn't have the *Loucuras do Diabo* cultures. But it's academic now that we know we're not dealing with an infectious disease." He looked at Karen. "I'm afraid it's back in your ball park."

Karen spoke slowly and deliberately. "It is possible to reverse the analog-caused disease. It happened with the X-ray technician and with Lauryn Hart. I have to learn what they received in time to save Hank."

Werner sighed. "That brings us back to Berkholt."

"Yes," she said heavily. "It all seems to come back to Berkholt."

44

$\mathbb{S}$igrid still couldn't reach Berkholt. Neither Percy Barnes nor the endocrine lab technician had seen him for a week. His answering service had no word from him.

Karen spent almost every moment in Hank's room. By now, he was taking food by mouth, his skin turgor had returned, and his urine output was up. His eyes followed her.

But he didn't know her name.

In a moment of desperation, she asked him, "Hank, think hard. Can you remember the password?"

"What?"

"The password," she pleaded. "The password to the CRH protocol."

He looked at her blankly.

She found herself shouting, as if she could break through to him if she could shout loud enough. "The password!"

His eyes melted as he stared at her helplessly.

She sobbed and buried her head against his shoulder.

She had so much to find out, and so little time left to do it.

Why had Berkholt used the flu vaccine as a clandestine route for giving the analogs when only a few months later the protocol would begin?

Why had the analogs *caused* the disease they were designed to *treat?*

Above all, why had some, like Lauryn, improved? If she could understand that, she'd have a chance to save Hank.

An answer, if there were one, had to rest with the analogs themselves.

Late that night, after Hank had settled into a solid sleep, she headed for her eighth-floor office. She rummaged through a file drawer filled with her CRH work from the year in Berkholt's laboratory and pulled out folders containing some of her early work with the analogs.

She opened one labeled RAT BRAIN CONCENTRATIONS.

Thirty-two analogs. All of them were coded and registered in the Novar-3 program, but only three were in the protocol. She sifted through the file, selected the data sheets for those three, and laid them out on the desk.

ANALOG NINE: heavy concentration in brains of rats sacrificed at ten hours, almost none left in brain tissue at twenty-four hours, none at one week. By far the shortest acting.

ANALOG FIFTEEN: heavy brain concentrations at ten hours, still heavy at twenty-four hours, one week, and two months. Very long-acting.

ANALOG TWENTY-SEVEN: brain concentrations only half those of Fifteen, but like Fifteen the concentrations were maintained for at least two months.

She closed the folder and gazed across the room. There'd been nothing from the preliminary rat studies to suggest that the analogs would cause dementia. But the lack of a clue to how they'd affect humans wasn't hard to explain—Alzheimer's is primarily a disease of the higher centers of the brain cortex, which is barely developed in rats.

She thought back to Fogelson's bombshell about the receptor studies on Duane's brain. The answer had to lie in that direction.

The receptors.

She and Berkholt had worked to design CRH analogs that could do what CRH couldn't—pass from blood into brain. They had adequately proved that the analogs in the protocol could do just that.

They hadn't proved that any of the analogs would perform the same functions in the brain as CRH itself. The protocol at Collier Hospital had been meant to furnish that information.

What happened after the analogs reached the brain? If they did what they were designed to do, they had found their way into the CRH receptors on the surface of the brain cells.

And filled them.

She pressed her knuckles to her mouth. What if the analogs then didn't function? What if they filled every available CRH receptor on the brain cells but didn't carry out the vital nerve functions of CRH? There'd be no way the victim's own native CRH could work if there were no open receptors for it to fill. If the analog didn't function—and it blocked all the receptors so that the victim's CRH couldn't function—*then dementia would result!*

Just as carbon monoxide poisons red blood cells by filling their oxygen receptors so that oxygen can't attach, so the analogs filled the CRH receptors so that the patient's own CRH couldn't work.

That's how the analogs had caused the disease!

She rose and paced the floor. If that were the case, why had a few patients improved?

She snapped her fingers as she remembered an accidental finding in her work in endocrine lab. She plunged back into the file cabinet, rifled through the top drawer, slammed it shut, pulled open the drawer beneath. From a hanging file labeled ABANDONED STUDIES, she pulled out a folder.

She opened it. When she'd goofed up on this particular rat experiment eighteen months ago, she could easily have thrown the results away. During the analog studies she'd mislabeled one rat and injected it a second time. When she sectioned the brain one week later, it had contained no measurable analog. She'd discarded it from the series after she realized that the rat had been mistakenly injected twice.

But its CRH receptors had been open!

What had she given it? She ran her finger down the first data sheet and stopped. The initial injection had been Analog Fifteen, which in all other studies had filled the rat brain receptors and kept them filled for the two months the experiment was followed.

She moved on to the second data sheet. Even before she came to the analog, she knew what answer she'd find.

There it was. Analog Nine. The one that was so short-acting that she'd questioned whether it belonged in the protocol.

She sat back in her chair. Her lips tightened. She hadn't even told Berkholt of this aborted experiment. It had just been a fluke, an error in protocol to be discarded.

Nine was the answer. The most active of the CRH analogs in concentrating in rat brain tissue, it had washed out and replaced the Analog Fifteen that had filled the receptors from the first injection. Then with its lifetime of less than twelve hours, it had disappeared.

Leaving CRH receptors open again.

She took a deep breath. That was what had happened to Lauryn. The analog she'd been given under the guise of the flu vaccine had poisoned the CRH receptors of her brain cells by filling them so that her own CRH couldn't function. The injection she was receiving at Collier Hospital had washed out the first analog, clearing the receptors. And it had been short-acting enough to then disappear and allow her own native CRH to function.

Lauryn had received Analog Nine.

She had to get Analog Nine for Hank. While there was still time. Before the poisoned brain cells made the transition from reversible receptor blockage to irreversible destruction.

She bit her lip. Although the existing supply of analogs was plentiful, all of it was coded by the computer. If she gave an unidentified one to Hank, chances were overwhelming that it would hasten his death.

Nor could she obtain a new supply. No new analogs had been produced in the endocrine lab for four months. To produce a fresh supply of Nine would require weeks of time as well as Dr. Berkholt's expertise. Neither was available to her.

She must find a way to break into the protocol's security code.

She had to do it without the passwords. Hank couldn't remember his. And even if she could find Berkholt in time, it was unlikely she could get his password from him.

What was left?

Ron.

Ron Olsen could do it.

She phoned him.

His voice was bleary. "Wha—what?"

"I need your help, Ron. I need it desperately. How soon can you meet me over at Collier?"

He completed a yawn. "Karen, my love. I'm always excited to hear from you—but do you realize what time it is?"

"Ron—please."

He groaned. "All right. I'll be in your office in about forty-five minutes."

He strode in through her open door and sprawled in the chair across from her. "Any other hour, and I'd think you'd finally succumbed to my lovestricken pleas. But at five in the morning, I suspect there might be other motives."

"Ron, you have to help me break into the security codes of the protocol."

He lifted his brows. "Can I believe what I just heard from the same lips that lectured me not long ago about waiting for 'statistically significant patterns'?"

"I was deluded. The protocol's meaningless. The analogs we're using to treat the disease have been causing it."

Olsen sat up straighter in his chair. "You realize that I don't understand a word you just said?"

She took a deep breath. "Berkholt handed us a program based on an elaborate lie." She went on to describe the function of CRH receptors, Fogelson's findings of the filled receptors on autopsy material, and her own conclusions from her early CRH laboratory data.

Olsen's face was sober. "Have you confronted Berkholt?"

"No one's seen him for a week. It's as if he's disappeared from the face of the earth."

"At least you could get one of the two passwords from your ex—I mean, Merrill."

She struggled to keep her voice level. "Hank *has* the disease. He was given one of the dementia-causing analogs. He can't even remember my name, much less the password." She swallowed. "He'll die unless I can break the code and find Analog Nine to give him."

Olsen looked at her incredulously. "How the hell did he get one of the analogs?"

"The same way as everyone else. At one of the Collier Hospital flu vaccine clinics. Berkholt substituted analogs for some of the flu vaccines."

Olsen's eyes widened. "You mean Ruiz's clinics?"

She nodded. "The ones that Will Hayes administered."

He leaped to his feet. "Oh, my God!"

She was baffled by his response. "What's going on?"

"I—I took the flu vaccine at last week's clinic!"

Karen stared at him. His face had gone pale. Drops of sweat covered his forehead. His lips trembled as he spoke. "I'm as good as dead."

She felt hopeless. "Ron, Ruiz checked over the Fieldstone list and didn't mention your name."

He fell back into his chair and buried his face in his hands.

She stood up and leaned forward with her hands planted on the desk. "Can't you hear me? Ruiz looked up the list of those who got Fieldstone! He didn't mention your name!"

He looked up at her through splayed fingers. His eyes were red. "What do you mean?"

"Only the Fieldstone vials had the analogs. Lederle and Merck are clean. You probably got one of them."

"I might not have gotten the disease?" He sounded dazed.

"For Christ's sake, that's what I'm trying to tell you!" She hadn't meant to shout and lowered her voice. "Let's go down to the microbiology lab."

He stared at her a moment longer, then leaped up and dashed through the door.

By the time she reached the basement lab, Ron was shaking the knob to the locked door. "He keeps the goddamned place locked!"

"I've got a key." She stepped in front of him.

The lock clicked. The door opened. Olsen ran to the desk. He tore through papers on the desktop. "I can't find any fucking list!"

"He's got his immunization programs on the computer."

Ron nodded quickly. Breathing hard, he jammed a stool beneath him in front of the computer. His hands trembled as they ran over the keyboard. "Shit!" he muttered as he punched a wrong key. He swiped his hand across his forehead. Fine droplets spewed off into the air.

Menus flashed across the screen. INFLUENZA 1988 appeared. His breath came faster. A list of names filled the screen. He scrolled down.

He stopped in the O's. His hands dropped to his sides. "Thank God!" he gasped.

The screen read, RONALD OLSEN, LEDERLE.

His breath slowed. He wiped his sleeve across his eyes. His lips still trembled, but they shaped themselves into a smile.

"Ron, you have to help me save Hank," Karen said. "He'll die unless we can break the security code."

"I didn't get the disease," he said unbelievingly.

She grabbed him by his shoulders and shook him. "Listen to me! You've got to break the code to the protocol! I have to identify the analogs to save Hank!"

He blinked. The smile left his face. "I can't."

"What do you mean, you can't? You told me there was no such thing as a foolproof system! You have to try, damn you!"

His shoulders slumped. "I already tried."

"What?"

"I wanted to discredit Merrill. I thought I could present you with the name of Lauryn Hart's analog. But I couldn't break the code."

She backed off until she struck the counter edge. She leaned back against it. "Then there's nothing you can do?"

"Without the passwords, there's nothing anyone can do."

She took a deep breath. "I have to get the passwords."

At seven forty-five the next morning, Karen stood outside the office of Dean Brigham Patterson at the medical school.

She herself had had little personal contact with the dean. The last time she'd seen him had been at Duane's funeral, when he'd made his interminable eulogy. Still, he'd been kind enough to appear at both Susan and Duane's funerals. He alone had access to both passwords. He had to help her now.

The dean's secretary, a mildly overweight middle-age woman wearing a crisp, navy wool suit, showed up at eight. "Dr. Formaker," she said as she unlocked the door, "can I do anything for you?"

Karen's last contact with the woman had been five years before, when she was a senior in medical school. She'd come to her for help in switching an elective from surgery to radioisotopes. "I have to see Dean Patterson," she said.

"I hate to tell you what his schedule's like today. Come with me while I check his appointments."

Karen followed her in. The secretary pulled a loose-leaf binder from her desk and shook her head as she studied it. "Let's see. Maybe I can squeeze you in between the department heads' meeting at nine thirty and Congressman Rafferton at eleven. I'm not promising anything, but how about showing up here at ten forty-five?"

"It's an emergency," Karen said. "I'll wait."

"He won't like it."

"I'll face that when he comes." Karen pulled a chair close to the door to the dean's inner office and sat.

At 8:37, Dean Patterson strode through the door. He wore a three-piece gray flannel suit. Every strand of his flowing white hair was in place. "Dr. Formaker!" He looked from her to his secretary and frowned. "I don't remember an appointment with Dr. Formaker."

His secretary gave a put-upon glance toward Karen. "She doesn't have one."

Karen had jumped up from her seat. "It's my fault. I have to see you, Dean Patterson."

Patterson looked at his watch and gave a final scowl at his secretary. "Come in," he told Karen. "I'll expect you to keep it brief."

Karen sat across his desk from him. "It's about the CRH protocol. I understand that the keys to the bank vault drawers that hold the two passwords are in your keeping."

"That's correct. They're in my office safe. Dr. Berkholt handed me sealed envelopes with them before your program began."

Her throat tightened. "Dr. Berkholt handed you *both* envelopes?"

Patterson looked at her curiously. "Yes."

So he did have access to the keys before they were stored away! Her certainty of his betrayal became a twisting pain deep in her stomach. He'd known both passwords from the beginning. "Dr. Patterson, I'm here to ask that the protocol be broken."

He frowned. "I shall give you ten minutes to explain."

Karen spoke hurriedly. She told him about the increasingly young age groups involved in the disease. Of the death rate that had grown to twice what would be statistically expected and was still growing. Of the filled receptors on autopsies, the improvements in a few, the findings of a CRH analog rather than virus particles in the flu vaccines.

As she talked, Dean Patterson repeatedly looked at his watch. She was describing the discarded experiment in which the rat mistakenly received two analogs when he interrupted. "Have you told all this to Dr. Berkholt?"

"He knows about the young age groups and the death rates and the blocked receptors. I haven't told him of the altered flu vaccines. I—I haven't been able to find him."

"And how long has that been?"

"Since Tuesday before last—nine days."

Dean Patterson spoke condescendingly. "Surely, Dr. Formaker, you realize that Dr. Berkholt has many projects going. If he had enough faith in you to entrust you with the administration of the Collier Hospital project, it would hardly be unreasonable for him to expect you to fulfill those duties for a week in his absence. After all, he does have many other important projects that depend on him."

Karen's hands gripped the arms of her chair. Her voice rose. "You don't understand, Dean Patterson. Unless I can break into the protocol and find a certain analog, a thirty-one-year-old man—someone who is very close to me—will die of the disease."

Patterson smiled tolerantly. "Now I understand what's going on. It's so easy to let emotional involvement color objective judgment. One of the lessons you'll learn with maturity, Dr. Formaker, is to avoid being a doctor for someone you're involved with." He folded his hands together. "If you wish, I'll certainly speak to Dr. Berkholt about your young man's problem."

"I didn't make it clear! I'm speaking of Hank Merrill—the biostatistician here at the medical school who programmed the project! Please! You've got to help me save him."

Patterson looked at his watch and cleared his throat. "I have a meeting to make. Ask Dr. Berkholt's secretary when she'll be able to reach him. You can leave word for him to call me."

"Dean Patterson, we're running out of time! Hank Merrill will die!"

Patterson gave a deep sigh of forbearance. "Dr. Berkholt entrusted me with the keys to the passwords to ensure that the double-blind protocol could be penetrated only if either person with a password died." He leaned forward, and his voice hardened. "Now, Dr. Formaker—in case I haven't made it completely clear—I will tell you once and for all that I have no intention of releasing the key to the passwords as long as Dr. Berkholt is alive."

"Damn it, you won't even try to understand! Someone already has broken into the protocol! Dr. Berkholt is the only one who could have done it! He's the only one who could have tampered with the flu vaccine!"

Dean Patterson sprang up from his chair. His cold blue eyes flashed with fury. "Young woman, you've gone mad! If you'd told me the dementia had spread to you, I would find your wild tale easier to believe. You're demeaning Dr. Arnold Berkholt, a Nobel laureate, one of the most brilliant men ever to honor this faculty. He is responsible for more grants to this medical school than anyone in its history. Do you realize that your own position on this faculty is purely a result of Dr. Berkholt's recommendation?" He spat out his words. "And now you come here behind his back to ask me to help you sabotage his work!"

Karen's taut frame barely touched the edge of her chair. "You don't realize what's happening! The program was flawed from the beginning! Please, for the sake of God, at least come with me to the hospital and let me show you the data!"

His voice dropped. Each word was ice. "If you say one more word, I shall personally convene the Faculty Committee to see that you are discharged from the faculty and from all institutions affiliated with the medical school." He pointed to the door. "Now leave this office!"

45

Berkholt knew both passwords.

He was the only avenue left to her. And he'd disappeared.

She drove from the medical center into Pacific Palisades. She'd gotten only an answering machine the times she'd phoned. She had little hope of finding him at home, but she had nowhere else to look.

If she found him, she'd confront him with the destruction wrought by the analogs. She'd force him to face the terrible toll among the unwitting guinea pigs who'd lined up at the flu clinics.

Hank was part of that list.

She'd plead with him, cajole him, threaten him, bargain with him. Whatever it took.

Yet the prospect of finding him in time to save Hank was slim. Sigrid still had no idea where he was, his answering service hadn't heard from him, the endocrine lab technician hadn't seen him for over a week.

Her hopes dwindled further as she neared the end of Mountainview Road and saw the empty carport. She walked up the path to the door and knocked.

She waited.

It had been futile from the beginning. She turned to leave.

The door jerked open.

She gasped.

"Where is he?" Will Hayes said hoarsely.

His hair was disheveled, his face drawn with weariness. His khaki slacks and blue poplin shirt looked slept in. He stared at Karen with haggard red eyes.

"You've got to help me find him," Karen said.

"He's not here. He's sick."

She stepped in. "Does he have the disease, Will?"

Will sank into a chair and buried his head in his hands.

Karen grabbed his head and jerked it up from his hands. "I asked you —*Does he have the disease?*"

He looked at her with wild eyes. "Yes, goddamn you, he's got the disease! And he knows it! It's tearing him apart!"

Her heart sank. She remembered the fear in his eyes when he forgot her name at the press conference. Even if she found him, would it be too late?

Could Berkholt have let Hayes in on the code? She took in a deep breath. "Will, I have to get hold of Analog Nine."

He looked blindly past her.

Her hands clenched. "Try to understand! Analog Nine reverses the disease. We can save Berkholt with it, too."

When he still didn't respond, she planted herself in front of him. "Listen to me, for God's sake! Hank Merrill's life is in the balance!"

He looked up at her hopelessly. "I can't help you. Everything's coded."

"You gave the injections! All I want is the analog Lauryn Hart gets."

"I just give what the computer tells me each Monday. I don't know what it is."

"What about the flu vaccines? They weren't on your computer program!"

"I give the three vaccines in sequence—unless Dr. Berkholt tells me to change it."

She clutched his shoulders and shook him. "Don't you realize he's been using you? You're just a tool! Do you understand how many lives you may have destroyed?"

He leaped up. "You're mad! He's the kindest man who ever lived."

"Will, you've been duped!"

"You think you know him?" Hayes cried. "Do you think working with him for two measly years gives you a right to judge? I've worked for him for sixteen years!"

Karen stared. "What?"

Hayes's face was covered with sweat, "My last year of training, I botched an insulin order and could have killed his patient. He caught it in time. He knew I was on drugs. He could've had me kicked out of the program and put in prison, but he changed his own order on the chart to protect me."

"What the hell are you on now?"

"Nothing!" he shouted. "I've been clean since then—I'd never let him down!" Tears glistened in his eyes. "Now he's sick. I've been taking care of him, giving him his injections. I shouldn't have gone to work this morning. The minute I got there I knew something was wrong. I came back—but he was already gone."

Her last hope gone, she walked out of the house.

She'd go back to the hospital and see Hank. Maybe then she could think more clearly.

She closed the front door behind her and slowly descended the four steps leading from the porch.

She stopped abruptly. Her heart raced.

The carport had been empty when she came in. Berkholt's Continental was in it now.

Something was draped over the hood.

She ran to it—and picked up the jacket she'd left at the abandoned Boy Scout camp.

She stared at it. This was his private message.

He'd known all along that she'd seen him in the canyon the afternoon following Henrietta's death. He was waiting for her.

She slipped her arms into the jacket, started for the fire road, and stopped.

She returned to her car, opened the trunk, and took her tape recorder from her briefcase. After she finished dictating, she stored the tape in the glove compartment and used her car phone to dial the hospital.

She left a message for Bill Horlich. Then she headed down the fire road.

This time, every odd-shaped boulder, canyon oak, and twisted manzanita was etched in her memory. When she crossed over the crest and descended to the creekbed, every stream crossing was familiar. She walked through the ruins of the abandoned Boy Scout camp, climbed the rise, and stepped around the large granite boulder.

Berkholt stood underneath the oak, facing the swimming hole. "Come down, Karen," he said.

Without hesitation she made her way down the rocky slope. A light wind blew across the meadow. "You left my coat on your car for me," she said. "You intended for me to come."

"Yes."

The anger that had smoldered inside her all the way up the trail fanned into a flame. "All the time you were telling me about your childhood visits to this place, you knew I'd seen you here."

He was silent for a moment before answering. "I told you about this place?"

"You know damned well you did!"

He turned and faced her. Stunned, she took a step backward.

His clothes were disheveled, eyes red, face drawn and haggard. He slowly shook his head. "I do not remember."

A terrible, sickened feeling gnawed away at her anger. She stared at him, unable to speak.

Then she said hoarsely, "What's happened to you, Dr. Berkholt?"

He spoke in a low, dismal voice. "It's too late to play games, Karen. You know what's happened to me."

She slowly shook her head.

His words came faster. "You knew what I faced. You knew what happened to my father in his thirties, my mother in her fifties." He sucked in air. "You've watched my mind crumble and pretended in front of me that you couldn't see it."

She swallowed. "I haven't seen your mind crumble. But I do know about your parents."

His eyes narrowed. "Wagoner told you."

She shook her head.

"You lie. She told you. I saw that she got Fifteen, but it was too late to stop her."

Karen caught her breath as the enormity of his words sank in. From the moment she'd learned of the substituted flu vaccines, she'd known that he'd tampered with the injections, but the cold-blooded deliberateness hadn't fully struck her until now. "Analog Fifteen—you knew of its effect on the receptors!"

His eyes stayed on her. "I didn't learn about the blocked receptors until the same time you did—at Duane's autopsy. After you saw Fogelson, I realized you would make the connection."

A wave of revulsion overwhelmed her. "My God, what kind of monster are you? You killed Duane, Cynthia, Pete! You're responsible for Susan's death. How many others have you killed?"

He ran his tongue over his lips. "I didn't expect it to turn out this way. But I felt myself slipping faster. My only hope was to find an answer before the disease overcame me as it did my parents." A pleading note appeared in his voice. "I had no way of knowing which analogs to use until I tried them on people. And I was running out of time. I couldn't wait for the protocol and then try to get answers from hopelessly demented souls in their eighties and nineties. The flu clinics were my chance."

Karen's horror grew. "You had me believe we were setting up an elaborate protocol with every conceivable protection. And all along you'd been secretly giving the analogs as though everyone within your reach were a laboratory rat."

A gust of wind struck the clearing. Clusters of brown leaves lifted from the ground and swirled between them. His voice rose. "Don't you realize how high the stakes were? You're talking about only a few people. I had a shot at a plague that destroys millions each year—one that had already destroyed my family." He wiped his hand across his forehead. "And is now destroying me."

He was truly mad. Could it all be the dementia?

How long ago had it struck him?

No matter. She desperately needed him if she was to save Hank. "You have Hank's password."

He looked off into the distance. The clouds were splitting raggedly as they floated across the sky. The sun broke through, and shadows of the overhead oak branches played across his face. "It was necessary. I've had it from the beginning."

She had to control her revulsion and break through to him. "Dr. Berkholt, it's not too late to save Hank."

"He received Fifteen," he said. "He will go quickly."

"No! Analog Nine clears the receptors! Those who got the disease from the analogs can be cured."

His lips moved before any words came out. "That is not true of all the analogs."

"What do you mean?"

"Nine doesn't work against the newest one," he said tonelessly.

She frowned. "It doesn't work against Twenty-seven?"

He turned back to her. His eyes had an uncertain look. "That's not the newest one."

"You don't mean Thirty-two?" It had been the last of the analogs to be developed in the lab. Karen had started animal trials on it while she was still in the laboratory year of her fellowship.

Berkholt gave a deep breath. "Yes. Thirty-two. I could not remember."

"But it isn't in the protocol!"

"I'm the only one who received it."

She stared. "I don't understand."

His voice was desolate. "None of the other analogs worked on the subjects. My only hope was to try the new one."

She felt sick. "When?"

"Nine days ago."

"How in God's name could you do that? You knew what was happening to those who received the analogs!"

"I had no choice. After the press conference I couldn't wait any longer. Nothing else had worked. Thirty-two had shown promise in the rat maze studies. It was my last chance, and I had to take it." His eyes filled with anguish. "It is as destructive as the others. My mind crumbles faster every day. I am running out of time."

"But what about Nine?" she cried.

A wave of despair swept his face. "Can't I make you understand? Nine doesn't work against Thirty-two. Hayes has given me daily injections of it."

She felt panic rise in her throat. Was she already too late? "Dr. Berkholt, we've got to end the protocol."

His breathing slowed. He seemed to study something in the far distance. Then he sighed. "Yes. In truth, the program has come to an end, hasn't it?"

The new, quiet tone to his voice chilled her. "Please," she said. "Analog Nine will work against Fifteen. I need both passwords if I'm to save Hank."

A fresh layer of clouds drifted in front of the sun. The shadowed pattern of oak leaves faded from his face. He slowly shook his head. "The passwords will do you no good, Karen. You're not going back."

"What—what do you mean?"

His hand reached into his coat pocket and came out with a gun.

He held it almost casually, but his eyes were piercing—terrible. "You were right—the program is dead."

This couldn't be real. She gave a sharp shake of her head as if to clear it of a bad dream. "I don't understand!"

He answered sadly. "The world must remember Arnold Berkholt as he was—not as a senile, mindless relic."

She tried to swallow, but her throat was too dry. "Why? Why do you want to kill me—and Hank?"

The gun steadied in his hand. "Three people knew enough to destroy my name. Sybil Wagoner is already dead. Hank Merrill has been taken care of. There's only you."

He raised the gun.

The ground felt as if it were heaving beneath her feet. She struggled to keep her voice steady. "What good will it do your name to face trial as a murderer?"

"I've faced my trial. I've already been sentenced—by my heredity." His voice was resigned. "When I leave here, I shall return to the medical school. Shortly afterward, I'll be found dead. There are many ways to make death look natural. The CRH program will die with my death. But the name of Arnold Berkholt will live."

"People come up here! You can't get away with it!"

Without taking the gun off her, he nodded up-canyon. "There's a cave

I once hid out in as a boy. I don't think anyone's seen it for years. Your body won't be found."

She'd seen plenty of gunshot wounds on her emergency room rotation. What did it feel like when the bullet tore through your chest or belly? She tried to answer him, but all she could do was shake her head.

No! If she let the terror paralyze her, both she and Hank were dead. She forced herself to speak. "It won't do you any good. I told Bill Horlich I was coming here to meet you."

His lips twisted. "You lie! You think I am so far gone that you can delude me!"

But a faint glimmer of uncertainty flickered in his eyes.

"I'm not lying. I prepared for this." She had to fight for breath between words. "Others—Mike Werner, Bill Horlich, Alberto Ruiz—know about the flu vaccine. Back at the house, just before I left to come to you, I dictated a report. It gives a full description of the Fieldstone product, the analog substitutions, and the deaths that resulted." Her voice grew stronger as she continued. "The tape also tells how you used Will Hayes as your murder weapon. That tape is now in Bill Horlich's hands. He'll take it to Detective Pritchard of Homicide if I'm not back by three o'clock."

Berkholt stared at her.

"If you kill me, after you're dead the headlines the world will remember you by won't concern themselves with your Nobel prize or your other achievements, but with your scientific frauds and murders."

His finger wrapped more tightly around the trigger. "You bitch! The analog has robbed me of my mind, and you would rob me of my name!"

The wind froze the sweat on the back of her neck. "It doesn't have to be that way. Your name is still intact. The protocol wasn't wasted. It was brilliantly conceived—it's already given us crucial new knowledge of neurotransmitter function."

The hesitancy in his eyes prodded her on. "Yours is one of the greatest minds in medicine. You've made inroads into a disease that no one else has been able to touch. Don't throw it away!"

He squinted. The gun stayed on her, but his entire body seemed to sag. A fresh layer of clouds drifted in front of the sun. The shadowed pattern of oak leaves faded from his face. "For a while I thought I'd found an answer," he said.

Her voice softened. "I thought you had too, Dr. Berkholt."

"I'd hoped to make a breakthrough in time to save myself. I've seen the signs developing in me for the past year. Just as I saw them develop in my mother twenty years ago." His eyes grew distant. "My earliest memories are of the signs in my father. I was five. I heard the gunshot. I was the first one in the room. I saw the blood and brains on the wall."

"I'm sorry," she said quietly.

He let out a deep breath. With one hand still holding the gun, he reached with the other into his back pocket and threw his wallet on the ground. "You'll find Hank Merrill's password in it."

"I need your password as well."

A fresh look of uncertainty crossed his face. For a moment his eyes flashed a gleam of anger, and his finger again tightened on the trigger.

She held her breath.

The gun wavered.

The gleam faded, and an overwhelming sadness took its place. "I cannot remember it." He turned the gun barrel, put it in his mouth.

"No!" she screamed, and lunged toward him.

He pulled the trigger.

She grabbed him just as the back of his skull exploded.

His body slowly slid from her grasp and crumpled in a heap onto the leaf-covered floor of the meadow.

She ran for as long as she could, breaking into a walk only long enough to catch her breath. Twice she stumbled, each time ending up sprawled on the clay-and-rock trail. When she crossed the saddle and reached the fire road, the going was easier, and she ran the rest of the way out of the canyon.

She reached her car and checked the glove compartment. The tape had been taken from it.

She picked up the car phone and dialed. First she called Detective Pritchard. Then she called Bill Horlich.

Two hours later, accompanied by Pritchard, she walked into the office of Dean Brigham Patterson. Patterson's secretary stared at her. "Oh, no," she groaned.

"Is he in?" Karen said.

The secretary nodded dumbly. Her eyes were fixed in wonder on Pritchard, who had just sucked in his jowls.

Karen pushed open the door to the inner office. Dean Patterson looked up from his desk with a start. The expression of surprise on his face quickly changed to fury.

Then he spotted Pritchard behind her.

"Dean Patterson, this is Detective Pritchard from Homicide," Karen said. "The body of Dr. Berkholt just arrived by helicopter at the hospital morgue. I need the deposit vault key to get his password."

46

Nine days had passed since Dr. Berkholt's death. With daily injections of Analog Nine, Hank had recovered dramatically. Analog Nine was now being given to every patient at Collier who'd received the Fieldstone product or the other two analogs in the protocol.

Karen and Mike Werner were sitting in Hank's hospital room when Bill Horlich came in to make his good-byes.

Karen took his hand with both of hers. "I don't know what we'd have done without you, Bill."

"Well, I sure missed the boat betting on *Loucuras do Diabo*," he said.

"We all did," Karen said. "I'm afraid Dr. Ruiz was badly misjudged."

Bill pulled up a chair. "You weren't wrong about one thing. He took me to his house. The incubator with the *Loucuras* virus is stored there."

She felt a wave of sadness. Only a while ago she'd detested the little man. "How much trouble will he be in?"

"Plenty. *If* he were reported. You may have forgotten that I'm not here officially." He leaned back in his chair and stretched. "Ruiz used excellent precautions—sealed incubator, closed room, disposable gloves and gown. I talked it over with my chief. He's excited to have an opportunity to study the *Loucuras* strain. I'm shipping it with very elaborate safeguards on the same plane I'm taking. And Alberto Ruiz has a six-month visiting professorship at the CDC."

"Good show," Mike Werner said. "Understanding the slow viruses may still help unravel Alzheimer's."

"The tabloids have had a field day," Hank said. " 'Nobel Laureate Blows Brains Out.' 'Dead Doc Revealed as Son of Henrietta Lee.' "

"That's only the beginning," Bill said. "Once the DA releases news of the flawed program, the lawsuits will start flying. The medical school hierarchy must be spending many long hours with its legal staff."

"What's left of the medical staff of Collier Hospital?" Hank asked.

"Until the university arranges replacements, it's decimated," Karen said. "Eisenberg is in a drug rehab center, and Olsen's returned to his old job at the VA in Wisconsin. With me scheduled to move back to the medical school to join the full-time endocrine faculty, that leaves only Frank Terhune."

Bill's face lit up. "Full-time faculty—Karen, that's great!"

"Dean Patterson offered it yesterday. He's been very solicitous of me lately."

"I wonder why." Bill grinned.

"Tomorrow after I'm discharged," Hank said, "we're going out to celebrate Karen's appointment. I'm sorry you can't still be here to join us, Bill."

"Thanks, I wish I could." Bill leaned forward. "You know, Hank, looking at you now, it's hard to believe you were so sick just a couple weeks ago. How much do you actually remember of that period after you got the so-called flu vaccine?"

"I remember very well waking up each morning to find that another part of my mind had slipped away." He looked at Karen and reached for her hand. "I'd think of you and try to recall things we'd said and done—as if somehow that would help me hold on to what was left." He bit his lip as he studied her hand in his. "Then there was the morning when I couldn't remember your name. All I could do was try to hold on to a picture of you."

Karen gripped his hand more tightly.

Hank looked back at Bill Horlich. "To get back to your question, Bill, there's a full week that seems to have dropped entirely from my life. Before that, the suspicion—and then the certainty—that I was losing my mind was the most terrifying feeling I've ever known."

"Berkholt must have experienced something like that," Mike Werner said. "I suspect that every time he forgot a name or an appointment, he went into a panic."

"He'd begun to act strange earlier," Karen said. "But he didn't really plummet until he gave himself the analog. It's almost as if he programmed his own retribution."

The door opened and the pathologist, Herb Fogelson, walked in. His face was grave. "I'm glad I caught all of you together. I have troubling news about Arnold's autopsy."

Karen looked at him with a feeling of sorrow. Fogelson had worked with Berkholt for many years. His death must have been particularly rough on him. "What is it, Herb?"

"I just finished reviewing the slides of his brain." His lips pressed into a thin line. "The slides are normal."

Karen gasped. "What?"

"They're entirely normal." The bewildered pain in Fogelson's eyes struck her with as much force as his news. "Arnold didn't have Alzheimer's."

Karen stared at him incredulously. "You mean he took the analog for no reason?"

Fogelson nodded grimly.

"My God!" Werner gasped. "Then until he gave himself the analog, all his fears that his mind was crumbling were groundless."

Karen turned to Fogelson. "But, Herb—if his deterioration was caused by the analog, why didn't it reverse? He had Will Hayes give him Analog Nine, just like we gave Hank. Nine reversed the dementia in everyone whose brain was poisoned by the analogs."

Fogelson shrugged helplessly.

"Karen," Hank said thoughtfully, "when did Berkholt give himself the analog?"

"It had to be after the press conference. That means it couldn't have been sooner than January twelfth. Probably a few days later."

Hank's forehead wrinkled in concentration. "Let's see. It was January thirteenth that I froze the codes." Suddenly his eyes flashed. He jumped up. "Let's go to my office!"

Hank ran from the hospital room with Karen dashing after him. "What's got into you?" she yelled.

"We've gotta get to the computer!" he called back.

They covered the connecting corridors between the hospital and the medical school. "Patients aren't supposed to act like this," Karen panted as they took the elevator to the basement.

Hank threw open the door to his office, perched in front of his computer, and typed the command to access the Novar-3 program.

He typed in his security password. "What's Berkholt's?"

Karen could repeat it in her sleep.

He entered it. Menus flashed across the screen as his fingers ran over the keyboard.

He stopped—and stared at the screen in disbelief. Then he turned and looked from Karen to Bill Horlich and Mike Werner, who'd followed them in. His voice was quiet, stunned. "There's a perfectly good reason why the analog's effect wasn't cleared up by the injections of Nine."

"I don't understand," Karen said.

"He never gave himself an analog."

"What are you talking about?" Karen said. "He himself told me it was Analog Thirty-two. He knew the code. He'd broken it long before."

Hank rose from the stool. "Karen, I told you I froze all the codes after I learned that the security database had been broken into. That meant that no new substance could be introduced into the protocol. Anything new would come out coded for the placebo or one of the three analogs already in the program."

Her eyes widened.

"Thirty-two was new, so far as the protocol was concerned," Hank said. "With the codes frozen, the Novar-3 would recognize no new substances. So it assigned Berkholt what would have been next in the old sequence. The last three patients to enter the program had received analogs—the placebo was due up next."

"Oh, my God," Karen said hoarsely.

"That's why the injections of Nine he gave himself had no effect," Hank said. "There was nothing to treat, because nothing was wrong with his brain. He'd given himself the placebo."

Karen felt a hollowness at the center of her chest. A long moment passed before she finally broke the silence that had blanketed the room. "Somehow that makes the waste even more horrible."

Bill Horlich's eyes were still fixed in awe on the computer screen. "He deluded himself twice. First, that he was developing Alzheimer's and was running out of time. And then that the analog he gave himself was destroying his brain"—he slowly shook his head—"when he had never even received it."

A heavy, penetrating sadness weighed down on Karen.

"His every moment must have been dominated by the fear that his heredity had doomed him to lose his mind," Mike Werner said.

"And in the end, the fear was self-fulfilling," Karen said softly.

EPILOGUE

"Hank."

"Uh-huh."

"You asleep?"

"Uh-huh."

She jabbed her elbow into his ribs. "No, you're not."

He groaned. "You're right."

She rubbed her cheek against his chest. "That was nice, Hank."

He slid his arm beneath her shoulders. "Yes, it was."

She lifted her head and gazed at his relaxed face. Her finger slowly traced lines over the fine crinkles at the corners of his eyes, first one side, then the other. "Was it any different?"

"Let me think." His forehead wrinkled in concentration. "Have you been practicing some new pelvic muscle exercises?"

"That's not what I mean! Was it any different making love to a married woman?"

He touched her lips with a kiss. "Absolutely. I'll need lots of practice."

She settled back on her pillow. "I got to know your folks while you were still coming out of it. I'm glad they were here."

"Well, at least Dad's almost satisfied," Hank said. "He didn't get a son to take over the Merrill Eye Institute, but he finally got a doctor in the family."

"He wasted no time taking me under his wing," Karen said. "Kept telling me the glories of moving to Dallas. He all but offered to endow a new chair of endocrinology for me at the med school there."

"It's hard to believe that after all these years, he still tries to take over," Hank said. "He would've taken charge of the entire wedding if we'd let him."

Karen grinned. "Actually, the wedding was more than any of us bargained for."

"I don't know how it happened," Hank said. "We finally managed to squelch Dad's idea of renting the main ballroom of the Ritz Carlton by insisting on our own quiet little ceremony at the Cinema Acres chapel." He shook his head. "Whose idea was it anyway to invite Lauryn Hart?"

"Well, we certainly couldn't have a wedding without Bev and Lauryn."

"Sure. 'Quiet little ceremony'—with four major TV news networks, several dozen magazine and newspaper reporters, and a few thousand drooling fans waiting outside. I guess we could've figured something like that would happen—with *Empire* breaking every Nielsen rating since Lauryn returned to the show." He chuckled. "That was especially devilish of you to invite Frank Terhune."

Karen sat straight up and burst out laughing. "Do you remember how scarlet Frank's face turned when Lauryn pinched his cheek in front of the cameras and announced that he was her 'little Frankie Doctor'?" Her eyes watered. "And then the way his head was almost torn off when his wife jerked him away?"

"Do I remember?" Hank shook with laughter. "The scene was repeated on all three networks' prime-time news shows for the next five nights!"

She wiped her eyes. "It was one helluva wedding, Hank."

"I'm glad Bill could make it back," Hank said. "He was a perfect combination of best man and . . ." He searched for the right word.

"And father of the bride," Karen finished. "Actually, it was more appropriate for Bill to 'give me away' than anyone." She sucked on her lip thoughtfully. "It's funny, though. I once had a crazy thought that someday Dr. Berkholt might fill that role." Her voice dropped. "I dreamed about how wonderful it would be to have someone like him for a father."

"He came within a hairbreadth of killing you, Karen. I can never think of him charitably."

She thought about that for a moment and nodded slowly. "You know, when I remember his eloquence at Susan's funeral or the tears in his eyes when we disconnected Duane's life support, I can almost forget that he was responsible for their deaths." She laid back down and rested her head against his shoulder as she recalled the grinding fear that had permeated every waking hour. "Oh, Hank, it's hard to believe that a little over a month ago I was afraid that he'd succeed in killing you, too."

His arms circled her, and he brushed his lips in her hair. "We 'computer types'—to quote your friend Olsen—are pretty hard to get rid of."

All of a sudden he started laughing again.

She lifted her head and glared at him with narrowed eyes. "What's so damned funny, Hank Merrill?"

He shook his head. "Karen, when you were at your most furious with me over the protocol, you complained that the Novar-3 had developed a mind of its own, that it had taken control."

"And exactly what humor do you find in that?"

"It's the irony. Until this minute I hadn't realized how right you were. After I programmed the Novar-3, I had to follow its rules just as you and everyone else working with the protocol had to." His face suddenly grew dead serious. "Then Berkholt tried to double-cross it."

She stared at him. Once again she pictured the gun wavering in Dr. Berkholt's hand and the desolation in his eyes as he told her he couldn't remember the password.

She swallowed. She wasn't sure whether she wanted to laugh or cry.

"And when it was all over," she said in a quiet voice, "it was the Novar-3 that had the last word."

She gazed down at Hank a moment longer.

Then she dropped back into his arms.